THE LOATHING

William H. Nelson

Infinite Worlds Publishing

ISBN: 978-1-7344642-4-5 (paperback)

Main Edits: Eris Hyrkas
Preliminary Edits and Final Proof Read: TJ Tranchell
Final Edits and Formatting: EbookPbook

Cover Art: Richard Luong

BOOKS BY WILLIAM H. NELSON

<u>The Awakening Wars Series:</u>

Within the Range of Reanimation
The Unnamed Town
City of the Lost (upcoming)
The Sacred Cenote (upcoming)

<u>Other Novels:</u>

Nathrotep
The Loathing

For Lisa Marie Paschke
You are a shining beacon of light in this world of darkness,
And a true inspiration to all those who know and love you.

ACKNOWLEDGEMENTS

First and foremost I would like to thank Lisa Paschke. Without her unfailing encouragement none of these books would ever see the light of day. I would also like to acknowledge Eris Hyrkas, TJ Tranchell, and all the good people over at EbookPbook. Their combined editorial assistance was indispensable, so many thanks go out to all those involved in helping me to make this the very best story possible.

In addition, I would like to express my undying gratitude to my readers. Your continued support of my writing endeavors is greatly appreciated. Thank you all so very much!

-1-

The alleyway was a dark and dismal place located in a section of town choked with the refuse of many years of willful neglect. Nestled between a boarded-up Japanese herbal shop and an unlicensed abortion clinic, it was a place of forgotten dreams and lost hopes, saturated with the unmistakable miasma of constant human suffering. For lack of any better alternative, it was also the place that Charlie and his best friend now called home.

After taking a mighty pull off the bottle of cheap whiskey, Charlie reached across the small fire barrel to pour a little on the ground for Simon, blinking his eyes back into focus while he tried to reorder his wandering thoughts. Memories, now blurred by the effects of the alcohol, drifted chaotically through his mind before tumbling back into a slightly skewed pattern.

"So you see, pal," he continued, recalling what he'd been saying, "life's not been so good fer me, not at all!"

Pulling the soiled burgundy curtains more closely about him, he scratched at his filthy beard, leaning back against the dumpster in an attempt to get out of the drizzling rain. The city had once been a shining example of culture and diversity. Now, corruption had eaten away at it from within, and crime ran rampant in the streets. Shaking his head at the bitter realities of life, he glanced back at his friend. Simon crouched on the other side of the fire, waiting patiently in the flickering shadows for him to go on. He truly was a good listener. Tilting his head back, Charlie took another swig from the bottle and then continued.

"I've been through three fuckin' wars, I have! Made it through every damn one uv' um too!" he said, his words slurred and almost indistinguishable. "And wad it get me? Not one damn thing! Bastards! Cut my fuckin' health benefits. Bastards."

Lapsing into silence, he gave Simon a chance to digest what he'd just said as he tried to suppress the overwhelming flood of emotions that always washed through him whenever he talked of the past. But it was no use; doubling over, he sobbed wretchedly, clenching his arms across his stomach as he rocked back and forth in utter despair.

It was a wasting disease. At least that's what the doctors had told him. There was nothing else he could have done for her. She'd faded away right before his eyes as the money went to line the pockets of the greedy physicians. He'd begged them to save her, pleaded with them. Oh, and she'd lasted a good long time all right—they'd seen to that! He struggled against the painful recollections, sensing Simon moving closer and appreciating his friend's compassion. He would understand, he always did.

"They let her die! Kept her. . . kept her hooked up to those damn machines!" he cried, the smoldering anger sharpening his enunciation. "Right up until the money ran out. What chance did that ever give her? No chance at all, I tell ya! Damn them to hell! No more money, no more machines. Bastards! Bastards. . ."

Sobbing and choking on bitter tears, he rolled over onto his side, pulling a fold of the curtains up a little more to cover his head. Oh, the things they'd done to her, had used on her. They'd violated her with their hideous instruments, their false medications, and he hated them for it—hated all doctors—for it was the doctors that had taken his beloved wife away from him. The doctors and the military.

"They cut me off, do ya hear, Simon? Cut *her* off! My sweet, sweet Judy. Oh, my beautiful Judy. She. . . she was everything to me. Her and our. . . our beautiful d-daughter." He felt Simon gently touch his arm, moving to nuzzle the back of his hand in sympathy as he convulsed, trapped within the darker, more frightening memories, the ones he'd never been able to share even with his best friend. After a few moments, he struggled back into a sitting position, reaching down to pick Simon up as he took another pull from the bottle. There would be no more memories tonight!

"I tell ya, Simon," he slurred, the liquor coursing through his system. "Yer the greatest frien' a guy like me ever had. . ."

Raising his gnarled, scabby hand up to his face, he peered closely at his companion, trying to focus. Simon had scuttled across his palm and now clung to the back of his wrist, staring at him and weaving his antennae in interesting patterns. The motion soothed Charlie, as it always did, and soon he was smiling. His friend was the best!

And the biggest, too.

Taking another swig off the bottle, he then tilted it toward Simon, nodding his head in encouragement. Seeing this, Simon bobbed up and down on his six chitinous legs, a trick Charlie had painstakingly taught him through much trial and error. Carefully setting the large insect back down, he then poured a small amount of the alcohol on a stale crust of bread and offered it to him. Crouching in the shifting shadows made from the rain and sputtering fire, Simon began to consume the morsel, his mouth parts clicking contentedly.

Chuckling, Charlie slid farther down on the low-backed couch, placing himself at eye level with his friend so he could watch him eat. Slowly, the pain fell away, and he was soon floating toward oblivion.

"Well, what do we have here?"

The obnoxious voice and hateful laughter that followed it brought him back to awareness, but not quickly enough.

Rough hands grabbed him, slamming him back into the dumpster. Head ringing from the impact, he attempted to wriggle free, but the youth's grip was unbreakable.

"Say, Gramps, you don't mind if we share your fire for a minute, do ya?"

It wasn't really a question, and so Charlie didn't even consider answering. He was too drunk to fight, and these punks would swarm all over him anyway, so why even try? Instead, he just smiled.

Wrong answer.

A fist slammed into his stomach, eliciting a hiss of pain from his lips before he spewed out his last few drinks. The blond kid wasn't bad for a street punk, but Charlie knew he could have taken him in better days. Now he was just too old, too broken. Besides, all that he'd ever cared about had been stolen—there was simply nothing left for him to fight for.

Except Simon.

Gasping for breath, he began to struggle against the boy's iron-hard grip, the end of the couch breaking off as he squirmed across it, seeking to wiggle free. But they only dragged him back, laughing and joking with one another as they prevented his escape. At this point, he wasn't afraid for himself. He only wanted to make sure that his friend would survive. And for that, he would need to remain alive as well, if only for a short period of time. Eyes darting around, he sought for a way out, but then he suddenly focused on the boy holding him instead. Something about the punk's voice had registered deep within Charlie's tortured mind.

"Hey, old man, come on—we're not going to hurt you," the boy was saying. "Maybe just slap you around a little!"

The voice was familiar, remembered from a long distance through a hazy, much-forgotten past. Amid the catcalls and laughter of the others, the recollections rose up, and for a moment, became crystal clear. Without thinking, Charlie's fist shot out, colliding with the gang leader's jaw and sending him sprawling into his cronies. In the silence that followed, Simon hissed, a thin sound that mixed with the popping of the fire and the patter of the drizzling rain.

The boy's reaction to this unexpected onslaught was a thin, baleful smirk.

Rubbing his jaw, he shook off the help of his crew as he regained his balance, his piercing eyes studying Charlie with newly heightened interest.

"I remember you now, Gramps!" he exclaimed after a moment. "You're the father of that sweet little piece of ass we had a while back. Hey, boys! Its old 'papa drunk' himself—'Oh, save me, Papa! Help me, Papa! Papa, get up!' Ha! You didn't even move when we had her screaming right in your friggen ear! Man, you ain't anywhere you don't belong, old man! What kind of a father would sleep through his own daughter's rape?"

Charlie cringed back, whimpering as his stomach knotted up and the rest of the gang dissolved into more hateful laughter. That wasn't the way it had happened, that wasn't the way at all! It was the doctors and the damn military! They'd taken his wife away, and they'd taken his life away with her. At the time, booze had been his only salvation. It had calmed him from his hysteria and helped him to hold up against the pain of her loss, but eventually it had come to rule him instead. On just such an evening, when he'd succumbed to the bottle, his daughter had been taken. He remembered only bits and pieces of it, but that alone was the stuff of nightmares. It was where his old life had ended and his new life had begun.

". . . Oh, Papa, save me!'" the street punk taunted. "'Save me!' You didn't even move! How does that feel, old man? Do you think that it makes you tough, huh, is that it? That you can hit me, in front of my men?"

The fist descended like an anvil, hammering him back into the cushions. Dust and feathers flew upward in a billowing white cloud as the sodden velvet of the ancient couch split open.

"Now, you worthless fuck," the boy said, grabbing a handful of Charlie's hair and placing a knife beneath his chin, "do you still think you're so tough? Do you? Well, I don't think you're tough at all. You know, your daughter was good. *Real* good. The things we did to her were. . . inventive! Do you even know what all we did? Did you even care?"

Charlie couldn't remember all of it, but he did care. When he'd awoken from his booze-induced slumber, he'd found his only child twisted and spent on the bed beside him. However, the memories he could recall of that night were filled with the sounds of the street punks' voices and her pitiful cries for help. He hadn't been able to do anything about it at the time; he'd just been too drunk, too broken.

Oh, how he wished he could make them pay, how he prayed for it! But he knew the chance for retribution would never come; this was the end, and he deserved it. He only hoped that Simon had gotten far away.

"She was good to us, old man. We made her do things even Rita over there would never do. Isn't that right, Rita?"

The sounds of girlish giggling floating up from the middle of the group sounded obscene mixed in with the brutish male voices. It was sickening, and Charlie tried again to shrink away from them, away from the knife pressed so tight against his jugular, but it was of no use. They held him fast.

"Yup, she was a hot one all right. And a real screamer! Do you remember her screams, old man? Can you remember? I remember. We picked her sweet little cherry right off the tree, didn't we, boys?"

More hurtful catcalls swirled around him as an icy chill ran down his back and then settled deep within his guts. He wanted desperately to strike out, to kill him and all the others who'd taken turns hurting his baby girl, but he couldn't even move. The knife was deadly insistent from where it lay against his bared throat.

"Come on, Bobby!" one of the others said. "It's almost time. We have to meet Sanchez at the warehouse or we'll miss out on all the good merchandise!"

"Yeah, yeah, just a fuckin minute!" Bobby growled, then turned back to Charlie. "You stink, old man. You're a filthy, yellow, drunken coward who failed to protect his own daughter. How does that make you feel, you pathetic piece of shit? And now I'm gonna do to you what we did to her after we finished turning her into a real woman."

The knife rose up, its silvery surface flashing in the firelight as the leather-clad hoodlum pulled him forward for the killing blow. With a silent prayer, Charlie closed his eyes and went limp. The punk was right—he was a worthless, old has-been, a broken-down shadow of his former self, and he deserved to die for his failures.

Then, he was suddenly falling backward as the boy screamed out in pain. Surprised by the unexpected reprieve, Charlie opened his eyes as he hit the back of the couch, staring up through a fresh cloud of exploding feathers in time to see Simon chewing his way through the soft flesh of the boy's cheek.

"Arrrggg! Get it off me!" Bobby yelped, dropping the knife to grasp Simon's writhing body with both hands.

"Simon!" Charlie shouted in renewed fear. "No!"

Tearing the creature from his face, the boy stumbled back as he threw the chittering insect to the ground. Quickly righting himself, Simon stood protectively in between Charlie and the others, hissing balefully as his chitinous body gleamed wetly in the dancing firelight.

"*Simon?*" the boy blurted, wiping blood from his cheek. "You have a *pet cockroach?*"

"Bobby, I don't like this," Rita said, moving to stand next to him and gripping his arm tightly. "Look at the size of that thing! What if there are more of them waiting in the shadows? Let's just get out of here, okay?"

Sneering, the boy shook her off. "One lousy cockroach ain't gonna stop me!" he declared. "Besides, roaches don't attack people; it's the other way around. This old guy's just got this one trained, is all. Now stop being such a baby or I'll have to punish you when we get home."

Rita smiled, gazing wistfully up at Bobby as she wiped some of the blood from his cheek with the tip of a finger. Then, moaning seductively, she sucked at the blood, staring at him with eyes glistening mischievously. "Oooh, I'd really like that. . ." she purred.

Charlie had struggled back into a sitting position while they were conversing, and now the alcohol in his system was rapidly wearing off in his desperate concern for his friend's safety.

"Simon, get the hell away from here!" he shouted. "I'm finished. There's nothing more you can do. Run, I tell you, before it's too—"

"Too late!" the boy chimed in as the sole of his heavy, black boot descended, crushing Simon right before Charlie's very eyes.

"Nooo!" Charlie wailed, rising to his feet in a surge of all-consuming rage. The doctors, the military, these punks—all of them had stolen his life away, twisting and distorting it into what it was now.

The loss of his family, and now the destruction of his only friend—he could take it no longer. With an inarticulate cry, he launched himself at the gang.

The struggle was brief; they had him outnumbered and surrounded. In mere moments, he was beaten within inches of his life and then left to die, sprawled out upon the broken couch he'd so recently called home.

As the gang moved away, their shouts and laughter receding, Charlie reached a shaking hand out toward Simon. One antenna still quivered feebly, lightly brushing his outstretched fingers as they both slipped ever closer to the edges of death.

It was then that Charlie noticed something shining dully from inside the exposed lining of the couch. With detached curiosity, he wondered why he'd never noticed a lump there before. In all the time since he'd dragged the large piece of furniture from out of the boarded-up herbal shop, he'd never even felt a bump in the padding. But now something glinted invitingly in the firelight. With his last ounce of strength, he pushed the remaining feathers aside to get a closer look. It was an urn of some kind, golden and compact, inscribed all over with tiny Japanese characters. Drifting closer to his impending demise, he pried at the lid, trying to get a final look at its contents.

As the ancient cap popped free, a greenish mist billowed out, covering him in waves of shimmering fog. Like in a dream, the pain was suddenly taken from him, and he felt himself floating away from the garbage-strewn alleyway, away from the rundown shops and illegal clinics, and away from his battered body itself. Beside him, he could see Simon glowing within the mists, wavering as he grew larger and more powerful.

And filled with newfound life.

Glancing up, he stared at the being who now stood before them both.

The Japanese warrior, clad in the armor of a feudal daimyo with a faceplate set in grim lines, clenched the hilt of a drawn sword in his armored hands. The vision didn't startle Charlie; at one time, he'd been an avid follower of Japanese history and culture. He could accept this vision and easily identify with it. Nodding in satisfaction, the warrior spirit offered him the point of his blade. Taking it, Charlie felt a tremendous power surge through him, a new aliveness that bespoke of imminent revenge. He would take the bargain this mysterious spirit offered and pay for it with the blood of his enemies. Accepting his commitment, the spirit bowed, saluted him once with the sword, and then faded away.

Charlie found himself back on the couch. For some reason, he felt different, more alert. Peering down at himself, he noticed that the filthy curtains he'd once wrapped himself in had become a sprawling burgundy cloak, its deep, purplish color faintly reminiscent of dried blood. Smiling, he reached down to grasp Simon and then placed him on the back of his other forearm. Things seemed strange, surreal somehow. Studying the huge cockroach, he sighed.

"So," he said, "it looks like we are back together again."

-Yes, Father, we are as one.-

Simon's voice rang strongly in his mind, and it came as no great surprise. It seemed to him that the voice had always been there, buried deep within his thoughts. As he sat pondering this revelation, he began to feel the subtle differences in his own anatomy. His skin, now tough and horn-like, was a dark reddish color reminiscent of a lobster's shell, and his body seemed shorter, more compact. Reaching up, he found that there were now nodes protruding from his forehead, which were supplying information to his brain at far greater speeds than he was accustomed to. Regardless of the rapidity, he could already distinguish between the overlapping images, sorting through them while gaining an incredible amount of useful information. Grinning in pleasure, he addressed his old friend, his voice taking on a vibrant, theatrical lilt.

"Well, what do you think of our new bodies then, Simon? I think that we shall grow to like them very much."

-Yes, Father, they suit us. If you are feeling up to it, then let us begin our task, for there is much work to be done.-

Chuckling, Charlie stared into the shiny black eyes of his companion, sorting through the multitudes of data now surging through his mind. It was a strange sensation, yet somehow very satisfying.

"Aren't you the rambunctious one!" he exclaimed, holding Simon up in the firelight to get a better look at him. "How do you propose we go after all those hoodlums when it is just the two of us, hmmm? We will need help, and lots of it, if we are to succeed."

-Father, your children are all around you.-

Searching the mist-filled alleyway with his newfound senses, he became aware of how the perceptions he was filtering through his new cranial nodes helped him to see. Closing his eyes, he could visualize whole sections of the city as if he were actually there. It was like having hidden cameras placed throughout the surrounding area, forever sending images to his brain of things that were happening all across town. Slowly, he came to realize the meaning of what his friend had just told him. Reaching out across his domain, he came to recognize the children of his new calling:

The Arthropods.

Staring back at him from over a trillion sets of different eyes were the masses of his newfound family, the endless, destructive forces he could now muster to defeat his enemies. Not even an army could stand against the waiting multitudes of his newly acquired host. He laughed then, a thin, screeching sound that bespoke the language of the night-spawn, the legion of the bug. His heart was now forever theirs, as was his commitment. The city would soon see a new master arise, and not just one of simple vengeance, but one of justice as well. Sitting there in the darkness of the alleyway, he met with his generals, his eight and six-legged minions of war. There, behind the ancient herbal shop, he plotted his first triumphant strike into the hearts of his foes, for they were many.

And now, they would pay.

-2-

"Fuck it," Jenkins muttered, grimacing a little as he realized he'd just said it out loud again. It was happening more and more frequently these days, but he couldn't seem to break himself of the habit. The two words were quickly becoming his mantra in life, like some kind of weird, early-onset Tourette's syndrome. Especially now, with everything turning to shit all around him.

Peering down at the half-finished report on his desk, he sighed, absently toying with his rumpled tie, and noticing as he did so that his ever-expanding gut was beginning to force the tie to curl upward. But that didn't really matter much anymore. He was single and not getting any younger, so who the hell did he have to impress? In fact, it seemed that lately his life had turned into one great big shit sandwich, and he was forever running out of bread. There'd been a time that the sardonic thought would have made him smile, but now he just frowned instead, glancing up at the clock.

Would this shift never end? It was beyond quitting time, and most of his fellow officers had long since departed. Now that it was getting on toward evening, he was looking forward to some much-needed downtime. Ten years on the force, and he'd been reduced to this—endless bullshit paperwork and nothing but small, worthless cases. Once, it would have made him furious, but the anger and resentment had dwindled, worn away by the unending tedium that had become his monotonous daily routine. He was used to it by now.

Well, mostly used to it, he thought with a small frown; these last few months had been tough to swallow. First, his partner had been reassigned. At least that's what they'd told him. But he knew it was a load of crap. He'd been out to Tom's house, and all his stuff was still there. In addition to that, after doing a bit of off-the-clock checking around, he'd been unable to find anything else out about this so-called "reassignment." No transfer records, no change of address—it was as if his partner had vanished from the face of the earth.

Leaning back in his chair, he ran a hand through his thinning brown hair, gazing around the large, cluttered office filled with battered desks, lopsided filing cabinets, and the remaining unfortunates who were also stuck with endless paperwork. He supposed this was what he got for being one of the last honest cops on the force. The whole damn city was going to hell in a handbasket, starting with the dirty politicians who ran things, then trickling on down to his own fellow officers, who no longer even batted an eyelash at taking bribes for doing "special" work on the side. It was disgusting.

Of course, when he'd first joined up, things had been different. But now it was like wading through a cesspool of corruption, and there was no one left to pull him out of it. Sure, his current captain was an okay guy, but everyone knew he was just here for the paycheck. In fact, it felt like his superiors had been trying to force him to quit ever since the old captain retired. Each annual review had been just good enough that he couldn't complain, but never quite good enough that he'd gotten the raises he deserved. The new captain was playing it by the book and taking his cues from the higher-ups, so for the last three years he'd gotten screwed. It wasn't fair, but there was nothing else he could do to change the situation. No matter how hard he worked or how much effort he put into it, he knew he'd never get another raise in this fucked up precinct. But he kept plugging away at it regardless and had continued to solve cases, day after day, with his partner.

Until his partner had disappeared.

Wiping a hand across his stubbled chin, he considered the problem. Sure, they'd said it was a transfer, but there was no evidence of that. And there was no one else he could reach out to since most of the other officers left in the precinct were all completely corrupt.

"Fuck it," he muttered again, turning to reach for his jacket. Time to get the hell out of this dump. He figured if he was going to find anything out about his partner's disappearance, he'd just have to do it on his own.

"Hey, Detective Limp Dick!" a voice rang out as a new set of files was slapped down on his desk. "Captain's got another case for you. Have fun tonight!"

Nick Resario, that worthless piece of shit. From his lumpy, shaven head and ridiculous handlebar mustache, right down to his low-brow, racist attitude, the man was a royal pain in the ass. And it was no real secret that he was on the local mafia's payroll, as well as accepting bribes from some of the city's most crooked politicians. But he was just one of the many, and it was all too much effort for Jenkins to try and deal with them anymore.

"Eat a bag of dicks, Resario," Jenkins growled, throwing the man an evil look.

Resario laughed, sauntering away with a huge cheese-eating grin plastered across his fat, ugly face. There was nothing else to do except go through the files and see what type of shit assignment had gotten passed down to him this time. It seemed likely he'd be pulling another unscheduled double shift no matter what the situation was. It sucked, but that was just one more thing he was slowly getting used to. At least tomorrow was his day off. Sighing, he grabbed the files, dragging them across his desk before flipping them open.

Just as he'd thought. It was another low-level investigation. Some two-bit smuggling with small-time gang involvement. Scanning the documents, he found that there were supposedly some shady dealings going on down by the docks tonight. And that, in a nutshell, was pretty much the gist of it. They'd been giving him nothing but these nickel-and-dime cases for months. Well, he was just here to do his job, no matter how insulting it was. Nobody was going to force him to quit, not after all the years he'd put in.

"Fuck it," he said again as he got up, throwing his jacket on before leaving through the battered front door. From here on out he would play by his own rules, and he'd find his missing partner as well, just for good measure. No one could tell him what he could or couldn't do in his off time. He would find out what happened to Tom and to hell with the rest of them.

With that thought firmly in the forefront of his mind, he made his way down the stairs and then out the main doors of the building, heading for his waiting unmarked squad car.

It was going to be another long night.

<h1 style="text-align:center">-3-</h1>

Shadows had already gathered within the darkened nooks and crannies of the dilapidated buildings as Florence traversed the litter-strewn sidewalk. There was simply no way she could have left any sooner. The big shipment of books from Europe had finally come in, and she'd been corralled into helping unpack and sort through it all. *Besides*, she thought, *it had been well worth the effort.* Patting the pocket of her battered trench coat to reassure herself, she walked faster, hoping to get home before her husband got too angry with her.

She didn't even know why she'd taken the dusty old volume. It seemed like a fever dream to her now, a momentary compulsion that she'd somehow been unable to resist. The book itself had fascinated her as soon as she'd pulled it from the bottom of the shipping crate, its smooth, leathery surface staring up at her with all its carefully incised glyphs and decorative filigree. When she'd flipped through it there in the musty back room of the used bookstore, its images had frightened her at first but then enthralled her with their graphic depictions and incomprehensible diagrams. She simply did not know what had possessed her to take the strange tome. Now, she was not only late, but she'd also managed to bring the bizarre manuscript home with her. Shaking her head in bemusement, she considered just how much trouble it had already caused her.

First off, Nico was going to kill her. He was always so insistent about her whereabouts. And about his dinner, if truth be told.

She'd felt the back of his hand on enough occasions to know what was expected of her. From here on out, she would just need to be more careful of the time, that was all. She'd explain it to him as best she could when she got there and then prepare a special meal to make up for her disobedience. For that was how she was sure he would see it. The thought made her shiver as she hurried along the garbage-strewn streets.

It would only be a few more minutes, and then she'd be back at their apartment. She was thinking about all of the ways she could placate him when she caught a momentary flash of blue from out of the corner of her eye. She'd been walking past the old abandoned herbal shop, but now stopped to turn toward the flicker of intense color. The building was a large, one-story affair, done in the traditional Japanese style. At one time, it must have been quite impressive but was currently in much need of repair, its roof tiles dingy and the tall ceremonial gates lining the walkway peeling layers of dull red paint. Adjusting her horn-rimmed glasses, she stepped over to the shattered storefront windows. Some of the plywood covering the gaps had fallen off, allowing her to peer inside.

And there Florence saw a rose.

A blue rose, to be exact. With an exclamation of pure delight, she leaned in to study it. The rose sat in a slim decorative vase that was inscribed all over with ancient Japanese symbols. *How did that get there?* She'd passed by this old shop twice a day, every day, for the last three years, and had never noticed it there before. And such a brilliant shade of blue! It really was her favorite color. Reaching through the broken window, she carefully drew out the porcelain vase containing the vibrant flower. *Well,* she thought, *this had been quite a day.* Such a day that had her pilfering books and stealing flowers! Not that there was anyone left to steal the flower from; the building had been abandoned since as far back as she could remember. Smiling a bit at her own foolishness, she set out again, heading toward the next block over which contained her run-down old apartment complex. *Oh my goodness, but I'm late!*

After entering the building, she hurried up the stairs. They lived on the fourth floor, so she was winded by the time she reached the door to their small corner apartment. Smoothing back her frizzy red hair, she tried to compose herself, her heart hammering in a frenzy of frightened apprehension. Then, taking a deep, shuddering breath, she reached into her pocket and drew forth the keys.

But as soon as her keys touched the lock, the door was jerked open from within.

"Where the fuck have you been?" her husband demanded.

He stood in the entryway dressed in a white tank top and jeans, his face livid. She swallowed heavily. He'd already changed out of his uniform, which was not a good sign. Trying in vain to rein in her fear, she reached up to straighten her glasses as she glanced down at the floor. She knew only too well not to make eye contact with him when he was like this—it would only make things worse.

"I. . . I had to work late," she began. "There was a big shipment that just came in down at the shop."

"Big shipment my ass!" he shouted. "Where the fuck is my dinner?"

She took an involuntary step backward, her heart fluttering inside her chest like a trapped hummingbird. But before she could say anything else, he lunged forward, grabbing her by the wrist.

"Don't you dare back away from me, you stupid little cunt!" he raged. "I don't give a fuck about your lame excuses! You've had this coming to you for quite some time now."

He'd been pulling her through the entranceway as he barked at her, crushing her wrist in his iron-hard grasp. She knew if she tried to pull away, the beating would only be more severe, so she meekly followed. Kicking the door closed behind them, he continued to yank her down the hallway, and then propelled her forward into the kitchen. As she caught her balance and turned to reason with him, he casually backhanded her across the face. Her lip split open as she fell against the stove, crumpling halfway to the floor while stars exploded behind her eyes.

"And where the hell did you get that fucking rose! You been two-timing me?"

Staring up at him, she was nearly blinded by pain and unable to comprehend his question. *Rose? What. . . Oh.* Glancing down, she saw that she still held the ornamental vase. The rose, such a striking shade of blue, was now speckled by tiny droplets of red. Her own blood, she realized. A trembling started deep within her and then worked its way outward. Soon she was shuddering uncontrollably, trying hard not to cry as she clawed her way up the oven door and then cowered back against the horizontal freezer standing next to it. Crying would only make him hit harder; he liked it when she cried.

"Answer me!" he roared, making her flinch.

"I. . . found it. . ."

Even though she saw the fist coming, it was like viewing it in slow motion, yet not being able to dodge out of the way. With the force of a sledgehammer, it struck her in the face, and she felt something break inside her cheek as her glasses flew off and then clattered across the linoleum floor. Time sped back up, and she found herself crumpling once more. As she hit the ground, she felt a searing wetness gushing from her mouth and nose. For some reason, she still had a hold of the vase. With the back of her free hand, she wiped at the blood now pouring from her battered lips and then stared at her reddened fingers in astonished disbelief.

"I'm going to teach you a lesson you won't soon forget," he said as he stood over her. "Then I'm going to take you into the back room and fuck the living shit out of you! When I get done, ain't no man gonna want to give you another rose ever again!"

She was dazed by the pain washing through her and confused by his actions. He'd hardly ever used closed fists on her before this; it had been mostly open-handed beatings up until now. Explaining away any marks left on her face had not been something he'd ever wanted to do, especially to his coworkers. Her thoughts were jumbled, the blood flowing freely from her battered features as she tried to climb back to her feet, tried to edge away from him. She was absently wiping her hand down the front of her jacket when it slipped into her pocket, and once there, she felt the book, hard and cold beneath her trembling fingers. As her blood soaked into the leathery cover and seeped down into the pages, the ancient tome grew warm beneath her touch.

Before she could react to this unexpected phenomenon, he lunged at her, grabbing the front of her coat and then pulling her up so they were standing nose to nose. His rage-infused features filled her entire range of vision as she stood on tiptoes, clutching his wrists to steady herself.

"You stupid little slut," he growled, his breath foul with the stale stench of whiskey. "Now you're gonna learn what it means to disobey me. When I get done with you, you won't be able to talk back to me ever again. Hell, I'll be surprised if you'll even be able to walk! What do you think of that, you smart-mouthed little cunt?"

"Why don't you go fuck yourself, you impotent pig!"

The angry words had flown out of her mouth almost of their own volition. She was shocked. Whatever had possessed her to say such a thing? Especially now? She watched in bemused horror as his eyes bulged out and a tide of crimson slowly spread across his cheeks to wash up over the top of his head in a sullen wave. Then, with an inarticulate cry of rage, he slammed her down onto the freezer.

The next few minutes were a patchwork of pain and nightmarish sensations. He beat her methodically, holding her against the top of the icebox as he struck her, obscenities rattling out of him in a spitting tirade like an out-of-control madman. Throughout it all, she somehow managed to keep ahold of the vase, the brilliant blue rose now drenched in gore by the blood spraying from the lacerations on her face. After what seemed like an eternity, he finally stopped, panting like a blown horse.

Gazing down at the carnage he had wrought, a degree of sanity returned to his bloodshot eyes. Wiping the sweat from his bald head with a bruised and bloodied hand, he let her slump back across the freezer's lid, stepping away to survey the damage.

"Holy crap!" he exclaimed. "Look what you made me do! If anyone finds out, I'll lose everything. Everything! I might even wind up doing time for this."

His small, piggish eyes darted about the room, searching for what she couldn't even begin to fathom. All she knew was that she was in agony and experiencing a strange weightlessness, as if she were floating. Her hand, still clasping the vase, moved slowly as she drew it up and cradled it against her chest, struggling as she did so to draw oxygen in through her shattered mouth and nose. Shadows gathered in the corners of her eyes as she gasped for air, and she could feel intense heat radiating outward from her jacket pocket. *The strange book*, she thought. Unable to focus, her thoughts unraveled, images both familiar and unfamiliar flowing through her fractured mind. She was afraid, yet the floating sensation seemed to free her from being overly concerned about it. Through eyes that were mostly swollen shut, she watched her husband rooting through the kitchen drawers. After finding whatever it was he'd been looking for, he hurried back over.

Without saying another word, he grabbed her by the waist and then hoisted her up over his shoulder like a sack of potatoes. Opening the freezer with his free hand, he leaned forward, and she flopped down inside it.

"They can't blame me for what they can't find," he said, grinning as he held up a butane lighter. "You're going to burn to death in this freezer, along with the rest of this shitty apartment. No one will ever know what happened to you—I'll make sure of that."

He slammed the lid closed, and she heard the latch click as he locked her in.

After a flash of panic, soothing blasts of cold air began hitting her wounds. She realized now that her death was inevitable and there'd be no fighting against it. Her thoughts cleared in the super-cooled compartment, and for the first time in her life, she became truly angry. Not only at her husband but at herself as well. She had let this happen; she'd been the one to marry into an abusive relationship, the one who was always so mousy and afraid. Her life had been squandered, and now she couldn't go back and rectify any of her foolish mistakes. She longed to have known love, true love, just once in her miserable existence, to have experienced what it must have felt like to have had real feelings flowing through her, to have known true happiness. But now it was over, and she'd never be able to feel anything ever again.

The rose was turning brittle in her hand as it began to frost over in the freezing environment. She could feel it, sense it somehow. Distantly, she heard a roar, like the cry of some ferocious beast, and then the inside of the freezer began to sweat, ice melting and reforming across her body as the heat of the flames outside mixed with the ultra-cool air within. She knew at that moment she was on the verge of imminent demise.

As the fire consumed the building and the freezer melted, warping in upon itself, her spirit rose up and she found herself in a place of glowing mists. A figure waited for her there, wearing the regalia of a noble Japanese house. The woman's face was concealed by a porcelain mask inscribed with brilliant blue characters, and her hair was elaborately piled atop her head, held in place with intricately carved jade pins. Her red and yellow kimono shimmered, its layers of silk sparkling like fireflies, and in her right hand she held an elaborately fashioned mirror. Reaching out with this beautifully decorated object, she offered power, a pact of vengeance, and a warning all at once.

Florence decided to take what was being offered, no matter what the cost.

But as she leaned forward to grasp the proffered mirror, a roaring, blood-red army of hideous, disjointed creatures reared up from somewhere deep within her, swarming out across her ethereal body, and then covering her from head to toe. Seeing this, the masked maiden swelled with righteous anger, her form wavering as she poured more and more of her power through the mirror, trying to stop the diabolical onslaught. But it was of no use. *It's the book*, Florence suddenly realized. Something from the ancient tome, come to lay its own claim upon her.

Power from both of the entities raged through her, stripping insubstantial flesh and bone away from her floating astral form. As the otherworldly creatures battled one another for the possession of her soul, Florence willingly accepted them both. Blood-red flames and ice-blue lightning engulfed her, and she bathed in these raging cataracts of energy, embracing what was being offered from both sources, then melding them into an uneasy alliance within her. Deep in her mind, she held tight to the image of the blue rose. The rose would now define her, would act as a focal point to channel her newfound powers from this day forward.

The world would now pay her back for all she'd lost, all she had never possessed, and the wicked would soon experience the strength of her conviction while feeling the wrath of her bitter regrets. She would take vengeance upon her husband and all others like him, and they would lament ever doing the things they had done to the innocents that they preyed upon.

The image of the blue rose turned to ice within her mind and was then consumed by the burning blood-red flames now surrounding her frozen heart. With these conflicting powers surging through her, she slowly dematerialized into the ethereal realm, formless and unseen.

- 4 -

S takeouts were incredibly boring, especially when working a shit case like the one he was on now. Sitting across from the old warehouse in his unmarked cruiser, he could see the two-story building looming quietly in the shadows amidst coiling tendrils of vaporous fog. It was weather-beaten and lonely, its windows partially boarded like so many missing teeth in a hobo's mouth. By all appearances, it was the perfect place for criminal activity. Unfortunately, there was a whole lot of nothing going on, and it'd been that way since he'd gotten there a couple of hours before. With a sigh, he took another sip of coffee and then glanced around. There still wasn't anything else to see. Just the ever-present fog and garbage surrounding rows of condemned shops leading off to the left. It seemed that this was going to be another long and fruitless night.

He didn't know why he was even on this case to begin with. These smugglers were all on the DA's payroll, and the gang involved was pathetically small. He supposed it was just another way to get him out from underfoot until he was fed up enough to quit. Well, one of these days they were going to push him too far, and then they'd see what he was truly made of—no one could back him into a corner without eventually paying for it. It was just that now wasn't a good time to rock the boat. He had to find out what had really happened to his partner first and then dig up some real dirt.

Enough dirt to hang them all.

But even if he could find the evidence he needed to prosecute, who was he going to show it to? There were very few people left he could trust, and they were all keeping their heads down and their noses out of it. Messing with the status quo around this town could get you killed. Not for the first time, he wondered if that's what had really happened to his partner. The disturbing notion frequently came back to haunt him.

He was still frowning, chewing over his nagging suspicions, when a flickering glow lit up the vehicle's interior. Startled, he glanced in the rearview mirror. A fire had erupted a couple of blocks behind him, and an explosion soon followed his wide-eyed discovery. Swiveling his head around to get a better look, he saw that it was an apartment building, and a large one at that. Keeping his eyes on the blaze, he grabbed the radio microphone.

"Dispatch, this is Unit 16. We have a structural fire over on 5th and Pine. Dispatch fire crews and emergency personnel. I'm proceeding to the scene right now. Copy?"

"Understood, Unit 16," came the static-filled response. "Fire trucks en route. Will send medical teams from Mercy General. Over and out."

Starting the car, he then threw it into drive before pulling out onto the street. Without a backward glance, he sped off, heading toward the building that was now completely engulfed in writhing flames.

As the taillights of Jenkins' squad car disappeared into the mists, a lone figure stepped out from behind a dumpster in the back of the vacant lot. Raising two fingers to his lips, he let out a piercing whistle, and then a leather-clad gang emerged from the deep shadows beside the warehouse. With a wave of acknowledgment, Bobby turned to face the rest of his cohorts.

"Man, I thought that pig would never leave!" he said, studying the inferno raging just a few blocks away. Shrugging, he turned back. "Come on, let's get moving. We're late, and these guys won't wait on us forever."

With that, he led his companions toward the doors on the opposite side of the building. They had an appointment to keep, and he wasn't about to let the police or any lousy slum fire keep him from this meeting. Once they had the merchandise from this deal, they'd be able to take and hold more turf in this section of town. None of the other punks in the area would be able to stand against the Brave Hearts then. The thought of it made him smile as he strode toward the future he'd envisioned for them all.

-5-

"Look, I know this establishment seems a little shady under the circumstances," Abraham said, "but I can assure you that it's all quite safe and truly aboveboard. We have state-of-the-art equipment here, even though it doesn't look like it from the outside."

Sitting in the chair across from his desk, the young woman twisted her hands together, seemingly on the edge of tears. Hell, she didn't even look old enough to be having sex, let alone a child. But that wasn't unusual in this part of town; he'd seen a thousand just like her since he'd been forced to set up shop here three years ago. Sitting there in her rumpled, floral-patterned dress with her hair in braids, she looked like someone's underage daughter, not someone's girlfriend or wife. He sighed.

"Listen, I know this is a big decision, and a difficult one," he said. "Are you sure you really want to go through with it?"

Tears welled up in her eyes, threatening to spill over and run down her freckled cheeks. Choking back a sob, she wiped at her eyes in angry frustration.

"What other choice do I have?" she demanded. "If I don't get rid of it now, I'll be stuck with another mouth to feed—we can't afford that! But it is my baby, my own flesh and blood! Do you know how hard this is for me? I just don't know what else to do!"

She hid her face in her hands, the anguished sobs now coming hard and relentless as he studied her over his long, steepled fingers. He sympathized, he really did, but after years of doing this job day in and day out, he'd become a little jaded. He was a fine doctor and took pride in his work, but he was also a scientist first and foremost. After he'd been forced out of his privately funded labs, he'd had to find a new location to carry on his experiments. His erstwhile colleagues hadn't understood him back then, didn't believe in the vital importance of his work. They probably never would. Still, he was not a complete monster. Sitting straighter in his high-backed chair, he tugged at the lapels of his white lab coat to straighten it.

"It's a tough choice and not one to be taken lightly," he said. Then, smoothing a hand down the front of his immaculate dress shirt, he considered her briefly as he sought the proper words to calm her. "I'll tell you what," he finally offered, "I'm going to let you speak with one of our counselors. She'll be able to give you advice, perhaps even ease your mind about some things, all right?"

The tear-stained look the young woman turned on him was one of hopeful gratitude mixed with resentful uncertainty. He'd seen it hundreds of times before on hundreds of other faces. This city was full of them, and he had helped them all. With another small sigh, he hit the intercom button on the desk phone.

"Monica, would you come in here please?"

"Yes, Dr. Orson," came the cheery reply.

Within moments, the door swung open and a woman dressed in casual business attire entered, her smiling face framed by ringlets of golden-blond hair.

"Monica, this is Libby," Abraham said. "Could you please take her over to the counseling department and see that she gets the best attention from whomever is available?"

"Yes, Doctor," Monica replied. "Libby? Please follow me. Everything is going to be okay. You'll see. We're here to help in any way we can."

As Libby stood to follow her out, Abraham shot Monica an appreciative look. She nodded in acknowledgment and then quietly shut the door behind her as they left.

Leaning back in his chair, he gazed unseeingly at the far wall of his office, memories taking him back to when he'd been able to make a difference. His scientific achievements in the past had made him a celebrity in certain circles, and he desperately missed it. Not the acclaim, but the access to new equipment and the unending flow of money that had once come from private backers to fund his ongoing research. Now he was stuck here in the sleazier part of town, running an illegal abortion clinic. Since the new federal regulations had been put into place limiting women from access to parent planning facilities and other related health services, these little establishments had sprung up like mushrooms all across the country.

He'd been lucky enough to be able to fund his own facility with the last bit of his savings, and in a location that was favorable to his continuing experiments as well. Only the money hadn't lasted long, and the clientele in this part of town left much to be desired. He'd been forced to take out loans from one of the local crime syndicates just to keep the police out of his hair and obtain the equipment he so desperately needed. It was a good thing that he'd figured out a way to tap into the city's power grid or else he would never have been able to afford the electricity required to continue his operations.

Thinking of his secret work made him anxious. He had to succeed before the Gargano family came looking for him. He was already behind on payments, and they didn't play around when it came down to money. He'd have to come up with something soon or suffer the consequences.

With that thought, he got to his feet, moving toward the filing cabinet in the rear corner and then stopping by a mirror on the way to straighten his red silk tie. He'd always been proud of his looks. The image staring back at him had a straight, aristocratic nose, expressive gray eyes, and thick, wavy brown hair. In the past, he'd had more than his fair share of romantic dalliances, but he'd always been careful not to get roped into anything too permanent. He'd known, even then, that he was destined for far better things than just a simple matrimonial existence. That was not the future he'd envisioned for himself—no, he was destined for greatness.

Completing the small adjustments to his wardrobe, he moved around the cabinet and then reached behind it to toggle an unobtrusive switch. When he'd purchased this old building for the site of his new clinic, he'd added some personal touches. The contractors he'd hired to do the remodeling work had all been from out of town, and he'd paid handsomely for their discretion. Now, as the hidden panel in the wall pivoted silently inward, he was glad, once again, that he'd thought of these precautions. Stepping inside the tunnel thus revealed, he closed the partition behind himself and then moved briskly down the steps into the corridor below.

One of the many reasons he'd selected this property was because it had been so close to the abandoned shop across the alley. There was a cellar partially blocked off from the rest of that derelict structure, and it was within that hidden sub-basement that he'd built his secret laboratory. His experiments ran day and night, and none seemed the wiser for it. Now, if he could only get them to come to fruition, all would be well, and he could pay off his debt to the Gargano syndicate.

So far, his results were encouraging, but his ultimate goals had yet to be realized, which left him in somewhat of a limbo as far as funding was concerned. Much of what he was doing would generate capital straightaway, but the main focus of his research could only be cashed in on once the final products were proven successful by extensive testing. Some of that could take years, but he was so close to unlocking it all now, and his facility provided a never-ending source of raw materials for his continual research.

Striding down a short, well-lit hallway, he soon came to a large steel-bound door. Drawing the key card from around his neck, he flashed it across a panel on the wall to the right, and the scanner blinked green. Pressurized air shot out from the edges of the door as hidden hydraulics slid it forward and then slowly retracted it into the wall to the right. The remodeled cellar beyond was spacious and filled with computerized scientific equipment, a vast area of his own design that he was immeasurably proud of. But as the door slid to a stop in the wall bracket, a hand shot out from behind him to grasp at his shoulder.

"There you are, Doc!" said a familiar voice. "We was just coming to talk with you about the debt you owe."

He was shoved forward into the room, and as he spun around in shock, he saw Ronaldo sauntering through the doorway with two of his goons trailing along behind him.

"How did you—"

"How did we know about your secret 'bat cave'?" Ronaldo chuckled. "Come, now! We know all your dirty little secrets. Just like we know you're currently broke and sucking the juice for this lab from the city's power grid and not ours. That's not nice, refusing to use our power like that. That's gonna cost you extra. We want our money, Doc. When can we expect payment?"

From the inside pocket of his sleek Italian suit, Ronaldo drew forth a straight razor, flicking it open with practiced ease.

"A straight razor?" Abraham exclaimed. "Who even uses those anymore? What is this, the 1940s? Somehow I expected more from you, Ronaldo."

Color spread across the thin man's face but did not quite reach the peaked edges of his slicked-back hairline. Carefully, he brought the razor up, turning it in the overhead lighting so that it reflected his cold, dark eyes. With his free hand, he brushed absently at his pencil-thin mustache, then refocused his attention on Abraham.

"You don't say?" he murmured.

At a slight nod from Ronaldo, the two goons burst forward, grabbing Abraham's arms and then pressing him back against the main computer console. Behind him, hundreds of tanks burbled quietly in the background as screens started flickering to life all across the walls of the large chamber. Most of it was automated, and as the mainframe sensed his presence, it started to activate certain critical key features.

"Good lord, Ronaldo!" Abraham cried. "What the devil are you playing at? My work is almost perfected, and soon you'll all be rich.

More than rich—famous! This technology is going to change the world. I just need more time."

"Then you won't mind explaining it to me and my pals here, will you? Call it a 'professional courtesy.' You see, I got to have something to take back to the boss, something more than just empty promises. He's done giving you leeway. That shit was okay for a little while, but now he's starting to get a bit sore at you. You been avoiding us, Doc. And you're late on your payments."

Struggling to shake off the henchmen's grasp, Abraham's anger got the better of him. "I can try and explain it, but I don't think you Neanderthals will understand the intricacies of my experiments!"

"Ouch! That hurts, Doc!" Ronaldo replied, grinning. "But I think we'll understand the important parts just fine. Like the part where we start making all this fabulous amount of dough you keep promising us."

Abraham glared at him, pointedly not looking at the goons that held both his arms. With a slight nod, Ronaldo signaled his men. They dragged Abraham to a chair and then sat him down hard.

"Start talking, Doc," Ronaldo said.

"I'll try and keep this as simple as I can for your limited intellect," Abraham spat. "My research, as you well know, deals with the applications of harvested living cells, as well as organs, tissues, and glands. At its most basic level, the embryos I rescue from unwanted pregnancies are cultivated here in my lab and will eventually provide many useful things to the scientific and medical communities. At its most complex, I am growing living, breathing beings that can be used for head transplants or programmed to serve in clone research. The applications are endless! Imagine, if you will, an unending supply of organs, skin, and cellular tissues for surgical use and burn grafting, stem cells to help develop treatments for hundreds of different ailments, not to mention the military applications of cloning. Why recruit an army when you can simply grow one? All I need is a little more time."

Ronaldo stroked his mustache thoughtfully, holding the razor up with his other hand to act as a mirror. The reflection off the blade caused patterns of light and shadow to dance across his angular features as he pretended to consider.

"It's really just as clear as the nose on your face!" Abraham cried, losing patience with the ridiculous little man. "If only you weren't too stupid to realize the ramifications of it all."

The razor cut through the air, and Abraham flinched back as it flashed before his eyes. Then, a burning pain exploded across his face. As if in slow motion, he watched his nose sail through the air to bounce across the pristine white floor tiles. It left a series of glistening red smears before coming to rest under a chair in the far corner. Crying out as fluids gushed from the large hole above his lips, his hands flew up in a futile attempt to staunch the flow of blood.

"You know, Doc," Ronaldo said, "I don't much like the tone of your voice. The boss says we gotta shake you down, but really, I think we're just done with you. You and your sick experiments. We'll tell him he refused to cooperate, right, boys? You're a nutcase, Doc. And now. . . you're dead. Boys?"

He felt himself being lifted by the goons. They carried him, struggling, back over to the computer console.

"You'll regret this, Ronaldo!" he shouted. "You and your whole family!"

"Oh, I doubt that, Doc. I really do."

Bucking and twisting within their grip, he was lifted higher but couldn't seem to break himself free. Swinging him back and forth a couple times, they finally hurled him over the console and into the far room, his body crashing down into the hundreds of burbling tanks of the experiments that were in various stages of development. As he smashed through them, they exploded, and energy channeled from the city's power grid surged forth in a violent electrical wave.

It was a pain like none other, and it felt as if he were melting within the masses of released embryos, flailing through hundreds of tiny bodies while sinking down through the thousands of gallons of surging embryonic fluids. Struggling to stay on top of the flow of protoplasmic goo, he was instead dragged deeper into its electrified embrace. He was dying and knew a moment of sheer panic as he struggled against this inevitable demise. Current ran throughout the chamber, exploding more and more of his experiments, and then the floor suddenly gave way beneath him. He was poured down into another room situated just below the lab.

It was a much smaller space and soon filled up with embryos and swirling fluids. As he sank into their lightning-shot depths, he saw from out of the corner of his eyes a shrine resting just below him. The room itself was like some kind of imperial temple out of a historical play, its columns and screens decorated in eloquently carved motifs. The rich simplicity of the space astounded him. When he'd created his laboratory within the herbal shop's abandoned cellar, he'd never imagined that this room even existed. A plaque engraved with Japanese symbols peeked out from the side of the shrine where it had broken open from chunks of debris striking it as they sank. Reaching out with his last ounce of strength, he grabbed at it, not knowing why he did so. Subjected to incredible amounts of torturous pain, his mouth finally spasmed open, and then he was drowning in electrified embryonic goo. Skin and hair sloughed from his bones as he succumbed to death's final embrace.

Suddenly, the pain was gone, and he found himself within a great expanse of shimmering mist. Standing before him was an old man dressed in ancient ceremonial robes, his head covered by an intricately fashioned mask resembling the face of a snarling lion. In his gnarled hand, he held forth a staff inlaid with ritualistic symbols and decorated with a round, sparkling jewel set at the top of its highly polished length.

Abraham instinctively knew what was being offered.

Reaching out, he grasped the jeweled staff and accepted the unspoken pact. His reemergence into the world of men would be one of vengeance but also one of rebirth, and he felt himself filling with the immense power needed to achieve such lofty goals.

Soon the criminal family that had destroyed his lab would be shown the error of their ways, as would the scientists that had once stood against him, scientists who even now were most likely copying his research for their own greedy benefit. He would avenge himself on all who stood in his way, and they would perish in anguish and fear. With a small bow and an inclination of his masked head, the priestly spirit accepted his dedication, then gradually faded from view.

Abraham found himself sitting alone in his office, illuminated by a faint fluctuating glow seeping in from the outer windows. The explosions in the lab must have blown out the rest of the power, he surmised. Climbing to his feet, he noticed his lab coat was different now, more elaborately constructed than it had been before. Its partitioned length, flowing around him like a robe, had Japanese symbols stitched all across it in shimmering white thread, and a high collar now encircled his slender neck. Raising his hands, he could see that they had regained their flesh but gleamed with an inner bluish radiance of their own. As he raised them up, holding them out to study them, he suddenly knew how to focus this newfound energy.

With a flick of his long fingers, small bodies of light and shadow materialized throughout the air. They floated in clusters of protoplasmic harmony, forming and re-forming when they touched, passing through one another in a never-ending display of arcane osmosis. It was like being inside a giant lava lamp. Fascinated, he watched them for a moment longer, coming to realize what they were.

They were the fetuses from his destroyed experiments.

He could control them, marshal them together from between the realms of time and space, and then send them out to do his bidding. They would fly for him, and attack in droves, overcoming anyone and anything that stood in his way. They were magnificent in their half-formed, fetal elasticity, beautiful to his eyes, yet deadly to any who would stand against him. Swarming through the air in globular masses of ever-changing reanimation, they were now his unformed family, summoned at his beck and call. With a wave of one hand, he dismissed them back into the aether from whence they came.

For now.

Wandering over to the mirror, he froze, staring at his reflection in growing dismay. Gone were the handsome features he'd once taken such pride in. The glorious wavy brown hair was burnt away from a head now swollen and distorted, the nose and ears almost nonexistent upon rippling, layers of scarred and patchy skin. Gazing back at him was the image of a large unblinking fetus, a bulging underdeveloped caricature of a man, glowing with a faint blue radiance and dominated by huge lidless white eyes. It was strangely fitting, yet it caused him a great deal of sudden, uncontrollable rage.

Swirling his robes about him, he turned and left the office. He would start with the Gargano family. It was only right that they should pay for what they'd done. Summoning all his dignity, he stalked out of the building and out into the fire-lit darkness of the surrounding alleyways. Turning away from the large apartment fire raging in the near distance, he disappeared into the shadowy mists, like a wraith on a mission of silent retribution.

-6-

Dust motes rose up and danced through the air as Bobby's heels echoed off the weathered floorboards. Resounding with the sounds of the rest of his crew's footsteps, they made an ominous counterpoint as the gang ventured further into the shadowy building. The main room was cavernous, liberally littered with piles of old wooden pallets and derelict machinery. The members of his team fanned out as they moved forward, scanning the darkness with predatory eyes, but they weren't really concerned. This meeting was prearranged, and they were to be expected.

A platform with stairs leading up to the offices on the second floor was situated toward the back of the large central area. As they stepped into the light coming from a series of single-bulb fixtures running along the top of the second-story landing, Bobby slowed to a stop, signaling his men to hold up. There was something wrong here, something that had his senses tingling like crazy. Scanning the encircling gloom, he hesitated, trying to pinpoint just what was setting off this sudden case of unease.

Charlie, watching them from the shadows, smiled to see his adversary pause in such conflicted indecision. There were five of them, including the leader and his woman, not to mention the three left outside to stand guard, whom he'd already dealt with. Letting his children move him forward a few feet, Charlie entered the pool of artificial light spilling across the middle of the wooden platform.

"Well, well," he said. "So here we all are, together again! Welcome, my old friends! I have been expecting you."

Bobby started, but then relaxed, disdaining to identify the old man confronting them as a threat. Rita, grasping his arm, pressed herself against him as the others closed in from all sides.

"We're here for the shipment," Bobby stated, glancing around. "Where's Sanchez? And who the fuck are you?"

Charlie shifted in his seat. It was a sprawling affair that fit around him like an oversized throne. Black and brown spokes radiated outward from the back of it, disappearing into the darkness behind him, while the armrests and base were like a solid mass of interconnecting shells. He had hoped that they'd recognize him, but he should have guessed that his new appearance would cause some small amount of confusion. It didn't help that the hood of his long burgundy cloak shadowed his features while the rest of its folds covered him like a mantle of dried blood.

"Ah, I see that you do not yet recall me," Charlie said. "Well, I can certainly rectify that, old friend. You see, I am Charlie, and you know me from the alleyway just beyond this building. Do you not remember? Hmmm. . . then perhaps you will more readily recognize my companion here. Simon?"

As Simon scuttled from the shadows to the very edge of the platform, the gang members shifted about, Rita letting out a small yelp of surprise. He was much larger now, a veritable nightmare sprung to life from out of the darkest depths of demented dreams, his antennae weaving in intricate patterns as he stared at them through cold jet-black eyes.

-Father, do you wish me to kill them?-

The thought sounded inside his mind alone, yet Charlie felt the need to respond to the question aloud.

"No, not yet, my overeager compadre. Let us just stick to the plan, shall we?"

"What plan, old man?" Bobby exclaimed. "Who're you talkin' to? That bug? I thought I already fuckin' killed you *and* your pet roach. What the hell are you doing here, anyway?"

He sounded brave enough in front of his men, but the sweat on his brow betrayed his fear. Charlie could smell the reek of it from where he sat on his spindly throne.

The other gang members tensed in the darkness, fingering their weapons. Their eyes were wide with anxiety, but they refused to back down in front of their leader. They were a loyal crew and trusted Bobby to figure this whole thing out. Besides, they had come for the merchandise, and they weren't leaving without it.

Charlie grinned.

"Why, I am here to pay you back for all you have done! And to take your woman from you, as you once took my daughter from me so long ago—"

"I've had enough of this crap," Bobby cut in, straightening to his full height as he drew a knife from inside his jacket. "Blake? Take that old fool out. Nobody messes with us on our own turf and gets away with it!"

Rolling his shoulders, Blake took a deep breath and walked up the stairs, swinging his metal baseball bat back and forth to loosen himself up. The muscles of his chest and arms bulged from beneath his black leather jacket as the bat swished through the air. When he reached the top of the steps, he rushed forward with all the arrogance of youth. But as he flew across the wooden platform, the boards gave way beneath him and he fell through the flooring up to his chest with a shrill screech of surprise. The other gang members lunged forward, ready for action, but Bobby raised his hand, holding them back.

"Yo, Blake, stop fooling around up there," he said. "Are you stuck or something? What the fuck happened?"

Blake shifted, dropping the bat as he placed both hands on the platform and tried to shove his way out. Yet it only increased his entanglement.

"I'm stuck," he shouted. "Some kind of sticky shit down here under these rotted boards."

"Did you know," Charlie said, almost conversationally, "that it takes about an hour for a spider to spin its web? Although, if you have a million spiders all working together, they can spin their webs in an amazingly short period of time."

Blake stopped struggling, staring up at Charlie with horror-chilled bloodless features.

"Spiders?" Blake ventured uncertainly.

"Oh, do not worry. I have sent them all away," Charlie purred. "And the termites who weakened the boards for me are gone now as well."

"What the fuck are you on about?" Bobby scoffed. "Are you trying to tell us that you can control insects? That's bullshit, old man. Blake, get your ass out of that hole and finish this guy off already. We got business upstairs. Enough fooling around. It's go time!"

"Bobby. . ." Blake began, but froze as a small creature with striped yellow markings crawled across his chest and then scuttled up his neck.

Charlie chuckled. "I sent the spiders and termites away, but the stinging insects are more than willing to do as I command. There are hundreds of different species living here in the city. How fortunate I am to have access to them all."

With that, the rest of the gang watched in disbelief as a horde of bees and wasps swarmed up from beneath the platform, covering Blake in a living blanket of buzzing black and yellow bodies. He opened his mouth to scream, but the insects poured down his throat before more than a sharp squeal could leak out. Then, they began to sting. Blake bucked and thrashed, whimpering and clawing at the surging multitudes covering him, but it was of no use. Within seconds, he was dead. As the droning, undulating mass that concealed his corpse sank back down into the hole, Charlie looked out at the rest of the gang with a feral grin.

"¡Dios mío!" Rita cried out, clutching at Bobby's arm.

"Enough!" Bobby roared. "Ox? Take that motherfucker out!"

Easily the largest of the group, Ox stood at a good six-foot four inches, a muscular youth filled with too much passion and loyalty to be afraid of anything. Without hesitation, he leaped onto the platform, jumped across the gaping hole in the planking, and then brought his machete down in a powerful, two-handed arc. As the blade struck Charlie square in the face there was a ringing noise like the sound of metal striking against granite. Bending under the force of the blow, the machete twisted out of Ox's hands, ricocheting off into the shadows.

Charlie looked at him, with amusement in his glowing eyes. "Oh, you'll have to do better than that," he murmured.

Charlie rose to his feet as the throne disintegrated around him, his movement punctuated by the maddened, clickering surge of its explosive deconstruction. The centipedes and cockroaches that made up the structure of his vile seat filled the air around him, boiling forth en masse to envelop Ox within their seething multitudes. The boy screamed, thrashing as the tide of insects rolled over him and bore him to the floor, continuing to wail as Charlie strode to the edge of the platform, the burgundy cloak flowing around him like a living, breathing thing.

Brushing back the hood, Charlie exposed the knobby surface of his chitinous skin, the nodes on his head standing out like the beginnings of proud horns, his dark liquid eyes flashing green in the dimness. "I will determine, in my own good time, when you have had 'enough,'" he snarled.

With a simple nudge of his newfound powers, thousands of fire ants covering the ceiling in an immense colony began to pour down upon Bobby's last remaining gang member. As the insects enveloped him, turning him into a pile of shrieking, thrashing limbs covered in layers of tiny stinging assailants, Bobby backed away, pushing Rita behind him as his eyes now sought any avenue of escape.

"You know," Charlie drawled, watching his adversary with undisguised glee, "there are at least five different species of ticks that can cause paralysis in humans."

There was a tickle at the back of Bobby's neck, and for the first time, he allowed himself to feel the fear that he'd held in abeyance for so long. Grabbing Rita's hand, he pivoted to run, but his limbs turned to jelly and he crashed to the floorboards instead, his back thudding against one of the support pylons at the center of the room. Rita gazed down on him, horrified, eyes going wide as a pitiful sob escaped her trembling lips. Turning in a circle, she looked for a way out, a place that she could run to, yet the floor now churned with hordes of insects. All different types and species were gathering there, in the millions, staring at her from trillions of shiny obsidian eyes. Twisting back around, she fell to her knees before Charlie, her hands upraised in shaking submission.

"Please," she whimpered. "I didn't do nothing to you. I wasn't even there when they killed your kid. Please. . ."

"Oh, it is far, far too late for clemency," Charlie said. "You are a necessary part of my plans, you see. I have need of a queen, someone that I can use to breed my new army of soldiers for the battles yet to come. You have everything I need to achieve this goal, and it will start here, tonight, in this warehouse. So, are you ready? Ready to become the mother of my new breed of children?"

She tried to scramble back to her feet, but there was a pinch at the base of her cranium. Crumpling to the floor, she was unable to move as Bobby watched on in paralyzed anguish. With a wave of his arm, Charlie ordered his swarm of cockroaches forward. Leaving the still twitching bones and ligaments that were all that remained of Ox, they ran beneath Rita's body like a living carpet. It took some maneuvering, but they eventually had her lying flat on her back with her legs spread far apart. One of her shoes had fallen off during the process, and her mini skirt was now hiked up at an odd angle, leaving herself partially exposed. She swallowed heavily, her eyes darting this way and that, unable to even scream.

"You see, Rita, I have gathered here the most vicious of my children, all the stinging, biting, deadliest of insects that infest this cesspool of a city. From them, my dear friend Simon has gathered the necessary components to make a new breed of warrior, a larger species—one with more stamina, a bigger bite radius, and a longer, more envenomed sting. They will be faster, smarter, harder to kill. Simon, of course, will be the father of my new children, my indestructible soldiers of retribution, and you, my dear, you will be his mate. . ."

She tried to scream then, to slide away, but her limbs would not obey her. Her eyes, blurred by tears of frustration and terror, followed the progress of the huge loathsome cockroach as it scuttled past her, heading toward her lower body. Soon, she could feel its antennae twitching and caressing the smooth surface of her legs as it moved past her trembling calf muscles and then scrambled inexorably up between her inner thighs. With an eagerness that was unnatural for such a creature, it eased itself into place before her pelvic mound, and then she could feel its oversized mouth parts tearing away at her panties, its hairy forelegs pushing the remaining folds of her skirt aside to obtain better access to her nethermost regions. As the material of her underwear parted, she felt its hard, bulbous head entering her body, sliding up into her vagina, its chitinous plates and stiff, bristly hairs abrading the interior of her endometrial lining as it forced its way into her abdomen. A single moan escaped her throat as the tears began spilling down her cheeks, her breathing now rapid and heavy with pain.

"Yes, you will most assuredly become our queen," Charlie said. "To be used in breeding all my new soldiers. Do not worry; we will keep you alive for quite some time yet. Your womb will be the birthplace of all our new brethren until we hatch out a new queen to serve us in your stead."

Bobby, watching from where he lay immobilized, could see that the immense cockroach had now completely disappeared inside of Rita. He struggled but could not even twitch a muscle as Simon penetrated deep into his girlfriend's waiting womb.

"And you, my *friend*," Charlie growled, turning back to him, eyes flashing. "You will watch as we mount your woman over and over again, breeding from her millions of my warrior children. We will use her until she can be used no longer—much like you once used my daughter. And through it all, you will be powerless to stop me, until you eventually witness her horrific death. Only then will you truly be able to know the depths of the anguish that you have caused me."

Rita's abdomen undulated as the large insect inside her began to fertilize and deposit thousands of specialized eggs. Tears of rage leaked from Bobby's eyes, and Charlie laughed, a thin screeching sound that echoed shrilly in the confines of the abandoned building.

-7-

Mercy General Hospital squatted on the west side of town like an overfed gargoyle, the architecture grim, the windows narrow, and the entire building looking like it could use a fresh coat of paint. It always gave Jenkins the creeps whenever he had to go there, and today was no exception. Having been up all night scouting the edges of the apartment fire and interviewing survivors only added to the sense of unease he was now feeling. But once he'd arrived at the scene, there was not much else he could have done. The inferno had raged out of control, and not even the fire department with all their ladder trucks could save it. The whole place had gone up like a haystack in the middle of a dry summer.

Which only made his decision to come here this morning all the more bothersome. There was something very wrong going on, something he couldn't quite put his finger on. All the people he'd interviewed last night had been evasive while answering his questions. No one was talking, and he wanted to know why. It was worth a shot to speak with those who'd been more seriously injured. Maybe being badly burned would loosen some tongues and get him the answers he needed.

The interior of the building was easier on the eye, probably from all the efforts made by the remaining staff to spruce up the place now that most of the personnel had transferred to the new facility in a better part of town. Harlson Medical Group, those rich, entitled bastards, always stole the best employees and left the dregs to deal with the lower-income clientele whenever they took things over. It was just the way of the world. In any event, plants were now strategically placed around the waiting area, and a large tropical fish tank dominated one whole wall. He was gazing at an angelfish as it fanned its fins in the burbling water when the intake clinician came out to meet with him.

"Detective Jenkins?" she said. "I'm Lisell Pachenke, hospital liaison here at Mercy General. I've been told that you want to interview some of our recently admitted patients?"

She carried herself with poise and grace, her natural attractiveness only enhanced by the lack of makeup or expensive clothing. As her hazel eyes gazed out at him through stylish oversized glasses, he stared back, taking in her loose auburn hair, perfectly proportioned features, and trim black-and-white outfit. She reminded him of a runway model taking the day off from the catwalk.

"Detective Jenkins?" she prompted.

"My apologies," he replied hastily, shaking himself out of his reverie. "I've been up all night at the fire."

"I'm sorry to hear that. Now, can you tell me why you need to interview our patients so soon after the incident? Most of them are in pretty bad shape."

"Well," he hedged, "we've been having some trouble determining the cause of the blaze. I thought it would be a good idea to go over some of the statements I've already taken from other witnesses and compare them to what the injured parties might have to say."

She looked him up and down, noting perhaps his rumpled appearance and the dark soot stains from helping firemen drag survivors out of the smoldering wreckage all night. Glancing aside, she waved over a passing orderly.

"Jerimiah? Can you please bring this officer a cup of fresh coffee? Thank you."

As the orderly nodded and walked off toward the cafeteria, she returned her attention to Jenkins with flattering solicitude.

"I understand your desire to obtain more information about the case, but couldn't it wait?" she asked. "The fire is out, and these people aren't going anywhere. Perhaps if you gave us a chance to get them all comfortably settled and let them rest a bit first, their minds would be clearer, more able to produce the results you desire?"

"I've found that the best results come from the freshest recollections," he said, giving her his most disarming smile. "Waiting could cause the memories of what happened to dim, make them harder to recall in as much detail. It won't take me long—just a few questions, then I'll be out of your hair."

"Well. . ." she drawled, teetering on the verge of capitulation.

Just then his phone went off, and he held up one hand apologetically while retrieving it from his inside pocket with the other. "This is Jenkins," he answered.

"Jenkins!" the captain's voice blared from the receiver. "Where the hell are you! I need you to get down to the park on Central Avenue. They've found a body, and you're the closest detective we've got."

"I've been up at that apartment fire all night, sir," Jenkins replied. "There's something fishy going on over there. I'm about to interview the survivors here at the hospital, and I think we may have a case of arson connected with the criminal underworld. A lot of the residents that I spoke with last night were clammed up pretty tight about it. They're afraid of something; I can feel it."

"I don't give a flying rat's ass about the fucking fire! Get over to the park and check out that dead body! Now!"

With a wince, Jenkins put the phone back in his jacket pocket. The clinician was looking at him with amusement sparkling in her lively eyes.

"Sounds like your boss is a pretty swell guy," she ventured.

"Yeah, a real cupcake," he replied, grimacing.

The orderly came up and handed him a steaming cup of joe. After taking a careful sip, he let out a sigh. "Well, it looks like I may have to postpone the interviews until later. Thank you so much for your time, Miss Pachenke. Can I call on you again soon?"

He hadn't meant it to come out sounding the way it did, but he was tired and not thinking too clearly. Besides, she was quite a woman, which also added to his inability to articulate, even though he knew he had absolutely no chance with her romantically. But watching her with a practiced eye for detail, he noted that she seemed surprised rather than offended by his unintentional advances.

"When you get the chance," she said, smiling, "come and find me in my office. Then we'll see about getting you access to those patients, alright? And, Detective?"

"Yes?"

"You be careful out there."

With that last remark, she turned and sauntered away. He tried hard not to stare but just couldn't help himself. The orderly cleared his throat, and Jenkins jumped a little, glancing over at him. Grinning, the orderly gave him a sly wink. With an embarrassed flush creeping up his cheeks, Jenkins turned and strode past him, leaving the hospital as he headed for his waiting squad car.

The park was only a few miles away, so he was there within minutes. As he pulled up, he saw a few lowly beat cops on the scene and an ambulance. The area had been cordoned off with yellow tape, and a hearse from the city morgue was just pulling in as he got out of the cruiser and walked over.

"What've you got for me, Moody?" he asked the officer standing by the taped-off area who was busily scribbling on a small notepad.

"Not quite sure yet, Detective," the man replied, scratching the back of his head and then repositioning his cap. "One dead guy, no signs of a struggle. No wounds, no tracks, no nothin'."

The corpse lay on the cold hard ground, the crisp leaves of autumn blowing around it. Right away, it sent unexpected chills up Jenkins' spine. He'd seen dozens of dead bodies over the years but had no idea why this one was affecting him so differently. Maybe it was the look on the corpse's face. Something about the way the eyes stared sightlessly out in absolute despair, or the way the lips were drawn back in a rictus of unbridled remorse. He'd never seen such an anguished look on a corpse's face before. Gazing down at it, he ran a hand over the stubble on his chin while he considered. There was no blood, no signs of a struggle. The man lay on his back, his arms and legs drawn up like he'd been trying to dig his way out of a grave, his hands twisted into claws.

"Heart attack?" he asked, glancing over at the medical examiner.

"Maybe," the man replied. "It's hard to say."

There was something else bugging Jenkins, something that tickled just at the back of his mind. He knew this John Doe from somewhere. Then it hit him.

"This is Chris Plunkett," he said to the other officer. "Long record of assault, child molestation, domestic violence—you name it. This guy was a total abusive asshole."

They both stared down at the rigid body as the coroner wheeled over a stretcher. There was nothing more of interest to see here. The crime scene itself, if it could even be called that, seemed clear of further evidence according to the officers already present. Besides, he was tired, really tired, and it was all up to the autopsy now anyway. Turning, he started strolling back toward his squad car.

"You leavin' already, Jenkins?" the younger officer called out after him.

"Yeah, this one's all yours, Moody. Good luck!"

It was just one more lousy, two-bit case like all the rest they'd given him lately, and he found that he just didn't care enough to linger. Giving Moody one last distracted wave of his hand, he got back in the vehicle and then headed home.

-8-

Luciano Gargano stood by the window in his study gazing down at the city spread out below the secluded hillside his mansion was built upon. It was magnificent to look upon, this place where he'd grown up, and now it was almost his to do with as he so pleased. Sure, it had its faults—what thriving metropolis didn't? But he was so close to overcoming the last obstacles left in his path, on the verge of obtaining absolute control of everything within it. Then he could reshape it in any way that he saw fit.

He hadn't been simply handed his current position of power. Far from it, in fact. As an illegitimate son of a younger Gargano family member, he'd needed to earn his place the hard way. From running the streets at a young age, to becoming an enforcer, and then a trusted right-hand man, he had worked his way up through the ranks until he'd become indispensable. His was a bestowed title and not one that he'd obtained by treachery or murder alone. Once he'd proven himself many times over to the entire Gargano syndicate, he'd then been chosen by the matriarch to succeed the old Don when he'd passed away.

As soon as he'd assumed the mantle of power, he had moved to consolidate the family's holdings, and they were considerable. More than two-thirds of the area was now owned by them, or by their affiliates, and they had many of the highest officials and members of the police force deep in their pockets as well. There were just a few loose ends left to tie up, and then the entire city would be his.

Sighing, he glanced over at the lower sections of town, the meanest neighborhoods, full of filth and degradation. It was there that he'd gotten his start, but he now sought to eliminate those despicable slums once and for all. His plans for them were many and filled with variation. The complexity was necessary to retain flexibility as he had several strategies in place that could result in total success at any moment. Or, instead, fail him utterly.

Such was the heavy burden of leadership.

There was a knock on the oak-paneled door. Turning from the window, his eyes slid past the luxurious paintings and handcrafted furniture, glancing toward the entranceway while brushing imaginary specks of dust from the sleeve of his immaculate cream-colored suit.

"Come," he called out.

The door opened, and Bernardo, one of his high-ranking servants, advanced into the room with a bow. "Mr. Gargano, the visitors you requested have arrived."

"Good," he said. "Have them escorted to the patio off the west wing. I'll be along directly."

"Certainly, sir."

As Bernardo bowed himself out, closing the door as he left, Luciano sighed again. He prided himself on knowing people. . . and knowing them well. What drove them, what frightened them, what they would do anything to possess, and the best way to inspire them to do things that the Gargano syndicate required. In some cases, it was better to use a gentle hand and forgiving attitude, to nurture and cultivate a mutual sense of trust, develop a sense of deeper loyalty.

Violence was not always the best solution.

Leaving the study, he strolled through his palatial estate and paused as he reached the west wing patio doors. Just outside was an expanse of rounded architecture fronted by a marble balustrade and flagged in creamy Italian tile work. A few decorative wrought-iron chairs clustered around a low table, and many potted plants stretched their foliage up and over the area to provide cool areas of shade on hot summer days.

Standing by the balustrade and gazing out over the city was Marco Giovanni, his head of operations in the lower district. Off to the left there was also a man with a pencil-thin mustache and slicked-back hair. He was paring his fingernails with a straight razor while two nondescript gentlemen with the look of competent street thugs stood beside him. Their eyes roamed everywhere and nowhere at once, and they'd placed themselves strategically. Without further ado, Luciano moved through the doors, passing two of his own guards, who straightened to attention as he walked by.

"Marco!" he exclaimed. "How good of you to come. How are things in the lower city?"

Giovanni had the good graces to turn with a look of mild embarrassment. A summons from the Don was almost never a good thing, especially when framed as an urgent request.

"Well enough, Mr. Gargano," he replied. "To what do I owe the honor of your invitation? As you can see, I've brought the men that you wished to speak with. What's this all about?"

Luciano strode forward with a practiced ease, extending his hand. Marco reached out, and they shared a firm handshake.

"Come, let us speak," Luciano offered, walking over to the railing and gesturing at the view. "Isn't it marvelous?"

"Yes, it's quite breathtaking, sir," Marco said, moving to stand beside him.

Luciano ran his hand across the fine marble of the balustrade, staring out over the surrounding area and letting the silence stretch on for a few moments. It was a calculated ploy, and one that displayed his power gracefully. Marco was well-mannered enough not to fidget. Luciano's estimation of him went up a notch at this show of respectful restraint.

"Well," he finally continued, "let me get right to the point. I called you here because I've heard some unsettling rumors from my informants. The word on the street is that Dr. Orson has been eliminated. Perhaps you would be good enough to explain—"

"I took that lunatic out for you, Mr. Gargano," the razor-wielding man interrupted.

Luciano turned, motioning his guards back with a small gesture. They had moved further onto the patio at this breach of etiquette, knowing how badly he detested such rude behavior. Locking eyes with the small man, Luciano then stepped over to him.

"And you are?" he inquired with great civility.

"The name's Ronaldo, sir. I work for Mr. Giovanni there."

"Are you telling me that you were ordered to kill Doctor Abraham Orson?"

"Well," the man hedged, cowed by Luciano's forthright manner and penetrating gaze. "Not exactly. But he was insane, sir. His experiments were a bunch of sci-fi baloney. We did you a favor."

"So, then," Luciano said, "you weren't ordered to kill him, and yet you took it upon yourself to do so, regardless of the consequences. Tell me, what exactly were your orders?"

Ronaldo fidgeted, painfully aware that he may have overstepped his authority. "My orders, sir, were to shake him down a bit, check on his progress, and then report back."

"And so you decided to kill him instead, on your own initiative, contrary to your direct orders?"

"Well," he said, "Rex and Patrick here helped, and then we destroyed his crazy lab in the process. The guy was a total nutcase, sir."

Gazing past Ronaldo's shoulder, Luciano motioned to one of his guards. Without hesitation, the man pulled his weapon and shot both of Ronaldo's co-conspirators in the back of the head. As they toppled to the ground, their brains splattering across the spotless cream-colored tiles, Ronaldo began to realize that he was on shaky ground indeed.

"So, you not only took it upon yourself to kill Dr. Abe Orson, but you also destroyed his valuable research lab," Luciano continued. "A laboratory on which I have spent a great deal of time and money. Research that, by all my previous reports, was very close to completion? Did you at least obtain his notes? Clean out his safe? Where are these valuable scientific documents now?"

Ronaldo was sweating buckets, the beads of moisture sliding down his high forehead and then trailing across his ashen features. His eyes shifted to Marco, then slid back to Luciano. Finally he had the good graces to stare down at his feet in shame.

"I don't have them, sir," he said, swallowing heavily. "Everything was destroyed with the lab."

"I see," Luciano replied.

Without warning, he snatched the razor from out of Ronaldo's lax grasp and then swiped it across the man's own throat. Grabbing him by the back of the neck with his free hand, he cast the razor aside before forcing his other hand up into the spurting wound. Digging upward through the neck cartilage, he reached into Ronaldo's mouth, grabbed a hold of his tongue, and then yanked it back down through the gash in his neck. As Ronaldo gagged and flailed, Luciano held him firmly against the balustrade, supporting his weight and watching as his eyes fluttered spasmodically, the blood spraying from the gaping slash to gush down the front of Luciano's expensive cream-colored suit. It took only a few lingering moments before it was all over. As the last light of life dimmed from Ronaldo's eyes, Luciano let the corpse slump to the ground at his feet. Then, he turned back to Marco, fishing a small handkerchief from his inside pocket.

"I am disappointed," he murmured, blood soaking into his jacket and dripping off the front of his slacks to add to the pool forming on the patio tiles. "When I gave you this assignment, I thought that I had been explicitly clear on how important it was to me. It took a lot of time, money, and effort to get Dr. Orson pushed out of his own privately funded labs uptown and then indebted to us so we could be the ones to reap the benefits of his research. And now, it is all gone, destroyed by your careless mismanagement."

Marco maintained eye contact with him. He respected that—the man had guts.

"It was my mistake, Don Gargano," he said. "My life is in your hands."

Luciano liked a man who could assume full responsibility for his own shortcomings. It spoke well of him.

"Perhaps then you would appreciate another chance to prove your worth to me."

"Yes, sir," Marco replied. "I won't let you down again."

With a small nod to his household guards, he signaled that the meeting was at an end. As one of the men led Marco back into the house, Luciano returned to the balustrade, staring out over the city he loved. In the background, a group of cleaners began to unobtrusively tidy away the bodies and wipe up the swiftly congealing blood.

Sometimes, he thought, cleaning his hands off with the silk handkerchief, *violence is the very best solution.*

-9-

Receiving calls on his day off was another thing that was getting really old. He'd only been sleeping for about six hours when his phone began ringing incessantly. No matter how hard Jenkins tried to ignore it, whoever was calling just kept at it. With a surge of frustrated anger, he groped after the irritating device.

"What?" he finally grumbled into the receiver.

"Jenkins!" the captain's voice roared back at him. "Get your ass down to the morgue! You were supposed to be investigating that crime scene this morning. What the hell happened? I need you to find out what the fuck is going on before the Chief starts chewing me a new asshole!"

"Captain Wolfe," he mumbled, rubbing his eyes and then rolling over onto his back. "Meaning no disrespect, sir, but there are at least twenty other guys you could put on this case. The victim was a known felon, and it was likely just a simple heart attack."

"I don't give a rat's ass about your worthless speculations, Jenkins. I need cold, hard facts!" Wolf shouted. "And unless everybody is suddenly having heart attacks in this town, we now have six more *homicides* just like him down at the morgue, and that's only in the last eight hours! It's a goddamn epidemic! So unless you want a *permanent* vacation, get your ass down there! Now!"

He winced as the captain hung up. So much for his day off.

After a quick shave and shower, he got dressed and then headed over to Mercy General. These types of cases usually wound up there, the city morgue uptown being reserved for more important clientele.

As he pulled into the parking lot, he began to wonder about all the unexplained deaths. Pausing for a moment, he did a little research on the squad car's computer and discovered that the victims had all been found within a five-block radius of the park, and none of the crime scenes had shown any signs of physical violence. Come to think of it, that park was right down the street from the fire last night. Was there a connection? He didn't think so. Still, it was a weird coincidence, and he didn't like coincidences. There was something going on in his town, and related or not, he was going to figure it out.

After skirting the hustle and bustle of the main lobby, he took the elevator down to the basement. It was there that they performed the autopsies, down where the bodies could be kept closer to cold storage. Hopefully, he'd be able to obtain some information from the forensic pathologist.

He walked down a long hallway and then pushed through the double doors leading to the autopsy room. The corpse from that morning was on a table with medical instruments and apparatus stationed all around it. A small man dressed in surgical scrubs, gloves, and a face shield held a scalpel and was preparing to make an incision into the chest of the subject. As Jenkins walked in, the man paused, reaching over to switch off his recording device before turning back and giving Jenkins a lopsided smile.

"Detective!" he said. "To what do I owe the dubious honor of your visit? I've only just completed the external examination and was getting ready to move on to the internal. I won't have anything concrete for you for another couple of hours at least."

"What? No music? No sandwich?" Jenkins asked.

The man pointed the scalpel at him. "You, my friend, have been watching too many movies. We have more respect for the dead around here in real life. This is an important job, and one we take very seriously."

He winked, grinning with his usual wry humor. Jenkins had always liked Miles McCready; he was a forthright guy and knew his job backward and forward. If there was any sign of foul play, he'd find it.

"Yeah, I knew it would take a while," he replied. "But the captain's already bustin' my balls—he says we got a bunch more just like this one that came in over the last few hours. You get anything from the external?"

"It's all pretty straightforward so far," Miles said. "No signs of a struggle, no bruising, nothing that would indicate cause of death yet. But there is one small thing that I find to be highly unusual. Come over here and take a look."

He pointed the scalpel at the victim's chest, and Jenkins walked over to stare down at it. But there was nothing there to see.

"What am I looking at, Miles?" he asked, scratching the back of his head.

"Here," Miles said, pulling the overhead magnifier over and shining the light down on the body.

As Jenkins bent over the magnifying glass, he could just make out a tiny round spot of darkened skin slightly to the left of dead center on the torso.

"Needle mark?" he guessed.

"Nope," Miles replied.

"Some type of skin condition, then?"

"Wrong again."

"Well, I give up. What the hell is it?"

"If I didn't know any better, I'd have to say it was severe frostbite."

Jenkins glanced at Miles, raising an eyebrow. "You're kidding me, right?"

"Not in the least," Miles replied. "Of course, I won't know for sure until I get in there. There's still a lot of tests to run. If you come back later, I may have something more for you then. As of right now, I really don't know what killed him. I just felt that this was unusual enough to point out."

Jenkins stroked his chin, staring down at the corpse as he considered. Frostbite? In August? It hardly seemed likely. And why just in one tiny area? It didn't make any sense. Taking a business card out of his jacket pocket, he laid it on the instrument tray.

"Do me a favor," he said. "Call me as soon as you know anything, alright? The captain's really frothing at the mouth over this. Have you had a chance to look over any of the other bodies yet?"

Miles gave him a sideways glance. "Are you kidding?" he said. "These things take time, my friend. I've got corpses piling up in the back, and my autopsy tech is on lunch break. Tell you what, though, I'll give you a call if anything pops up as unusual during the internal exam, okay? It'll take time to get the labs back, of course, but if I see anything that indicates the cause of death, I'll be sure to let you know straightaway."

"Thanks, Miles. I owe you one."

"You owe me a sandwich—just don't bring it down here!"

They shared a companionable laugh, and then Jenkins turned with a parting wave and left the room. He had one more thing he wanted to do while he was at the hospital. As he rode the elevator back up to the main floor, he straightened his tie and made sure his shirt was tucked in all the way. He was wearing one of his best suits, and he wanted it to look tidy.

It was a long shot, and probably unrelated to the case, but he planned on checking in on those burn victims as long as he was there. Plus, that intake clinician had smiled at him. That was well worth following up on in and of itself. As he finished tucking in the shirt, he glared down at his belly with a frown. He was going to have to start doing something about that if he was serious about dating again. Time to bust out the dieting app on his cell phone and start counting calories. About five pounds should do the trick. Even if he struck out with the clinician, it was still a pretty good idea to get back into shape.

After inquiring at the information desk Jenkins eventually found her office located down a long hallway close to the records room. Upon reaching it, he paused to take a deep, steadying breath and then let himself in. Lisell was sitting behind a desk, working on the computer. The light from the screen reflected off her glasses and highlighted her face as she sat frowning in concentration. As she looked up and saw him, the frown brightened into a genuine smile that just about took his breath away. Damn, but she was one fine lady. Getting up from the chair, she came around the desk and offered him her hand.

Smiling in return, he clasped the proffered hand, glancing around. Her office was small and neat with one window facing a courtyard and a bookshelf on the back wall. There was a stuffed animal resting between two stacks of books—some kind of three-toed sloth. Glancing back at her, he let go of her hand with some reluctance.

"Detective. . ." she began, "you know, I never did get your first name."

"Dan," he replied politely. "I came back in to see about those survivors. Are any of them up to answering questions yet?"

She seemed confused for a moment as she smoothed a hand down her blue and white sweater. "Well, they are, but another officer already came in earlier and did those interviews himself. In fact, I was beginning to think that I wouldn't be seeing you again."

It was his turn to be befuddled. Another officer? Something wasn't right here; he hadn't even filed a report yet. Why would the captain send someone else to question the witnesses right after telling him that it wasn't a top priority?

"I see," he said. "Did you get that officer's name by any chance? I'd like to correlate my findings with him if I can. Today was supposed to be my day off, but I've been called in on another case and just thought I'd drop by to do a follow-up."

She moved back around the desk and then rummaged through a stack of papers. "Here it is," she said, pulling out a single sheet. "The release form that he signed. His name was Officer Resario."

Resario? What the hell was that dirty bastard doing poking his nose around the arson victims? Jenkins stood lost in thought until Lisell cleared her throat with a polite grin.

Refocusing on her, he smiled back. "Sorry. That kind of caught me off guard. I didn't know he'd be following up on this. Did he find anything out, do you know?"

"Well," she said, "we don't generally chaperone the officers, but I can tell you that there were very few patients willing to speak to him. Most of them are still in pretty bad shape. We've sadly lost a few since this morning, and most of those that remain are heavily sedated. I went by to check on the ones that he did speak with, though, and they all seemed unusually subdued after his visit. Is there something going on here that I should know about?"

The honest concern in her eyes was very touching. He could tell she cared deeply for her patients and wanted to make sure that they weren't in any trouble. He hesitated, not willing to lie just to protect Resario, but unable to tell her of his suspicions either. He would have to settle for a half-truth.

"It's probably nothing," he reassured her. "Officer Resario is pretty hotheaded and not very good at doing these follow-up interviews. I've always considered him to be a bit too abrasive for this type of an assignment. I'll speak to him personally and make sure that he doesn't have any further contact with any of your other patients. I'm very sorry to have caused you any trouble. Can I buy you lunch to make up for it?"

That was smooth, he thought. *Way to hit on her right when she's worried about her patients.* Well, there was no calling it back now. He tried not to sweat it too much as he stood awaiting her reply.

She pretended to consider for a moment, a smile teasing at the corners of her mouth. "Are you asking me out on a date, Detective?" she finally said.

"I suppose I am," he replied.

"Well, I can't do it today, but if you leave me your card, I'll give you a call sometime, okay?"

It wasn't a flat-out "no." At least that was something.

"Sure," he said. "Here's my card. Call me anytime. And if you see Officer Resario come back around here, you just let me know, and I'll take care of it."

The smile she'd been marginally holding back blossomed across her face, transforming it, and he felt his heart turn over in his chest.

"I'll do that," she said. "But if you'll excuse me now, I have to get back to work—there's a lot of reports to finish."

"Alright, I'll just leave you to it."

With a parting nod, he turned and left the office. He'd have to get a hold of Resario straightaway. Somehow that douchebag was involved with the fire, he just knew it. He wished he could've spoken with those survivors before Resario had gotten to them, but whatever it was that he'd said, it would probably shut them up good and tight now. It would be a waste of his time to even try. With a sigh, he headed back toward the parking lot and his waiting squad car.

-10-

Rita was doing quite well for someone who was filled with thousands upon thousands of specialized insectile eggs. She lay as before, spread out on the floor of the warehouse, her legs splayed, her vacant eyes staring out into empty air. Her belly, round and distended now, rose up in the caricature of a pregnancy, while a yellowish fluid continually seeped from her womb, collecting in a pool on the cold wooden floorboards. Every once in a while, she made a low sound in the back of her throat, almost like a detached groan. It was an animalistic noise, much like that of a creature awaiting its foreordained fate after being worn down by the constant threat of imminent slaughter.

Meanwhile, Bobby was like a man tied to the railroad tracks with a train due along at any moment. He continued to struggle against the tick-induced paralysis, attempting time and time again to move even a muscle, but with no apparent success.

Charlie knew he could keep them both immobilized indefinitely, although if it went on for too long the effects would become irreversible. Either way, it made little difference to him. They would suffer for what they had done, and then they would die. It was as simple as that. As far as he was concerned, they both deserved what was coming to them.

As he sat lost in thought upon his reformed throne, Simon, who was now resting on the back of Charlie's chitinous forearm, continued cleaning himself with a practiced ease. Watching Simon run long antennae through his fast-working mouth parts, Charlie considered their next move.

They had to find another place to lair, and soon. His insects were innumerable, and for the most part unbeatable, but the warehouse was far too vulnerable. There was only so much he could do with the swarms and hordes that were now his children. In a full-on frontal attack, a firebomb or explosion could wipe out thousands of them at a time. Not that he feared such an attack was imminent. It was only the survival instinct of his kind bleeding through and affecting his innermost thoughts. They must find someplace away from the docks, somewhere underground perhaps, with easy access to heat and water. He was running a search even as he pondered it, but he hadn't located anything suitable yet. The abandoned subway tunnels would be too hard to defend, the condemned power plant was much too sprawling and open, and many of the cave systems nearby were either too small or lacked proper access to the resources they would require. He would just have to keep looking.

His mind now processed millions of images sent from his children, working them into understandable patterns that he could sort through at incredible speeds. He knew that once he found the perfect spot, he would be able to move his children, and his captives, on to greater safety, but he needed to do this before the first of his new brood could hatch out of Rita's swollen womb. Once they were birthed, they would need time to grow, to fan their fragile wings, and to harden their new bodies into his unbeatable soldiers.

However, the power within him was driving him to start his tasks as soon as possible. Although he could see everything his children could see, he was discovering that there were limitations to what he could do with such information. He'd found that he needed to concentrate on a certain thought or idea in order to bring what he wanted into greater focus. Vague notions were of no avail to him in these searches, and the process tended to be frustrating in the extreme. Also, there were still areas of the city that his children did not have access to. It was hard to believe, but there were buildings out there that were sealed up tighter than he could have ever imagined.

Because of these limitations, he'd been unable to locate the doctors he was looking for. The hospital where his wife had died was still located in its accustomed place, but the machines that had kept her alive and the doctors who'd tended them had all been moved. Where they'd been taken, he did not yet know. His children had shown him only empty spaces where the machines had once been installed, rooms that were dark and shrouded, and medical staff that he no longer recognized. It was becoming apparent that he would need a reconnaissance mission to the hospital itself in order to check the records there and then perhaps discover just where his enemies had fled to. He would find them, oh yes!

And when he did, they would pay dearly for their crimes.

But that presented its own unique set of challenges. He'd never been very good with computers. As an infantryman in the army, he'd been a typical grunt more or less. Tough and able to hold his own in the motor pool, yet never trained in the ways of complex technology. It was a reasonably safe bet that he could access the computers once he'd gotten to the hospital. Any of his children could spy out the proper security codes by watching the staff log in. But once inside the computer system itself, he was unsure of how to locate the specific information he desired.

Another thing that caused him concern was the distance he would have to travel to get to the hospital. Between him and the building in question were many city blocks filled with gangs, hoodlums, and drug dealers. How was he supposed to fight his way through all of that without being spotted or detained? He supposed that he could go in under the cover of darkness, through the sewers perhaps, or wearing some sort of disguise even, but these options held little appeal for him. He was the master here, not some sneak thief who had to skulk about in the night and hide from those who would dare to accost him.

His other option was even less desirable. He could simply use his children to clear a way between here and the hospital with overwhelming force. It would be easy, and he had already decided to take control of those territories anyway. However, he did not wish to inflict harm upon the innocents who still lived in those areas, of which there were many. Collateral damage was one thing, but an all-out slaughter would be too much like genocide. It appealed to him even less than sneaking around did. Besides, if he went in that way, the forces that protected the city would rise up against him and he would be forced into a premature confrontation with the possible loss of thousands of his tiny soldiers. Not to mention that it would reveal his enhanced presence far too soon for his own liking.

He wanted to be able to move from a position of strength, take control without having to injure innocent civilians, and then conquer his enemies when they least expected it. It only made good sense, and it was the way that he'd decided he would go about honoring his sworn pact.

In light of that, he was determined to wait until his new breed of warriors were ready and he'd found out just where his enemies were hiding. The army base outside of town would then be his next objective once he'd taken care of the doctors, but he intended to consolidate his power even further before he attempted to infiltrate that nest of vermin.

He knew only too well that control over the city was the best position to start from when dealing with the military, and he would have to become indomitable before overrunning their fortified position once the time finally arrived.

As he sat pondering all the many ramifications of his goals and strategies, the images that his children constantly fed him were filling his mind with millions of scenes from all across town. He sorted through them, always on the lookout for things he desired, things that could be of use in achieving what he'd set out to do. Signs of the doctors' whereabouts, a new home for his growing brood, anything that could help in his ongoing efforts to succeed at his sworn tasks.

It was thus that he took notice of a man dressed in white robes standing in the alleyway across from a mafia-run eating establishment.

It caught at his interest because the man glowed with a faint blue radiance that surrounded his hands and face. As he stood in the darkness of the alley, he was gazing across at the two men standing guard in front of the restaurant. Everyone in town knew that this was a Gargano family business. No one in their right mind would ever go there alone to challenge them. Yet this man seemed unafraid, determined even.

-Father, what is it? Do you wish us to eliminate this creature?-

"No, Simon," he replied with a tolerant grin. "Let us simply watch and see what happens next. Have all of our children in that area concentrate their numbers in and around that building, but out of sight. I do not wish our presence to be known. Instead, I would like to hear what is going on, see what this man intends to do. The Gargano family is powerful. That man is either incredibly brave or incredibly foolish. Let us just see which one it proves to be, shall we?"

As he focused on the imagery unfolding within his mind, he was able to watch as the man in question stepped out from the darkness of the alley and then advanced straight across the street. It was a move that only a fool would make. Still, Charlie was intrigued. The guards glanced up and couldn't help but see him as he was making no attempts at all at stealth.

Charlie's children did not hear like a human would, they used vibrations. Yet, with his vast powers, Charlie was able to transform these vibrations into actual sound.

"Hey, buddy! Halloween ain't for another couple months!" one of the guards said.

"Yeah," the other chimed in. "What are you supposed to be, anyway?"

They both laughed as the man in white drew closer. When he didn't stop, they quit laughing, and the taller one pulled a handgun from beneath his jacket.

"Alright, alright," he said. "That's far enough there, pal. This here is a private establishment. You best be on your way before someone gets hurt."

The glowing man stopped and stared at the guards with large unblinking eyes, studying them, judging them. The eyes were colorless, gazing out from a scarred and swollen face that lacked even a rudimentary set of ears or nose. Reaching up with unconscious effort, he tugged at the lapels of his white robe, straightening it as he continued to regard the two men like a child contemplating a strange and puzzling new toy.

"I have come to see Ronaldo," he finally said. "Kindly step aside."

The guard with the handgun gave his companion a long-suffering look. "Well, that ain't going to happen, which I think you already knew," he said. "Look, I don't know what's going on here, and I don't wanna know. But you go tell whoever sent you that it ain't funny. Practical jokes is one thing, but have some respect for the dead for cryin' out loud!"

The strange man's bulbous eyes widened even further as he stared at the two men in shock. "Do you mean to tell me that he's already dead?"

Leaning forward, the guards tensed with pent-up aggression.

Charlie was fascinated with what he saw through his children's eyes. *Cannot the strange man see that he is in grave danger?*

The smaller of the two guards pulled out a truncheon.

"Listen," he said, "whoever you are, and whatever it is that you think you're doing here, you need to stop it right now. It ain't funny, and we ain't laughing, see? Now go on, get on outta here before I beat your ugly face in."

The man in white considered a moment, ignoring the smaller man's posturing. Then, drawing himself up to his fullest height, he addressed the man with the gun in dignified tones. "Then I shall need to speak to his superior. It's about my laboratory, you see."

Glancing at each other in astonishment, the guards seemed to reach an unspoken agreement.

"Whelp," said the gunman, "we did try an' warn ya."

With a firm nod from his associate, the smaller guard stepped forward, raising the truncheon as if readying it for a tremendous blow.

But before he could initiate his downward swing, the man in white raised a hand, flicking his glowing fingers. From out of nowhere, a swarm of repellent creatures materialized and enveloped the two men. Charlie could see that the clustered blobs were embryos in various stages of development, but it almost looked as if white blood cells were attacking a virus. The men dropped to the ground, covered in heaving mounds of writhing protoplasmic goo, and Charlie could hear the sounds of muffled screaming and bones cracking as the interconnected embryos tightened their hold upon them. Within moments, it was over. Then, the hideous globs of animated cellular life vanished as if they'd never been there, leaving behind two hemorrhaging piles of compacted flesh and fractured skeletal remains. Charlie was utterly entranced.

"Did you see that, Simon?" he exclaimed. "That man has rare talent! Is he like us, do you suppose?"

-That is unknown, Father. Perhaps he would make for a good ally if it is so.-

Filing that thought away for later, Charlie continued to watch as the man in white calmly walked through the front doors of the building. Once inside, all conversation ceased as the eyes of the patrons were drawn toward him. With an almost simultaneous reaction, hands then began reaching beneath jackets, while the bartender's nimble fingers crept along a concealed shelf toward the double-barreled shotgun hidden there.

"Who is in charge here?" the strange man inquired.

At the back of the room, a fat mafioso sat in a corner booth. His three companions moved to stand up, but he waved them back down.

"I am," he answered. "What the fuck do you want?"

"I need to know where I can find Marco Giovanni," the man said, his fingers twitching.

"Well, it looks like you're about to be disappointed then," the man replied, making an expansive gesture with one pudgy hand.

At this signal, weapons were drawn throughout the room and then pointed toward the intruder. He remained unconcerned. Without a shadow of fear coloring his bizarre features, he began walking toward the back booth.

Exploding into action, everyone attempted to fire their weapons at once, but as they did so, the lifeforms that the strange man seemed to control flowed outward from within the jammed gun barrels, oozing along the cold hard metal, before writhing up arms to encase their bodies in a heaving, ever-tightening fetal embrace. Falling from chairs and stools, the inhabitants of the restaurant screamed in agony as bones broke and tendons popped. With sweat glistening along his furrowed brow, the fat mobster rose from his seat, staring in horror at the carnage while attempting to back toward the rear exit.

The man in white cocked his head to the side. Then, with another flick of long fingers, a thick layer of protoplasmic tissues rose up to seal off the back door in a slimy wall of undulating flesh-colored membrane. Looking over his shoulder, the gangster wiped the sweat from his face with a meaty paw before glancing back at his antagonist.

"Okay, okay—you got me, pal," he said. "Take it easy there. I'll tell ya what you want to know. He's at his club, uptown. The Gleaming Gypsy. You'll find him there almost every night of the week."

Standing in the middle of the room, lumps of oozing, compacted flesh surrounding him on all sides, the strange man gazed back at the gangster with his huge unblinking eyes. Then, slowly, he nodded his bulbous head. "I believe you," he said.

From behind the mafioso, the wall of living cells and interconnected embryos crested like a wave and came crashing down, covering him like a flood of amoebas bent on a feeding frenzy. As the mobster's wails of agony grew sharp and distinct from within the seething mass, the man in white turned and walked out the front door, disappearing back into the night.

"Oh, I like him!" Charlie exclaimed. "Simon! Keep an eye on this one. The man is positively inspiring! In fact, I have just reached a very important decision. Starting right now, have the children begin to quietly take care of the less desirable people living in this section of town. Touch no innocent soul and harm no animals or children, but at the same time let no one see us at our work. We shall begin the cleansing of the city this very night!"

The abnormally large roach's antennae quivered in anticipation at this forthright command.

-Yes, Father, it shall be done.-

-11-

"Please," the girl pleaded. "I have to get to school. . ." He had her up against the wall in the alley, his arm propped in such a way that she couldn't possibly escape. "Come on, sweetie," he cooed, leaning in, "just one kiss and you can go, okay?"

His uniform was crisp, the dim light from the overcast morning glinting off the objects on his utility belt and reflecting from his official badge. He had one hand on the butt end of his service revolver as he nuzzled the side of her neck. Turning her head away, tears formed in the corners of her eyes as his moist lips brushed against her cheek.

"But I'm only twelve years old!" she sobbed. "Please, just let me go! I won't tell anyone!"

"Of course you won't, pumpkin," he said, releasing the gun and then forcing her head back around with a ridged forefinger. "Now just give me one little smooch, and then you can be on your way."

Reluctantly, she gave in, squeezing her eyes shut and whimpering as the tears tracked down her cheeks. His lips were hard and insistent, his breathing labored and tasting of stale coffee. With his tongue, he forced her lips apart, clenching her chin in a painful, rock-hard grip while his wet, disgusting mouth covered her own. After a moment, it slid inside her, probing, licking, twisting around, his saliva filling her mouth as she struggled. She tried to push him off as she gagged, but he was just too strong. After what seemed like an eternity, he broke away, panting heavily. Then he turned her around and twisted her arms up behind her back. As he frog-marched her deeper into the alleyway, he fumbled at his belt with his other hand.

"Now I'm going to show you something you'll really like," he said. "Have you ever sucked a man's cock before, my sweet? I want to feel your mouth on me, and if you do it really, really well, then I just might let you go. . ."

She squirmed and struggled even harder, but to no avail. He simply dragged her around a corner and then pushed her down behind a filthy dumpster. As she fell to her knees sobbing in abject terror, he was unbuckling his belt, smiling down at her with a sadistic glint in his eyes.

From behind him there came a sudden flash of blue light. Squinting hard against the glare, she stifled a scream, scrambling backward until her backpack slammed up against a brick wall.

"Stop!" a sibilant voice rang out, its metallic intonation echoing off the walls and then rebounding all around them in the small confines of the secluded alley.

The cop froze, startled by the strident command and unsure of how to react. His pants halfway undone, he shot a glance over one shoulder while reaching for his gun. A low growl of frustration escaped his lips as his eyes narrowed in rage.

In the alleyway beyond them, sputtering bands of blue and white radiance, like tiny bolts of violent electrical energy, swirled into a vortex of flashing colors, coalescing into the vague suggestion of a woman's form. She floated several feet above the ground, her eyes twin points of fire as she beheld them from above. The blue energy cascaded around her in a sphere, reflecting across the surrounding walls as the air grew suddenly cold enough that frozen particles of moisture drifted through the mist like an early frost. Snarling, the officer spun the rest of the way around, drawing his weapon.

Florence stared down at him, anger warring with compassion as she saw that the girl was frightened. Inside her, the dark spirits cried out for blood. They wanted this patrolman's soul and lusted after his perpetual torment. They whispered to her—dark things, evil things, suggesting ways that she could make him pay, ways that she could make him writhe in agony, bleeding from a thousand different wounds, ways to make him scream himself hoarse from brutal, unrelenting pain. Yet she fought these urges down. They had grown stronger with each kill, but so had she. Drawing upon all of her innermost fortitude, she subsumed their temptations within the bright blue radiance of the mystical spirit's influence. As the power of the two entities coiled within her, never truly in sync, but forced into uneasy alliance, she gathered her will and then poured herself into making the conflicting energies submit to her own desires once more.

The cop was a perverted lecher, but a brave one, nonetheless. His gun pointed unerringly in her direction as he reached down to re-buckle his belt with his other hand. "Lady," he said. "I don't know who or what the hell you are, but you best back the fuck up right now. This doesn't concern you."

Glaring down, she raised her hand, pointing at him with an insubstantial finger. "A great many things in this city now concern me," she said. "I can see into your soul, and I know about everything you've done. For all the suffering you've caused, for every life you've ruined, you will now offer up restitution. I will have your reparations in full before I'll give you your release."

Sputtering in indignation, he tightened his grip on the revolver, but before he could even pull the trigger, her power wrapped him in its chilling embrace.

He fell to the frosted, garbage-strewn concrete, the gun dropping from nerveless fingers. Within him, emotions roiled like a storm, boiling through him and emptying his soul as tears formed within the depths of his eyes. Throughout his life, he'd given much pain, yet there were times that he had known true love, felt the warmth of another's kind regard, or experienced the elation of justified recognition. Those brief and fulfilling moments were suddenly brought to the forefront of his mind all at once.

There was a girl, back when he was young, a stolen kiss, a promise of mutual desire. A puppy that he'd raised, strongly bonded to him, the joy of sharing an unconditional partnership, the rewarding feeling of knowing that an animal loved you without reservation. His mother, when he was a child, her arms wrapped tightly around him, her concern for him when he was ill, all her caring and nurturing while he was growing into manhood. Even the feelings of belonging, safety, and warmth that he had known inside her womb while he developed before he was born. All of this and more he experienced again, all the past loves, all the caring and sacrifice of those who had ever shown him any kindness, rose to the forefront of his thoughts. He was bursting with it, filled with it, until he was moaning in ecstasy like an over-satiated lover.

And then, Florence drew it out from him, siphoning it off like a surgeon drawing fluid from an abscessed boil.

Falling forward onto his hands, he was gasping at the enormity of the loss. Bleakness ran through him, an all-consuming sensation of destitution and abandonment. All his hopes, all his dreams, all of his memories of ever being cherished or loved, gone in one flashing instant of absolute emptiness. A surge of despair welled up within him, a desolation of spirit that there was no coming back from. His were now the feelings of crushing defeat, the unending pain of losing everything you've ever loved, and the never-ending punishment of regret. He relived every failure he'd ever experienced, every slight given him, every lost opportunity. He was drowning in shame, wallowing in hopelessness, longing for surcease from the overwhelming feelings that now ruled him mind, body, and soul. Gazing up at her with tears streaming down his face, he managed to whisper one single word.

"*Please*," was all he said.

That was all, but that one word spoke volumes.

Within her shimmering electrical field, Florence blazed now with the glory of his cherished moments. All the feelings of joy that he'd ever had coursed through her, every hope and dream, his successes, and all his deepest, most heartfelt longings. She was filled with them, overcome by them, bursting with an ecstasy that was larger than life itself. It swelled her energized astral form to three times the normal size as she basked in the afterglow of all the love that he had ever known.

But soon it dwindled away, and she shrank back down, the feelings of warmth and joy draining out of her until she could feel them no longer. She was more powerful now for the experience of it, more able to focus and use her abilities to achieve her ultimate goals, but the intense feelings of love never stayed with her for very long, and the brief moments in which this man's life had included such things had been few and far between. She stared down at him as he crouched sobbing upon the wet pavement, and she took pity.

Focusing her powers once more, she formed the image of an ice-blue rose. It floated in the air beside her, perfect and eerily distinct, like an object carved from the purest heart of an ancient glacier. Rotating slowly, tiny particles spun off from it, floating toward the ground like a sprinkling of delicate snowflakes. Inside the rose, a storm of another sort was forming, this one blood-red and filled with the all-consuming fires of hell. They burned with a blazing intensity, a bright crimson flash of light that split the morning air like a smoldering volcanic caldera.

"*Please,*" he whimpered once more.

As she hovered there, glaring down upon this pathetic misbegotten soul, she decided that she would grant him what he now craved more than anything else in the whole world. Staring up at her, he silently pleaded, begging her with his eyes, and she relented.

With a flick of one supple, insubstantial wrist, she sent the rose, stem first, sailing straight into his despairing heart.

The young girl had witnessed it all from her hiding place behind the dumpster. With widening eyes, she had seen the officer begging for death, watched as the terrifying electrified spirit cast the rose into his chest. And then she had seen him topple onto his back, clawing at the air with hands and feet while the rose melted, disappearing within him and causing him to struggle against what must have been an incredible amount of agonizing pain. It lasted only a few moments, but it was horrific to behold. Once he'd stopped scrabbling like a poisoned roach, she'd stolen a glance back up at the bright and shimmering spirit, clutching her cell phone and shaking her head in silent denial. As the phantom turned its blazing, red-hot eyes her way, she jumped to her feet and ran.

Florence watched her go, knowing she had at least saved this young one from a fate worse than death. She realized that she was strong enough now, more in control, and finally able to use her powers at peak efficiency. The first few victims she'd taken had went to feed her growing corporeal presence, yet she now knew she was ready to take on more of the people that deserved her attentions, siphon off more of the love she so desperately craved. Soon she would be able to confront her husband and his despicable fellow officers at long last, to take from them that which they had never given freely in life. With this thought shining like a beacon of hope within her mind, she faded from view, back into the ethereal realm from whence she came.

-12-

Jenkins arrived at the office early that morning and now sat staring bleakly at the computer screen. The previous night had been a total bust; he'd visited several of the crime scenes, read the first responders' reports, and had spoken with several potential witnesses, but he'd still come up empty-handed. It just didn't make any sense that these people were dead. There were no signs of a struggle, no wounds on the bodies, and no one had seen any evidence of foul play. The only thing they had in common was that they were all scumbags. In each and every case, the people being killed had had a rap sheet a mile long, many with a history of violent domestic abuse or sexual assault. That could easily have provided motive, especially if these were some kind of revenge killings, but until he got the autopsy results back from the morgue, he had absolutely nothing else to go on. Sighing, he completed another entry in his report and then eased back in the chair, yawning while extending his arms out in a joint-popping stretch. This case was becoming maddening and he was nearing exhaustion. Then the phone rang, and he reached over to answer it.

"Dan?" the voice on the line said. "This is Miles over at the morgue. I think you'd better get down here as quick as you can."

"Why?" Jenkins asked. "Were you able to determine the cause of death?"

"Well. . . yes and no," Miles replied. "It's hard to explain—you'll need to see it to believe it."

"Yeah, sure. I'll be right there."

Hanging up the phone, he grabbed his coat and headed for the door.

Ten minutes later, he was riding the elevator down to the basement of the hospital. Miles came to meet him, looking a bit frazzled.

"Dan, you gotta see this," he said. "I've never come across anything like it in all my years as a forensic pathologist. Come over here and take a look, would you?"

They walked over to the medical station on the far side of the room. There were several corpses laid out on tables now, all in various stages of examination. As they neared the area Miles indicated, he saw there were an assortment of internal organs laid out in pans at the grossing station.

"What have you got for me, Miles?" Jenkins asked.

"Here you see a heart that I've removed from one of the victims. Tell me, what do you make of it?"

Jenkins peered down at the organ resting in the metal pan. It was black, almost like it had been injected with indigo ink.

"I don't know what's wrong with that heart, Miles, but I do know that they aren't supposed to be that color. Is this some form of cancer?"

"No," Miles said. "It's severe frostbite, just as I suspected when I saw that pinpoint of blackness on the chest of the first victim. But, and now here's the really weird part, take a look at what happens when I cut it open."

Selecting a scalpel from a tray on the counter, he bent over the pan and made an incision, splitting the heart lengthwise, and then prying it open with his gloved hands. The inside of the organ was filled with soot, almost like blackened wood fibers. Jenkins leaned back, drawing a hand across the bottom of his face and then rubbing at his chin.

"Is that charcoal, Miles?"

"No—it's burnt-up heart tissue. The outside of the heart is severely frostbitten, while the inside has been burned from the center outward. I just don't understand it. I got three more just like this one laid out there behind you, each one exactly the same. Every corpse has had that same black mark on the torso as well. And now I find this. It's as if something went in through the chest, froze the heart solid, and then burned it from the inside out."

"What could do something like that?"

"I have absolutely no idea. I've sent all the lab work out, but you know how that goes; it could take days, maybe even weeks, before we get the results. I really don't know what else to tell you. Hell, I don't even know what to write in my own damn reports, except the obvious, but who's gonna believe that? It's the damnedest thing, I tell you."

Jenkins stood lost in thought. There had to be some kind of scientific explanation.

"What about some type of new, undocumented CDC infection?" he asked. "One that we haven't heard about yet. Could this be caused by some new super virus?"

Miles tilted his head, raising an eyebrow. "Dan, we've established the times of death here. I'm telling you, a virus like that takes hours in order to do this kind of damage. In addition to that, there would be all kinds of other signs and symptoms if these bodies had been ravaged by a disease. In all these cases, the victim seems to have died within minutes. No virus works that fast. Even the most infectious of diseases can take up to twenty-four hours to kill you. This was like a lightning strike, or a sudden cardiac arrest, but combined with the effects of extreme cold, and carried out with pinpoint accuracy. In addition to that, the black marks appearing on every cadaver are in exactly the same spot; they are precisely above the heart without any measurable deviation. It's uncanny."

Staring down at the frozen burnt-out organ lying in the tray before him, Jenkins considered. There had to be other possibilities, like maybe a new experimental weapon of some type, but until he had more to go on, he had to take control of the situation before the media got wind of it and had a field day.

"Who else knows about this?" he asked. "Who have you told besides me?"

"No one," Miles replied. "My autopsy tech was here during part of it, but he just deals with the bodies. He's not sufficiently trained to do the internal exams. I called you straightaway, once I'd discovered that the hearts were all similar. I've only opened up the three so far, but the rest of them all have that same black mark on the torso. I'd wager that I'll be finding this type of damage in all the other cases as well."

"Listen, not a word of this to anyone, then. I have to lock this thing down until we find some answers. No one gets in here without prior authorization, got it?"

As Miles nodded in agreement, Jenkins fished the phone out of his pocket and then called the station.

"This is Detective Jenkins down at Mercy General Hospital," he said into the receiver. "Send a couple of units down here to run interference with the press for me. No one is to have access to the morgue until I say otherwise, got it? Thanks."

The next call was to the captain to fill him in and then ask for a rush on the autopsy lab results. The captain agreed with his assessment for a change, and then told him to keep at it. They had to find out what was happening, and fast, before they had a full-blown panic on their hands. If the population got wind of this before they were ready to explain it, all hell would break loose. Fortunately, the victims thus far had been found in a bad area of town, and none of them would be missed. They were all human garbage.

Jenkins had the uncomfortable feeling that he was overlooking something. Blowing out a lungful of air that puffed out his cheeks, he decided he'd better go back to the drawing board and recheck everything they had so far on these mysterious deaths. Telling Miles to keep investigating and inform him if there were any other new developments, he headed back to the precinct to search through the files again. There had to be something, somewhere, that he was missing.

-13-

His hands shook, and he twisted them together to stop their incessant trembling. It wasn't as if he'd never killed before. But those had been accidents, deaths from patients who hadn't made it during surgery, not cold-blooded murder. He was a scientist, first and foremost, but he was also a doctor, and a damn good one. Seeing those bodies crushed and broken, strewn across the floor of the restaurant like that—it had affected him in ways that he hadn't expected.

But they were evil men, he told himself, and they'd been trying to kill him at the time. Plus, they were employed by the Gargano family. He'd taken them out to save his own life, as well as gain the information that he'd sorely needed. They were miscreants, all of them, and worse. Shifting in his chair, he glanced around the room, hoping to distract himself from the dark tangle of his thoughts.

They'd also done this, all of this destruction. His apartment was a total wreck. They'd tossed it, looking for his research notes no doubt, but he'd never kept anything at his residence; it was all in the safe at his lab, a lab they had destroyed. And now it was gone forever. Anger surged anew, washing away the fear and anxiety in a red-hot wave.

Everything he'd worked for, an entire lifetime of research leading up to what would have been his greatest scientific achievements, swept away in one ignorant act of senseless destruction. And he hadn't even gotten to kill the man who'd instigated that act. Ronaldo had already passed beyond his reach.

But the family he'd worked for was still alive and well.

Abraham untangled his hands, smoothing them down the front of his robes and then straightening his lapels. He had to come up with a plan. The Gleaming Gypsy was a large club, and it would be filled to the rafters with mobsters and their sympathizers. He couldn't just waltz in there as he'd done at the restaurant. He would stick out like a sore thumb and immediately be attacked and overwhelmed. No, he had to play this one smart, get more intel, find out where Marco was located within the club itself. Information was what he needed now, and once he knew where the rest of the Gargano family was headquartered, he would then be able to wipe them all out in one fell swoop.

And why stop there, he thought. There were other crime syndicates living in this town, all just as bad, and they'd only move in to take over the Gargano territories once he'd taken them out of the picture. It would be a better plan to simply eradicate them all, one family at a time. Or all of them at once, if he could manage it. He really didn't know the true extent of his newly acquired powers. All he knew was that he must cleanse the city of these criminal elements and then instigate a time of rebirth within the affected communities. How to go about that was a puzzle he needed to solve before he began.

First things first. He would need a disguise to infiltrate the club and obtain the much-needed information.

Climbing to his feet, he then moved through the small apartment and into the bathroom. Switching on the light, he saw himself in the mirror. It was hard for him to look at the damage; he had once been so handsome. Now, his features were changed forever by the attack on his lab and the assumption of his new powers. The swelling had gone down some, but his head was still slightly oversized, the eyes bulbous, his nose nonexistent. Not to mention that he had no ears to speak of and now glowed faintly with a bluish radiance. There had to be something he could do to alter it.

Summoning some of the embryonic tissues that he could manipulate at will, he studied the problem as the cells floated in a featureless blob just above his hand. He could manipulate this blob into almost any shape he wished; why not make new skin with it? He'd done his fair share of reconstructive surgery in the past. This should be no more difficult, but without any stitches or recovery time. Stretching the floating materials into a long thin strip, he then used his powers to apply the newly formed substance to his cheek.

It took quite some time, and a lot of false starts, but he was eventually able to stretch a layer of new skin across the entire surface of his head. The nose and ears had been the hardest parts as he had had to sculpt them from fetal materials and attach them in such a way that they appeared natural. The results were less than perfect. He now looked like he was wearing a frightening Halloween mask on an oversized skull. Drawing on all of his power, he modified his brow and cheekbones, altered the chin a little, and then added some scar tissue in strategic places.

When he was finished, he found himself staring at an image in the mirror that reminded him of a longshoreman or a dockside worker. His features were rough, his face the type that only a mother could love. The eyes were still pale—there was nothing he could do about that. But the baldness he could perhaps fix. Concentrating once more, he manipulated the skin cells to grow new hair. It spouted in tufts, a short, uneven crop of bristly black filaments. It was the best he could do for now, but at least it matched the brutish facial features he'd been able to achieve. Now to do something about his clothing.

He was loath to take off the robes. They seemed to be part of him now, increasing his awareness of everything around him at the same time as they energized his strength. Underneath them, he still wore his old dress clothes from the day that he'd died. Perhaps there was something left in his wardrobe that he could put on over the top. Moving into the bedroom, he opened the closet and peered within.

Most of what was left by the mob who'd ransacked his personal belongings was unsuitable, but there, way in the back, he located a trench coat that he'd saved for no other reason than he'd once found it to be an interesting-looking garment. Pulling it out, he held it up. It was long enough, and although beaten up and dusty, he thought that it might just do the trick. Shaking it off, he swirled it about himself, pulling it on over the brilliant, white robes. As it fell to the floor in a slither of rough material, he straightened it around him, then buttoned it up. Moving back to the bathroom, he shut the door to have access to a full-length mirror attached to the back of it.

The image staring out at him now was that of a thug, scarred and heavy browed, covered by an Australian outback-style long coat. He looked mean and, better yet, like someone you wouldn't want to mess with. Just the sort of fellow you'd find frequenting the Gleaming Gypsy close to quitting time on a weeknight. The eyes were still pale, but as long as he didn't make direct eye contact with anybody, he doubted anyone would truly notice. He still had to do something about his hands, though.

Moving back into the bedroom, he rummaged through some dresser drawers until he came up with a pair of black driving gloves. Once he pulled them on, his disguise was complete. Now he just had to figure out how he was going to go about his infiltration and then determine the best methods to obtain the information he desired.

After that, he would pull the entire club down around their ears.

But how to do it all without getting himself killed? It was true that he wasn't sure that he could even be killed, since he was already dead to begin with, but there was no sense in taking any chances. Plus, the last thing he wanted was to get shot full of holes. He'd have to think on it and come up with something clever. Darkness was still hours away; he had plenty of time to figure it out before he had to make an appearance at the infamous Gleaming Gypsy. He only hoped that whatever he came up with would be good enough.

-14-

Charlie was ecstatic. He had not only found a new lair for his swollen queen and massive swarms of children, but he'd also figured out a way to get the information that he needed to carry out the rest of his plans.

The city had been originally built over the top of a much older mining community. The tunnels and caves that still existed below the antiquated subway system were secure and little remembered by those that lived so far above them. His children had found a large cavern with a mining base that sat unused and now long forgotten. It was situated by a small underground lake fed by hot springs and had a geothermal warmth about it perfect for hatching out the thousands of eggs incubating within Rita's womb. Getting her and Bobby down through the passageways and into the cavern itself had been mere child's play for him and his many children, and they were now locked away deep beneath the earth in one of the buildings that had once been used as a headquarters for the miners who'd lived and worked there so long ago.

In addition to that, the plan that he'd put into motion only the night before had already resulted in unexpected benefits. His children had begun a stealthy and systematic takedown of the undesirable elements within the neighborhoods running between the warehouse and the hospital, but like most covert operations, there had been some bleed over. During the night there had been a few unfortunate sightings of them at their task no matter how secretive they'd attempted to keep things, and the results had been positively brilliant.

Now a sullen fear built within the populace, a deeply ingrained terror that had spread with rumors and gossip like wildfire. Most of the criminal elements in these areas had stopped operations altogether, some even fleeing to other parts of town. The rest were not taking any chances. Some suspected their rivals were moving in and prepared for war, while others simply locked their doors and windows and prayed for the attacks to be done with. Whichever way they played it, the end results were the same. Many city blocks were now either quiet and holding their collective breath or locked up tight and plotting against one another. He could not have hoped for better results.

And, on top of all that, he had found a solution to his computer problems as well. There was a man living in a penthouse apartment not far from the docks. The place was fortified and booby-trapped, with extensive surveillance systems in the form of cameras and other listening devices. It seemed that Charlie's children had located a survivalist, a conspiracy theorist who was also an accomplished hacker. His whole place was crammed full of technical equipment. It was a dream come true for Charlie. If he could get this man to work with him, then he would have no trouble whatsoever at the hospital and finally be able to obtain the information he so desperately needed.

He'd sent many of his children on ahead of him to disarm or circumnavigate the traps the man had laid throughout his ventilation system, and this had allowed Charlie to scuttle through it without mishap. Now, as he kicked in the ceiling grate and dropped down into the man's living space, he made no further pretense of stealth: it would have been a waste of effort.

The man looked up from his seat behind a large desk, his eyes bright and with no shadowing of fear within their brown depths. He was middle-aged and fit, dressed in a loose-fitting sweater and comfortable jeans, and he sat with the air of a man resolved to his fate, whatever that may be. Behind him, and all along the wall to his right, were banks of computer monitors, and his desk had keyboards and other electronic devices scattered about it. As with much of the other clutter filling his apartment, there was a pattern to the mess, one that matched the man's own peculiar way of thinking. He stared at Charlie like he was an expected guest, albeit an unwelcome one. Reaching under the desktop, he wrapped his hand around the grip of the .45 he kept duct-taped to the underside in a battered old holster.

"Who sent you?" he asked. "It's the military, right? They've finally hired someone to take me out. After all this time, I expected someone better trained. I saw you coming a mile away. You know that you tripped off about a dozen alarms coming through that ventilation system, right? How the hell did you manage to disarm all those traps? That, I have to admit, impresses the hell out of me."

Charlie gazed at him, grinning fondly. He could feel a budding affection for this man already. "I am not here to kill you, my friend," he said. "Far from it, in fact."

The man didn't smile back, instead pulling the gun from its holster and then standing. "Well, if you're not here to kill me, then what the fuck do you want? You have to be some kind of special operative then, am I right? Look at you—you've got some type of new cloaking technology wrapped around you and your eye optics are glowing. Or maybe you're one of those aliens the government has been covering up? Here to control my mind? Well, whoever you are, you ain't gonna take me that easily. You just stand right there and don't move, or I'll put a bullet right between those beady little eyes of yours. *¿Comprendes?*"

"I wouldn't do that if I were you," Charlie murmured.

"Why not?"

"Because I've clogged the barrel of your weapon with hundreds of honeydew-enriched aphids," Charlie said. "So, if I were you, I would put that gun down and listen to what I have to say—unless you want to risk a muzzle breach."

The man stared at him and then slowly raised his arm so he could sight along its length while still aiming. The entire weapon, from the chamber to the end of the barrel, was crawling with aphids, the sticky fluid of their honeydew excrement saturating and dripping from the shiny black muzzle. The man's eyes widened slightly, but he still didn't quite panic. Returning his focus to Charlie, he lowered the weapon and then tossed it contemptuously onto the desk.

"Okay, then," he said, wiping a sticky hand down the front of his sweater. "Who the hell are you, and what do you want?"

"What if I were to tell you that all of your theories about this city, and the government that runs it, are correct?"

"Tell me something I don't already know," he said. "Like how you fit into it all. And, more importantly, what exactly is it that you want from me?"

Charlie moved to stand before the desk, then reached up to remove the hood of his cloak. The man resisted any outward reaction to the features thus revealed, yet Charlie could tell that he was shocked. A faint sheen of sweat appeared along his brow line, and he shuddered ever so slightly like he was resisting a sudden flight-or-fight response.

"I am the one who is going to set things aright," Charlie said. "I have already started within this very community, and I don't plan on stopping until corruption is removed up to the very highest levels, including the military who run the bases just outside of town. I plan to make changes, my friend, sweeping, life-altering changes. And I need your help to do so."

The man thought for a moment, the thumb of his right hand circling the pads of his middle two fingers as he stood in silent consideration.

"And then you plan on running it all?" he finally asked. "The city? The government? Even the military? I don't know who you think you are, but that ain't ever gonna happen. Friend."

It was Charlie's turn to stop and think. He had never considered just what he would do when he was finished. He'd seen himself as a liberator, someone who now had the power and the divine direction to make changes for the better. But could he see himself running this city after it was all said and done? The military? It seemed ludicrous even to him the more he pondered it.

The man shifted slightly, bringing him back to the present. His mind had wandered far, his thoughts seeking answers that he simply did not have. Returning his attention to the man standing before him, he sighed.

"You are right," he said. "I cannot run this city after I am done. Or the military, for that matter. I will have to find others to do that, people who are worthy of such great responsibility."

The man visibly relaxed, running a hand back through his blond hair and blowing out a breath that Charlie had not even realized he'd been holding. Then he abruptly sat back down.

"Well," he said, "as long as you understand that, then at least it's a start. You still haven't told me who, or what, you are, though."

He pointedly did not look at his desk, which was now crawling with well-fed aphids.

Charlie grinned. "I am a man, much like yourself, but one who has also been granted great powers, powers that can be used to effect change within this city. As to how I have gained those powers, that is a story for another time, perhaps. All you need know is that I have made it my goal to cleanse this city and its government of all corruption, to make it a better place, a safer place, for me and my children, for everyone, and to also take out the foul-minded military commanders that run things out at that base. My name, by the by, is Charlie."

No smile had as yet cracked the man's features. He was wary and did not trust so easily, this recluse who had lived in self-inflicted solitude. It would not be so simple to win this man to his cause. It may even take a great leap of faith on his part.

"Your… children?" the man prompted.

"Yes," Charlie replied. "The arthropods. I can control them, feel them, see through them. They are mine as I am theirs."

"And you plan on having these 'children' coexist with the population of the city once you're through? I hate to break your bubble, pal, but most people round here just kill bugs when we see 'em. I find it hard to believe that you're going to find a way to get people to accept them on a day-to-day basis."

"Oh, but they already do," Charlie exclaimed. "My children are around you all the time, only you do not see us, nor feel our presence so regularly. We already coexist, my friend, and will continue to do so, in many ways within a somewhat symbiotic relationship. Insects do many, many things that it would be very unwise to remove from normal everyday existence. They provide a necessary function, and all benefit from their unending toil. I suspect that, once things have settled down, life will return to as it has always been. They will live amongst you, and you amongst them, and yet you will have little or no contact with one another."

The man eased back in his chair, considering this.

"So," he said, "you wish to use this. . . power. . . a power that gives you control of, did you say *all* the insects? Gives you this power over large amounts of tiny soldiers, let's say, to take out the corrupt government, and then the military leadership that is so grossly abusing its privileges outside of town, and then you wish to replace all of these people with fair-minded, hard-working citizens chosen by their merit and ability to lead once it's all over?"

"In a nutshell, yes."

"Count me in then—when do we start?"

Charlie did not fully trust this sudden capitulation, but the man was not lying; he could tell at least that much. This man would try and push his agenda when the time came, but as it so seamlessly coincided with Charlie's own desires at the moment, it hardly seemed worth worrying over. Besides, he could always kill him if he became too much of a hindrance. But so far, he liked the man's panache. Perhaps he would become a valuable asset, someone that he could count on to help find the type of people that would be needed to carry on after he was done with his own sworn duties. It was the best that he could hope for at this point and time.

"Simon," he said, making his decision, "you can come out now."

The man started a bit as Simon crawled from behind the main monitor to crouch on the desk by the central keyboard. In the light from the multiple computer screens, he looked like something straight out of a nightmare. The man swallowed visibly.

"This is my friend, Simon," Charlie continued. "He was waiting, just behind you there, this entire time. In case you did not agree with us, you see."

Nodding his understanding, the man's eyes took on a little more of the fear and respect that Charlie felt he deserved. Good. It would help keep the man's ambitions in check.

-Father, you have made a good choice. This man can do things that we cannot. And his knowledge of the government and of the politics surrounding us will serve you well.-

"He says that he likes you," Charlie explained. "For now. . ."

As the man stared down at the huge cockroach on his desk, he reached up to rub at his eyes briefly, perhaps checking to see if he were truly awake.

"So," he finally said, "you're Simon? Nice to meet you, I guess. Hey, can this thing really talk to you? You're not pulling my leg, are you?"

Simon scuttled over to the man's keyboard, and with a few deft keystrokes, words formed on the central screen.

It is nice to meet you, Demitre.

"Hey! He knows my name!"

Charlie grinned.

Getting down to business, Charlie quickly explained his need to access the records at Mercy General Hospital. Demitre listened but shook his head after Charlie was finished.

"That's going to be tough. Those systems are all self-contained. I can't just hack into them from the outside; I'll need a linkup to remotely access them."

Charlie considered this. "How can we best establish such a link?" he asked.

Reaching over to the other side of his desk, Demitre dug through a pile of equipment and pulled out a small device.

"With this. You just have to get into their data processing room and then connect this to the USB port on the main computer. Once you signal me that it's connected, then I can break in remotely and download their files. When this light here turns green, then you just unplug it and bring it back to me here. I'll be able to decode it, and then we'll have all the info you need."

There was no time like the present, Charlie thought. Taking the unit from Demitre's hand, he placed it inside his cloak. He would leave immediately, travel across this vast area of mostly deserted streets, and then break into the hospital records room. Once he had done this, he would then return and get the information they needed to pursue the ones who'd killed his darling wife. After that, he would begin to focus his intent upon all the other people who so richly deserved his attentions. Soon, they would pay.

They would all pay.

-15-

"Night Of Terror Leaves Residents Loathing To Return To Homes"

Jenkins read the headline again, shaking his head in bemusement. He didn't know what the fuck was going on in this town, but he had enough to deal with right now without this adding to it. He needed to find a break in the case before things spiraled out of control. So far, he'd been able to keep things buttoned down over at the hospital, but if word got out, the press would descend on the place in droves, seeking to cash in on the story. The last thing he wanted was the papers spreading more panic amongst the populace. Without even reading the article, he shut down the news website in disgust and then slumped back in his chair with a groan.

A commotion near the front of the precinct drew his attention as Resario walked in talking and laughing with a bunch of his cronies. Well, he'd been meaning to speak to that jackass sooner or later, so it might as well be now. He got up and moved to head the man off.

"Resario," he called out. "I need to talk to you."

The bald prick actually smirked as he turned toward him. Shouldering past the rest of his crew, he met Jenkins in the center of the room.

"Well, if it isn't Detective Dickless!" he sneered. "What the fuck do you want?"

"I want you to keep away from the arson victims recovering at Mercy General," Jenkins said. "I don't need you messing around with my case."

The bulky man actually took offense, swelling up like a balloon that was getting ready to burst. "I have no idea what you're talking about," he said. "So why don't you just get the hell outta my face before someone gets hurt?"

Keeping control of his mounting anger, Jenkins stared the younger man down. "I'm talking about you interviewing those witnesses. You're overstepping again, and I don't like it. I've got it handled, and I don't need you screwing around with the people I'm supposed to be taking statements from."

"Why do you give a shit if I talk to the survivors?" he shot back. "You're not even officially assigned to this case. Besides, it was *my* apartment building that got burned down. I lost my wife in that goddamn fire, you heartless bastard!"

That caught Jenkins off guard, yet Resario didn't seem like a man who was overcome by grief. Something wasn't quite adding up here. "If it was your building that got burned down," he said, "then I'm sorry to hear it. But shouldn't you be out on bereavement leave then? I got this covered, and I'm warning you right now, you'd better steer clear of it from here on out."

Color spread like a rash across Resario's features, moving up over the expanse of his lumpy head. The other cops who'd clustered around them stepped back, sensing trouble on the rise as Jenkins shifted his weight onto the balls of his feet. If this froggy wanted to bounce, then he'd put him down quick enough. The man had the height and weight advantage, but Jenkins was a survivor, and he knew how to handle himself in a fight. The room grew still like a calm before the storm as Resario leaned forward, lips twisting into a silent snarl.

Stepping from his office, Captain Wolfe took in the whole scene at a glance.

"Hey! What the fuck is going on out here?" he said. "If you two chuckleheads are done playing house, I'd love for you to get your act together and stop being such a personal pain in my ass! I just got a call, and it looks like the killer's struck again over in an alleyway off of 5th and Treacle. It was Officer Lewinsky this time around, and he was one of ours, so I need you two to start behaving like we're all on the same team here, you got that? So let's pull it together and stop acting like five year olds! Jenkins. Get your ass down there and canvass the area. You're the highest-ranking detective we got available right now, so don't fuck this up, okay? I need you on point for this. Resario, you and your cohorts are all on crowd control. Don't let the press get within a hundred feet of the body. I got the first responders taping off the alleyway, and the crime scene technicians are en route. Let's look alive, people! This one hits too close to home, and we need to find out what happened ASAP. Understood?"

The room had fallen into a hushed silence while he was issuing orders, but now a murmuring rose amongst them, building in waves and threatening to wash them all away in a sea of simmering resentment and anger.

"I said, *do you understand*!" Wolfe shouted.

A chorus of acknowledgments rang out as the precinct burst into a madhouse of activity. Wolfe turned to coordinate their efforts with other top-ranking officers gathering around him while the rest of the department scrambled into action.

The scene of the crime was a total shit show. The press had gotten wind of it, and it was already becoming difficult for the first responders to hold them back from the taped-off area. After Jenkins stepped from his car, he was forced to work his way through a throng of shouting, microphone-waving news correspondents while calling out "no comment" the entire way.

There were police photographers and medical personnel surrounding the body while a stretcher crew waited off to one side. Jenkins moved across the alley, careful not to disturb anything as he made his way toward the dead officer lying on the cold, wet concrete.

Upon reaching the rigid corpse, he stopped and stared down at it, its positioning so similar to the other victims that he was almost unfazed by the sight of it. The deceased lay on his back, arms and legs raised as if he'd been trying to fend off the armies of hell, his expression one of total anguish. Jenkins had known Lewinsky for well over six years now. He wasn't a good cop—in fact, he was dirtier than most—but he didn't deserve this. From what seemed like a vast distance, he heard himself speaking to the medical staff in a detached way, asking them what they'd found.

Their answers were the same standard replies that he'd heard a dozen times over in the last couple of days, and about as helpful. But there was at least one thing he could verify for himself. Requesting a pair of latex gloves, he put them on and then crouched down to unbutton the middle two buttons of Lewinsky's shirt. Once he had the white undershirt exposed, he took out a small penknife and cut a hole in the material directly over the man's heart. There it was, that same black dot that had been on all of the other victims. He couldn't even begin to imagine what had caused it.

Glancing around, he tried to reconstruct what had happened in his mind's eye. The officer had come down this alley for a reason. Allowing his vision to go slightly out of focus, he scanned the crime scene with the heightened perception that this allowed him. There, over by the dumpster. The trash in that area appeared to have been disturbed. He got up and worked his way over, crouching down once he got there to study it. There were definite signs of someone else being present at the time of Lewinsky's death, maybe even a suspect that he'd been grappling with. It didn't look like much of a struggle, though. More like someone had been pushed down and then scooted backward until they hit the wall. A person of interest that Lewinsky was questioning? Perhaps. All he knew for certain was that it meant there was an eyewitness out there somewhere. Now all they had to do was find them.

"Marsh?" he called out to one of the first responders.

"Yes, Detective?" the man said, hurrying over.

"Did anyone come forward yet? Have we taken any statements?"

"No, sir," Marsh replied. "Did you find something?"

He glanced up at the eager young face gazing down at him with such restrained curiosity. Had he ever been so young? "Possible movement in this area," he pointed out. "See how the trash has been shoved around here? These markings could indicate a scuffle. You can tell because the trash is still wet around the edges from this morning's fog yet some of the papers and cardboard are dry side up indicating they've been flipped around. Then there are these slide marks through the dirt heading back to the wall over there. I think someone was forced to the ground here, possibly a perp that Lewinsky was questioning, maybe even the killer himself. You see anything when you got here? Hear anything?"

"No, sir," Marsh said.

"Well, keep your eyes and ears open. There's no telling what we might find in this alleyway. I'm going to need you to get the whole place quartered off. The tech boys are going to have to go over it with a fine-tooth comb when they get here. He was one of ours. They don't get to do this to one of ours, you hear me, Marsh?"

"Yes, sir!" came the crisp reply.

"Well, then, hop to it, Officer!"

As Marsh hurried away, Jenkins continued surveying the littered concrete, his eyes traveling over the disturbed filth before being drawn to something lying just at the edge of the dumpster: a purple hair clip shaped like a butterfly. He retrieved it and then held it up to study it in the hazy light of the overcast day. What would a young girl be doing back here? Glancing over at the body, he had a few sinking suspicions. Lewinsky's reputation was well-known, and it wasn't a good one. Focusing on the rest of the alley, he tried to envision exactly what had occurred there, but his mind was still unable to fill in the missing blanks. There wasn't enough information yet to go on. His cell phone went off while he was still pondering, and he fished it out of his jacket pocket.

"Detective Jenkins," he said into the receiver.

"Dan?" came the voice on the other end. "This is Lisell. From the hospital."

"Hey, Lisell, it's great to hear from you, but I'm sorta in the middle of something right now. Can I call you back at another time?"

"Are you down at the alley where that officer died this morning?"

He was completely taken aback. The press couldn't have gotten that information out yet. "Forgive me for asking," he said, "but how did you know about that? It's not common knowledge, and we've only just arrived at the scene."

"I've got someone here that you need to speak to right away," she replied. "It's about that deceased officer, and it's also somewhat personal. I'm afraid that I'm going to have to ask you for a favor, Dan."

Staring hard at the hair clip he was holding in his other hand, he wondered why he suspected that he wasn't going to like the answer to his next question. "What have you got for me, Lisell?"

"It's my niece," she said. "She has information about the crime, but she's terrified. Please, I know that you don't owe me anything, but if there is any way that we can keep this just between the two of us for the time being, I would very much appreciate it. There are some things you need to know, things that could place my niece in terrible danger."

He considered a moment. Lisell's niece having information that presented a personal danger to herself could mean only one thing. He glanced back at the corpse, a surge of bitter anger almost choking him. "You have my word," he said at last. "Just between us. For now. Where are you? I'll come meet you right away."

"We're at my office in the hospital," she told him. "And, Detective?"
"Yes?"

"Come alone, okay? I'd like to do this without your fellow officers knowing where she's at right now."

"Absolutely," he reassured her. "Sit tight. I'm on my way."

"Thank you, Dan," she said and then hung up.

Pocketing the cell phone, he took one last look at the hair clip and then slipped it into his other pocket before straightening up.

Pretending to dust off his pant legs, he took the opportunity to glance surreptitiously around. He was going to have to throw the dogs off the scent somehow. Searching the edges of the taped-off area, he located Resario and called him over.

"What the fuck do you want now, Jenkins?" he said as he walked up. "I'm trying to do my job over here."

"I'm going to have to ask you to do more than that," he replied. "I've gotta go check out a hot lead, and I need you and your men to keep this place buttoned down. I've ordered the scene quartered off, and I need someone who knows what they're doing, someone who can go over it inch by inch with the technicians. I don't like you, Resario. But you're the best man we got for this job, so I need you to find out what you can while I'm gone, okay? Don't fuck this up. I want the bastard who did this. You understand?"

It was just the right combination of insult and backhanded praise. Resario swelled up with importance as he bought it hook, line, and sinker. The man wasn't very bright, but he did know how to canvass a crime scene, so at least that much was only a slight exaggeration. Time to put the icing on the cake.

"Alright, everyone, Officer Resario is in charge until I get back," he called out. "Stay sharp and do what he tells you until then, got it?"

The other officers acknowledged the order and got back to work. Giving Resario one last long, calculated look, he turned and walked over to the yellow tape. Ducking beneath it, he once again fought his way through the shouting reporters as he headed back to his squad car.

By the time he drove into the hospital parking lot, it was late in the afternoon. As he got out of the car, he noticed there was a chill in the air that was unusual for this time of year. Shivering, he pulled his jacket closer around him as he walked to the main doors, nodding at the plainclothes officers stationed there before going inside.

As he moved through the lobby, heading toward Lisell's office, he saw that there was a great deal of increased activity, but not from the expected influx of reporters. The people wandering the halls weren't all staff members either. Many of them appeared to be street-level thugs and low-rent hoodlums. He wondered what could have happened to swell the number of questionable civilians here so drastically. Pausing at the information desk, he greeted the receptionist and asked her what was going on.

"We've had a lot of injured people being admitted in the last several hours, mostly down at the emergency room," she said. "There's been a ton of accidents happening over on the lower west side of town for some reason and a whole bunch of fairly serious bug bites. We have a lot more friends and family here today because of it."

"Bug bites?" he asked, raising an eyebrow.

"I know, right?" she said. "It's crazy! It gives me the heebie-jeebies just thinking about it. But there are a lot of people coming in right now complaining of being attacked by swarms of insects. Weird, don't you think?"

He nodded in assent and thanked her for the info before continuing on his way. So that's what the headlines this morning were going on about. The whole city was deteriorating into chaos, with things getting worse each day. Shaking his head in exasperation, he made his way to Lisell's office, but when he tried the door, he found that it was locked. Glancing around, he made sure the hallway was clear before rapping on the frosted glass of the window.

There was a rustle of movement inside, then whispered conversation. After a moment, the door cracked open and Lisell peeked out, keeping a firm hand on the knob while blocking the entrance with her body.

"It's just me," he said quietly.

She ushered him in, locking the door behind them before turning around. He could tell she was upset. The high spots of color in her cheeks brought out the brightness of her eyes.

"Thank you for coming," she said. "I appreciate you taking the time to see us. And for keeping this confidential."

"My pleasure," he replied. "Now what's this all about?"

She glanced toward her desk, and Jenkins saw that there was a small figure slumped in the chair behind it. The young girl had the face of an angel, but her nose was reddened from crying, and her hair was in tangles. She had a purple butterfly clip still holding back some of it, but the rest hung in a hopeless snarl around her face. So here was his eyewitness. What were the odds? Glancing back at Lisell, he inclined his head politely, waiting for her to speak.

"My niece, Abigail," she began, gesturing toward the girl. "This morning, she had a run-in with your patrolman. I'm sure that once you've heard her out, you'll understand my concerns. She was in that alleyway while he was being murdered, but it's what happened to her before he died that has me worried. If anyone finds out what she knows, it could be dangerous for her. I need your assurance that you'll do everything within your power to protect her. She's too scared to go back to school or to even return home right now. Please, can you help us?"

"I'll do what I can, of course," he said, "but you do realize this is a murder investigation? If she's a witness, then I'm afraid she'll have to testify. We need to arrest whoever is responsible and then prosecute them to the fullest extent of the law."

The girl was listening as he spoke and now dropped her head to her hands, bursting into huge heart-wrenching sobs. Lisell knelt beside her, placing a protective arm around the girl's shoulders. Shooting Jenkins a wounded look, she returned her attention to her niece.

"Honey," she said gently. "This is Detective Jenkins. He's here to help. Please, just tell him what you told me earlier, okay?"

The girl sniffled, wiping her face with trembling hands. Glancing up at him, her reddened eyes sparked with sudden anger. "He put his tongue in my mouth!" she spat. "Then he d-dragged me behind the dumpster and was going to f-force me to. . . to s-suck his. . . his. . ."

Breaking into a fresh bout of weeping, she hid her face again in shame. Lisell patted her back awkwardly, then got up to lead Jenkins over to the other side of the room.

"She's still pretty upset," she said. "If she makes a statement and says these things about that officer, it's going to put her through a lot of public scrutiny. And if there are others like him on the force, then I'm afraid she'll be targeted for immediate retaliation. You know as well as I do that these sorts of people tend to stick together when an accusation like this comes up. This could ruin her life! Or worse, put a target on her back for every other maladjusted cop in town. No offense."

She was right, of course. Staring into the depths of her eyes, he knew that he would help her in any way that he could. Yet what more could he do beyond what his job already required? This was a murder investigation, and interfering with it was a crime in and of itself. Still, if word got out, Abigail's life would be forfeited, even more so than Lisell realized. The type of officers who sanctioned such behavior would have no trouble at all in taking the girl down and then making it look like an accident or suicide. He had to think this through, find some way to handle it that would keep them all safe yet still help with the investigation.

"Listen, I feel what you're saying, and I agree with you," he told her, taking her arm and moving her even further away from the distraught young woman. "But I have to take a lot of different factors into consideration here. Did she get a good look at the perpetrator? We need to identify the person responsible and arrest them as quickly as possible. Anything that can help the case along without exposing her to further danger would be a good place to start."

A multitude of conflicting emotions crossed Lisell's features as she stared at him. Then, shifting her eyes to her niece and back again, she lowered her voice. "I'm afraid that the situation is more complicated than you realize. This experience, it's altered her, made her somewhat. . . unstable. Her mind has fabricated a story to gloss over the horror of the attack. I don't believe you will get what you're looking for as far as any insight into who the killer really was—"

"I can still hear you over there," the girl interrupted. "I'm not deaf! And I'm not crazy! It was a ghost! An electrical ghost, and she killed him with a flower made of ice!"

Jenkins glanced at the girl, and then returned his attention to Lisell, trying to keep shock and disbelief from coloring his features. She had a helpless look on her face, an unspoken pleading that struck directly at his soul. Damn, but this was a bad time for her niece to turn delusional—he needed cold hard facts! Turning back to the girl, he went over and crouched down next to her.

"Why don't you start from the beginning and just tell me everything you remember, okay?" he offered, peering into her deep-blue eyes.

With many false starts, and much angry exposition, the girl told him a tragic tale of magic and woe, with an avenging spirit who seemed to have materialized right when she was needed the most, saving the girl from what would have certainly become a horrible sexual assault. It was not a pretty story, and all of it rang true, except for the ghost. Of course, the ice flower and electricity might have explained the frostbitten, burnt-out hearts, but that part all sounded bat-shit crazy. There were no such things as ghosts.

The girl glared at him, somehow sensing that he didn't fully believe her.

"You think I'm nuts!" she cried. "You both do! Well, I'm not crazy! She saved me, and then she killed him with a flower! Why would I make any of this up?"

Jenkins glanced at Lisell, seeking her support. Moving to stand beside him, she placed a hand on his shoulder, then focused all her attention on her niece.

"Abby," she said gently, "sometimes when the mind has undergone a traumatic experience, it often creates a false memory to cover up the things that are causing it distress. It's a common occurrence and nothing to be ashamed about. We don't think you're crazy, we just think that you've been very badly traumatized and need our help."

"Well, I *have* been traumatized!" she cried. "But I'm not making things up. In fact, I even took a picture of it! I'd forgotten until just now."

Leaning down, she rummaged around in a backpack that was resting by her chair and came up holding a pink cell phone with a unicorn blazoned across the case. Activating it, she proceeded to flip through her image files and finally flourished the phone at them both. Jenkins peered at the screen while Lisell leaned over his shoulder, gazing down in curiosity.

The image was blurry, but it was definitely a picture of an electrical field surrounding the shape of a woman. The phantom floated within this defined bubble, and Officer Lewinsky was on his knees in front of it. There was a stream of energy running from his forehead back into the spirit. It was not something this twelve-year-old girl could have put together using Photoshop in less than a day. Jenkins swiveled his neck to glance up at Lisell. She seemed quite taken aback, staring at the cell phone with her lips parted and her eyes widened in shock. Before either of them could comment, the hospital intercom sputtered to life.

"There is a code gray in the records room," it blurted. "I repeat, a code gray. . ."

Lisell glanced down at him with panic in her eyes. "That's right down the hall!"

Jenkins shot to his feet. He didn't know what was going on, but he did know that a code gray meant there was someone dangerous on the loose in the hospital. Motioning Lisell to step aside, he started for the door, calling back over his shoulder as he went.

"Get under that desk and keep quiet. I'm going to go check this out. Stay hidden until I get back, okay?"

"I'm going with you," Lisell said.

"You got keys for this office?" he asked.

"Of course!"

"Then let's go. We'll lock it behind us to make sure she's safe until we return."

Abigail had already crawled beneath the desk and was now hidden from view. Jenkins and Lisell left the office together and moved down the hallway, following several security officers who had come running from the main lobby.

As they reached the records room, they found a couple of guards already in place on either side of the door, while the ones just arriving slid to a stop and hunkered down beneath the large glass window running the length of the hall. Everyone was staring inside the room with eyes as big as dinner plates.

"Detective Jenkins," he introduced himself, flashing his badge. "What've we got?"

The man crouching beside him didn't reply. Instead, he merely pointed.

Jenkins followed the guard's finger, and his eyes locked on to the strange scene unfolding within the room itself. There was a small man in a long burgundy cloak standing by the main computer terminal. His face was concealed by a hood, but his hands were the color of burnt umber and looked as if they were formed of interlocking plates. Some type of body armor? Maybe, but it appeared more like it was a part of his natural skin, perhaps even a medical condition of some sort. As they watched, the man pulled a device from the USB port of the computer and tucked it up under his cloak. As he turned toward them, Jenkins got the impression of glowing eyes under the shadowy hood. With a flash of gleaming white teeth in a crooked smile, the man spun around and leapt onto the wall. Scrambling upward, he headed toward a busted ventilation grate on the ceiling, scuttling across the ceiling tiles like an oversized cockroach to disappear into the open shaft in a swirl of reddish material and flashing limbs.

Lisell gasped from behind him, gripping Jenkins' arm as he just stood there flabbergasted. What the fuck was going on in this town anyway? Ghosts, mysterious deaths, bug bites, and now whatever the fuck this guy was. He didn't know what to make of it all.

With a sudden return to mobility, the hospital guards burst through the door and then into the room, fanning out and checking for more intruders. Jenkins had the sinking feeling that they wouldn't be finding anyone else.

The thief, or whatever the hell he'd been, had already taken what he'd come for and fled. Leaning back against the wall, Jenkins ran a hand across his face. He was getting too old for this shit.

-16-

braham had been circling the club for over an hour and still hadn't come up with a foolproof plan to gain entrance without attracting undue attention. The main doors were manned by two intimidating bouncers, the back door was covered by extra security, and all the fire exits were locked from the inside. A roof area was also accessible via the fire escape, but that was guarded by men with rifles. It was a good thing that this was a busier part of the city or he might have been spotted already. For now, he was just another nameless face in the crowd, an unknown stranger wandering the sidewalks as part of the nightlife in this section of town. Unfortunately, the hour was growing late and he had to find a way in soon or risk being noticed.

The Gleaming Gypsy was a popular club offering a variety of adult entertainment, and there was a river of overstimulated humanity going in and out of the main doors at all times. If he could just find the right moment, he might be able to slip in without having to interact with the bouncers. The less attention he drew to himself, the better. Circling around again, he saw a small confrontation going on at one side of the entrance. The bouncers had a man cornered and were asking him a lot of questions. Coming toward them from the opposite direction, Abraham noticed a group of rough-looking characters laughing and joking around as they prepared to enter the building. Moving up to the rear of this group, he then sidled in behind them. It was a very near thing as one of the bouncers glanced over, but the man leading the group was well-known and just nodded as the bouncer waved them on through.

Once inside, he left the group and moved over to the bar on the right. Standing in the shadows at the end of the long highly polished oak counter, he was able to glance around unobtrusively. This part of the building was lit up by rotating lights, which flashed down on the crowded dance floor in an ever-changing, multicolored display. The patrons bumped and ground to the sounds of pulsating music while on the other side of them, there was another area filled with well-lit gaming tables. He could also see a stage along the rear wall. It was dark right now with its curtains drawn, but Abraham could tell that it featured an orchestra pit with rows of seating just in front. Off to the left of the main doors were stairs leading up to the second story, guarded by two burly thugs dressed in matching black suits. Following the stairway with his eyes, Abraham caught sight of a row of tinted windows overlooking the rest of the establishment. That might be where Marco's office was located, but he couldn't see any way of getting up there without being detained. He would have to bide his time until he figured out what to do next.

After a few moments, the bartender approached him and he ordered a drink. He'd been able to scrounge together a few bucks before he set out from his apartment, so he had that covered. Once the drink was in hand, he meandered over toward the gambling area and pretended to be engrossed by the action at one of the craps tables. All the while, his eyes roved the room, taking in everything. He had to figure out a way to get into those upstairs offices, some way that wouldn't get him shot on sight. As he stood sipping his drink and puzzling over his options, the club patrons moved around him in a dizzying display of frivolous hedonism.

It occurred to him that he could easily overwhelm everyone in the club by summoning his multitudes of prenatal fetuses, but at this time of night there were still too many innocent people filling the room. A lot of folks came here just to enjoy the simple pleasures of gaming, dancing, and drinks. Not all of them were good people, but that didn't automatically make them worthy of killing. Besides, he was beginning to get the deep-down feeling that keeping the true extent of his powers out of the public eye would be a good idea. He didn't need the police involved in his affairs. Keeping the cops off his back was one of the many things that he'd been paying the mob to do in the first place. With that in mind, he decided to wait until more of the civilian riffraff left before making his move.

Picking a quiet, out-of-the-way booth in the corner, he bided his time, and after a short while he was rewarded for his patience when he saw a man coming down the stairway. He was dressed in a dark suit of the best quality, the lustrous waves of his hair glinting in the lights coming off of the dance floor. The men at the bottom of the staircase were deferential to him as he passed, and as he moved through the crowded room, he was treated with the utmost respect by everyone around him. Although Abraham had met the man only once when first establishing his clinic, there was no mistaking him now—it was Marco Giovanni. Power and influence oozed from him as he crossed to the gaming area and then claimed a private booth just beneath the second-story windows. Once there, he proceeded to hold court with various men and women approaching him for an audience throughout the rest of the evening.

As the night waned and the crowds began to thin, Marco remained at his table, conducting business as the club's patrons swirled around him. When the remaining clientele started trickling out the main doors after last call, Abraham decided that now would be the perfect moment to corner the mob boss and force him to disclose the locations of the rest of the Gargano businesses and headquarters. It was his intention to make them pay for destroying his life's work while at the same time freeing the rest of the populace from the burden of their presence within the city. Starting with Marco Giovanni, he would squeeze the life from them one by one until their entire organization was no longer a threat to anyone.

Approaching the private booth, he considered his plan of attack, making note of the other mobsters in the immediate vicinity. This was a much larger venue than the restaurant had been, so he would need to spread his fetuses out over a far greater area than the previous time. He decided it would be best to immobilize first, killing only those employed by the club itself. It would be easy to tell them apart from the rest of the remaining patrons once he began his assault as they'd be the only ones left who were holding guns. Twitching his fingers, he readied his minions to burst forth from the aether and overwhelm all those around him while he closed in on his target. But as he stepped over to the table itself, Marco grinned broadly up at him.

That was all the warning Abraham received. Before he could summon his fetuses, there was a sound like a firecracker going off, and he felt the sudden impact of a bullet ripping through his right shoulder. Blasted from his feet, he flipped around in the air and hit the floor hard, overcome by an uncomfortable sensation that was not quite pain. His focus wavered as he lay curled up around the wound, and he lost control of his abilities. At that moment, he felt the disguise he'd so painstakingly wrought sloughing from his face. It melted away in peeling swaths of flesh-colored cellular matter that bubbled in the flashing lights as it faded from view. His true features thus revealed, he lay paralyzed in shocked dismay.

A deep sounding chuckle made him glance up. Marco was now standing over him, glaring down with a look of triumph scrawled across his blunt features. As Abraham tried to gather his will and focus his powers, Marco pulled a large handgun from beneath his jacket and casually shot him again. The force of the high-caliber round entering his body hammered him back against the unforgiving hardwood floor, leaving him gasping for air.

"Doctor Abe Orson, I presume?" Marco said. "You look. . . terrible, I guess is the word I'm groping for here. I don't know what the hell happened to you to make you look like that, but you know what? We're going to find out. And then we're also going to get your experiments back on track as well. What do you say to that?"

"How. . ." Abraham managed.

"Ah, I see that you consider us stupid and easily manipulated," Marco said, making an expansive gesture with the weapon. "Well, we're a lot smarter than you think. Didn't you realize we'd have security cameras, that we'd know all about you after your blatant attack on our restaurant? You may have left no living witnesses, but you forgot to take out the video feed during your little caper. That was sloppy of you, Dr. Orson. Very sloppy. All we had to do was wait for you to show up here and then nab you. In fact, it was far easier than I'd expected. I'll have to admit that the disguise did throw us off, but I'd instructed the sniper to shoot anyone approaching my table that he didn't recognize. You, my weird-looking friend, are simply not a recognizable person, and so here we all are."

Marco's grin split his face from ear to ear while he stood gazing down with a smugness that was almost proprietary. "I'll be making a call to Luciano to let him know you've been captured," he said. "He'll be glad to hear it. Your lab blowing up was an unfortunate accident, one that he didn't sanction and now deeply regrets. You see, he's the one responsible for allowing your experiments to continue in the first place. Who do you think got you pushed out of your cushy digs uptown and then made sure that your research was funded down here this entire time? Oh! Did you think that it was me? I don't give a fuck about your crazy experiments. It's the Gargano family that runs things around here, see? Luciano owns everyone and everything in this city, you understand? And now, you sorry-looking sack of shit, he owns you, too."

Abraham's eyes darted about, searching for any avenue of escape, trying desperately to summon his minions, but the discomfort was too great. He was having trouble thinking, difficulty functioning. The images of the men surrounding him swam in and out of focus, their laughing faces and cold hard eyes kaleidoscoping around him as he remained pinned to the floor by waves of something that now felt very close to agony. *Is this the end?* he thought. *Shot down like a common criminal, trapped by my own ignorance and stupidity?*

It seemed that the Gargano crime syndicate was a greater threat than he'd let himself believe. Secure in his power, he'd badly underestimated them. Marco had known he was coming, had prepared for it like the professional killer he was. These people owned businesses and ran things in ways that Abraham could not even begin to comprehend. All they'd had to do was conceal a lone sniper, probably behind the curtains of the empty stage, and then wait for him to approach Marco's table. Even with all his tremendous new abilities and a disguise that he'd felt to be foolproof, he'd never even been a challenge for them. Curled in a fetal position upon the floor of the Gleaming Gypsy, despair made him flush in angry self-loathing.

"I see by your pained expression that you're beginning to understand," Marco said. Then, with a sardonic lift of an eyebrow, he shot Abraham again, this time in the leg.

It felt like a spike of white-hot metal driving into his thigh. He'd known pain before, but this was different. It wasn't the expected intensity of a bullet entering flesh, but instead an uncomfortable sensation of wrongness, a pulsating feeling of pure unease that throbbed throughout his entire being. Did they know that he was already dead, that it would take much more than mere bullets to put an end to him now, or did they simply not care either way? As he groped through his mind for a way out of the situation, it occurred to him that this was what the rest of his existence might be like now—abused and controlled by the very family he'd hoped to destroy. How could he have been so naive?

"We don't know how you're even alive, or what really happened when your lab was destroyed," Marco said, "but I have orders to take you to see the boss. He has big plans for you, and for those weird powers that you've somehow acquired. Personally, I don't give a shit. You took out some of my best men over at the restaurant, and now it's payback time. This is going to be a long night for you, *capisce?* A very long night. Boys? Take this *figlio di puttana* to the back room. Let's see how much damage we can inflict before turning him over, shall we?"

Rough hands grabbed him by the shoulders as Marco's men prepared to take him to an area of the club that was hidden from the eyes of the public, a place where they could do with him as they pleased without any fear of retribution. His sacred pact was over far too soon, and he knew a moment of all-consuming regret. Immobilized by discomfort and trapped within the tangled folds of his robes and trench coat, he tried not to whimper as they made ready to drag him away.

Just then, a sudden wail of inarticulate sound came surging up from the front of the club, the resonance of a hundred voices crying out together in horror and pain. The mobsters holding him dropped him like a hot potato, and as he lay peering around in gaping astonishment, he watched as Marco and his men were overwhelmed by a rippling tide made up of millions of tiny brown specks. It was like an ocean of animated sand particles swelling upward from the floor in a seething wave to engulf all those around him.

As utter chaos ensued, a man appeared by his side, throwing an arm around his shoulders to help him sit upright. The swirling folds of a dark burgundy cloak concealed him from head to toe, its billowing hood riding low across a shadowy face. From within this pocket of darkness, Abraham could just make out lambent eyes staring back at him from over a large beak-like nose. The skin of the man's arm was rough and pebbly against his back and felt covered in plates, like that of a crab or insect. However, the compassion that lit the man's strange features was genuine, and he seemed filled with absolute glee just to be there.

"Come, now," he said, grinning like a madman. "We must get you away from here while they are still busy with my host of fleas. I will create a further distraction to cover our escape. Behold!"

With a wave of his free hand, the air filled with swirling clouds of horseflies that came pouring in through the ventilation system with a sound like the roar of a thousand chainsaws. Abraham stared in shocked incomprehension. He'd never seen so many bugs all in one place at the same time before. There were millions of them, and they blackened out the lights in the room, throwing it into almost perpetual darkness. Under the cover of this artificial eclipse, the strange man dragged him the rest of the way to his feet, then helped him limp unsteadily toward the door.

"Who. . . who are you?" Abraham asked.

"Someone very much like you," came the jovial reply. "We are alike, you see. For I believe we have both been given powers and a sacred duty to use them. Now come! Let us be on our way. Once you regain your strength, then these miscreants will taste the fullness of our wrath! Together we will be unstoppable!"

Chuckling, the man dragged Abraham the rest of the way through the club and then out into the night, moving unseen past the indistinct shapes of screaming mobsters who were now completely covered in masses of unrelenting, bloodthirsty fleas and shrouded by clouds of buzzing, painfully biting flies.

<h1 style="text-align:center">-17-</h1>

Jenkins hadn't slept very well. Right now there was just too much going on, so much to worry about. After witnessing the break-in at the hospital, he'd pulled the surveillance footage from their security system and loaded it onto a thumb drive. Then he'd confiscated Abigail's cell phone. She'd been upset about it, but it was the safest way to handle things. If she'd sent that picture to him in an email, then there would be a way to trace it back to her, but by having control of the phone itself, he could take it to a guy he knew and get the image pulled off before having it wiped.

He'd told her she'd have to stick with Lisell for the time being, and then took them both to a safe house that only he knew about. Lisell had called Abigail's parents from a landline at a gas station on the way there in order to reassure them, and he'd also given them a burner phone, one that couldn't be traced, not even to him, to use for emergencies. He was taking no chances that they could be tracked by anyone in the department before he'd had time to figure out what to do next. There was no doubt in his mind that other corrupt cops were already searching for her by now. He wasn't the only one who could read a crime scene, and he'd left Resario in charge. Not his brightest move, as it turned out, but it was all he could have done under the circumstances.

Shaking his head, he brought himself back to the present, focusing on his current surroundings. It was morning now, and he was sitting in Captain Wolfe's office with Resario. Their boss was already in rare form, puffed up and breathing fire as he grilled them over their poor handling of the case. At the moment, he sat rubbing his temples in frustration, then stopped to run his hands back through his short, dark hair, leaving it sticking up in spikes.

"So, in your infinite wisdom," Wolfe said through gritted teeth, "you left Resario in charge of the alleyway to go running off on some wild-goose chase? What the hell were you thinking!"

"Sir," Jenkins said, "I had a hot tip about something that was absolutely vital to the case. I had to follow up on it or lose any chance of obtaining the information. Resario was more than capable of handling things, and I figured he'd be able to go over the crime scene just as well as I could."

"I don't give a goddamn what you *figured!*" Wolfe shouted. "I assigned this case to *you*, not Resario! You had no right to go charging off on your own without my authorization. Now I've got the Chief riding my ass, the District Attorney is breathing down my neck, and I have to explain to them both why it got passed off to a junior officer. What the hell was this 'hot tip' anyway? It better have been worth it."

Jenkins shifted in his chair. There was no way he was going to say anything in front of Resario. The man was rotten to the core. "It didn't pan out."

"Didn't pan out!" Wolfe exploded. "You risked screwing up an entire investigation into the death of a fellow officer, and it *didn't pan out?*"

Before he could reply, Wolfe turned on Resario. "And you!" he said, stabbing a meaty forefinger in the bald man's direction. "What have you got for me, and this had better be good!"

Resario looked somewhat uncomfortable but not intimidated. In fact, he looked like he was halfway enjoying himself. Risking a glance back in Wolfe's direction, Jenkins saw that his face had turned an interesting shade of red. With his short salt-and-pepper goatee and the streaks of gray running through his spiked hair, he looked like an angry badger defending its kill.

"Sir," Resario began, "me and the techies went over that alleyway inch by inch after Jenkins left. There wasn't much to go on, but we did find evidence of a struggle behind the dumpster, and we also found a footprint. It looks like it belongs to someone with small feet, maybe even a woman or a young girl. So far, no witnesses have come forward, but we did obtain some fibers and hair off of the wall there. The team is still at it, and they'll be going over everything again until we find something more concrete. We also have several units out on patrol speaking to the people who live in the area, but so far no one's talking. There's no cameras in that part of town either. It's in the slums, and those streets haven't been updated with the new traffic cams yet. Plus, none of the local businesses in the area have any security footage showing that corner of the alleyway. It's a blind spot, sir."

"So you're telling me that so far we have next to nothing," Wolfe said.

"Well, if we could find out who the print and hair belong to, we could have a potential witness. Whoever Lewinsky was shaking down back there may have seen the whole thing." At this point, Resario gave Jenkins a suspicious sideways glance.

Jenkins refused to rise to the bait. "Before I left I was able to ascertain that the spot on Officer Lewinsky's chest may be identical to the ones we've found on the previous victims," he offered. "It's obvious that we have some sort of serial killer on the loose, but until we get those lab results back from the autopsies, we won't have anything further to go on. However, there was a break-in yesterday over at Mercy General. I retrieved the security footage, and it's pretty compelling, sir. The perpetrator used a thumb drive to steal data from the main computer and then escaped through a ventilation shaft in the ceiling. I traced the conduits to the roof, but the suspect had already fled the scene. The two crimes could be related."

The captain leaned back in his chair, his hands resting on the edges of the desk. "You don't say," he stated with a flat look. "And on what evidence do you base this assumption, Detective?"

"Well," Jenkins replied, "the perp was very unusual. You'd have to watch the footage to see what I mean. And the fact that he would break into the data processing center in the middle of the day with patrol officers stationed just down the hallway shows that it was important enough for him to take that kind of a risk. We currently have all those autopsies going on at the morgue down there, so I think he could have been after information pertaining to the case. It's just too much of a coincidence for me to swallow, sir. There has to be some sort of connection."

Resario snorted. "That's weak as hell," he scoffed. "You know what I think? I think you know something you ain't telling us and now you're trying to cover your own ass by throwing out this bogus theory."

Jenkins turned to glare at him. "You weren't there," he said. "This guy had on some type of tactical gear and he crawled straight up the wall and then right across the damn ceiling to get to that vent."

"And what exactly were you doing there in the first place?" Resario retorted. "Can you tell us that, Detective? Why don't you climb down off your high horse and get with the program? We're in the middle of an investigation here, in case you hadn't noticed."

"Oh, you mean the program where I take unsanctioned mafia payoffs to look the other way?" Jenkins shot back.

"Enough," Wolfe roared, slamming his hand down upon the desk. "Resario—get out. Now. And shut that door behind you."

"But, Captain. . ."

"I said get the hell out of here," Wolfe shouted again, pointing at the door.

Resario got up and stormed out of the office, slamming the door so hard that the pictures on the wall jumped. Jenkins calmed himself, taking a deep breath before turning back to the captain.

"Sorry, sir," he began. "I lost my temper."

"Are you trying to get us both killed, Jenkins?" the captain asked.

The question took him by surprise. "Sir?" he ventured.

Wolfe leaned back in his chair, running his hands through his hair again, and then letting out an exasperated sigh.

"Look, you know as well as I do that most of the force is corrupt," he said. "And I got the Chief and the DA to deal with on top of everything else. I'm walking a very fine line over here. You can't just come out and accuse people of that kind of stuff right now, you just can't. That sort of thing is only going to cause us both a lot of trouble. You may not give a fuck, but I've got a wife and four kids! We gotta play this smart and try not to rock the boat, you understand?"

"I've been holding back for years now, Captain," Jenkins fumed, "and where does it get me, huh? You don't back me up on anything, give me all the shit cases, reassign my partner. And I don't even get the raises I so clearly deserve! I've been thinking about walking outta here for quite a while now. But you know what? I put in too much goddamn time here and I've paid my dues. I don't give a crap what you think anymore—this is all bullshit and I'm tired of it!"

"You can't quit!" Wolfe exclaimed. "You're one of the last honest cops I got in this department. I know things have been hard for you, but you gotta understand that I have to do whatever the hell they tell me to do right now. The Chief's been holding the reins good and tight since I got here. If I don't do what they want, well. . . there are worse things than just losing your job, you know. Much worse."

Jenkins was shocked by the captain's unexpected candor. Seeing the man with fresh insight, he began to understand what he'd never realized had been there all along. The captain did care, but he was under a tremendous amount of pressure because of it. They had him between a rock and a hard place. Jenkins could read between the lines as well as the next guy; the DA had something on Jonathan Wolfe, something more than just the threat of firing him. The way the man stared at him now with that pleading look in his eyes was downright disturbing. What were they holding over him that could make him so afraid? How high did this corruption go? All the way up to the mayor? He didn't doubt it for a second.

Sighing in defeat, he reached up to rub his eyes. "Sorry, Captain. I didn't get much sleep last night and I'm not thinking clearly. You gotta believe me, though, there's something going on in this city, something more than just these murders. We got all those weird reports coming in from the lower west side of town now, people either leaving their neighborhoods or locking themselves in, and I'm beginning to hear rumblings about the Gargano family as well. There's some kind of stir-up going on with them, if the rumors are to be believed. What do all these things happening at the same time add up to? Something bigger than the both of us I'd wager, and we've got to get ahead of it before it buries us alive."

"That's why I put you in charge of this investigation," Wolfe said. "Look, I know you got an angle you're working, I can tell. That's another reason I sent that idiot Resario out of the room. But I don't even want to know what it is you've discovered until you can bring me something conclusive. It's safer if I don't know anything specific right now, you understand? But you gotta be more careful. Resario is hot for your blood right now, and that's not good. You'd better watch your back out there, you hear me? I'll do what I can on my end, but you know how it goes. My hands are mostly tied right now."

"Yes, sir. I read you loud and clear."

Wolfe's beefy fingers drummed the top of his desk as he considered Jenkins from across its cluttered expanse. "Well," he drawled after a moment, "then what the fuck are you waiting for? Get out there and find me something I can use, Detective!"

"Yes, sir," Jenkins replied, getting up to exit the office.

There were so many things in motion now that it was hard for him to decide what to do next. Ever since the reports had started trickling in about the strange goings-on in the lower end of town, they'd had every crackpot in the city trying to file a report or claim credit for the unrest. There were so many conspiracy theorists and outright con men making statements right now that it was nearly impossible to sort through all the bullshit and get to the meat of what was really happening. As he walked out of the captain's office, shutting the door behind him, Resario swaggered over with several of his cronies in tow.

"We know you're covering something up," the big man began, reaching out to poke a finger into Jenkins' chest, "and we're gonna find out what it is. You might as well just come clean right now and get it over with."

"Get off my case, Resario," Jenkins growled.

"So that's the way you wanna play it?" Resario said. "Well, me and the boys know all about your little side hustle down at the hospital. Lisell's her name, right? Well, maybe we'll pay her a *special* visit, find out just what it was you two were talking about yesterday. We know you're holding out on us, and we're going to find out what you're up to, one way or another."

"I'm warning you—" Jenkins began, but was cut off by an Asian teen who had walked over from the intake area.

"Detective Jenkins?" he asked in heavily accented English.

Jenkins gave Resario one last hate-filled glare before turning to the boy. "Yes, I'm Jenkins. How can I help you?"

An elderly gentleman dressed in casual attire followed the spindly youth. His white hair was short and neatly trimmed while his fathomless brown eyes stared out of a leathery face that appeared ageless. With an air of quiet confidence, he swayed to a halt and stood with his arms clasped loosely behind his back.

Resario snorted and turned to walk away with the rest of his posse following along at his heels. Jenkins decided to ignore them for the time being, focusing all his attention on these unusual new visitors instead.

"My grandfather wishes to speak with you," the boy said, "and it is very important that you listen to what he has to say."

"Please follow me then," Jenkins replied.

He led them over to his desk and watched as the boy held out a chair for his grandfather. After making sure that the old man was comfortably seated, the boy positioned himself just to the right of him. Jenkins went around behind the desk and took a seat himself. Looking them over with unfeigned curiosity, he came straight to the point. "So, what can I do for you today?"

The man looked up at his grandson, who was rapidly translating the request into what sounded like Japanese. Nodding, the man returned his piercing gaze to Jenkins and then began to speak fluidly in his native tongue. The boy listened, bobbing his head when the old man had finished.

"My grandfather wishes you to know that the harmony of the city is out of balance," he translated. "The interrelation between it and the natural world must be restored."

Great, Jenkins thought, *another whack job.* He looked over at the intake desk and saw that several of his coworkers had paused to smirk in amusement. Apparently they'd sent this guy over on purpose just to waste his time. Sighing, he refocused his attention on the old man.

"I see," he said. "And what does this have to do with me, exactly?"

The boy translated this, and the man gazed back at him with some uncertainty. After a moment of hesitation, he replied through the boy.

"You are the officer in charge of the investigation into the murders, yes?"

"Yes," Jenkins answered, a little taken aback. "What does that have to do with anything? Is he a witness? Do you have information for me regarding the case?"

"My grandfather says that he has felt the influence of very powerful kami in the last few days. He wishes to warn you that they must be appeased or things within the city will only continue to get worse."

Jenkins tried not to roll his eyes. "Well, okay then. Thank him for the tip, would you? But really, I do need to get back to work right now. Perhaps we can talk again at some other time when I'm not so busy?"

The boy translated that, and the old man nodded. Then he replied in rapid Japanese, and the boy tried to hide his amusement at his grandfather's brusque words.

"He says that he will speak with you again soon and also thanks you for your time," the boy said diplomatically. "He would like to leave you with our address, for when you do decide to seek him out."

Jenkins plastered a pleasant expression on his face as the elderly man rose, nodding his head respectfully. Reaching into his pocket, the boy brought out a slip of paper, placing it on the desk with a small bow. Then he turned and led his grandfather back out of the precinct. Jenkins shook his head in bemusement. Why did he always get all the crazies?

-18-

Luciano watched as Marco's men were subsumed by the onrushing tide of fleas that rose up in unending waves from the floor of the club. Panning the cameras around, he located Dr. Orson but then lost the image as a massive cloud of flies occluded the view. It was the third time that he'd run the video logs, and he was not surprised by them in the least. Having dealt with the metaphysical and paranormal all his life, he was used to the strange and unusual. Glancing up, he let his eyes touch upon the painting of his great-grandmother before shying away from it, unwilling to allow himself to dwell for too long upon her stern and uncompromising features. She glared down at him on a daily basis from above the fireplace in his study, her likeness painted in exquisite detail, right down to the traditional Roma headscarf covering her silver-white hair. But it was her eyes that bothered him the most. It felt as if she were watching him through the painting, spying on him from out of those ancient, all-seeing orbs. Refocusing his attention on the monitor, he played the recording again, running it in slow motion this time, and then panning around from camera to camera to view Dr. Orson's position.

There. For the briefest of moments he could see another man, this one short and squat, covered by an immense, burgundy cloak. A flash of glowing eyes flickered from within the depths of his hood before the flies covered the camera's lens and blocked the image from view. Interesting.

He leaned back in his chair, running a hand down the front of his fine Italian suit jacket. He'd worn the blue one today. It was a shade of azure that was accentuated by the lighter color of his cream-colored shirt and matched well with the darker silk of his indigo tie. It really was one of his favorites, he had to admit.

He let his thoughts wander for a moment and then glanced over at Marco, who was slumped disconsolately before the desk. He was trying his best to sit up straight and ignore the pain, but he was not doing well at it. It looked as if the man was about to topple from the chair and go into cardiac arrest. Which, actually, might not be too far from the truth at this point. The flea bites covering him from head to toe made him resemble nothing more than a formless mass of swollen red flesh. However, Marco seemed determined to hide his discomfort as best as he could under the circumstances, and Luciano liked that about him. Perseverance in the face of adversity was a character trait he valued highly in his underlings.

"So," he said, steepling his fingers, "tell me again why you thought it was wise to shoot the good doctor before even attempting to speak with him?"

Marco shifted about in his chair. The movement appeared an involuntary reaction to the bug bites, so Luciano excused it this one time. "Sir," he began, "the guy wiped out an entire room full of my best men just the night before. You'd already warned me that he might be wearing body armor, so I was only trying to incapacitate him before he could bring those weird powers of his into play. Which I did. We would have had him, too, if it wasn't for that other guy who helped him out. There was nothing we could do once those bugs got on us. It was just sheer luck that one of my men had the foresight to jump on a table and flick his lighter under one of the fire sprinklers. The water seemed to help, and after Dr. Orson and his colleague had disappeared, the bugs began to lose interest in us anyway."

"So you think these two men were in collusion?" Luciano asked.

"How could they not be?" Marco countered. "We was just about to wrap the scientist up good and tight for you, and then here comes this guy with all the bugs. He had to have been waiting for his pal, maybe sort of in reserve in case things went south, you know?"

Luciano considered this. It did appear that way from what he'd seen in the video. "How did you not spot this new assailant beforehand?" he asked. "Where were your lookouts at the time? I'd like to know how he managed to waltz into the club just as you and your men were about to procure the doctor and then escape with our prize unchallenged. Weren't you prepared for such a contingency?"

"With all due respect, sir, we never saw him coming. There were fleas everywhere, then the flies, and we wouldn't have even known he was there except for watching the video footage afterward. I'm embarrassed by this whole situation, Mr. Gargano. I've failed you twice now. But the circumstances were extraordinary. I don't point that out as an excuse—I take full responsibility for my actions, sir. I only mention it because I would like for you to consider sparing my men. Those of them that survive the bug attack, of course."

Luciano detested begging. It showed a flaw in the man's character, and it was one that he considered a weakness. Still, it was admirable of him to bargain for the lives of his subordinates, especially as they were not entirely at fault. These new assailants had powers beyond human comprehension and thus were outside the realm of expectancy for what they'd normally be required to defend against. It did not excuse their lack of success, but it did mitigate it somewhat.

"I will consider it," he granted.

The failure to capture Abraham Orson was the true setback here, one that presented its own special set of difficulties. There was a great deal of money involved, of course, for the Gargano family had been invested in the research that he'd been conducting, the results of which were of great importance to his immediate superiors. Back in the old country, they were expecting him to handle this situation and had tasked him with obtaining the results they required from Orson's work. He could not fail them, not now, not ever. It was unthinkable.

That Dr. Orson had somehow obtained these new abilities during the destruction of his lab was in itself bothersome. Luciano had some of his best people looking into that, but so far, they'd come up with no viable explanation. It was ridiculous to think that such a range of capabilities could have come from the experiments alone. Yes, the man had been thrown into the middle of a room filled with research equipment and had subsequently been electrocuted and submerged within embryonic fluids and fetuses. Still, that did not explain the powers he now somehow wielded. Any normal man would have simply died. And it was even more troublesome to consider that this scientist may have been withholding further discoveries from them, scientific breakthroughs that might explain his survival and the assumption of his newfound identity. There had to be a plausible explanation that was based solely on fact. And it was part of his job to find out what this explanation was and then procure such knowledge for his family's exclusive benefit.

Yet now there was this new player thrown into the mix, and that made it a more complex situation. Who was he? How did he go about manipulating the insects? Was it some sort of trick, a chemical compound introduced into the air of the Gleaming Gypsy to attract them? If so, how was he then able to get them to attack only the people that were employed by Marco? And how did he manage to have such a dense cloud of flies fill the air within the club just as he and Abraham Orson were making their escape? Were his abilities somehow linked with those of the doctor? Were they in cahoots? To all these questions and more he needed the answers, but even more than that, he had to be ready to deal with these people on an equal footing. Fortunately, he had the resources to make that happen.

His eyes wandered again, gazing out through the windows, across the picturesque landscaping, and then down to the city beyond. As he came back to himself from this unintended woolgathering, he glanced over at Marco once more. There would have to be an example made of him, but now would not be an auspicious time for such a demonstration. He needed the man's far-reaching criminal network intact in order to help flush the doctor and his companion back out into the open. Hence, an act of clemency was in order.

For now.

"The physicians at my private labs are the finest in the country," he said. "You and your men will get the best treatment available. You are to avail yourselves of this care immediately. I want you fit and ready for duty as soon as possible. We are at war, my friend, and we will need all of our resources to emerge victorious. Once you've been treated, I want you to dig in over at the club. I want it barricaded for a long siege, and I'll be sending you new equipment and a special backup unit to help subdue these two individuals that have so damaged your reputation. They've thrown down the gauntlet, and it's a challenge we can ill afford to ignore. But for now, you're not to engage with them in any way until your backup arrives and I give you more detailed instructions. Is that understood?"

"Yes, sir, Mr. Gargano," Marco said. "I won't let you down again."

"See that you don't. You are dismissed."

As Marco rose stiffly from the chair and was escorted from the room by one of Luciano's men, Luciano turned to the phone and considered it a moment before deciding that it was high time he called in some debts.

After picking up the receiver, he dialed a number and then waited to be connected.

"General Anderson's office," a feminine voice answered. "How may I help you?"

"This is Luciano Gargano," he replied. "Connect me to Anderson immediately."

There was a click as the phone was transferred, and then a gravelly voice at the other end. "This is Anderson. What can I do for you, Mr. Gargano?"

"Why are my calls being screened by a secretary?" Luciano asked. "Our agreement was that I would have direct access to you whenever I so wished. Is this a secured line, General?"

"A moment," came the response. There was a series of clicks and beeps, and then the connection obtained a slightly tinnier sound.

"Okay, we're secure," the general said. "I have a secretary for obvious reasons. You can't expect me to be at your beck and call twenty-four-seven. I'm a busy man. Now, what's this all about?"

"Are your wife and daughters enjoying the palatial estate up in Coventry Hills?" Luciano inquired. "What are they now? Ten and five, I believe. Ah, what a time to be alive! When I saw them just the other day, running and playing around the lawn in front of your new mansion, I could not help but notice how happy they seemed! I remember when I was that age, growing up back in the old country. Such mischief that I got into back then!"

"Are you threatening my family?" Anderson growled.

"Not at all," Luciano said. "I simply remind you of where your loyalties lie. It was my patronage that allowed you to be able to afford all these nice new luxuries, and I just wanted to reassure you that, as a friend to the Gargano family, you can be confident that your own interests are being looked after and protected. Why, I can have men at your home in less than a minute, should the need ever arise! We're always prepared to do our best to make sure our friends stay happy and secure. Surely you can do no less for me? After all, it's our money that's been filtering into your pockets for over a decade now, correct?"

"You've made your point," Anderson grumbled. "Now what the hell do you want?"

"First of all, I'm to have direct access to you whenever I call and you're to make it a top priority to be available whenever I make contact. Is this understood?"

"Yes," came the gruff reply.

"Secondly, I'll need Epsilon Squad. Have them equipped with our newest experimental weaponry and then dispatched forthwith to my estates."

"Those weapons aren't fully tested yet. I can't release them to you, let alone have such an unauthorized military task force put at prominent risk of being caught out in the public eye. You can't be serious!"

"Oh, but I am," Luciano replied. "And you will do as I say. I desire their services, and I want them here *now*! Is that clear enough for you, General?"

"Yes, sir," came the grudging response. "But if things go sour, I'm washing my hands of the whole operation, do you hear me? I'm not going down for something you put into motion against my better judgment!"

"Your objections are duly noted," Luciano replied smoothly. "Now get me those men!"

As he hung up the phone, his gaze swiveled, once again, to the view from his study windows. Everything seemed so peaceful from this vantage, so tranquil. Folding his hands in his lap, he sighed. There was a war brewing, and he was about to embroil himself in a fight that could very well rage from one end of the city to the other. Yet these men with their incomprehensible powers must be caught and pacified. The Gargano family would have all their dark secrets and more—they would have their utter obedience.

One way or the other, he would have his way in this. Any other outcome was unthinkable.

-19-

Charlie led the wounded and bedraggled man back to his new lair deep beneath the city. Now that he'd had the time to set it up properly, it had taken on quite a homey feeling. The first generator he'd found had been destroyed over the years by rust and algae but the backup generator had been covered and was in pristine condition with an auxiliary tank of treated diesel fuel to prevent its decay. He may not have been a computer specialist in the army, but his days in the motor pool and machine shop had been time well spent. Now the generator provided warmth and light to the underground mining compound, as well as additional power.

The man in white had recovered somewhat as they made their way through the tunnels until they finally reached the cavern where the hidden mining facility was located. Now he was resting on a cot within the foreman's office and seemed to be getting stronger by the minute.

Grinning in pleasure as the man regained consciousness, Charlie nonetheless continued to puzzle over his new companion as he sat looking after him. His guest reminded him of an underdeveloped child scarred by some hideous tragedy, and the lab coat he wore under his failed disguise had somehow been modified into a luxurious robe. Its intricate stitching glowed faintly in the dim lighting, revealing Japanese characters of unknown significance. Just who was this person who appeared to have such similar powers to his own? Charlie intended to find out.

"Well," Charlie said. "How are you feeling today, my mysterious friend? You took quite a few bullets back at that club. It was foolish of you to go there on your own."

The man returned his gaze through colorless eyes that seemed far too large for his face. Glancing down, he groaned low in his throat, his body tensing as his chest heaved upward. The faint blue glow about his face and hands intensified but then subsided as he slumped back, his energy spent. After resting a moment and taking in a deep, steadying breath, he reached beneath his robes, running long nimble fingers along the length of his torso. When his hands came back into view, they were clasping slugs that had miraculously been extruded from his body by sheer force of will.

"Who are you?" he asked, staring up at Charlie with the wariness of a cornered animal, "and where exactly are we?"

"Relax," Charlie said. "We are safe. You are in my refuge below the city. It is here that my children and I congregate, and it is a secure place that those above have long since forgotten. My name is Charlie, by the by. And who, may I ask, might you be?"

"Abraham," the man replied. "Dr. Abraham Orson."

"Ah!" Charlie cried. "The good doctor from the clinic near the docks! I knew who you were back then, but how did you become what you are today?"

"I could ask you the same question," the man replied, swinging his legs off the cot as he sat up. The slugs made a faint tinkling sound as they cascaded from his slack fingers on to the hard cement floor. "Did you send those insects to help me?" he asked. "How were you able to accomplish such a feat?"

"They are my children," Charlie said by way of explanation. "My story is a long and complicated one, but I would venture a guess that it must have similarities to your own."

The doctor glanced away, his face growing taut with poorly concealed rage. "I accepted a bargain from a mysterious spirit the night my lab was destroyed. There was a great deal of pain involved. In fact, I'm pretty sure that I died. And yet, here I am. It's all very confusing. My research once meant everything to me, but now I find that I'll not rest easy until I cleanse this city of mob activity. Of course, I'll have to root out the ones who did this to me first, and after that, pay a visit to my erstwhile colleagues who think they can steal my discoveries for their own benefit. Well, they deserve what's coming to them and more. I'll make them pay, all of them, for what they've done!"

"Easy, friend," Charlie said, patting him on the shoulder. "I too was visited by a spirit as I lay dying in that alleyway behind your clinic. A gang of hoodlums had beaten me within an inch of my life, but the spirit offered me vengeance and a chance for redemption. I aim to honor that bargain. But first, I must destroy certain doctors who allowed my wife to die, and then take care of the military who cut off my health benefits. However, you should know that I have also sworn to liberate this city from its corrupt influences and then install a new leadership who will perform their duties in a fair and equitable manner. It is a heavy burden, but one that I take quite seriously. It sounds to me as if you and I have similar goals. Now we just need to decide how best to begin."

Twisting his hands together in his lap, Abraham stared down at them while deep in thought. "Marco Giovanni," he said after a moment. "He let it slip while he was lording it over me that Luciano Gargano was the one who'd made certain I'd be thrown out of my privately funded labs. He insinuated that they'd been interfering with my work for years now. My continuing research, establishing the clinic, even my hidden laboratory—all of it was a set-up from the start. They've been using me this entire time! We've got to find out where this Luciano is hiding. My original laboratory is probably under his control by now if what Marco said is true. They must have needed me out of the limelight because my research was taking too much heat from the press. All this time, all the money they've given me, it was all just so they could get their hands on my discoveries once I'd succeeded."

Charlie sympathized with him, he really did, but things were suddenly falling into place with the information he'd obtained from the stolen computer files. "That new hospital uptown was built around a research facility, quite possibly the same one that you were forced to vacate," he said, "and it was bankrolled in part by the Gargano family. The doctors I seek are now situated inside hermetically sealed buildings located within this very complex. Perhaps if we work with each other, we can accomplish our goals more efficiently. We can infiltrate that club, gain the information you need from Marco, and then ferret out these elusive doctors that killed my wife. Once we have accomplished all of that, then we can both go after Luciano together as a team. Think on it! With your fetal assailants and my swarms of children combined, we would be unstoppable."

-Father, our new brethren are about to emerge.-

Charlie tried to contain his mounting excitement as he glanced over to where Simon had just landed on the floor by the open office doorway. His new warriors were about to be born into the world. Shooting to his feet, he grinned in Abraham's direction, noting his shocked silence.

"Do not be afraid," he said. "This is Simon, my closest friend and confidant. He has just informed me that the specialized eggs we have lain within the womb of a harlot are about to hatch out into a new species."

"A new species?" Abraham said. "I should very much like to see that. How did you achieve the specialization within the eggs?"

As they walked out the door together, heading for the unit in which Rita and Bobby were housed, Charlie explained how he'd used his powers to collect specific biological traits from different insect families and had then melded them together to form a new type of hybridized egg cell. The doctor was fascinated and asked many questions as they walked along the well-lit pathway, their conversation echoing throughout the cavern as it mixed with the vocalizations of a trillion different arthropods now infesting the underground area. As they passed by the small lake, the water was burbling quietly, heated by geothermal springs that caused a faint sulfurous stench to hang in the air. Insects lining the walkway parted before them like a living carpet as they proceeded along the path until they reached the large shipping container that housed the two prisoners. Charlie stopped, holding the doctor back with an outstretched arm.

"I must warn you that what you are about to see is not pretty," he said, "but it is necessary. These two have more than earned their fate. The boy was leading the gang that raped and killed my daughter while the girl was a party to it. So I must ask that you forgive me if I have treated them less than gently during their stay here."

Abraham's expression changed to one of instant outrage. "If that's the case, then I'm sure I won't blame you for whatever you've done. A crime such as that deserves to be punished most severely."

Charlie appreciated the man's understanding and liked his moxie. He only hoped that Abraham felt the same way once he'd gotten a good look inside the cargo unit. Reaching out, he grabbed the handle and dragged the door open.

Flickering illumination from the overhead fixtures revealed Bobby propped up in the back corner, drool oozing from his slackened mouth but eyes still blazing with undiminished anger and indignation. He'd soiled himself several times, but there was nothing Charlie could do about that. The ticks could not stop all bodily function. Legs splayed out before him, he sat in a pool of his own filth, arms laying lax at his sides. A thousand daggers seemed to fly from his burning stare as he watched them enter through the open doorway.

Rita, on the other hand, lay spread-eagled in the middle of the floor, her once beautiful face now covered in sores. She gazed sightlessly up at nothing as her swollen belly, its distended surface awash in sweat, heaved with internal activity. As Charlie and Abraham approached, a low gurgling sound escaped from deep within her throat.

"How have you kept them immobilized?" Abraham asked.

"There are several species of tick I have found to cause a form of paralysis as one of the side effects of their bite," Charlie explained, motioning him forward. "In this way, I have kept them stationary for the last couple of days now. It suits my purposes well enough, and

Bobby there gets a front row seat to the violation of his girlfriend while also having to witness the birth of all my new warriors. I dare say that he does not seem to enjoy being on the other side of things. Is that not so, Bobby?"

Chuckling, Charlie watched Bobby's face quiver as the boy struggled to break the bonds of his captivity, the anger inside him boiling like molten steel. But after a few moments, he subsided once more, eyes going glassy from the strain.

"But how are you keeping them hydrated?" Abraham asked. "I understand the need for paralysis, but surely you must be giving them fluids? I don't mean to criticize, but it only makes sense from a medical standpoint because of the female's condition. It would also prolong the male's suffering until you've finished with him."

"Oh, I have several thousand insects attending to that," Charlie assured him. "Ants bring them water held within cups made from leaves. They simply drizzle the liquid into their slackened mouths, and they are forced to swallow or choke on the fluids draining down their throats. I leave them enough of a muscular process to carry out simpler tasks such as that. For the sake of keeping them alive, you see."

"That's quite ingenious," Abraham said.

Just then, Rita's back arched, liquids jetting from her swollen vagina as her arms and legs danced across the floor in uncontrolled spasms. As her heels and elbows drummed against the flooring, she twisted her head back and forth, her face now a mask of unrelenting horror as the paralysis was overcome by irrepressible agony. Watching the lumps that dimpled the surface of her distended belly wriggle like tadpoles churning beneath the surface of a pond, Bobby's eyes leaked tears of frustrated rage.

With a moan and a final flutter of limbs, Rita slumped back again as tiny insects began to boil outward from her body by the thousands, spilling forth from her uterus into the flickering illumination of the overhead lighting. Charlie cooed in pleasure.

"My new children!" he proclaimed proudly. "Oh, I cannot wait until they grow and begin to spread their fragile wings. It will be glorious!"

Abraham watched with heightened interest as the smaller man's modified insects swarmed across the floor. *His powers must be incredibly strong to have achieved all this,* he thought. The new brood was tiny for now and clustered together so that he could barely make heads or tails of them just yet, but he had a feeling that they would be unstoppable once they achieved their adulthood.

His own powers seethed within him in response to what was happening on the floor of the storage container. He now realized that he needed to learn more, find new ways to utilize his fetal material, before venturing out again to confront the Gargano syndicate. Once he might have been shocked by what was going on in front of him, but no longer. His brutal murder and assumption of powers had changed him in ways he couldn't begin to fathom, allowing him to accept things that may have once frightened or confused him. One thing that he did know for certain was that with the help of this strange theatrical-sounding man he would soon learn all he needed to complete his objectives. Then he could begin an era of rebirth within this festering cesspool of a city and fulfill the pact he'd made with the spirit. The thought of it made him flush with newfound confidence.

Rita appeared spent, her breathing shallow, but then she groaned, her back twisting upward beneath her. The deflated folds of her stomach rose as something larger and more powerful heaved against its constricting weight. Blood started flowing from her nose and mouth as the sagging flesh expanded and then ripped open from within.

Forcing its way out from the gaping wound it had chewed through the lining of her abdomen was a creature quite shocking to behold. Its multifaceted eyes swept the room, searching, and then focused on Charlie. With a proud, possessive screech, it launched itself out of Rita's body to land at the little man's feet.

"Ah," Charlie breathed in wonderment, "it seems that we have a new queen! Isn't she lovely?"

Abraham stared down at the grotesque, multi-legged horror that rested before them and suppressed a small shudder. Never in his wildest nightmares had he seen anything remotely like it. He was suddenly very glad that Charlie was on his side.

-20-

Jenkins didn't have any solid leads and knew he needed more information before deciding his next course of action. He considered shaking down some of his street informants or looking into the strange occurrences down by the docks, but the things Resario had said to him earlier were weighing heavily on his mind. The thought of that goon showing up at Lisell's office, even though Jenkins knew that he'd already relocated her to a secure location, was just too great a threat to ignore. He decided that the rest of the investigation could wait until he'd followed up at the hospital first, just to be on the safe side.

Upon reaching Mercy General, he climbed out of the squad car, thinking about all the crazy shit that was going on as he walked toward the entrance. They had a killer on the loose that could freeze a man's heart and then burn it from the inside out, there was some kind of a bug infestation happening in the slums, and now the Gargano family was up in arms over some as yet unnamed threat. On top of all that, there was also the theft of the hospital computer files to deal with. There had to be some sort of connection to it all, but exactly what that connection was, he hadn't the foggiest of ideas.

As he was passing by the patrolmen stationed at the doors, he paused. "Have you guys seen Resario or any of his crew around lately?" he asked.

The first officer avoided his eyes, ignoring him. Jenkins had been about to enter the building, but the man's willful obstinance infuriated him. "I asked you a question, Officer!" he barked.

"We ain't seen nothing," the man sulked. "Have we, Jake?"

The other patrolman glanced over, his face impassive. "Nope," he added.

So, two more clowns willing to follow Resario's lead, he thought. *Great. That was just great.* The last thing he needed right now was for the rest of the force to band together against him. Snorting in disgust, he let it go for now and went inside.

The attitude of the two officers only added to his mounting anxiety. Making his way over to the security desk, he hailed the two guards on duty, recognizing them from the day before. "Hey, have you guys seen any other officers come through here? I'm trying to coordinate with one of my men. His name is Resario."

"Yeah," one of them replied, "he was here. Came by to look at more of that security footage from yesterday. We played it back for him here on the monitors."

"Did he say what he was looking for?" Jenkins asked.

"Well, he said he needed to see more footage from the hallways leading up to the records room," the man elaborated. "Mentioned something about checking for other suspicious activities. He had us run through the camera locations just outside of Miss Pachenke's office, and once he'd noticed that you'd been down there with Lisell and her niece, he was asking a lot of questions about them."

"That makes sense," Jenkins replied, trying to remain calm. "Did he mention anything else? Like maybe where he was heading?"

"Once we'd told him about Abby, he seemed real interested in checking in on her," the other guard chimed in. "She's a sweet kid. I'm guessing he's probably on his way to her house right now to make sure she's okay. Her family lives not too far from here, just a couple blocks away, in fact. You could try there for starters."

"Thanks," Jenkins replied.

With an urgency he hoped wasn't too obvious, he steered toward the exit. Even though he knew that Abigail wasn't at home, he was afraid of what might happen if Resario and his flunkies stopped by her parents' house. He needed to make sure that her family didn't get caught up in what was quickly becoming an internal conflict within the police force itself. He owed Lisell that much.

Within minutes of getting back in his squad car, he was in front of the girl's home. Studying the house from inside the vehicle, it seemed peaceful enough. For right now anyway. After a quick glance around the yard, he turned to check out the rest of the surrounding area, and it was then that he noticed a white van parked just across the street. As he stared at it, wondering who it belonged to, the tinted driver's side window slid down, revealing Resario's smiling face. He gave Jenkins a knowing wink and then blew him a kiss as the house behind them exploded in a violent roar of sound and energy.

Their vehicles rocked back and forth as the blast wave struck, pieces of wood and other building materials ricocheting off the side panels. Twisting around in his seat, Jenkins was just in time to see a huge cloud of fire and smoke billowing outward from where the house had just been. Then a board the size of his arm punched through his back window, lodging in the seat cushion. Shaking his head to clear the ringing from his ears, he turned back to the van, but it was already pulling away, heading in the opposite direction.

With adrenalin pounding through his veins, he threw his sedan into gear and started to execute a U-turn, but as he was halfway through the maneuver, several other police cruisers pulled up, blocking him in.

"Out of the way!" he shouted, leaning on the horn.

The officer in the lead vehicle rolled down his window. "What was that, Detective?" he said with a smirk. "I couldn't hear you."

"Move that goddamn car right now, or I'll ram it out of the way!"

With studied nonchalance, the officer backed up, taking his time about it.

Swearing like a dockside sailor, Jenkins floored it, sparks flying as he scraped against the other car and swerved off after the van. But he found that the road before him was now quite empty.

A helpless anguish built up inside him. Lisell's sister, the rest of Abigail's family, they might have all been inside at the time of the explosion. Taking a deep breath, he tried to fight through his raw emotions long enough to regain a sense of clear reasoning. If Resario knew the girl's home address, just what else did he know? Could he have already located the safe house?

There was only one way to find out.

Taking a roundabout way through town to make sure he lost any possible tail, he drove to where he'd stashed the women. The whole way there he was filled with so much apprehension that it almost drove him mad. In his mind, the safety of the witness was paramount, but on top of that, he also had Lisell to consider.

He didn't know her very well, but he'd thought there'd been a connection building between them, something that he hadn't felt with anyone in a long time. When this was all said and done, he hoped he could somehow make amends for the way he'd fucked up her life. It was clear to him that this whole situation was his fault.

Protection was the one thing he was sure he still had left to offer her now.

The safe house was in the middle of an industrialized area where there were very few other residences. Pulling the squad car around into an alley behind it, he parked between two dumpsters to avoid suspicion should anyone else happen by. After exiting the vehicle, he checked his surroundings, making sure the coast was clear before moving up the back staircase.

Being squeezed in between two other buildings, the small house had a pinched appearance, which helped it to blend in with the surrounding factories and warehouses. It was left over from a time when he and his partner had still been together and the old captain had trusted them to do the job they were being paid for. Until this case, it had stood empty for years. Unlocking the back door, he let himself into the kitchen and then paused a moment to get his bearings.

There was a table and chairs along the wall to his right and some traditional appliances off to the left. The floor plan was an open concept, with the dining area leading into the living room before angling around toward the front of the house. Because the windows had been boarded up long ago, the interior was dark and quiet. After locking the door behind him, he placed his hand on the butt end of his revolver, unnerved by the disquieting silence. "Lisell?" he called out. "It's me, Dan."

After a few moments, Lisell came around the corner, the dark circles under her eyes betraying her exhaustion. "Abigail's finally asleep," she said by way of greeting. Then, leaning forward, she focused on his appearance. "What's the matter? You look like you've seen a ghost."

He didn't even know where to begin. "You'd better sit down," he offered, gesturing at the table.

Her face scrunched up, the blood draining from her already pained expression as she realized that he had more bad news to impart. Moving to the table, she collapsed into a chair, peering up at him with a pleading look in her eyes.

Sitting across from her, he reached out and took one of her hands. It was soft and warm. He didn't want to tell her, didn't want to be the one to bring her such gut-wrenching news. Steeling himself, he stared into her beautiful hazel eyes, hoping that his heartfelt compassion would somehow help to soften the blow.

"I'm sorry," he said, "but your sister's house was just destroyed in an explosion. I'm not sure if anyone was home at the time. I came here straightaway to tell you and don't have any further details yet, but I do know that it was done by other officers from my own department, ones that have known mafia connections. I can't explain everything to you right now—it's a complex situation. But, if they knew your sister's home address, then there's no telling what else they may have already discovered, what else they might have figured out about us. I have to get you guys out of here right away."

Tears welled up in her eyes, spilling down her cheeks, and he longed to hold her, to comfort her in some way. However, it was painfully clear to him that he hadn't yet earned that right, and probably never would now. So instead, he held her hand, hoping that she could take strength from it despite his own pained realizations. Sucking in a ragged breath, she reached up under her glasses to wipe away the tears and then met his gaze with fresh determination. "Can we at least call her?" she asked. "I could try her on her cell, just to see if she's. . . she's still okay."

"It's too dangerous," he cautioned. "Once we leave here, I'm going to be taking you both somewhere that's a lot safer. There's a guy I sometimes work with. He's a survivalist, and his place is extremely secure. He should be able to check in on your sister for us without tipping anyone off. But for right now, it's just too dangerous, even with the burner phone. These other officers, they know about you and Abigail now. If they find you, they will kill you."

"But why?" she cried. "I haven't done anything wrong!"

He wished that he didn't have to say anything but knew that she deserved the truth, no matter what it cost him. "Because of me," he admitted, hating himself. "They know I've been speaking with you, that I'm. . . interested in you. I'm sorry, but this is all my fault."

She searched his face, studying the sincere remorse evident in his earnest expression, marveling at the honest compassion she also found there. Then, making an effort to pull herself together, she retrieved her hand from his comforting grip. "Well," she said, "I'll go and get Abby right now then. The faster we get to your friend's place, the sooner I'll know if the rest of my family is—"

The sound of a board breaking away from one of the windows interrupted her, then something hit the living room wall, bouncing off it to clatter across the hardwood floor. Instinctively, Jenkins threw himself forward, covering Lisell with his own body and knocking over the table as they crashed to the floor together. There was a flash of blinding light and then a wave of force as an explosion rocked the small house, plaster raining down around them as they were slammed against the back wall in a jumble of arms and legs. The aftereffects of the blast left him deaf and blind. Beneath him, he could still feel Lisell, but other than that, the world was a blank canvas of searing white light. Struggling to shake the fog from his mind, he attempted to climb to his feet, but his limbs had turned to jelly and his body wasn't responding to his desperate commands. Through a haze of scattered thoughts, he realized they'd been hit by a stun grenade, probably launched from the street out front.

Rolling to the left, he was able to flop over onto his back. From previous experience, he knew that this type of grenade was meant to incapacitate, but the force that it generated was considerable. In the past, he'd trained for this type of situation and had even participated in raids where these types of deterrents were used, but that didn't make it any easier to deal with. His head felt too large for his body, his ears were ringing like crazy, and he was unable to get his limbs to coordinate long enough to stand. Even though he knew the effects were temporary, the loss of sight and motor function were unsettling. In frustration, he tried rubbing his face while rolling over onto his side in an attempt to restore his lost faculties.

When his vision at last began to clear, he struggled onto his elbows and knees, making a grab for the edge of the broken table. It overbalanced again, and he toppled to the floor, his legs folding beneath him. Forcing himself to work through the pain, he managed to slide himself up into a sitting position by placing his back against the wall and then shoving with his legs. Peering around through the tears that still blurred his eyesight, he saw beams of white light crisscrossing the smoke-filled living room. He was still trying to clear his befuddled senses the rest of the way when men in riot gear came around the corner.

Resario held the point position.

A grin split the man's broad features as he caught sight of Jenkins, the ends of his ridiculous handlebar mustache framing his mouth like a huge hairy caterpillar. As he strode across the dining area with his shotgun held at a forty-five-degree angle, he shouted back over his shoulder to the rest of his team, "Spread out and find the girl. I've got things handled here in the kitchen."

Squatting down, he rested an elbow on his knee, the shotgun held upright across the front of his body. With mirth crinkling at the corners of his eyes, he considered Jenkins, pursing his lips a little in thought.

"Well, lookey what we have here," he said after a moment. "I'm surprised at you, Detective! You must think I'm stupid or something, trying to hide a witness from me like that. Well, I got news for you, my squeaky-clean compadre—nobody likes you, not even the guys you got assigned to that crap detail outside the hospital. It was nothin' for me to just ask them to slap a tracker on your squad car while you were poking around inside. And I knew you'd come running to the rescue as soon as I threatened this juicy little cunt of yours. Blowing up her sister's house was just icing on the cake to make sure of it."

Leaning over, he poked Lisell with the end of his weapon, eliciting a frightened squeal from her as she tried to crawl away. The lecherous hunger that spread across his features in response to her reaction was terrifying to see. Jenkins tried to move, tried to reach out and stop him, but the effects of the grenade still had him incapacitated. It was a wonder that he could even hear. The ringing in his ears was still so loud that Resario's hate-filled words were faint and indistinct.

But there was no mistaking his intent.

"And now, we're going to have us some real fun," Resario continued. "Once we finish interrogating the girl, me and the rest of the guys are going to have us a little party. And guess what? You get to watch! This piece of ass you been hiding looks like a real sweet ride. I bet by the time me and the gang here are through, these two young fillies of yours won't even know what hit 'em. Hell, they might even enjoy it."

The other officers who'd clustered around him were laughing and jostling one another for position now as the house filled with the disquieting sounds of their amoral intentions. Reaching out, Resario slid his free hand up one of Lisell's legs, his smile widening as she tried to pull away. With a forceful yank, he jerked her back across the rubble-strewn floor, licking his lips in anticipated lust.

Another officer came around the corner, calling out to Resario as he joined the rest of the pack. "We found the girl in the back bedroom," he said. "She's dead. Looks like she took some shrapnel when the grenade went off."

Resario glanced over at the man, then nodded before returning his gaze to the still struggling Lisell. "That's too bad," he mused. "Looks like this party's just gotten a little smaller, boys! But don't you worry, there's enough to go around for everyone. We'll just have to interrogate Jenkins after we're done plowing his little fuck toy here to figure out what we need to know about our missing perp."

The laughter spread, and Jenkins redoubled his efforts to shake off the effects of the grenade. But it was no use. He still hadn't regained his full range of movement yet, and he knew that they'd be handcuffing him anyway before they started in on Lisell. Shame and anger flooded through him in equal parts. How could he have let this happen? How could he have been so stupid? It didn't matter anymore; they'd both be killed after Resario and his goons were done raping Lisell. And there was nothing he could do about it.

Tears of frustrated rage ran down his face as he lay amidst the brutal laughter, trying desperately to regain control of his uncooperative body.

-21-

They hauled Jenkins off the floor and were now finishing handcuffing him to one of the chairs. Meanwhile, Resario had cleared off the kitchen island and had slung Lisell down across it. She was still dazed from the grenade but struggled against him, crying out in pain and terror as he began ripping off her clothing. There was general laughter from the other officers at this while the musky scent of anticipated lust permeated the air. Jenkins pulled against the handcuffs but was too weak to break free of the chair. With his head bowed, he tried to think of a way out of the situation while harboring his strength and grinding his teeth in frustration.

Over in the living area, there was an unexpected buildup of pure static electricity. It started out as a few tiny wisps of energy roving over the discarded furniture, crawling along the baseboards, and running the length of the frayed carpet. Then a feeling of suppressed air filled the space like oxygen being drawn up out of a diving bell as the electricity suddenly coalesced, swirling about in the middle of the room. Chain lightning flickered across the resulting charged atmosphere, gaining power as it zigzagged across the ceiling. It accentuated the hard lines of the wooden fixtures and boarded-up windows with crackling illumination as it cascaded into intersecting patterns before combining to form the outline of a figure hanging in midair. Within seconds, the figure took on definition, and then a glowing woman materialized, floating within a globe formed by the brilliant electrostatic fields and pulsing like the heart of a supernova.

Jenkins was the first to witness her appearance, but the bursts of light and sound that accompanied her manifestation had also caught the attention of the rest of the officers. One by one, they turned, raising their weapons and forming a defensive line around their leader. Resario, who was still focused on attacking Lisell, was the very last to become aware of her, his hands still grasping the bared breasts of the clinician as he glanced over his shoulder to see what the commotion was all about.

The sounds of crackling energy rose to a deafening level as coils of electricity snaked out from the apparition, writhing around the room like the tendrils of a living organism. Their whip-like caresses snapped across the papers, littering the floorboards, lifting and sending them spiraling in a tattered whirlwind of torn confetti. Within this central field of elemental effulgence, the female figure hung encapsulated, bathed in the dappled patterns of her sparkling supercharged power.

Staring down at her husband and his cohorts with glowing red eyes, Florence was filled with a sense of righteousness that she'd never before thought possible. She'd spent the last few hours siphoning the love and contentment from so many other corrupt officers and officials, that the energy running through her now was like a barely contained nuclear reaction. Her form had taken on more of a corporeal presence because of it, the feelings she'd consumed lending her the substance she needed to solidify as she gazed down upon the last remaining officers left of the force that she'd spent so much time and effort decimating.

Jenkins was transfixed by her appearance, eyeing her smooth and hairless body of light with rising amounts of hope as well as dread while the other officers just stared at her like she'd been thrown up from the very bowels of hell. Resario, on the other hand, gaped in slackened confusion, his jaw working back and forth as he tried to comprehend what was going on right in front of him. After a brief moment, he snapped out of it, shouting at his men with all the rage of a dumb animal, "Take her out! Fire! Fire, you morons!"

As the men discharged their weapons, a small number of the shots went wide, blasting gaping rents through the boards covering the windows. As light streamed in through these newly created holes, it slashed across the room, resulting in random beams of sunshine that illuminated the walls and flooring in shafts of blinding radiance. Suspended within these beams like an avenging angel, Florence blazed, her inner power pulsating as the shots struck and melted into her opalescent skin.

Deep within her, the blood lust of the demons clamored for her attention. In that moment of wavering vulnerability, she was almost overcome by their demands, considering the suggestions that sprang, all unbidden, into her mind from the darkened depths of their most twisted desires. As her own anger swelled, rising to match their demonic outrage, the influence they had upon her strengthened. The arrogant police officers, unaware of her inner turmoil, continued to fire their weapons from close range while she fought against these impulses. By sheer force of will, she managed to hold firm against the almost undeniable urge to torture and flay, to rend and to maim, to satiate herself on blood and feast upon the anguish of their mutilated flesh.

Battling back the demons' desires, she denied the influence of their baser emotions, collecting what remained of the shotgun slugs that had melted within her superheated body of light as she did so. Taking the white-hot metal, she then formed it into a sphere of coppery-silver liquid, drawing it out and suspending it in the air before her. The officers, seeing this, stopped firing, their eyes going wide in shock, many cowering away, some even seeking to flee. Yet there would be no escape, not now, not ever, for these unrepentant fools. Now was the time of their reckoning, and she would claim them one and all. Raising her arms, she blocked all the exits by sheer force of will, covering them in the cascading intensity of her vibrant electrical fields.

Resario, recovering some of his lost bravado, pushed through his demoralized men, drawing out the .44 Magnum from his shoulder holster and then aiming it straight at her face. He had always been such a fool. She didn't even know what she'd ever seen in him when she'd still been alive. With a twitch of her hand, she dropped him to the ground, his teammates falling to their knees around him like overripe apples plummeting from a tree. With an impressive show of willpower, he was somehow able to keep the ridiculous handgun aimed at her. It was a pitiful display of defiance that was almost laughable.

"Nicolas Resario," she intoned, melting the barrel of his weapon with a mere thought. "You and your men have been judged and found to be devoid of even the most basic elements of human morality. Because of your past indiscretions, as well as your willful disregard for all life, I now condemn you and your followers to death."

"Who the fuck do you think you are?" he spat, eyes going wild as his burned fingers dropped the heated gun. "You don't have the authority to judge us, you crazy bitch! I demand a trial by jury. I demand to see a lawyer! You can't do this—we're police officers! We have rights!"

Floating to the ground, she stepped toward him, her simulacrum shimmering in waves of elemental power. Then, gazing down into his eyes, she swirled the globe of molten metal above her upraised hand, considering well his desperate declaration.

Did she really have the right to judge these men? Wasn't what she'd been doing since obtaining her powers going against the very ideals that she now claimed to uphold? What gave her the authority to do the things she did, to control the fate of so many deviants who now infested this grim and morally unbalanced metropolis? The thought gave her pause.

But then she considered all the innocent lives that these men, and others like them, had taken—all the sexually abused children, all the raped and battered women and housewives, all the old people brutalized and left to die alone in their own filth. Who would protect their rights, who would avenge them if not for her? These men—these horrible rapists and murdering psychopaths—knew no compassion and gave no quarter. There were no lawyers, no fair trials, for the victims of their violence-fueled crimes. Just who did they think they were to commit such acts of atrocity on so many without ever worrying about the consequences?

While they continued to walk the streets, no innocent woman or child was safe from their predatory pursuits. While they were in positions of power, no justice would ever be brought down upon them for what they did. They truly thought that they were above the law. The knowledge that so many of the men she'd punished this very day had seen it as their God-given right to inflict such pain and suffering made her anger boil like molten lava while the demons within her cried out in delight.

Glaring down at her husband, the fire in her eyes painted his features in flickering ruddy highlights as she let the demons of the strange book surge to the surface. "I have held back from this, tried to suppress it within the tenants of my most sacred duty," she said. "The powers I've been given are compassionate and merciful, and I take from those who have sinned only what they ask of me after their redemption is complete.

"But," she murmured for his ears alone, "for you, my dear husband, I will make an exception."

Staring into his shock-widened eyes, she looked through them and beyond, delving into the very depths of his blackened soul as she slowly tilted her hand, letting the molten metal flow down over his face, covering his entire head and then coursing across his shoulders and chest. He didn't even have time to cry out; the liquefied bullets were so hot that they melted his features away, consuming them all as his skull collapsed inward, leaving his body to topple forward into the dust. With a loud clunk and a splatter of bubbling minerals, he hit the floor hard, his limbs spasming as the final traces of his ill-lived life drained out there upon the cold, hard floor.

She could feel the terror in the rest of his men now, beating against her in waves. Forcing the minions of the dark book back down, she turned to the kneeling officers, raising her arms. From each of them, she took what was her due. All of their feelings of joy and happiness she stole, all of the love that they'd ever known, she consumed. Rising back into the air, she floated in the middle of a vortex of cascading emotions, basking in the luxuriant warmth of its passionate embrace.

Jenkins watched all this from where he was handcuffed to the kitchen chair. He didn't know who or what this spirit was, but he was grateful for her intervention. As she continued to collect streams of blue energy from the men kneeling around her, he glanced over at Lisell. She'd come to her senses enough to clutch the tatters of her torn shirt back together and now lay staring at the scene playing out in front of her. It was a vast relief to realize that she was safe, that she still lived, and had not been completely molested. With a thankful sigh, he turned back to see what this strange apparition would do next.

The officers, at first rigid, their chests thrust out with arms splayed back behind them, now slumped forward as the electrified field began to dissipate, funneling back into the shimmering spirit. She grew larger with the absorption of so much raw energy, her astral body expanding to fill the entire center of the room like some finely crafted sculpture sprung to life from out of a Byzantine cathedral. With her back arched and head thrown back, her eyes, like twin points of fire, reflected off the chipped plaster of the weathered ceiling as the lightning crackled all around her. Highlighted by the beams of sunlight pouring in through the holes the shotgun slugs had made, she took on a further ethereal quality, like some ancient deity painted by motes of celestial light. It was such a beautiful image that Jenkins found he had forgotten to breathe. Wishing he could move his arms, he instead blinked away the tears he felt flowing down his cheeks, staring at her in helpless awe.

After she'd finished subsuming these swirling tendrils of emotional residue, she glanced down at the men who were bent over on the floor before her. Each of them in turn looked up, raising their arms, beseeching her in silent anguish with eyes now devoid of any emotion save despair. With a silver-shot hand, she gestured, and a dozen gleaming blue roses appeared in the air around her, spinning like toy ballerinas in a music box. These exquisite flowers, sculpted from what appeared to be ice, shed tiny flurries of crystals so that the room became chilled by clouds of frost as they rotated around in the shafts of sunlight streaming down through the busted window boards. Gazing at the kneeling men, a smile graced her features that was almost too beautiful to behold.

"I grant you your release," she murmured.

With a flick of her supple wrist, she sent the ice roses flashing, stems first, into the hearts of the men, where they disappeared with a sizzle and a small puff of frigid air. Jenkins now realized that the cause of death in all of his murder victims must be this mysterious spirit. As to the motive behind her actions, on that he could only theorize. But he knew that all of the victims lying dead here today were scumbags, and most of the bodies down at the morgue belonged to child molesters, rapists, and other abusive assholes. This fact gave him a pretty good idea of what the driving force behind such slayings was. Hell, he'd wanted to kill most of these bastards himself at one time or another. They deserved what they'd gotten, and ten times over, in his humble opinion.

The men were now convulsing in agonizing death throes, arms and legs spasming as their fingers drew up into rigid claws. In a short amount of time, nothing but corpses lay sprawled across the floor, limbs locked and twisted into abnormal positions, their lips pulled back in petrified rictus. As the last light of life faded from their despairing eyes, the woman floated down to the floor again, turning her red-hot attention upon Jenkins.

Florence could sense nothing evil coming from the man chained to the chain, in fact, just the opposite. Moving toward him, she tasted the emotions flowing out from him like a connoisseur might sample a fine vintage of wine. Here was someone true of heart, noble of spirit, and fair of judgment. She could see that his deepest concerns were only for the safety of others and that he lived his life by a rigid code of ethics. He was everything her husband had never been, and more. She took from him his fear, yet touched nothing else. With a wave of one hand, she then released him from his shackles before turning to regard the woman.

Lisell slid off the countertop and tried to stand, but her legs wouldn't hold her. Sinking to the ground amidst the contorted lumps of once-living, breathing human flesh, she clutched at her torn shirt, shivering in absolute terror.

Florence felt a great sorrow for all that had befallen this young woman, yet a soaring pride as well. Here was someone of true virtue, with a mothering instinct honed by close family ties and a heart that had much love left to give. She was a kindred spirit, and as such, Florence was drawn to her. Offering a hand that was now more solid than it had been just moments before, she spoke in reassuring tones. "Please," she said, "let me help you. These men, you need fear them no longer—they can't hurt you anymore."

Staring in wonderment at the beautiful spirit, Lisell reached out with a cautious amount of shyness and then grasped the offered hand. It was smooth and cool to the touch. Then the spirit raised her up, embracing her like a sister, and Lisell felt a new strength flowing through her.

"Thank you," she whispered, stepping back. "Who. . . what are you?"

"I came here for those who don't follow the true path," she replied. "My Lady has given me the power to protect the innocent, and any who seek to abuse them will experience my swift and just intervention. I'll leach from them their precious emotions before relieving them of their worthless lives, and in this way, I now fulfill part of my sacred duty to help restore balance within the city."

Lisell was confused, yet no longer afraid. As Jenkins came and put his jacket around her shoulders, she continued to take in the shining spirit, basking in the love and affection she felt radiating off her in waves. Reaching out, she blindly sought and then clasped Jenkins' free hand, taking further comfort from his solid presence.

"Treat this one well," Florence told her with a warm smile, "and he will always hold faith with you. I sense in him none of what these others had eating away at their souls. He's one of the good ones, and you'll be hard-pressed to find anyone else half as worthy of your true attention."

And then, like a dream fading away with the dawn, she dissipated and was gone.

-22-

As he walked through tunnels carved from solid rock by the machines of long-dead miners, Abraham thought about how he'd come to this point in his life. He'd gone from being a respected scientist, to becoming the owner of an abortion clinic, to being transformed into. . . well, he didn't know exactly what he was now, not with any surety. The powers granted him by the spirit when he'd died were still growing, still developing within him. While he felt that he could understand what he'd been tasked to do with these powers, he didn't yet have the ability to know how to use them in the most effective manner. Coming up with a strategy for defeating Luciano and his henchmen was foremost in his thoughts as he strolled through the abandoned tunnels.

The Gargano family had really pulled one over on him, and now it appeared that his old labs were all owned and interconnected with all their other holdings uptown. The mafia-run syndicate had its fingers into nearly everything in the city, or so it would seem. From that new hospital, Harlson Medical, to the police force, and even right on down to the military itself if Charlie was to be believed. It would take a great deal of effort to defeat them now, even with all of his new abilities.

And though he'd been given these powers by an ancient Japanese spirit, he was not entirely sure of the reasoning behind its mysterious intervention. He'd come to an agreement with the being who'd appeared to him out of sheer necessity and not from any deep, mutual understanding of its underlying intentions. Charlie seemed to know more about it than he did, yet by unspoken agreement they didn't discuss it. It was a subject that they both seemed compelled to shy away from. The less said the better, he guessed, about the spirits who'd created them as instruments of justice and revenge.

Now, as he moved through these forgotten corridors lit only by an occasional safety lamp attached along the edges of support beams, he was trying to determine how best to use his powers to greater advantage. Those gangsters had taken him out with ridiculous ease, and it had shown him his limitations as well as his vulnerabilities. He couldn't have that happen again. He had to become better than that, stronger. There must be something he could do, something within the range of his previous human capabilities that could help him right now.

He came upon an open area that stretched out before him, an enormous space covered in rusted-out mining equipment and huge pillar-like stalagmites. Coming abreast of one of the larger machines, he stopped and then leaned back against it, thinking things through. He was a doctor and also a scientist. Shouldn't there be some way for him to use all of that hard-won knowledge to better his cause?

Strength was what he needed the most, as well as protection against bullets and other piercing weapons. He was dealing with the mafia here, so that seemed like a sensible place to start. To obtain this new strength, he needed more muscle mass, and he didn't have time to work out down here in the darkness, exercising until he became more physically fit. He needed to become stronger *now*. So, what else could he do about it?

Rubbing at his jaw, he stood awhile in thought. Could his musculature be enhanced, perhaps even encouraged, using the powers he'd been given? With a wave of his free hand, he summoned some of the protoplasmic goo that he could control with a mere thought. It was like a free-floating ball of cells swimming within a gelatinous substance that, for lack of a better term, he'd been referring to as protoplasm. Since these cells were not contained by any type of overall cell membrane, he supposed that it was a close enough analogy. A few of his embryonic minions winked into life as well, floating around his head and watching him with unfeigned curiosity. Studying the living globule of cells, he began to formulate a plan.

It would be radical, and potentially dangerous, but could he, in fact, grow the cells within this glob into any type of building blocks he needed? He was about to find out. Concentrating, he focused all his willpower, applying his extensive knowledge of the human body and all that it contained to force changes within the cells that now floated above his hand. It took him quite some time, but after a while he was able to achieve the results he desired. Now that he'd found he could do it, he would need to learn how to apply this newfound talent.

Closing his eyes, he centered himself, entering into a trance-like state and then delving deep within his own body. It was like traveling through the pages of an anatomy book, only these were his own systems, his layers of skin and tissue and blood. There, behind his closed eyes, he saw everything that made him the man that he was and more. He found that the basic structures of his human physiology were still as they should be, yet much of it had been altered by the powers he now possessed. He saw where the bullets had damaged him and realized how he'd repaired that damage, marveling at his capability to withstand more than any normal human being could endure. Now he needed to modify himself even further, to make changes that would help him confront the Gargano family and triumph over all of their evil machinations.

Working with a great deal of deliberate care, he began to splice the new muscular tissues he'd created into place along his own preexisting skeletal frame. It was difficult, tedious work as he not only had to continuously create the different types of tissues he needed, but also had to produce multiple strands of connective fibers and tendons to hold them all together, as well as nerve bundles to power them. On top of that, he soon realized that he needed the support of a stronger, more resilient bone structure to compensate for the extra weight.

Time flowed, passing him by, as he worked at a deeper level of concentration than ever before, increasing his bone density, layering on thick slabs of new muscle and connective tissues, enhancing his circulatory system, and making adjustments to his heart and other remaining organs. He was so involved with his work that it became almost like art, something that he wanted to perfect and make flawless before he completed the task. After what seemed like days, but was perhaps only hours in real time, he came back to himself and opened his eyes.

He felt more powerful, more alive than ever before, which was really quite an interesting sensation for a dead man. Bending at the knees, he grasped the giant rust-covered machine he'd been leaning against and then raised it up over his head. Swiveling around, he hurled the heavy piece of equipment away from him, tossing it through the air like it was nothing more than a child's toy. Crashing to the ground several yards away, it rolled end over end before coming to a stop in a cloud of settling debris. After that, he crouched like a football player, setting his feet and bracing the knuckles of one hand upon the ground. Shoving off with his powerful new leg muscles, he sprinted toward one of the massive stalagmites. With a sound like a miniature explosion, he shouldered into it, smashing all the way through it before skidding to a stop on the other side. Yes, he was more powerful now, more able to confront those that would try and stop him, but what to do about bullets?

Observing his new partner's impressive range of powers had given him a few ideas about that as well. Of the insects Charlie controlled, most had a hard exoskeleton, a covering of plates that were tough and resilient, yet flexible. Was there some way that he could use this simple knowledge of insectile anatomy to increase his own defensive capabilities?

Once again, he summoned some of the protoplasm from out of the aether as his floating minions watched on with their tiny bulbous eyes. This time, he wanted to make the cells change into something different, something dense, like leather or horn.

It took him a great deal of experimentation, but he was finally able to figure out how to make a series of armored plates. They were fashioned from hardened skin cells that were woven into many fibrous layers placed at slight angles to one another. Now penetrations would have to break between two parallel levels before reaching the next layer, thus absorbing the force of the projectile as it went in. In this way, bullets or other piercing weapons would have to expend their energy breaking the bonds of the uppermost fibers along their strongest axis before running into each consecutive layer beneath.

He worked these into multiple configurations, and by trial and error, soon had his entire body covered in an interconnected, overlapping carapace. It was a good thing that he'd started out by upgrading his skeletal and musculature systems as the new segmented plating was somewhat bulky and difficult for him to manage at first. But after a great deal of practice, he was able to move unencumbered by its layers so that it became very much like the shell of an ant or other similar arthropod. Even his head was encased, and he now peered out through lenses that he'd fashioned to prevent himself from being shot in the eyes. Gazing down at himself, he found that he liked these new changes. With more practice, he would be able to summon this protective suit at will, encasing himself in its bulletproof protection with the speed of thought.

Now that he had defensive capabilities, it was time to think about offense. He could summon his minions in droves, overpowering multiple targets and then crushing them within their wet and slimy embrace, but what else could he do with them? He knew his access to these embryos was not limitless, but he also realized that he knew where to find more. There were several fertility clinics in and around the city, as well as many other illegal abortionists working at various hidden locations. It would be easy to collect thousands of these tiny fetal assailants from all over town if need be.

Having figured that out, he tried to determine what more he could do with these tiny, amorphic fetuses. How could he manipulate them to an even greater effect? What could he do with them to cause the maximum amount of damage? Were there any limits to his newfound powers, and how could he best learn to control them in new and more efficient ways?

For the longest time, he stayed within that chamber deep beneath the earth, practicing with his minions, forming and reforming them into weapons he could summon at will, honing the skills he'd been given to a precision that he'd previously never dreamed of.

The next time he struck a blow against the Gargano family, he would be prepared. The next time he went up against them, he would not fail.

The Gargano family, and all others like them, would most certainly die.

-23-

There were so many people waiting at the main entrance to the precinct that they spilled out into the hallway. Jenkins had to push his way through just to get in the door. Once inside, it wasn't any better. The place was crammed with citizens, from scruffy-looking homeless derelicts to men and women dressed as if they'd just returned from an elite social event.

Glancing around, he wondered what the hell was going on. He'd taken a huge risk in coming back here, one that he didn't yet know if he was going to live to regret. Even so, there weren't that many officers on duty at the moment, and the ones he did see working the desks were all female. The sight was almost surreal.

After the apparition had killed Resario and the other men who'd been following his lead, Jenkins had taken Lisell to Demitre's penthouse. The man was not happy to see them, but once Jenkins let slip that they were in the middle of a conspiracy involving supernatural beings taking out government officials, Demitre had become positively enthused. After letting them in, he'd listened to their story, asking an inordinate amount of questions about the female spirit as he'd copied the image from Abigail's phone onto his own computer. Jenkins now carried a digitally enhanced photo in a manila envelope, along with some still shots of the bug guy Demitre had pulled from the hospital security footage.

Now, if the captain would only listen to his explanation and provide him with some sort of assistance, he could try and dig his way out of the hole he was currently buried in. It was a long shot, but they had to get a handle on things before the entire city came crashing down around their ears. He was hoping that having the captain on his side for the rest of the investigation would outweigh the risk he was now taking. There was just no way that he could solve this case all on his own.

Where Lisell was concerned, the situation was more complicated. Although he felt that he could rely on her, she was a civilian and still shaken up by all that had happened to them at the safe house. She'd been inconsolable about the loss of her niece ever since, and the fact that they'd been forced to leave the girl's body with the rest of the dead officers had not helped matters any. Now, for the time being, at least, she was safe and had been relieved to find out that the rest of her family was alive and well. Demitre was able to discover that they'd been out shopping when Resario blew up the house and that they currently still had no idea what had happened or even that their daughter was deceased.

Before Jenkins left, Demitre had assured him that he would keep things locked down tight until he could arrange to get the help they needed. Thinking back on it, there was something odd about the way the reclusive survivalist was reacting to all of this. He wasn't shocked by the pictures he'd enhanced and not in the least bit surprised that there was a specter out there somewhere killing government officials. He'd taken it all in stride like it was an everyday occurrence and his strange acceptance of these events had warning bells going off in Jenkins' mind. Still, there was nothing to be done about it right now. In order to solve this crime, they were going to need his help, even if he did have ulterior motives. Shrugging off the uneasy thoughts, Jenkins pushed the rest of his way through the crowds, moving with a purpose toward the captain's office.

Before he even reached the door, it was opened from within, and Captain Wolfe leaned out. Upon seeing Jenkins, he grabbed him by the arm and yanked him forcibly back into the office, slamming the door behind them.

"Where the hell have you been?" Wolfe growled. "The whole city's in an uproar, and we're so short-staffed right now that I've had to call in officers from other precincts just to fill out the roster!"

As the captain moved to take a seat behind the desk, Jenkins settled into a chair facing him, fingering the manila envelope with mild trepidation. He didn't quite know how the captain was going to take the revelation of his current findings. Clearing his throat, he decided on a direct approach.

"Captain," he began, "we've got some kind of spirit on the loose, and she's been taking out a lot of our men. And there's also this other guy, the one from the hospital break-in, who's somehow mixed up in this as well. I don't know how else to say this, sir, but we have some weird shit going on in the city, and it appears to be supernatural in nature."

"Tell me something that I don't already know, Detective," the captain scoffed, picking up a newspaper from the top of his desk and then scanning the front page. Snorting in derision, he lifted his eyes to study Jenkins' shocked expression before tossing the paper across at him.

Jenkins caught the folded projectile before it could hit him in the chest and flipped it around so he could read the headlines.

There was a huge full-color shot of the phantom, albeit a blurry one, and the tagline read, "Love of Life Leached from Lawless Lawmen." Oh boy. The press would be having a field day from here on out, and there was likely to be panic in the streets. Whistling through his teeth, he looked up to see how the captain was handling it. He actually seemed calm and in control for a change.

"So, as you can see, we've got the press to deal with on top of everything else," Wolfe said, rubbing his eyes, "and most of our boys are either turning up dead or currently unaccounted for. We're receiving more reports about murders related to this serial killer every hour, but the victims are all government officials and officers known to be shady. It's almost like this 'Love Leach' is doing us a favor, right, Detective? At least thus far anyway. Oh, we've still got the

DA and the Chief breathing down our necks, but they've got to run damage control on their end first. The whole city's in turmoil. And people are coming here in droves now, reporting more of those bug stories from the lower west side of town."

He flung his hand toward the chaos going on in the outer office with a look of disgust. "Seems like your hospital perp may have something to do with that, but honestly, that's just a wild guess. There's a lot of folks either dead or missing from that area, but so far, they're all drug dealers, gangbangers, and pimps. The rest of the population seems to be either too afraid to leave their homes or are making ready to get the hell outta Dodge. Not only that, but because of our loss of manpower, we've got a whole crew of women from other departments running things in the front office. It's like a goddamn wall-to-wall estrogen fest out there! I knew we had some dirty cops in the ranks, but I had no idea that there were so many across the board, and almost all of them men from our own department!"

Jenkins leaned back in his chair while he digested this information. These spirits, if that's even what they were, seemed to be targeting those in the city who had a bad rap or were corrupt in some way. While on the one hand, it was cutting down on the overabundance of crooked politicians and cops, it was also so far outside the law that it made his hackles rise. Vigilante justice, especially on such a large scale, was a crime, and no two ways about it, even if this so-called 'Love Leach' had saved his bacon earlier at the safe house. He tried to wrap his head around it, but it was a lost cause. How the hell were they supposed to capture something made of pure energy? He didn't have a clue. Glancing back at the captain, he saw that the man now sat in his chair with a look of bemused frustration. But he was in charge here, so he had to have some sort of plan, some directive that would help push the case along, didn't he? Jenkins was all but counting on it.

"What are your orders, sir?" he asked hopefully.

With the suddenness of a striking snake, Wolfe's fist slammed down on the desktop, rattling office supplies and upsetting a half-full cup of coffee. "You're going to get out there and find me some answers!" he roared. "That's what we're paying you for! I need to know what these spirits are! I want to know who else they're targeting, where they're likely to strike next, and who's still alive out of our missing boys! And I want this 'Loathing' character found and brought in for questioning!"

"*Loathing* character, sir?" Jenkins asked in some confusion.

Wolfe waved his hand through the air. "That's what they're calling your bug guy. Something to do with what was written in the papers a couple days ago, and now it's stuck. You know how people generally latch on to things like this and then just run with it. Everyone coming in here from that part of town is going on and on about him—'The Loathing killed my friend,' 'The Loathing ate my brother'—that sort of stupid-ass bullshit. The reports we're getting are all so conflicting that it's like none of these knuckleheads has ever actually seen him in the flesh. All we got is a bunch of unsubstantiated, speculative hogwash with very few verifiable facts. You get a handful of people being stung by insects and all a sudden it's the boogeyman out to get everyone! Fucking morons!"

Jenkins knew that as soon as the media got word of any noteworthy criminal, they liked to tag him with a moniker. He guessed that it just made for more colorful coverage and therefore sold more copies. Running his hands along the seams of the manila envelope, he supposed he should be focusing on his job and not worrying too much about what the rest of the world was calling these miscreants. Right now, right or wrong, they were wanted felons and he had to try and resolve this mess before more people got hurt.

And the first step was gathering more intel. He had Demitre running some internet searches using his extensive technical knowledge, but he needed more than that. He needed concrete, verifiable proof of just who these beings were, what they were doing, and why. If he could figure that out, then he might be able to determine just what it was that they wanted and then discover how best to safely detain them. Opening the envelope, he extracted the photos and slid them across the desk.

"Here are some better shots of the perps," he said. "I had a guy enhance them for us, but they still don't tell us much more than we already know. The phantom is a woman. She seems to be able to manipulate electricity. When she strikes, she lashes out with this energy and then somehow draws the life force out of her victims. After that, she freezes their hearts with a rose-shaped dart made from ice, which also somehow incinerates the organ from the inside out before melting away without a trace. I'm not sure how exactly that works yet; we're still waiting for test results to come back from the morgue. As for the bug guy, I don't really know what his angle is. All I've got besides the hospital break-in is that there's a lot of people over there being treated for bug bites right now and they're all coming in from that part of town. But you already know as much as I do about that."

"The lady with the darts, how did you figure all that out?" Wolfe asked, slapping the back of his free hand across the images he'd lifted from the top of his desk. "These pics of yours don't even have that much detail."

"Well, sir," Jenkins said, fiddling with his tie, "for starters, I had an eyewitness I was protecting until I could find a way to bring her forward."

The captain slouched in his chair, throwing the pictures back down. "Why didn't you tell me this earlier? We could have been further along in this damn investigation by now!"

"No offense, sir," Jenkins said, anger coloring his response. "But the way things have been going around here, I didn't think it was wise. Anyway, it doesn't matter anymore—Resario and his men killed her yesterday."

"I suppose I deserve that," Wolfe replied with a sigh. He suddenly looked older than his thirty-nine years. "Look, I'm sorry about your witness, but we both know that I've had to do what I had to do just to survive. That's not an excuse. It's just the way things are, you understand? But it'll be different now. Speaking of which, where is that idiot Resario? You'd better steer clear of him until we can bring him up on charges—sounds like he's turned into even more of a dirty bastard than I am!"

The captain tried for a smile, but it died on the way to his face, a look of shame crawling across his blunt features instead. Jenkins just stared at him, at a loss for words. Was this some lame attempt to save himself from the attentions of the Love Leach or was he really trying to turn over a new leaf here? There was no way to know for sure, but in his heart Jenkins felt that the captain was an honest man. That didn't mean he could fully rely on him, though. Not just yet anyway. Raising an eyebrow, he waited for the captain to continue.

"Look," Wolfe finally said, "I know you don't trust me right now, and I can't say that I blame you. But you gotta at least level with me. This city is falling apart—it's total anarchy out there! If we don't do something about it, there'll be nothing left to protect. I don't know about you, but I believe in the oath we both took when we accepted this job. I know I haven't been doing all that I could have done to uphold it, but that's going to change, and it's going to change right fucking now. The DA can kiss my big, fat, hairy ass, and the Chief of Police can take a long walk off a short pier. Besides, they're probably already fleeing the country by now if they know what's good for 'em since it's a safe bet that they're already on the hit list for this phantom of yours. She seems to have a taste for the corrupt ones, and they're as black as they come."

Jenkins knew that Captain Wolfe was right, but that didn't make things any easier. He didn't know what these spirits were just yet, but he was going to find out, and for that, he needed the captain's support. Making a difficult judgment call, he decided that he'd have to start trusting him if he was going to get the resources he needed to solve the case.

Over the next few minutes, he explained what had happened in the investigation leading up to and including the safe house incident. Certain parts he glossed over, like his affection for Lisell and some of the things that were said between them, but he spared no other important fact or detail. As he got to the end of the report, he leaned back, folding his hands in his lap. "So, if you go to that safe house, that's where you'll find a lot of our missing officers," he finished. "I'd appreciate it if you could send someone over there right away to take care of Abigail's body. She was innocent, sir, and she deserves better than what she got."

Wolfe considered this and then nodded in somber agreement. "From now on," he said, "you'll get all the help I can give you. I want you to start by going over what we have so far, then get out there and see what you can do about rounding up better leads on where we can find these two suspects. If we can get on top of the situation, we'll be saving a lot of lives. I don't know who or what these things are, but they can't keep doing what they've been doing. This is our city, you understand me, Jenkins? It's our job to serve and protect it, so get your ass out there and get it done!"

It was a dismissal, but Jenkins felt that he was on firmer ground with his superior for the first time in years. Leaving the captain's office, he wandered over to his desk and took a seat. Yet he was at a loss as to where to begin. He'd already been over the files a million times. With a sigh of resignation, he went over it all again. The female spirit seemed to be concentrating all of her efforts within a radius spiraling outward from that burned-down apartment building. Was there some kind of connection to the fire?

The idea was a weak one, but it was all that he had to go on where she was concerned. Over on the lower end of town, there were plenty of informants and other less-than-desirable folks who owed him favors. He could go down there and start shaking some trees to see what monkeys flew out, but he wasn't so sure just what that would get him. It might turn into a colossal waste of time, and time was of the essence right now. As he sat staring down at the files while pondering his limited options, he became aware of a group of people quietly gathering around him. Lifting his eyes, he was startled to see that quite a few of the female officers were now surrounding his desk, staring at him with varying degrees of determination coloring their individual features. What the hell was all this now?

"Detective Jenkins?" one of them said, stepping to the front of their ranks.

"Yes," he replied with unfeigned curiosity. "What can I do for you, Officers?"

"We just wanted to let you know, sir, that we aren't like the other cops that you had working here before." There were nods of agreement all around, accompanied by hardened looks of pure conviction.

He waited, and after a moment she cleared her throat and then continued. "We wanted to tell you that you can count on us, sir. We're here to do our job to the best of our ability, and we know what this badge means, not like the others." Leaning forward, she placed her fists squarely on the desk and stared him straight in the eye. "To put it plainly, sir, we don't take bribes, and we don't work for the criminal families that think they can run this town. This is *our* city, not theirs, and we aim to keep it that way. If there's ever anything that you need, anything at all, you can count on us."

Straightening up, she then gestured around herself, indicating all her fellow compatriots. "Every single one of us here right now, and some of those still out on patrol even, I can personally vouch for. What I'm saying, sir, is that you have our unequivocal support. We've been following this case and watching what our fellow officers have been doing about it, and we don't agree with their methods. Some of us have been at the crime scenes, and most of us here are fully trained crime scene technicians. We think that things should have been handled a lot differently, if you take my meaning. It could be that we may have found some things that the other officers somehow missed or overlooked. We just wanted to let you know that we're here to help, and we'll do whatever it takes to back you up, sir."

For a moment, he could only stare back at her while his throat closed up around a lump of gratitude. Striving to remain in control of himself, he denied the emotions that threatened to overwhelm him. It would not make for a good impression to shed tears in front of these dedicated women, but their offer made him proud, damn proud, and he felt as if a huge weight had just been lifted from his shoulders. With the help of incorruptible officers, ones that he could count on, he knew that he'd make better progress, perhaps even get ahead of things. With his spirits soaring to greater heights, he stood up, extending a hand.

The officer smiled and took his hand in her own firm grip. With a strong, decisive handshake, she introduced herself. "I'm Officer Mattie Williams," she said, then went on to introduce the other officers that stood with her. He shook all of their hands, overwhelmed by their show of solidarity. By the time they were done introducing themselves, he had a stack of new files already laid out on the desk and a core group of honest cops that he could trust without reservation. He felt like bursting into song.

After sharing some further information on the case, he dispersed them, sending some off to ask questions on the lower end of town and still others to research the burned-down building and other areas within the radius of the spirit's activities. Once they'd left to begin their assigned tasks, he sat down again and began flipping through the reports and extra field data that they'd presented him with. While he was perusing this fount of new findings, he noticed a slip of paper sticking out from beneath one of the older files. With a finger, he caught the edge of the note and drew it out into the open.

A name and address, nothing more. As he studied the precise, neatly written information, he remembered the old man and his grandson who'd come to discuss the case with him a couple of days ago. What had the man said? Something about the "harmony of the city being out of balance"? It was a long shot, but perhaps it would be a good idea to pay this Japanese gentleman a visit. Leave no stone unturned, and all that, especially since he had so little else to go on. After pocketing the note, he gathered up the rest of the files and headed for the door. He would check in with Demitre first to see what he'd come up with, but then go seek out this man who was apparently named 'Takashi'.

It was worth a shot, and right now they needed all the help that they could get.

-24-

Charlie had planned the raid for the middle of the day. They'd be expecting them to come at night, and from the images his children were sending him, their enemy's preparations were only making them stronger by the minute. They couldn't afford to wait any longer; now was the time to strike, before they lost the element of surprise. With that in mind, he and Abraham were making their way through the back alleyways and progressing toward the Gleaming Gypsy at a steady pace that still kept them well out of view of the general populace. Not that there were that many people around to begin with. Since he'd instructed his children to start cleaning out the less desirable folks in this part of town, there were very few left who were still willing to brave the streets, even in broad daylight.

"You say your insects can see everywhere," Abraham said as they strolled along. "What do they see right now? Do we have sentries to deal with? How dug in are they over at the club?"

With a sidelong glance, Charlie studied his companion, who was currently walking along beside him in his white lab coat, face and hands glowing a faint blue in the afternoon sunlight. "Oh, I have already taken care of their sentries," he replied. "They are getting smarter about us now. These men had on beekeeper outfits with duct-taped seams. There were six of them stationed at various points leading up to the club, but don't worry—I have taken them out with my hordes of insects. The beekeeper outfits were a smart move, but they could not prevent my children from subduing them by sheer overwhelming multitudes. They will not know we are coming until these men fail to report in, and that will give us a short window in which to make our assault."

"I still don't understand why you couldn't have just sent in the ticks like you did with those teens back at the base," Abraham said. "It seems to me like that would be the easiest way to defeat these mobsters without any actual bloodshed."

Charlie laughed, slapping Abraham on the shoulder as they moved out of one alleyway, crossing a deserted intersection before heading down another. "Those specific species of tick are hard to come by in this area, my blue-faced friend. And that would only have made it so we would be unable to speak with our captives. With those teenage gang members, it was different. I had to work out how many ticks it would take to do the job and at what precise juncture of the neck to have them coordinate their bites. I needed just enough of an effect that it would immobilize yet still keep them alive and aware, you see. There were also weight ratios involved, and I knew my targets intimately in advance. Yet even then, it was a delicate process.

"This is an entirely different situation. We are going into battle, and we aim to take no extraneous prisoners. The people who work for the Gargano family that I have captured and questioned in the last few hours say they have no idea where Luciano's base of operations is located. They all say the same thing—that it is somewhere in the upper part of town, and well-guarded. None of them has ever been there. No, my friend, we need to capture Marco himself and then question him to get the address. He is the only one who they all say has made several trips to see Luciano in person."

Abraham considered Charlie's explanation while some of his bulbous-headed minions floated in the air around him, watching with their oversized lidless eyes. "Well, that being the case, then why a full frontal assault?" he asked. "Couldn't we perhaps sneak in the back and take them by surprise? Don't get me wrong. I've prepared for this fight, and I've developed protections against the weapons that they're sure to have. Yet I can't help but wonder what the wiser course of action in this confrontation might be. I want to win this without sustaining any injuries to us or to your children."

It warmed Charlie's heart to hear the sincere concern in his friend's voice. It seemed that he was considering all options and trying to minimize any possible damage. He glanced down at Simon, who rode on the back of his wrist like a falcon waiting to be released, and winked at him. Simon's antennae whirled in intricate patterns, indicating his shared feelings and ultimate agreement.

"You have the right of it, I'm afraid," he replied as they skirted around a cluster of overfull dumpsters. "But that will no longer be possible. They suspect we are coming, and even now continue their preparations to repel our attack at every possible entrance. My children have been forced out of the club by a series of exterminators who have been through there in the last few hours, and I can no longer get reliable images. Because of this, I have lost many of my best-placed infiltrators. They have covered the building in a vast sealed tent and then pumped it full of poisonous gases, you see.

"Normally, they would have vented this tent after they had killed or driven out my forces, yet still it remains. Before my last spy succumbed to the fumes, I was able to see that Marco and his most trusted henchmen are waiting for us inside. Yes, they wear protective clothing and gas masks so they can withstand it, but I sense that there is something else they are planning, something beyond what they have already had time to put into place. I worry, my friend, that we may have waited too long, given them too much time to ready themselves for our attack. Our best chance now is to go in guns blazing, so to speak. If you can knock a large enough hole in their defenses, I can fill that building with such an abundance of arthropods that they will not even know what hit them. After that, we can pick them off one at a time as they flee into the streets, and when Marco eventually emerges, then we shall have him!"

Shrugging his massive shoulders, Abraham decided that Charlie's plan made sense. A surprise attack in the middle of the day like this just might give them the advantage they needed, especially if they were able to fill the building with Charlie's brood. They were getting close to the club now, so he sprang his new armor into existence with a mere thought, encasing himself in its multilayered protection. Within seconds, he was staring out through the bulbous lenses of his helmet. The surprised look of pleasure on Charlie's face was priceless.

"Oh-ho!" Charlie crowed, marveling at his friend's choice of armament. "I see that your time spent alone within our underground lair was not wasted on idleness! You look magnificent!"

Abraham's body, already hulking with its new muscle growth, had sprouted plates that were not unlike the ones covering many of Charlie's own children. Bronze in coloration, and overlapping in many areas, the new suit also sported articulated joints like those of a crab. The helmet that encased his features was rounded in the front, but then tapered to a spike at the back, and his colorless eyes now stared out from behind transparent lenses shaped like orbs. The long white lab coat that had always reminded Charlie of an elaborate, Japanese kimono finished out the look, its embroidered stitchery flashing in the sunlight as its exquisitely tailored panels rippled in the light autumn wind. The effect, he had to admit, was quite dazzling.

-Father, he is truly one of us now, isn't he?-

"Yes, Simon, he certainly is," Charlie replied with a feral grin.

Flexing his upper body to settle the armor more comfortably about him, Abraham waved his open, chitin-encased palm through the air and a glob of protoplasmic tissues formed, growing larger as he concentrated. Once it was about the size of a small medicine ball, it solidified into a hardened mass covered in lumpy nodules.

"I think I can knock a hole in the wall with this," he said.

Charlie nodded in approval. "Yes, that does look like it will do the trick quite nicely. Let me ready my troops then, shall I?"

With a wave of his own hand, an enormous cloud rose up off the surrounding rooftops, blacking out the sun as the air was suddenly filled with a great buzzing roar. Exiting the alleyway, they stepped out onto the street directly across from the Gleaming Gypsy, Charlie's warriors massing above them.

Right away they could see that the club was still covered in heavy material that puffed out at the sides, its rounded edges taut with the poisonous gases it held within. There was no sign of anyone else on the streets around them, and no men were posted on the rooftops either. For all intents and purposes, the entire block was devoid of life, except for the billions of insects now swarming in an impenetrable black cloud overhead.

Without hesitation, Abraham cocked his arm back and then hurled the large, dense ball of hardened skin cells out at tremendous speed. Rocketing across the street, it tore through the Gleaming Gypsy's tent-covered wall with a monumental explosion, the canvas crumpling inward as gases belched forth, vomiting up into the cloudless sky. Once the poisons had cleared, they could see that the hole it had blasted through the side of the building was about the size of a city bus. Abraham stared, surprised by his own success. He'd had no idea that his projectile would be so devastating. There'd been only a short period of time in which to practice the maneuver inside the old mining cavern before Charlie had come to collect him for the assault.

While waiting for the poisonous fumes to dissipate, Charlie continued marshaling his forces about them with an insane grin plastered across his craggy features. While he did so, a great throne of roaches and centipedes rose up around him as millions of his land-bound arthropods scuttled from every crack and crevice, pouring over the pavement in uncountable multitudes before entering through the jagged hole in the side of the club. Seconds later, the hovering swarms followed them in, funneling through the rent in the canvas like they were being sucked into an industrial-sized vacuum cleaner. From inside the building there came the sounds of gunfire, and then hysterical screaming.

Leaning back in his spindly multilegged throne, Charlie laughed aloud, the spikes radiating out from the back of his newly formed seat causing long shadows to play out across the concrete in front of him. "Well, Abraham," he said, "it appears that now we have only to wait. Soon, my friend, we will get the answers that we desire."

After only a few minutes, men wearing gas masks and modified beekeeper suits began boiling out from the hole caused by Abraham's projectile, fighting against an overwhelming number of both crawling and flying antagonists. Covered from head to toe in the seething insects, they looked like formless lumps of wildly flailing limbs coated in millions of tiny chitinous bodies. Yet still they came on, surging against the irrepressible horde in order to reach the relative safety of the street. As soon as they'd cleared the building, they began to open fire with automatic weapons, bullets peppering the surrounding area with no apparent regard for aim or precision.

Abraham waved a hand, and a large oval of hardened skin cells appeared before them. Its rigid thickness absorbed the random gunfire with a deadened chiming, transforming the projectiles into slag as the bullets fell from the shield in a tinkling red-hot rain of deformed metal slugs. With his other hand, he then made a splay-fingered motion, and hordes of his prenatal fetuses appeared out of the aether to sail across the open spaces and engulf the men. As the gangsters screamed from within the compacting tissues, insects flew up in waves, escaping through the permeable outer membrane of the pulsing globules as the men inside were crushed by ropy masses of living embryonic cell clusters.

Soon bodies began dropping to the ground in lifeless, mangled heaps, blood splattering the concrete and smoking a little in the chill autumn air. Abraham was nauseated by the sight of it but shook off the feeling. He would not allow himself to find sympathy for these hedonistic scum. They'd not only destroyed his life but had also taken away everything that he'd once held dear. They deserved to be annihilated, all the way down to the lowliest, most insignificant member of their far-reaching family. He decided that he would kill every last one of them if he could manage it. Within the confines of the helmet, his face took on grim, hard lines as he steeled himself against the carnage filling the street before him.

Charlie glanced over with a satisfied expression, denoting a feeling of pride that Abraham clearly did not share. "Well, this all seems a bit too easy," he began. "Not that I enjoy this sort of thing overly much, but I had thought that they would put up more of a fight." His smile suddenly faltered, then slid from his face. "Something's. . . coming," he added haltingly, his voice suddenly growing hollow with foreboding.

As he lapsed into confused silence, gouts of flame erupted from the interior of the club, incinerating the insects swarming within the opening. Through the resulting smoke that poured from the rent in the wall emerged two men wearing elaborate combat suits. Between them they carried some kind of small contraption resembling a portable generator which they then set down on the pavement before kneeling with their weapons poised defensively. Striding through the billowing flames behind them came several other soldiers, who swiftly moved into a protective formation around the device. The gear they wore appeared specialized, a type of armor the likes of which Charlie had never before seen.

The hi-tech outfits covering them from head to toe were configured of close fitting, articulated plates and had mirrored helmets of unconventional design, making them appear more like space travelers than soldiers. In addition to that, they each had canisters strapped to their backs that were not unlike those of a flamethrower crew. The tubular-shaped wands they carried were connected to these tanks, and some appeared to already be belching fire. But the other devices distributed evenly amongst their ranks were more uniquely constructed. Charlie wasn't sure what to make of it all.

While the newly arrived defenders maintained their strategic positioning, the kneeling soldiers switched on their machine. This unusual device then somehow produced a field which crackled to life around them, encasing the entire party within a dome of flickering violet-colored energy. Abraham glanced over, arching a questioning eyebrow at Charlie from behind the transparent lenses of his own protective headgear.

Considering these unfamiliar foes for only the briefest of moments, Charlie raised his arms and summoned the most vicious of his stinging arthropods, sending them forth in countless droves. From out of the afternoon skies, he called down dense swarms of hornets, yellow jackets, and wasps while the streets simultaneously filled with millions of bark scorpions, hobo spiders, fire ants, and centipedes. In unstoppable waves, these tiny minions of war poured forward, converging upon the unit of battle-ready soldiers who still held their position inside the purple radiance of the energy dome created by their peculiar device.

But as the leading edges of his combined assault force came into contact with the shimmering field, there was a tremendous flare of electricity. Charlie watched on in mounting dismay as his battalions of tiny antagonists sizzled and fried all along the crackling barrier. With the bodies of his slain warriors piling up in rising mounds of twitching electrified death, he suddenly found himself at a loss. Ever since he'd gained his powers, there'd been none who could stand against him. Yet now, these new enemies with their unfamiliar technology had effectively rendered his vast armies useless. In the few brief moments that he sat his living throne in shocked perplexity, Abraham flexed his massive shoulders and then strode forward.

The insects parted before him as he moved across the intersection, the iridescent robes he wore swirling around his hulking body which now gleamed in the sunlight like a statue carved from living bronze. Raising his arms high above his head, he summoned huge numbers of his fetal minions, forming a gigantic blob of living protoplasm that coalesced into being with the churning internally-heaving appearance of liquid lava. Then, bringing his arms forward with palms facing outward, he sent this mass of living cells boiling forth in an unending tide of repellent, all-consuming destruction. With a roiling, amorphic liquidity, this outpouring of primordial viscosity hammered into the barrier with the full force of an unstoppable avalanche, but then melted away into clouds of vapor with the hissing resonance of red-hot metal being squelched in a barrel of ice-cold water.

They were in trouble, and Charlie knew a moment of concern, perhaps even fear, as he considered his opponents. This was obviously a battle-hardened, well-equipped tactical strike team, he realized, glancing over at Abraham, who'd stepped back as his minions continued to evaporate against the shielding. Their eyes met, thoughts mirrored within each other's grave expressions, and then they turned as one, raising their arms together in readiness for a devastating combined attack.

But before they could bring their powers into play, the soldiers kneeling by the machine switched it off while blasting the air around them with great gouts of flame. At this signal, the other six men stepped forward, aimed their weapons, and then began to fire.

From three of the strange nozzle-shaped wands came streams of dark green gel that blasted out in high-pressured arcs. This thickened fluid, bubbling with internal heat, struck Charlie full on, toppling him from his throne of centipedes and roaches, and then binding them all into a sticky, coagulated ball. He tried to move, to get his limbs out from underneath his sprawling cloak, but he was now saturated with a substance that was as thick and unforgiving as tar. The more he struggled, the worse it became, and he sank even further into the congealing wad of smoking-hot adhesives.

Abraham witnessed this and then turned back just in time to raise multiple layers of hardened skin cell barriers in the air before him. But the other three men on the strike team had concentrated their attack in his direction, and from their weapons came gouts of freezing-cold liquids. Abraham could only assume that this was some new type of cryogen-based attack, and as his shields froze in midair and then splintered into a thousand pieces, he backed away, reaching deep within himself to pull forth even more of his offensive capabilities. Yet before he could mount a counterattack, the streams of nitrogen-based chemicals shattered his remaining defenses and hit him full force, slamming him onto his back and sliding him across the pavement toward the alleyway behind them. He struggled against the freezing embrace of this continuous onslaught but was soon entombed within an icy crust that froze the joints of his armor and completely immobilized all his movements.

Fighting against their separate but equally dire predicaments, Charlie and Abraham both tried desperately to escape, but it was useless. Trapped within their chemically induced confinement, they couldn't concentrate enough to use their powers. As they sought to regain control, to burst forth from the restricting compounds, the strike team leader moved to stand over them. Raising a hand to the side of his odd helmet, the man touched a button that caused his mirrored faceplate to turn transparent. Grimly staring down at them while the rest of his men gathered around him, he spoke into a small microphone located next to his chin.

"Mr. Gargano, we have them," he said. "You're clear to send in the recovery team now."

Charlie searched through his mind for a way out of the situation, appalled by this turn of events, and reached out with all of his remaining power to try and retake command of his disorientated children. But he couldn't focus his energies. Even Simon, his most trusted lieutenant, was stuck, wrapped within the confines of the tar-like substance covering the voluminous folds of Charlie's burgundy cloak. Abraham was having similar difficulties, his massive form coated in layers of ice that frosted his flowing robes down across the cooled plates of his gleaming armor. Although he struggled with all of his not inconsiderable might, he simply could not break free.

With waves of panic threatening to overwhelm him, Charlie's eyes were somehow drawn to a glimmer of light growing above them in the cloudless sky. Captivated by this strange event, he watched in stupefied wonder as a woman appeared, floating within a globe of crackling electrical energy. As bald as a newborn babe, she hovered there just a few feet above them, her nude body shimmering with a stunning amount of self-contained incandescent power.

"Cease and desist your acts of hostility," she intoned, her strange, metallic-sounding voice echoing from the buildings around them.

⚌╫ ╫⚌

Florence had been drawn to this location by the soldier's inhumane thoughts and actions, yet there was something more that had attracted her here. The two beings who were now immobilized below her had powers that called out to her, spoke to her of a close kinship the likes of which she'd never before experienced, not in this lifetime nor the last. There was an almost harmonious balance between them when they were all within close proximity, and one that she was sure that they must also feel within themselves. The smaller of the two was stuck to the pavement, his magnificent cloak wadded around him within a syrupy mass of bubbling greenish tar, while the larger and more armored of the two was frozen solid, his beautiful white robes frosted to his gleaming bronze plating. With a wave of her hand, she released them, her energy cascading around them to melt and dissolve the ice and goo covering them both. As they began to break themselves free from the rapidly deteriorating chemical compounds, she turned her attention back to the group of soldiers now staring up at her.

"You have been judged, and I have found you all to be wanting," she told them. "But do not fear, for yours will be a just retribution. I will now drain you of all your wasted passion before I grant you your final release."

The men paused only for the briefest of moments before they trained their weapons upon her, their wands belching forth streams of fire, tar, and ice. Florence was engulfed in liquid napalm, freezing nitrogen, and bubbling adhesives simultaneously. Although her body of light was impervious to such attacks, her form had only just begun to take on more solidity. It was because of this that she found herself being pushed back up into the sky, her shielding quickly coated by the bombardment being brought against her. Through a mounting anger that nearly blinded her, she fought against the continual streams of their weapons' discharge while the demons within her clamored for fresh blood.

Charlie saw the exquisite lady falter as she struggled against the chemicals being fired her way and instinctively knew that the power she held within her was not enough to stem the tide of the triple attack. The adhesives were covering the ice that formed around her impenetrable globe, the flames searing the resulting layers with intense, solidifying heat. This unrelenting assault caused so many additional coatings per second that Charlie could see she was having trouble just trying to stay airborne. Soon it would be too late and she would fall to the ground, immobilized just as they had been but moments before.

Concentrating all his will, he seized control of his powers and then reached out toward the commandos. With a suddenness that was satisfying to behold, they dropped their weapons, stumbling around while yanking their helmets off, and then violently rubbing their eyes.

"Code Red! Code Red!" the leader shouted into his microphone. "We've been blinded. I repeat, we have been blinded! Where's that damn extraction team? We're losing them, dammit! Immediate backup required!"

With a flicker of her immense inner strength, Florence shrugged off the layers that had formed around her protective globe of energy, blazing brighter than the sun as the chemicals melted away in a multicolored rain of toxic sludge. Reaching out, she then brought the men's hopes and dreams to the forefront of their thoughts, caressing them, stroking them into intolerable levels of desire and wonderment. With a collective gasp, they stopped what they were doing and dropped to their knees, some of them bursting into uncontrollable sobbing.

Seeing this, Florence balled her hands into fists, drawing forth their deepest emotions, their innermost enthusiasm for love and life, and then absorbed it until she grew larger than the buildings around them. She was glorious in her consumption, radiant in her electrified field of overwhelming power. And as the combined emotions tore through her like a tropical storm, they filled her with feelings so pure and poignant that she rode on waves of boundless ecstasy. But all too soon their emotions were exhausted, and she once again subsided back down to her original shape and size. At this point, she summoned her ice-blue roses, swirling them through the air so that they danced in the sunlight like fanciful concoctions spun from the heart of an ancient glacier, yet beating internally with the pulsating blood-red aura of encapsulated hearts.

Glaring at the men with cold-eyed disdain, she then cast her deadly darts out in a glistening arc.

With uncanny precision, the icy projectiles pierced the men through their hearts, causing their backs to arch as they flopped to the pavement, jerking about like a school of beached fish after a tidal wave. Within only a few moments, it was all over. Floating to the ground, Florence stepped over their still-twitching bodies, her bubble of energy dissipating as she offered Charlie a hand.

Climbing back to his feet with her aid, he smiled. "Thank you, dear lady," he said. "Allow me to introduce myself. I am Charlie, and this is my good friend, Simon." Raising his arm, he displayed the giant cockroach who was now busily cleaning his antenna. "And our blue-faced companion over there," he indicated Abraham, who was shaking ice melt from his shimmering robes, "is Abraham. Well met, I say, well met indeed!"

Gazing at the bizarre little man, Florence took a moment to study his unusual features, noting his glowing eyes, the knobs that grew like stunted horns from his forehead, and his long, pointed nose. He really was quite an extraordinary individual, she decided. "I agree that we are well met," she replied with a warm smile. "Yet, tell me, what did you do to them there at the end? I was having difficulties, but then you blinded them somehow."

"Ah," he said, "it was a simple enough thing, really. You see, there are many tiny insects, demodex mites to be exact, that live on the surface of human skin. I simply ordered hundreds of them to gather together and then invade the soldiers' eyes. It was not enough to truly harm them, only to blind them momentarily. If it would not have been for you, we would have been captured, or worse. Might I inquire as to who you are and how you came to be here?"

"My name is Florence," she said, continuing on to explain how she'd sensed the soldiers from the immaterial realm and had come from there at once to claim them.

While they were conversing, Abraham finished collecting himself. *Who is this amazing woman?* he wondered, trying hard not to stare as he shook the last of the frost from his robes. She was the most captivating creature that he'd ever laid eyes upon. And now she was speaking with Charlie like they were the closest of companions. Jealousy rose within him before he could squash it, causing him to narrow his eyes as he stepped forward.

"I'm Dr. Abraham Orson," he said. "Thank you. Thank you so much for saving us both. We are in your debt."

"Nonsense," she replied. "You would have done the same for me, I think. Now come, we must leave this place before the other strike team arrives. The two of you need time to regain your strength before we can face such a challenge again. Do you have somewhere to go, someplace where we could recuperate while we talk?"

"Of course!" Charlie exclaimed, eyeing the still-smoldering nightclub with a look of hopeless regret. "I suppose that Marco will just have to wait for another day. Please, follow me."

The three of them left by the alleyway that Charlie and Abraham had entered through earlier. They were not in the best of shape after their ordeal, and so it was that they were unaware of their erstwhile prey watching them from within the shadows of the gaping hole in the wall of his establishment.

Out in the street, the strike team lay sprawled in various positions of agonizing death, their specialized armor a silent testimony to the ineffectiveness of the protection it should have provided. Mounds of insects were also in evidence, and as a light wind began to pick up, it caused their tiny carcasses to blow in small whorls across the surface of the concrete. The machine that had allowed the soldiers to hide behind an electrified barrier sat alone and inert, its functionality now betrayed by the men it had failed to protect. As the sun beat down on this scene of dismal carnage, reflecting off the pools of blood, ice melt, and greenish bubbling tar, Marco drew a cell phone from the pouch on his belt.

It was hard to dial it through the gloves of his beekeeper's suit, but he managed it with grim determination.

"Sir?" he said as the call was connected. "Did you see all that? We almost had them, but then some broad came outta nowhere and took out your team without even trying. I'm sorry, sir, but I ain't got nobody left down here to help me get a handle on things. I respectfully request that you put a rush on that extraction team so we can get rid of this mess before the cops show up."

"It will be done," Luciano's menacing reply echoed back through the receiver. "Oversee the cleanup operation personally and then come meet me at the villa when you're through."

The call ended abruptly with a chilling disconnection.

Standing in the shadows of his destroyed club, Marco felt a rush of all-consuming rage. Those filthy bastards had ruined him, destroyed everything that he had worked so hard for, and had most likely just signed his death warrant as well. Luciano wouldn't be as forgiving after yet another failure, especially one of this magnitude. Marco realized that he couldn't just let them walk away from it all scot-free. Thinking things through, he impatiently awaited the extraction team, formulating a plan that only a madman would willingly follow through with.

-25-

emitre's penthouse was only accessible via a service elevator at the back of the building that was also monitored by several well-placed surveillance cameras. And even though he was a highly suspicious introvert by nature, Jenkins and he had somehow managed to form a mutual bond of respect over the years. Demitre recognized that Jenkins was one of the last cops left in town who wasn't on anyone's payroll and so grudgingly lent him a hand with the trickier cases. At the same time, Jenkins had learned to look the other way on some of the man's more quasi-legal interests and activities. Now Jenkins was just glad that he'd formed a working relationship with the recalcitrant recluse. As he rode the elevator up to the top floor, he hoped that they could make some real progress on the case now with this influx of new data he'd received.

The files Mattie had given him were crammed full of useful details taken from scraps of evidence uncovered by her fellow officers at the scene of each murder. Using this information, Jenkins was hoping he could find some sort of a correlation between the victims besides the fact that they were all scumbags. It would be helpful to know what they were dealing with here, and why. Having a female spirit that leached the life out of people was not exactly a textbook case. Fingering the file folder he held in his hands with a nervous anxiousness, he waited for the elevator doors to open and then stepped into the corridor.

In addition to the ongoing investigation, Lisell's situation was also weighing heavily on his mind. He'd ruined her life when he'd gotten her niece killed, and he also felt responsible for her sister's house being destroyed. Shame threatened to overwhelm him as he thought about how much he'd screwed things up for her. It would be a miracle if she ever spoke to him again after all that had happened in the last couple of days. But for now at least she was safe. Demitre's apartment was like a fortress; nothing could get in or out without him knowing about it. Her safety was first and foremost in Jenkins' thoughts as he strode down the hallway toward the apartment's front entrance.

Demitre's penthouse was protected by a large metal door with no visible doorknob mounted in a triple-reinforced frame. The whole thing was wired, and the only way to gain entrance was with a special key card that could be used on a panel just to the right. Cameras looked down from five different vantage points, and there was also a screened microphone set in a square plate to the left for communication.

After pressing the call button, he stood waiting impatiently, and in a few moments was rewarded by an electrical buzzing sound. There then came a series of loud *ka-chunks* as bolts in the doorframe released from their sockets. With a second, there was an even more audible thrum of motors, and the door cracked open before sliding back into the wall to the left. Stepping forward, Jenkins entered the foyer, and the door hissed back into place behind him with an audible thump and a whir of hidden electronic gears. The sounds of the bolts ramming home into their slots followed him as he moved further into the small reception area.

The foyer was deceptive, designed to put unwanted visitors at a false sense of ease. It was rectangular in shape and appeared comfortable enough, with its rich wood paneling and attractive hardwood floor. A few well-placed chairs and a coat rack rounded out the décor while a couple of landscape paintings brightened up the walls. But to those who were unwary or simply unwelcome, it was an absolute death trap. Vents along the ceiling and floor could pump gas in at a moment's notice, and there were also decorative holes situated in the wall around the secondary doorframe that could be used to launch projectiles of any variety into the room.

Also made of sturdy metal, the main entrance had a regular knob and several large deadbolts that could be unlocked either by a set of keys from this side or conventionally from within. Jenkins knew that an electrical current could also be generated into this door and through its doorknob as an added precaution against unexpected intrusion. Demitre was nothing if not thorough about his security measures. Being a conspiracy theorist and a survivalist had made him very distrustful over the years, and it was a paranoia that Jenkins could now fully appreciate.

After a moment, the deadbolts on the second door began to click back one at a time. He waited for it to open and then saw Demitre peering out at him. With a grim smile, the man waved him forward. "Detective," he said in greeting. "I didn't expect you back so soon. Did you have any luck down at the station?"

The man had seldom changed his looks since the day they'd met, and as always, his hair hung in loose strands around his thin pasty-white face while a scraggly mustache still colored his upper lip. After Jenkins entered, Demitre immediately turned and then relocked all the deadbolts before leading him deeper into his spacious abode.

Following him into the main living room, he ran the fingers of his free hand along the spine of the file folder he carried. "As a matter of fact, I did have a bit of luck for a change," he said. "The captain seems to have finally taken a stance, and it's one that will benefit the entire city if you ask me. As long as he sticks to it, that is." Glancing around as they walked toward the back of the penthouse, he noticed that Lisell was fast asleep on the couch, a fuzzy blanket snuggled up tight around her. "How's she doing?" he inquired.

"About as well as could be expected," Demitre replied. "Come here for a minute. I want to show you something."

Leading him over to the far side of the room where he housed his extensive computer equipment, Demitre took a seat behind the desk and began pounding away at the keys. The main monitor went through a series of overlays as schematics started cycling across the glowing screen. "Give me a second to get these aligned," he said, "and then I'll show you what I've come up with so far, okay?"

Jenkins nodded, turning away briefly as he pulled out his cell phone. He needed to check in with Miles down at the morgue to see what developments, if any, had been made on the autopsy front. As he hit speed dial, his eyes stole another glance toward Lisell. She lay sleeping with one arm thrown back over her eyes, her glasses sitting next to her on a small coffee table. Watching her from where he stood, she seemed so fragile and lost that his heart tied itself into knots as the phone rang through at the other end. After a moment, it was answered by Miles.

"Mercy General Morgue, this is Miles," he said. "How may I help you?"

"Miles, this is Dan. What have you got for me?"

"Well, not a whole helluva lot, I'm afraid," came the apologetic reply. "I've had a bunch more of your victims coming through here in the last day or so, all of them in identical condition. The official cause of death as of now is trauma to the heart, but of course that can change when we get the labs back in a couple of weeks. It's a good thing you have officers stationed at the doors or we'd have had reporters barging right into the examination room! I'm so sick and tired of saying 'no comment' every time I walk past 'em that I feel like I'm losing my voice!"

"Well, I just thought I'd check in—no harm in asking, right?"

"Yeah, no harm in that at all," Miles said. "But I gotta tell ya, Dan, it's the damnedest thing. We've got so many other dead bodies coming through here right now that I've had to call in extra help from uptown. Not only are we still getting all the ones with the frostbitten, fried-out hearts of yours, but now we're also receiving a lot of corpses from the lower west side as well. And if you can believe it, the cause of death on those is even stranger! It's all from insect stings and bites, and I mean on a massive scale. These people are literally covered from head to toe, and we're not just talking about one species here, either. I've never seen anything like it. Most of these insects aren't even communal ones.

This type of coordinated, full-scale insectile attack on a human being has never been recorded anywhere before in the history of medical science. What the hell is going on out there, Detective?"

"I'm still looking into that, Miles," Jenkins said, "but I can assure you that I'm going to get to the bottom of it, one way or another."

"Well, let me know what you find out, okay?" Miles replied. "The whole thing is giving me nightmares, for Christ's sake, and I work in a damn morgue!"

"Will do," Jenkins said, repressing a grin. "I gotta go for now, but I'll touch base with you again soon. Thanks, Miles. Keep up the good work, alright?"

"You got it," Miles replied before ending the call.

Putting the phone back in his jacket pocket, Jenkins turned to the desk and saw that Demitre had pulled together a map with colored overlays on his large central monitor screen. The details were so accurate, it felt like he was looking at an aerial view taken from a helicopter. As he studied it, Demitre turned to him, waving his hand toward the screen.

"So here we have a map of the city and its surrounding areas," he said. Then, reaching down, he toggled in a few keystrokes, and blue dots suddenly appeared on the overlay. "I was able to take all of the information you've given me so far and then correlate it with addresses across the map in order to see what sort of a pattern, if any, would emerge. These dots represent all the attacks that have happened over the last few days which resulted in corpses with frozen hearts."

Jenkins stepped forward, stroking his stubbled chin as he gazed at the images. The dots seemed to spread outward from a suspiciously familiar central point. "What's in the middle there, right at the center of all these attacks?" he asked.

"It's the location of the building that burned down, the one you told me about from just before these attacks all started." Reaching down, he performed another set of keystrokes, and this time, red dots appeared.

"What am I seeing now?" Jenkins inquired, coming around the desk to get a closer look.

"These marks are also from the last couple of days, but they illustrate all of the bug attacks I've been able to find out about from hacking into police databases and researching local hospital reports. The really weird thing here is that they also started happening the same night your murder victims began turning up."

The red dots spread out in a circular pattern as well, but all of them radiated outward from another location, one that was only a couple blocks away from the building fire. "What's right in the middle of all these occurrences then?" Jenkins wondered aloud.

"It's just an old warehouse, as far as I can tell," Demitre said. "I've tried to pull up more information on it but haven't had time to do a really deep search yet. From everything I've gotten so far, though, it's just an abandoned building with no further significance."

What in the hell could an old warehouse have to do with anything? Jenkins wondered. Then it hit him. That night, the same night that the building had caught fire, he'd been on a low-level stakeout, and it was one that he'd never completed.

"Demitre, that's the warehouse where we've had reports of smugglers and some sort of gang-related activity going on," he said. "I was supposed to be looking into it on the night in question, but then the apartment building behind me exploded, and I rushed over there to help out instead. See if you can reference anything based on those details while I make a quick call, okay?"

"Sure thing," Demitre said, his fingers flying over the keys with a rhythmic tapping.

Turning away, Jenkins pulled out his phone again and hit a different speed dial option. "Mattie," he said when the call was picked up, "this is Jenkins. I was wondering if you could do me a favor and send some officers down to that warehouse by the docks, the one with the low-level smuggling reports from a few days ago?"

"Sure thing, Detective," she replied. "What have we got?"

"It might be nothing," he said, "but the insect-related attacks that have been happening in the lower end of town seem to spiral outward from that location, and they also started the same night as the fire. Those other murders, the ones caused by this so-called 'Love Leach', they began at the same time and have a similar pattern. You know what? Come to think of it, let's not take any more chances with our people. Send in a couple more units as backup and then have them all wait until everyone's ready before proceeding into that building, got it?"

"Yes, sir, we're on it. I'll call you when we find out what's inside, okay, Detective?"

"Sounds good. Thanks, Mattie."

Pocketing the phone, he turned back to Demitre.

"Anything?" he asked.

"Hmmm. . . all I can find is what you pretty much already know. There's been reports of some smugglers using that warehouse as a base to sell weapons out of. Mostly just sidearms, maybe a few rifles. It's all nickel-and-dime arms dealing, you know? A lot of the gangbangers around here like to try and gear up when they're expanding their turf or defending it from rivals. It looks like what we have here is street-level crime at its finest."

Jenkins studied the map, noting the locations on the overlays. There had to be something they were missing. "What else have we got in that area?" he asked, pointing at the map. "Can you tell me about those buildings sitting in between our other two locations of interest?"

Demitre pounded away at the keyboard again for a few seconds and then sat back.

"Just more of the same," he said. "A few abandoned warehouses, a row of long-vacant stores. . . wait—the building that's the most centrally positioned between the other two locations was once a Japanese herbal shop." His fingers flew over the keys once more, his eyes searching through data being brought up on his secondary screens. "From what I can tell, it's been there for years, but it's remained empty now for quite some time. The family who owned it doesn't seem to be around anymore. It's my best guess that they moved away after that whole area turned into slums. With the corruption in the police force, and city officials doing next to nothing to keep the peace or to clean up that section of town, you can hardly blame them. No offense, Detective."

An abandoned Japanese herbal shop, Jenkins thought as he put his hand in his pocket, fingering the slip of paper with the address on it that he'd intended to visit earlier. Maybe that old man could provide some insight into this puzzle after all. At this point, anything was worth a shot.

"Keep at it," he said, placing the file folder on the desk. "Here's all the new info my fellow officers have gathered. Try and work through it to see if you can discover anything useful, okay? If you could find any correlation between the victims, or even between those being taken out by these insect attacks, it would be a huge help. Right now, I have another lead to track down, and if it pans out, it may just crack this case wide open."

-26-

Florence was astounded that she'd found such fitting allies who also had abilities so similar to her own. Since she'd begun her new calling, she'd spent most of her time battling to balance the internal struggle going on within her while also learning to regulate and control the energies that continually raged throughout her entire being. The demons from the book she'd stolen were a constant drain on her attention. They waited, potent and predatory, just below the surface of her conscious thoughts, always ready to leap up at a moment's notice and fill her with feelings of perversity and bloodlust. In counterpoint to this, the shimmering power that the maiden had gifted her with rippled through her like a raging electrical storm, reminding her of the bargain she'd struck and reinforcing the terms of that agreement. It had only been after she'd drained enough of the spiritual energy from her many victims that she'd become more solidly anchored within the physical plane. Before then, she'd spent most of her time as a non-corporeal being, existing as fluctuating, insubstantial particles like a ghost in the realms of aether.

Now that her astral body could become more tangible, she'd found that it could also be taken out of sync with the physical world in the blink of an eye. With this control over how she materialized, she purposely kept herself in flux to deny the people she was harvesting the ability to damage her in any way. With her form in this constant state of instability, their weapons could do her no harm, and that was the way she preferred it as she scoured the city of its degenerates and other abusers.

For the time being, she had drawn the light into herself to form a physical presence that could be more readily interacted with as she walked through the abandoned subway tunnels with her newfound companions. It was all for the sake of her new friends—these two men who could not have been more different from one another if they tried, yet were strangely alike all the same.

Charlie walked at her left side swathed in his burgundy cloak with the hood pulled up to cover his chitinous head. His body was short and compact, covered with rigid plates that intermeshed smoothly like the ones on his strange and wondrous comrade, Simon. His staunchest ally was the largest cockroach she'd ever seen, but that didn't frighten her one bit. He was actually very sweet and liked to fly around her in amusing patterns as they walked, often foraging on ahead to scout out the way for them as they moved along.

The man on her right, however, was quite different. Once his armor had melted away, it revealed a head that was slightly out of proportion, its hairless expanse glowing a faint bluish color in the shadows as his wide lidless eyes gleamed with a milky-white sheen in the surrounding darkness. Something had also been done to his nose and ears at one time, leaving only the slits and holes remaining. Adding to the strangeness of his appearance were the white robes he wore. They reminded her of a scientist's lab coat, yet one that had been altered in many ways. Now the collar stood up stiffly about his neck while the rest of it flared out around his large, well-muscled frame almost like a kimono. The runes embroidered in iridescent white thread across the voluminous material were ones she didn't recognize, yet they seemed to be some type of stylized Japanese symbols. The entire effect of it was quite striking.

However, these were simply his outward physical attributes. Regardless of what he looked like, there was just something about him that she felt drawn to, a warmth and refinement, perhaps, that Charlie somehow lacked. It had been a great pleasure for her to unobtrusively use her powers to clean away the dirt and residual filth from their clothing as they'd been traveling together so that they now strode along in spotless harmony with her own shimmering form. She enjoyed the way that her glow lit the way for them within a circle of radiance that also reflected from their freshly turned-out garments. It made them appear to be more of a team as they progressed across the uneven ground of the tunnel, and it suited her to have done them this simple act of kindness. The thought of it made her smile as she followed them further into the darkness.

After a while, they took a series of switchbacks through some abandoned subway trains. Charlie led them down the middle of each car, winding in and out of them until they reached the other side of the tracks. The area beyond them was littered with a tangle of old machinery, but behind this jumble of rusted-out parts and towering pieces of twisted metalwork lay a hidden set of stairs. They went down them, and then the stairs appeared to end at a blank wall. She was delighted, however, to discover that this was but an optical illusion. As they went around to the left, there was a gap between the wall and the other side of the stairwell. Once they'd eased past this, they found themselves standing in front of an ancient boiler resting within a chamber that had not been used in many years. Charlie led the way to the metal doors of this huge device and then stepped within. From the interior of the unit, Florence saw that the back wall had been blown apart by some long-ago explosion, and it was through this aperture that they ventured, then out again into the more rough-hewn tunnels beyond.

"Where are we?" she wondered aloud.

Charlie glanced up at her, his green luminescent eyes sparkling with barely contained mischief. "These, my dear lady, are old mining tunnels that have been abandoned for eons. My children scouted them out for me a few days ago, and I have since been able to make them somewhat more hospitable." He waved her forward with a graceful twist of one arm. "Up ahead are the remnants of a small mining compound, one that rests beside a natural hot spring. It is my own hidden world down here and quite well-guarded, as you can see."

And then she did see, once she knew to look for it. All along the walls and in every nook and cranny bugs were crawling and slithering, an astounding variety with many different types that she didn't even recognize. It was an entomologist's dream come true, and it shocked her that there could be such a profusion of different species living here together in mutual harmony.

"So the power granted you is control over insects?" she asked. "How do you feed so many of them down here alone in the dark like this?"

He chuckled, warming to the topic. "Ah, they are my children now, you see. I but ask them for assistance when needed, and they comply. As to their feeding habits, these hordes and swarms are always in a state of constant flux. Many children depart to find sustenance when the need arises and then return here to gather together again when they have been satiated. Most of the ones you see here now are used to living communally while still others have adapted under my leadership. I have called in all of the ones that might be helpful to our cause, and that is why the bulk of them remain—to be closer to me should I have need of them."

"And your cause, it's like my own then?" she asked.

"Of course!" he said. "We three are alike in that way it would seem. For example, I have been tasked with ridding this city of the gangs that infest it, the doctors who use their medical expertise to provide unnecessary and overly expensive treatment options, and those in the military that have been coerced into serving the crime syndicates that currently rule them all. Abraham here has a similar agenda. He is focused on taking down those same mafia families and destroying the labs that house the corrupt medical practitioners themselves, all while bringing us closer to a time of healing and rebirth. I can feel that you have been given duties that parallel our own in some way. Am I correct in this assumption?"

She thought for a moment, then nodded in agreement. "I've been asked to seek out and punish all those who are physically and morally abusive, especially those who're in positions of power. This will eradicate their influence from the local governing bodies and make sure that the city can return to a time of true harmony. It's a sacred duty, and one that I take very seriously."

"Lest we forget," Abraham added, "these powers were also given so we could exact our revenge upon those who've wronged us. I can only assume by your appearance, and by your similar power set, that you've similarly been visited by a mysterious spirit who offered you a choice, another chance at 'life.' When we each agreed to these separate yet seemingly interrelated bargains, we accepted this as part of that arrangement and then paid for it with our own humanity."

Glancing down at her nude and hairless simulacrum, Florence found that she tended to concur with him. Yet she had no regrets. "There is no right or wrong in this," she told him, staring back into his pale, colorless eyes. "We may have made our choices based on revenge, but the greater benefits of what we do now outweigh that petty consideration a thousand times over. People like to label things good and evil, but that's a misconception. We are what we are now, and the things we do from here on out will change the world and bring it into greater balance. I, for one, have accepted this and continuously strive toward a better tomorrow. Not just for myself but for all of humanity. Would you not agree that that's why we're here in the first place?"

He studied her, his eyes roving over her shimmering form and then coming back to meet her gaze squarely. "Yes, I would agree wholeheartedly," he said. "And yet, I cannot help but wonder what will come after? Once we've completed our mission, what then? It's not as if we'll be able to walk the streets again as we are now. What will become of us when all is said and done?"

She considered this question from all angles. To walk amongst the general population, breathe air into actual lungs, feel the warmth of sunlight caressing her skin, taste the sweet flesh of a ripened peach, and feel its juices running down her chin. Yes, she would miss these things. But she was far more than what she once had been. The enjoyment of such earthly delights could never satisfy her in the same way now—she was beyond all that. It made her sad to realize that she would never be able to interact with people on a regular basis, never again move amongst them and be seen as truly human. But she didn't regret becoming what she now was; it had saved her from herself as much as anything else.

"What becomes of us afterward is inconsequential," she said. "We must live in the now without any thought for what's behind us or what the future might hold. Our previous lives were but an illusion, and this is now our only reality. Seek a purity of purpose, my friend, and be content with the fact that we work together for the greater good. The past, present, and future—these are all concepts that we three are not truly bound by anymore. We are as one with the spirits that awakened us from death and should focus solely on making this land whole again. It is enough for me, and it should be enough for you as well."

He nodded at that yet remained thoughtful as he studied her. His gaze was quite frank, and she found that she might have been blushing had she still retained the ability to do so. Even though she truly believed in what she'd just said, the admiration in his pale eyes stirred to life many of the longings she'd kept secret even from herself. Would she ever really know true love? Could she even experience it anymore without using her powers to draw it forth from others and then fill herself with those secondhand feelings? She didn't know the answers to these questions and glanced away from him before he could see the confusion and longing hidden deep within her fiery gaze.

"Well, such speculation is useless at this point," Charlie said, breaking the awkward silence that had grown between them. "I, for one, will be most content to continue living here with my family. What have the people of this world ever offered me anyway? I gave them everything I had in their endless wars, and yet afterward they discarded me, oftentimes treating me with nothing more than thinly veiled contempt. I have no need for the world in which they live in, even after we are done putting it to rights. I will remain here, potent and powerful, ready to do battle whenever I am called upon by the spirits that now guide us. That, my friends, should be enough for any one of us I would think."

They'd continued walking during their discussion and now stepped out into a large chamber dominated by structures that looked to be industrial trailers resting beside a small bubbling lake. Mining equipment and storage containers also dotted the floor of the cavern, while a small power station housing a generator was situated off to the right. In the illumination cast by the lights that were strung along the walls and ceiling, she saw that there were millions of insects covering every square inch of the place. This living carpet of chitinous bodies parted before them as they moved down the path, closing in behind them as they progressed.

Stopping beside the lake, Charlie suddenly cocked his head, as if listening to something that only he could hear. Then, he smiled. "My new children have been busy while we were gone!"

Motioning for them to follow, he moved toward one of the larger storage containers, and as they got closer, Florence could see that the doors to the boxlike structure had burst apart at the seams. Fibrous filaments were now growing from the cracks and crawling out along the sides and roof. It seemed to be spider webbing, but it more closely resembled the pale questing roots of some hideous albino tree. Stepping forward, Charlie grabbed both edges of the sagging double doors, then dragged them open the rest of the way.

Florence's shimmering radiance cast more illumination than the flickering overheads within the container itself. Lit by her vibrant glow, the interior of the rectangular chamber was revealed to be festooned with more of the glistening wet strands which grew outward from the back. Lying in the middle of the floor was the corpse of a young woman, her body sucked dry of life so that it bore an uncanny resemblance to an unwrapped mummy. Her clothing hung in tatters from a desiccated, skeletal figure while her cloudy, lifeless eyes stared unseeing from a thin and shrunken face. Covering her emaciated frame were thousands of strange creatures that Florence had never before seen. They were undoubtedly insects, yet larger and fiercer than any she'd ever encountered. Raising her eyes from this disquieting spectacle, she noticed a much more sinister presence wrapped within the shadows at the very back. As she stepped closer to get a better look at what was lurking there, the crackling essence of her inner energy revealed a being straight out of the realms of nightmare.

It was unbelievably grotesque—a veritable horror—sporting long, spindly legs like an oversized king crab and an enormous, pulsating abdomen. The webbing that hung about it supported its swollen length from the ceiling while many of the other new insects tended it, moving all along its rotund lower body in a scuttling frenzy. Piled in the far corner beneath the back end of this being's immense shuddering bulk she could see a cache of faintly glowing eggs, but her eyes were inexorably drawn back to the creature's elongated plate-crowned head, which reminded her vaguely of a prehistoric triceratops. She could not help but stare as it continued to feed.

Resting just beneath the creature's clickering mouthparts was the body of a young man, his skull split open like a soft-boiled egg. The creature's dainty forelimbs were grasping the edges of his shattered cranium, and while Florence stared on in utter shock, its oversized labial palps brought small portions of his exposed brain up for its other mouthparts to consume. His eyes were glassy, but Florence could tell he yet lived, could feel the pull of his life force beckoning her, tempting her to use her powers to draw from him the most powerful of his remaining emotions. Under different circumstances, this young man would have been a prime candidate for her attentions; she could see all of the corruption in his soul, sense his many immoral sins like the heat of a roaring fire.

But right now, all he truly felt was terror and pain.

"It seems that our new queen has matured," Charlie mused aloud. "It's a pity about Bobby, though—I had hoped that he would have lasted much longer than this. What he is now experiencing is but a fraction of what he deserves for all that he has done. Yet the newest members of my current brood must feed and grow strong. Ah, well.

At least they will be satiated for a while yet until their next molting." Waving his arm toward one of the nearby buildings, he turned away. "Come, my friends! Let us take our leisure in the foreman's office and talk more of what will come next for us in the cleansing of this foul city. There are many plans yet to be made, and time grows short."

Florence found that she agreed with him. Taking one last look at the dying teenager and the malevolent arthropod that was still gorging upon him, she shrugged and then followed Charlie toward the closest trailer, Abraham walking alongside her as Simon flew around them in gleeful circles.

From within the storage unit, Bobby stared after them, unable to do more than strain helplessly against his paralysis as the large insectile queen feasted upon his flesh. Tears rolled down his haggard cheeks as the unbearable pain and horror of his situation sunk in. They were leaving him here to die and there was nothing he could do to prevent it. In utter despair, he watched as they left him there, feeling the horrid queen's spidery palps as they continued to delicately slice off portions of his fading intellect for her to daintily consume.

-27-

This was no longer just a problem for the Gargano family alone; this was an all-out war on criminal activity throughout the entire city. Luciano pondered this, considering his options as he stared out the window of his study, gazing down at the picturesque landscaping surrounding his palatial estate.

The strike team had failed, but it wasn't from any lack of planning on his part. It was due to the unexpected arrival of yet another supernatural entity. He'd reviewed all the helmet cam footage and the video feeds taken from security cameras in the surrounding area, and the debacle at the Gleaming Gypsy was most assuredly caused by this woman who'd appeared right out of thin air. But studying the problem had also made him realize that most of his recent problems could be attributed to her direct interference.

It had become quite clear that the men he'd lost over the last few of days were a direct result of her ongoing efforts. Because of her meddling, almost all of the people that he'd bought and paid for on the city council and within the police force itself had now been either killed or driven from town. For the first time in his life, the empire he'd so carefully constructed was resting on shaky ground, and he would be a fool not to recognize what was happening for the serious threat that it was. This woman, this "Love Leach," as they were now calling her, was a thorn in his side to be sure, and one that he could ill afford to ignore. There had to be a connection between her and those other two unusually gifted opponents that he could somehow exploit. He just needed to find it.

Turning away from the window, he strolled over to his desk and took a seat behind it, leaning back in the chair with his hands folded across the comfortable expanse of his midsection. These people, or whatever they were now, were really beginning to get on his nerves, and that was never a good thing. He'd always prided himself in his ability to remain calm in the face of adversity, but after taking so many losses, and now this failure to capture the ones responsible, he was beginning to get truly irritated. Maybe it was time to contact the leaders of the other crime syndicates and bring them in on this. After all, it wasn't just his holdings that were being decimated—this affected everyone associated with the criminal underworld. If they lost this ongoing battle against these supernatural antagonists, it would put them out of business for good.

Over the last two days, the reports coming in had all indicated that he was taking huge losses in other areas as well. Drug trafficking was down; smuggling, gunrunning, even prostitution, had all seen a marked decrease in profitability. The numbers didn't lie, and right now they were hemorrhaging money on several different fronts. That damned bug guy had insects crawling all over the lower west side, killing his most highly skilled operatives and driving the others into hiding, while his accomplice, Dr. Abe Orson, was trying his best to shut down the most profitable clubs in the whole city. And now this woman comes along, and by all the evidence he'd been able to gather thus far, she was the one taking out the police and other government officials whom he'd once held so firmly under his iron-willed control.

Mind churning with plans and contingency plans to deal with the situation, he sat rubbing his thumbs together atop his clasped hands. He still had the labs, the new hospital, and all of his more legitimate businesses here in the upper part of town, but how long would that last? It was only a matter of time before these people finished mopping up in the lower districts and then came snooping around up here, looking to shut him down for good. There had to be a way that he could come out on top of the situation, a way to somehow move this conflict out of the public eye and then fight it on his own terms.

His gaze wandered, sliding across the painting of his great-grandmother hanging above the mantle before shying away from it again. There would be repercussions, he knew, for the setbacks he'd suffered, but he could mitigate them somewhat with the capture of these newfound foes of the Gargano family. Somehow, he needed to incapacitate them, harness their powers for the sole use of his organization alone, and then find a way to duplicate their unusual abilities in a controlled setting. Either that or just kill them outright if it came right down to it. There was still time, he could still get a handle on things, but only if he acted quickly.

Unfolding his hands, he leaned forward and picked up the phone. For the next several minutes, he spoke with the heads of each syndicate that controlled other large portions of the city, arranging an emergency meeting for later on in the day. Once he'd finished the last call, he hit the intercom button.

"You can send them in now," he told his assistant.

Less than a minute later, the door opened and eight men dressed in military fatigues shuffled in, lining up in front of the desk. Studying them, he saw that they all slouched in various poses of internal misery, their sullen expressions making it quite clear that they weren't happy about their current situation. This was the extraction team assigned to cleanup duties after their comrades had been slaughtered, and they were now all that remained of the two original units that he'd created. Luciano detested sloppiness, and in fact abhorred the overall attitude these men were projecting. Searching their faces, he tried to find even an ounce of moxie left in any of them, but after the humiliating defeat they'd suffered, they all appeared to have lost their edge.

That's when he noticed that Marco was no longer with them.

Now there was a surprise. Keeping his emotional response from reaching the stone-cold features of his face, he thought about what the man's absence could possibly mean. Marco was neither a coward nor a fool, and ignoring a direct order to report in was just not in the man's nature. There had to be something else going on, something that must have delayed him. If they needed to chase him down, it would not end well for him, and that was something Luciano knew the man was quite aware of. In any event, it was a problem for another time perhaps. Right now, he needed to focus on the business at hand. Leaning back in his chair, he steepled his fingers, trying to decide how best to deal with this group of sad-sack soldiers and their obvious lack of self-discipline.

Was it to be the carrot or the stick today?

In the past, he'd found that it was often best to start right at the top and then work his way down. Their leader, Jace Whitmoore, was second in command and in charge of the extraction team, but now the duty of leadership had fallen on his broad shoulders alone. These men were the best of the best, and Luciano had seen to their specialized training at the military base outside of town after they'd joined the clandestine operation just over a year ago. He'd monitored their progress from behind the scenes ever since, implementing changes in the rigorous structure of the program over time to increase their effectiveness. Originally, there'd been two teams of twelve men, but a few of them hadn't been able to cut it and were let go in favor of a tighter, more trimmed-down tactical unit. In the end, he'd wound up with two detachments of eight men apiece, all specialists, all veterans of many conflicts, with each team consisting of one commander and seven sergeants.

Now, however, through no fault of their own, they had suffered this embarrassing setback. These men had arrived on the scene soon after their comrades had been slain, having been forced to watch it all from their own monitors while en route. Without making it there in time to aid their fellow soldiers, they had instead been burdened with the unpleasant task of cleaning up the bodies, with no further outlet for their seething anger and deep-rooted resentment. Given the chance, Luciano knew that they would channel that impotent rage into a killing frenzy. But how best to harness this untapped potential?

"Commander Whitmoore," he said. "What is your assessment of the failed mission?"

"Begging your pardon," the man replied, "but it was total bullshit. If it weren't for that electrified bitch, we would've had them all wrapped up good and tight for you. Perhaps if we'd been told beforehand of this extra level of threat, we could have been better prepared for it. Sir."

Eyes staring at a point just above Luciano's head, his body assumed a rigid pose, hands clasped behind his back. The other men shifted around and then came to attention as well. Their leader was on shaky ground, and they all knew it.

Luciano toyed with a button on his vest as he studied them for several long minutes, letting the tension draw out. Then, leaning forward, he tapped his meaty forefinger on the desk for emphasis as he spoke. "If the threat had been known beforehand, you would have been informed, Commander. Unfortunately, this person is a new player, one that we had no knowledge of prior to the mission. Do you not think that we would have prepared you for such a contingency had we but known of its existence?"

This gave the man pause. Luciano could see him struggling to process this new intel, the muscles on his jawline clenching as he thought things through.

"In fact," Luciano continued, pressing the issue, "we not only would have prepared you for her attack, but we would have also made certain that you'd defeat her without any difficulty. We have the means to do so, and after studying the footage, I can assure you that the next time she strikes at us, it will be her last. What say you to that, Commander?"

"Sir," the man replied, standing even straighter, "nothing would give me greater pleasure than to take that bitch out for you. Tell us when and where, and we will gladly avenge our fallen brothers."

Luciano leaned back in the chair, studying the rest of the team as he considered. It seemed that the fire was back in their eyes again, their faces now grim with brutal determination. Yes, they would do nicely, perhaps even more so now that they were all fired up about it. There were still a few other things to take care of—some modifications to their armor, a few injections to increase their combat effectiveness—but all would be in readiness the next time they faced these superpowered foes.

It was the carrot today, but if they failed him again, there would always be time for the stick.

-28-

The old man's residence was in midtown, and while it wasn't a trip of any great length, it began to seem that way to Jenkins. Wrapped in an awkward silence, they drove through the city streets, Lisell seeming to be lost in her own thoughts as they made their way toward the address written on the small slip of paper he had stashed in his pocket.

He'd been surprised when she'd tearfully followed him out of Demitre's penthouse and insisted on going with him. But she seemed to be in much better shape now after they'd stopped by her small apartment so she could freshen up and change her clothes. Now sporting worn jeans, tennis shoes, and a warm coat over her button-up sweater, she looked a lot more comfortable than she'd appeared wearing Demitre's oversized sweatshirt. And he supposed that her quick run through the shower had helped as well. He hadn't been invited up, and he hadn't asked to be. It was bad enough that he'd ruined her life; there'd been no need for him to exacerbate the situation while she was getting herself situated.

Now she sat staring out the window with a face bereft of all emotion. After a few moments, she reached up to adjust her glasses and then pushed a strand of her still-damp red hair back behind one ear. Glancing at him out of the corner of her eye, she cleared her throat.

"So, this man that we're going to see," she said, "how do you know of him?"

"He came into the station with his grandson the other day, but I didn't think it was worth the effort to speak with him at the time," Jenkins replied. "To be honest, he sounded a little crazy. It was only today after I'd been sorting through some things at my desk that I remembered something he'd said to me. He was going on about the 'harmonious balance' of the city being disrupted or something of that nature. When Demitre showed me that there was an abandoned herbal shop at the epicenter of our little murder spree, it reminded me of what he'd said because he's also Japanese in nationality. With everything that's been going on right now, and these supernatural creatures wreaking havoc all across town, I figured it would be a good idea to see if he knows anything more. Pretty weak, though, isn't it?"

"I suppose that it wouldn't hurt to ask him about it," she said. "After all, the Japanese community is a pretty close-knit group of people. If he doesn't know anything, then maybe he can point us toward someone who does. Are you going to fill him in on what you've found out so far?"

"I can't tell him everything, of course, but I can show him a picture of the female entity that we encountered and see what he says about it. Maybe it'll be something that he understands better than we do. He appeared to be a pretty spiritual old man, so he might have some further insights into where these beings are coming from or why they're here."

"How are you going to show him the picture?" she asked, raising a skeptical eyebrow. "You dropped those files off with your boss, remember?"

"Oh," he said, reaching into his coat pocket to pull out Abigail's cell phone, "I haven't had the chance to wipe the memory yet, so I was going to show it to him on this."

The sound of her quickly stifled sob was like a stab through the heart. How could he be such a thoughtless idiot! He went to put the phone back in his pocket, but she reached out, stopping him. With a gentle touch, she tugged it out of his hand, rubbing her fingers across the animal emblazoned on the protective case as fresh tears rolled down her flushed cheeks.

"She loved unicorns," she murmured, her voice thick with emotion. "Oh, Dan, I just can't believe that she's really gone! Why? Why did this have to happen to her? She was only a little girl! I used to take her camping with me in the summers, did I ever tell you that? She was one of the only people I knew that could keep up with me on a long hike. For her birthday this year, I was going to buy her a new camera, a real one, not like the crappy one on this stupid cell phone."

Sitting there holding the pink phone in her lap, he noticed her cradling it as if it were a living, breathing child. Tears drained down her cheeks, falling from her chin as she continued to sob.

"I'm sorry," he managed. "I shouldn't have taken that out right now. Listen, I realize that I've really messed things up for you and that there's nothing I can say to make your loss feel any less painful. But I want you to know that I am sorry. I'm sorry that I got you into all of this. I'm sorry that I got your niece killed and your family's home destroyed. I screwed up, and this is all my fault. But once I resolve this investigation, I intend to do whatever I can to make things right. I know that I can never bring her back, but I want to help your family pick up the pieces afterward, if I'm able. I'll understand if you don't want my help or if you never want to see me again after today."

"You think that this is all your fault?" she exclaimed, staring at him in shocked outrage. "Why are men so stupid? Dan, I don't blame this on you, not any of it! You didn't make that officer take advantage of my niece, and you didn't cause that spirit to save her by killing him. You weren't even there! How can you try and take the blame for everything that's happened to my family over the last few days? You're the only one who's been trying to keep us safe!"

"If it wasn't for me," he said stubbornly, "Resario would have never even known about you. He wouldn't have blown up your sister's house. If it wasn't for me, Abigail might still be alive right now—"

"If it weren't for you," she cut in, "Resario would have killed her anyway. Who do you think would have come by the hospital if I'd have called the station after Abigail ran to me? And if she had gone home, then they would have just tracked her down there instead and blown up the house with her in it. Dan, you can't blame yourself, not for any of this! If you hadn't been around for me to rely on, who knows what might have happened? My whole family could be dead right now, me included, if it weren't for you!"

He thought about that for a moment as they crossed another busy intersection, maneuvering around the slower moving traffic. Her logic seemed sound, but that still didn't make him feel any better about the role he'd played in it all. Glancing over, he saw that the tears had dried up and her face had taken on a determined look. She wasn't going to back down on this, he could tell.

"You may have a point," he conceded. "But that doesn't make my part in this any less of a factor. I failed you, Lisell. I didn't protect her, or you. That safe house wasn't a good choice. I should have known that it would be compromised. I should have taken you to Demitre's in the first place. I don't blame you if you hate me now. I've made some poor decisions, and people got hurt. All I can promise you from here on out is that your safety is my top priority. Once we're done interviewing this guy, I'm taking you back to Demitre's, where you'll be protected until I can see this thing through to the end."

Reaching out, she placed her hand on his leg, leaning over to gaze into his face while he continued to concentrate on driving. "Dan, I don't hate you. I could *never* hate you. You're the only thing that's holding me together right now. Can't you even see that?"

He risked another glance her way and saw that she was completely serious. Her features had softened, her demeanor pleading and full of hope. How could he ever deny what was swimming in the depths of those beautiful eyes? His heart swelled with emotion. He would protect this amazing woman with every fiber of his being, and once this was all over, he would pray that he merited the regard she currently held him in.

"Well," he said gruffly. "I just hope that I can continue to hold you together until this whole thing is finished." Reaching down, he gave her hand a gentle squeeze.

Blushing a little, she smiled as she reluctantly pulled her hand away, and it was as if the sun had come out from behind a bank of dark clouds. As she sat back, he breathed a sigh of relief. It was a blessing that he'd found out she didn't hate him for all he'd done. Although he would have to work twice as hard now to make sure that he deserved the trust she'd placed in him, he found that he relished the challenge and that his heart felt much lighter for it.

As they parked in front of the address written on the slip of paper, he was taken aback by the nature of the dwelling. It was done in the traditional style of Japanese architecture, with a well-manicured lawn and minimal décor, just like in pictures he'd seen of small temples from that island nation. Turning off the car, he got out and went around to the passenger side to open the door for Lisell. She stared at the house in frank admiration as they walked up the stone pathway to the front door and seeing the childlike wonder in her eyes made bringing her along with him that much more worthwhile.

He knocked, and after a moment the door slid open to reveal the grandson he'd met the other day at the station. The kid did not look the least surprised to see them. "Hello," he said. "My grandfather is expecting you. Please come around to the back of the house. He is waiting for you there in the garden."

The boy moved out of the entranceway, sliding the door closed behind him. Then he motioned for them to follow as he led the way around the side of the picturesque home on a walkway made from polished river stones. Jenkins had a chance to marvel at the view while they circled the house, and everything he saw spoke of minimalistic order and tidiness. It was very soothing to the eyes, an aspect that had a definite calming effect upon his inner turmoil. *This case has really been getting to me*, he realized, breathing deeply and just enjoying his surroundings for a few brief moments as they walked along.

When they reached the back of the property, he saw that there was a formal garden with paths and fountains spreading outward from the building. It was planted with a profusion of flowers and blooming fruit trees, some of which were dormant this late in the season. The boy led them down a spiraling trail of crushed white gravel until they reached the old man where he sat on a plain wooden bench beside a pool filled with lily pads and cattails. In the depths of the water, Jenkins could make out fat koi fish swimming, their multicolored bodies moving in and out of the lily pad's dangling roots.

Approaching his grandfather, the boy gave him a formal bow before speaking in rapid Japanese and indicating Jenkins and Lisell. The man glanced over his shoulder at them, then stood, turning with a slight smile. Folding his hands together at the waist of his long rolled-collar sweater, he greeted them with a small bow. The garment he wore was knit in shades of oranges and browns similar to the autumn colors surrounding them, and his eyes were as bright and inquisitive as those of a curious bird. His short-cropped silver hair gleamed in the wane sunlight as he began to speak and the boy translated.

"My grandfather wishes you to know that he is happy to see you. He has been waiting for you to come to him and bids you welcome to our home. Will you take tea or other refreshment?"

Jenkins politely shook his head to decline the offer before replying to the older man. "Tell your grandfather that we appreciate his time. Then please find out if it would be okay if I asked him a few questions about what's been going on in the city."

The boy relayed this, and the old man smiled again, speaking through the boy. "My grandfather says that he would be happy to talk with you about what has happened. He has sensed a great imbalance in this city's harmony. The laws of nature have been corrupted here for far too long, and he has felt that there are kami at work even now trying to restore the balance and move things back into alignment with the natural order of all living things."

Jenkins blinked. Clearing his throat a little, he spoke again. "Please tell your grandfather that I don't understand. I'm here to talk about the murders that are happening throughout the city, and I hope that he can shed some light on the creatures that are connected to these killings. We're not really sure if he can be of any help, but we'd be interested in hearing his thoughts on the nature of these mysterious beings if he has any."

The boy's eyes grew wide before he turned back to his elder and explained. On hearing this, the old man grew increasingly grave. When he spoke again, it was in a much more serious tone.

"My grandfather wishes you to know that he is a Seikai of the Shinto order," the boy told them. "That would be sort of like a head priest in your language. As followers of Shintoism, we believe that all things in this world are connected and that one should strive to live in a manner that promotes aligning yourself with the life forces of nature. This life force allows everything in the universe to develop, evolve, and harmonize within the natural laws. It was thus that he was able to feel this imbalance that has been occurring and also sense the forces already at work trying to restore it. He respectfully asks that you tell him more about these creatures that you mention."

Jenkins didn't know what to think. The old man seemed legit, but all this talk of spiritualism and forces of nature was way beyond him. It sounded a little screwy, if he was being honest with himself. But there was no harm in showing the priest a picture of the Love Leach. She'd been all over the papers today anyway. Holding out his hand, he motioned to Lisell, and she gave him the pink cell phone.

"Please tell your grandfather that this is a picture that was taken of a spirit that's been plaguing the city," Jenkins said as he activated the phone and pulled up the pic. "She seems to be able to suck the life out of her victims and appears in a ball of energy that sorta looks like it's been infused with lightning. She can speak pretty good English and seems to fully understand us in return, but we haven't been able to make much sense out of anything that she's told us so far." His ears burned a little as he remembered what she'd said about him to Lisell back at the safe house.

The Shinto priest took the phone and studied the image, his features unreadable. After a few moments, he lifted his eyes, piercing

Jenkins with a look of deepening concern. Then he spoke again at some length.

His grandson's expression grew taut with suppressed emotion as he listened. Afterward, with awe filling his voice, he translated. "My grandfather wishes you to know that he thinks this spirit may be a new type of kami. In the Shinto religion, we believe that all things possess a spiritual essence or energy that we call a kami, or divine spirit would be the closest in your language. This essence is not restricted to just living things but is also imbued within everything around us, such as the trees and rock formations, and even in the forces of nature itself, like wind and lightning. But sometimes members of a clan can become deified after they have departed the earthly realm if they were able to embody certain virtues and values throughout their lifetimes. The spirit you have captured in this photo is very powerful and appears to be a type of kami that he has never seen nor heard of before. He says that she could be a part of what he's been sensing and that she was obviously called upon to help restore the harmonious balance to this area. These type of spirits must be appeased and their honor satisfied or they will continue to visit retribution upon us all."

Jenkins was taking it all in, but he still wasn't sure how much of it he believed or even understood. Although he knew that these creatures were real, and had even been in the same room with them, he remained skeptical. "Can you ask him how these evil spirits were summoned?" he ventured. "And how exactly do we appease them if we don't even know anything about how they got here or what they really want?"

The boy translated, and then the old man replied. "My grandfather wishes you to know that kami are not necessarily good nor evil but possess many positive and negative characteristics. They are manifestations of musubi, which is the interconnected energy of the universe, and can be ambiguous in their actions because of this. In the Shinto religion, we believe that everything is always changing, always interacting with the world around us in a constant state of fluctuation, so there can be no absolute right or wrong. And while there are less benevolent spirits called *yōkai,* he believes that this creature is not one of them but is instead a force of nature and has been summoned in some way that he cannot yet fathom.

"He has only just arrived in this country in the last few weeks to take care of me." The boy stopped for a moment, swallowing visibly, then continued. "But he has heard rumors of a family with strong ancestral ties to Japan that moved here several years ago to establish themselves and build a new shrine, the first of its kind in this area. They have had many illustrious ancestors who were considered worthy enough for their kami to become enshrined, and he believes that this family may have performed a ritual to transfer some of these guardian spirits to this city when they consecrated their new place of worship. What that has to do with the being in this picture you have shown him, he does not yet know, but he thinks that they are all interconnected in some way. Perhaps if you could find out more about this family, then we could discover just how, and why, this spirit of yours is active right now."

Jenkins' phone rang, and he raised his hand, pausing the conversation with an apologetic smile. After fishing the phone out of his inside jacket pocket, he answered it. "This is Jenkins."

"Sir, we're at that warehouse you sent us to, and we've found evidence of a struggle," Mattie's voice said. "There are three deceased teenage males between the ages of seventeen and twenty-three on the main floor. Cause of death appears to be from multiple insect bites and stings, but we're not one hundred percent certain of that yet. A couple of known smugglers were also found dead in the office upstairs, and we've recovered cases of weapons that were up there with them, mostly handguns. I have officers canvassing the surrounding area, and so far we've located two other victims. The ones found on the main floor of the warehouse are all from the same gang, and so are the bodies that were discovered just outside, possibly what's left of their lookouts. I've already sent for the forensics team as well as a coroner. What are your orders, sir?"

"Have the tech team start investigating as soon as they get there, and then keep everyone else out of the building for now," he said.

"Also, I want you to post additional officers in a five-block radius around the warehouse and station some men up on the rooftops as well. Make sure that everyone goes out in teams of at least two and stays within visual range of each other. We aren't losing any more of ours on this one, Mattie. Do you copy that?"

"Yes, sir. Loud and clear."

"Good. Then hold out there until I arrive, and don't let anyone else contaminate the crime scene. We need to figure out all we can about what's happened there, and fast. The more we know, the sooner we can track down this damn bug guy and lock him up for good. I'm on my way right now and should be there in the next twenty minutes or so. Jenkins out."

He disconnected the call and pocketed the phone, noticing that the look in the older gentleman's eyes was forthright and inquisitive. Jenkins decided that he could trust him with another tidbit of information. "Please tell your grandfather that we really appreciate his assistance," he said. "Inform him that there is also at least one other of these spirit creatures that we know of, this one with some kind of control over insects, and there may even be others. Tell him that I have to go right now, but I'll be back as soon as possible to speak with him some more about all of this. If he wouldn't mind?"

After the boy relayed the message, the old man nodded and then bowed. After saying something in his own language, he turned back to the quiet pond, contemplating its still waters.

"My grandfather wishes you to know that your next visit will be most welcome," the boy said. "But he also tells me to ask that you be very careful. These spirits, if they are kami, do not distinguish between right and wrong in the way that you Americans do. Please, for your own safety, do not get in their way, Detective."

With a sharp nod, Jenkins agreed with the old man's assessment. These beings were nothing to fool with, and that was an understatement. Then, gathering up Lisell, he headed back to the car.

-29-

They'd been discussing their plans for a few hours now, and Abraham was getting heartily sick of watching Charlie and Florence conversing together like an old married couple. He'd tried to interject his own ideas into the conversation, but his jealousy of the way that the other two were hitting it off was making him a bit tongue-tied. It wasn't as if he didn't have anything important to add; he knew that he was the smartest man in the room. It just irked him that he couldn't control his rising annoyance long enough to speak to her as he would speak to anyone else. Frustration ate away at him the longer he sat there with his newfound companions. He needed a break and some time alone to himself so he could think things through.

So far, they'd decided that their next step would be to go back to Demitre's apartment and ask him to research the Gargano family. It was what they should have done in the first place, but Abraham hadn't known that that was an option at the time, and so they'd chosen to confront Marco at the club instead. Now that they'd failed in that regard, Charlie had conveniently remembered that his acquaintance was a technological genius.

Even though Abraham knew that they would have had to take out the men at the Gleaming Gypsy anyway, it made him livid to think that they could've just gotten the info from this computer hacker and then gone straight to Luciano's house in the first place. They would still have had to mop up all the rest of the mob bosses and henchmen in the city afterward, but it would have been so much easier if they'd just taken out Luciano to begin with. Abraham's resentment of Charlie's lack of foresight was further fueled by the fact that his friend was now monopolizing Florence's attention in deep, intimate conversation. Their obvious preoccupation with one another left Abraham to sit alone on the sidelines, watching them with a sense of mounting dissatisfaction.

He needed to get out of there and go do something positive, something to distract him from the puzzling loss of his normally eloquent perspicacity. That and there was also a need for him to resupply his stock of embryonic materials. Unlike his new friends' powers, he had to rely on the protoplasmic tissues and fluids of live embryos collected and then held in the aether until he summoned them. Fortunately, he knew just how to go about obtaining all the specimens he would ever need to complete their mission and then clear the city of corruption before ushering in a new era of rebirth and healing. He just needed the time and a quiet place to think before going about it all.

Watching his companions laugh together, he fumed on in silence while deciding what he should do next. *Just what did she see in that troll anyway?* he wondered, and not for the first time. The man was positively grotesque with his chitinous skin, glowing eyes, and the nubs of horns protruding from his forehead like they did. Then, glancing down at himself, he realized that he was even more hideous than Charlie was. He'd completely forgotten about his own appearance. When he'd made the modifications to his body, his clothing had split apart, and he now looked like he was dressed in filthy rags. Without thinking, he'd even increased the callouses on his feet after they'd burst through his shoes and had never thought to replace any of his once-fashionable attire. Thankfully, his new robes had grown with his physical modifications and continued to flow around him in all their shimmering perfection. But the rest of him still resembled an oversized, poorly dressed hobo with a burned-up, glowing head.

Realizing how unattractive he looked was the absolute last straw.

"I have to go out for a while," he told them, rising from his chair and then retrieving the trench coat he'd draped across the back of it.

They glanced over and acknowledged his declaration—Charlie admonishing him to be back soon so they could all depart for Demitre's penthouse together—and then went back to their discussion about the nature of the universe. Taking a deep breath and letting it out slowly, Abraham left the foreman's trailer, making his way toward the lair's hidden exit.

It took some time, but with his trench coat pulled tight about him and the longshoreman disguise that he'd used earlier set firmly back in place, he made it to his old apartment without any mishaps. Once there, he set about finding himself a new set of clothing, but everything he had was now too tight, and he didn't have any shoes that fit him anymore. After doing the best he could with what he found in the back of his closet, he was able to squeeze his oversized feet into a pair of dress boots that had always been far too large on him in the past. From a hidden spot behind the nightstand, he then retrieved his emergency credit card. He hadn't planned to use it unless he got into dire straits but figured that if there was ever a time for it, then that time was right now. He needed a whole new wardrobe, and he needed it to be of the finest quality. His intention was to outshine Charlie so spectacularly that Florence would be forced to take notice.

But when he checked his image in the bathroom mirror, it was a real wake-up call. His longshoreman disguise was ugly, and there were no two ways about it. *Like dressing a pig in an ill-fitting Armani suit,* he thought, noticing that the clothes did nothing to enhance his overall appearance at all. The buttons on the shirt were strained to the breaking point over his newly defined muscles, and the pants were too short and almost bursting along the seams. Combined with the coarse features of the face he now wore and the bristling shock of his patchy, ill-grown hair, he looked like a joke. More than that, he was by far the ugliest man that he'd ever laid eyes on. It was no wonder Florence preferred Charlie over him.

There had to be something he could do, some way he could rectify the situation. Moving back into the central living area, he sat down at the desk and thought about it for a few moments.

It would be necessary to obtain new materials beforehand, but he figured that now, with all the experience he'd gained over the last few days in using his abilities, surely he could do better for himself. Settling into a relaxed posture, he rested his hands on his knees and focused his energy. Then, closing his eyes, he took a deep breath, reaching out with all of his not inconsiderable power.

There were dozens of fertility clinics all over town, in addition to hospitals and other small, quasi-legal businesses like the one that he'd once owned. He could sense the small sparks of life, the twitches of curling energy that signified to him the presence of millions of tiny fetal cells and other materials related to the growth of embryos. Reaching out with his power, he gathered them up, drawing them forth from all the sources he could feel around the city. Stretching his senses to their limits, he sought out every available venue, plundering them for the raw materials he needed to increase his powers to their maximum potential. Soon, he'd collected an immense amount of the needed cells and fluids, a pool so vast that he knew nothing could ever stand in his way again. This enormous reservoir of protoplasmic goo and living fetal cells filled his power levels to the brink. As he opened his eyes, he felt renewed and bolstered by the resources he now had at his beck and call. Rising from the chair, he went back into the bathroom and gazed at himself in the mirror once more.

It shouldn't be too difficult, he decided. He would just need to make the modifications necessary to obtain the best possible results. His true features were well-known to him, and he'd once taken great pride in his appearance. The body he had now was more powerful, corded with muscle and strengthened by his increased bone mass, but it no longer sweated, shed skin, or needed to void wastes, so therefore he had no need to shower. His personal cleanliness he took care of with the merest thought, expunging the dirt and soil from himself with waves of radiant energy. Afterward, he studied his face in the mirror, and then set to work with a will.

In a couple of hours, he felt confident enough to stop the process and study the fruits of his labor. The results were stunning, if he did say so himself. The image looking back at him once more had that proud, straight nose, those arched eyebrows and sculpted cheekbones. His chin was yet again chiseled to perfection while brown hair now flowed from his head in wavy locks that shone with health and vivacity. There was nothing that could be done about the largeness of his head, but the swelling had gone down somewhat over the last few days, so he'd just adjusted his overall height and width to compensate. He now looked even better than before, he realized. With a tight little smile, he promised himself that he would talk to Florence, would regain his natural eloquence, and make sure to be included in all of their conversations from this point forward. The new confidence flowing through him was quite invigorating.

But why stop there, he wondered. Could he do it, could he really create for her the perfect gift?

She'd spoken of living only in the moment, had said in fact that she needed no promise of a future where she could walk amongst mortal men again, freely and without fear of ridicule or causing a panic. He agreed that the concept of being able to blend back into today's society seemed laughable at this point, but what of leading a normal life, one that was outside of their commitment to healing this vast metropolis? What of their just rewards for all the battles they must fight? Should they be regulated to living in a cave beneath the earth like Charlie, with no culture, no interaction at all with the finer things in life?

No, he simply could not accept that, could not let it happen, not to her, or to himself.

Focusing all his will and energy once more, he began to form a body created from one perfect embryo. It was female, vibrant and pristine, just a cluster of cells at this point, with no soul or consciousness. Slowly, he fed power into it, growing it, nurturing it with fluids and sustenance, modifying it in ways that would make it stronger, more agile—an exquisite specimen of the human form. As it grew in front of him, filling out and expanding into the body of a young woman, he began to manipulate its other attributes.

The hair he made a shining copper waterfall cascading down to a slender waist, the eyes, like the greenest leaves of summer. He dusted freckles across the pert little nose, gave it full, sensual lips, and formed these all within a beautiful, heart-shaped face. The body was long-limbed and athletic, the shoulders and arms delicately muscled, and the breasts small and perfect. Nicely rounded hips that flowed down into well-toned legs filled out the rest of the simulacrum, and as he stood there gazing at his creation, he fell in love with her all over again.

Here was the perfect vessel for such a wondrous creature. Surely Florence would see how much he cared when he presented her with this masterful work of art, would notice that his was the better range of powers, that his will brought forth the very creation of life itself. What sort of woman could choose a father of insects over that? With the wave of a hand, he stored the empty receptacle away, hidden in the aether to be summoned again at the appropriate time.

Then, with mounting anticipation, he left the apartment, flipping the credit card through his fingers and across the back of his knuckles. Now he had only to go down to the haberdashery and get outfitted with an entire new ensemble. He would spare no expense. The next time his companions saw him, it would take their breath away and turn Charlie positively green with envy.

Whistling a tuneless song, he wandered out onto the sidewalk and then set out toward the closest of his favorite row of clothing shops.

-30-

Staring down at the body, he felt his guts twisting but managed not to hurl in front of the other officers. The corpse was in the preliminary stages of decay, but he could still see that livid welts covered the youth from head to toe and that he'd died while frothing at the mouth. The swelling and redness suggested a venom of some type, possibly wasp or maybe even scorpion. On the other side of the warehouse doorway was another teenager who appeared to be in the same condition. This bug guy was really something else if he could cause insects to go wild and kill like this. Seeing just what this spirit could do was making Jenkins that much more eager to find him and take him off the streets for good.

Nodding to the attending patrolmen, he entered the building, heading for the taped-off region at the center. There were many small, numbered tags posted all around, and the technicians were swarming across the area, gathering clues and bagging evidence. Being careful not to disturb anything, he moved around the crime scene and then approached Officer Williams, who was standing with one of her compatriots comparing notes. As he walked toward her, she glanced up and then motioned him over to a less busy spot by the stairs.

"What have you got for me, Mattie?" he asked as he joined her there.

"The ones outside are all from the same gang; we got three more of them here in the main room, plus the five smugglers we found in the upstairs office. It looks like there was quite a tussle going on down here, but the smugglers show no signs of a struggle, almost as if they'd been taken unawares.

"In addition to that, there are another two victims, one on the roof and one on the next street over, who match the profiles of other known members of the smuggling ring. All of the deceased were done in by what appears to be insect-related attacks. We also recovered some boxes of small arms, most likely brought here to be sold to the gang members, and out in the back alleyway there's another area where it looks like someone was beaten pretty badly. There's blood everywhere and some broken-up furniture, but it doesn't exactly fit with the M.O. of what was going on in here. I currently have the forensics team going over everything while the coroner is waiting to bag up the bodies. And I've taken the liberty of calling in an entomologist from a nearby university—he should be here any minute now. I have all of our current findings compiled for you right here, sir, if you'd care to look through them?"

"Put some feelers out on the rest of the gang," he said, accepting the proffered tablet and scanning through the notations. "Let's bring them in for questioning. Maybe one of them saw something, or maybe someone got away. You feel me? We also need to figure out where these smugglers were based out of and then send a unit over there to round up the rest of them while we're at it. Let's try and gather in any stragglers on this thing and see what info we can squeeze from them. Meanwhile, fill Captain Wolfe in on the operation's status and alert the station that we're going to be bringing more people in for questioning. Let's get some of those interrogation rooms cleared out in advance—I want to move quickly on this. And, Mattie? You've done well here, real well. I appreciate all your hard work and support on this."

She stood straighter, a flush of pleasure coloring her cheeks as she accepted the praise. "It was nothing, sir. Just doing our job. We got your back on this, Detective. Let's get this son of a bitch before he hurts anyone else."

Staring into her eyes, he gave a crisp nod. Then, after handing back the tablet, he circled the perimeter of the central area, checking things out on his own.

A hole had been broken through the boards of the platform in front of the stairs, and there was a corpse tangled in spiderwebs dangling just below it. Off to one side was another body, this one stripped of flesh, which appeared to have once been a very large young man. Now it was just a pile of bones and ligaments. He wasn't even sure what type of insects could do that. Wandering over to one of the support pylons that were spaced at intervals across the middle of the structure, he bent down to study what he found there.

Another corpse lay twisted and bloating close to the concrete post, this one done in by fire ants from the looks of it. There were crushed ant carcasses still gripped inside his clenched fists when the technicians had pried the fingers open. It must have taken thousands of bites and stings to kill the boy—his face was distorted and unrecognizable now, a red and white blister of swollen flesh that had split along the sides. Fluids continued to leak out and wet the ground in a creeping yellow stain as he watched, nausea still churning his stomach. It was a gruesome way to go, and no doubt about it.

But what was drawing his attention now were the scuff marks on the hardwood planks of the floor. Someone else had fallen here, and he saw traces of black rubbed off on the cement post, perhaps dye from a leather jacket. So, one of the gang members had survived and had been propped up against this pylon before being dragged away. Edging around to the left, he found signs of another scuffle right in the middle of the floor. Could there have been additional victims here that had gotten out somehow? It was hard to say. This could simply be where the ant boy had first fallen before flailing his way over to where he'd died in agony just a few feet away.

After letting the tech crew know of his observations, he proceeded to make his way back outside. He wanted to check the alleyway and investigate the area that Mattie had said showed signs of violent activity. Maybe what he found there would give him some clue as to if anyone had actually made it out of this mess alive. As he exited the warehouse, he saw Lisell fiddling with her cell phone while standing in front of an adjacent building. What the heck was she doing? He'd told her to stay in the squad car, for crying out loud. Shaking his head in annoyance, he changed direction, moving toward her while trying not to appear too overly concerned.

Once they'd finished speaking with the old man, he'd planned on taking her back to Demitre's, but they'd gotten sidetracked by the need for caffeine. It was no big deal that they stopped off to get coffee along the way but doing so had put him several minutes behind schedule. She'd pointed out then that it would save time if she just tagged along with him. Not only was he unable to say no to her after all they'd been through, but she'd also convinced him that she would be just as safe with him as she would be back at Demitre's penthouse. A subtle stroke of his ego that he was quite aware of, but had fallen for, nonetheless.

As he walked up, he realized that she was consulting her phone and then glancing back up at the structure she was standing in front of. "I thought you were going to stay in the car?" he said after clearing his throat to alert her of his presence.

Glancing over at him, she wrinkled her nose, then focused her attention back on the building she'd been studying. "I think that, as an adult, I can take care of myself, Detective, especially when the surrounding area is literally crawling with other officers." The smile that briefly touched her lips took the sting from her words as she looked down at her phone again, reading something on the display screen.

Taking the admonishment with a grain of salt, he decided that it wasn't worth arguing about. Turning to stare at the building himself, he tried to determine just what the hell it was that she was so focused on.

Like something right out of a Japanese travel brochure, the structure had a gabled roof with curving, stylized edges. Decorative pillars and intricately carved motifs also covered many of its outside surfaces, and it seemed almost like a palace of sorts. Except for the fact that there were regular storefront windows running along one side with additional modern embellishments built into the main level. In fact, now that he stood staring at it, the entire layout just seemed off for some reason.

As he stood puzzling over it, he noticed that the doors were situated in the middle of a long corridor, giving the rest of the building a lopsided horseshoe shape. To enter the edifice, you'd have to pass down a walkway going through the middle of the corridor thus formed, traveling beneath two large archways built into the walls on either side. Taking a closer look at the entrance, he saw that there were also two fantastical dog sculptures flanking the double doorway and a stone basin, almost like a drinking fountain, resting just to the right of them. At one time, the whole place must have been magnificent to look upon, but now it was badly in need of repair, with garbage littering the surrounding lot and overflowing out into the street.

"Is this the herbal shop that was at the center of the chart Demitre showed us?" he wondered aloud.

"It is," she responded as if he'd actually been asking. "And look here, I've pulled up some information about Shinto shrines, and this place matches some of the criteria. See? Those two arches could be torii gates. They have the two crossbars and were once painted orange and black by the looks of it. And the doors are guarded by *komainu*, those stone lion-dogs. They're there to keep out *yokai*. And it also says here that Shinto shrines often had a *temizuya*, or place of purification, to wash your hands in before entering. Could that fountain have been placed there for that purpose, do you think?"

As she spoke, he was nodding in agreement, even though he really didn't really know what she was getting at yet. It was obvious there was a point she was trying to make, but he just wasn't sure what it was. "I can see what you're saying," he said, "but what does all of this have to do with the case?"

Her sidelong glance made him feel foolish. "And you're supposed to be the detective here," she lamented, then winked to show she was kidding. "The old man, he's a Shinto priest, right? Didn't he say something about there being a venerable, Japanese family who came here a few years ago and that they may have brought their ancestral kami along with them? Wouldn't they have had to have built a temple or something to put those kami in once they'd arrived? From everything I've read online, you have to have a place for these kami to reside when they visit our plane of existence, a location they can inhabit while being worshiped. If we're going to find a way to appease these entities, then we have to find out where they live first, don't we? This building is at the center of where all the criminal activities in your case first started, so it is possible that this could be the actual shrine they built for them here in the city, don't you think?"

Studying the structure, he was still more than a bit skeptical. "But it's an herbal shop—you can see the old display cases covered in pieces of cheap pottery through the broken windows over there. Plus, the rest of the architecture is all wrong for it. Much of the building has been Americanized, like with the Japanese restaurants you see all the time over here. It takes away from the solemnity of the place and makes it seem less than holy if you ask me. Wouldn't that offend any kami that you were supposed to be honoring?"

"Window dressing," Lisell replied confidently. "What better place to hide a shrine than in plain sight? This way, they could have the shop as a front to throw off the non-believers and still allow people in who wanted to worship the kami with proper reverence. If you were from another country, one with radically different religious practices, and you wanted to stay out of the public eye here in America, wouldn't you disguise your temple in such a way that you didn't have a bunch of looky-loos coming by at all hours of the day and night just to gawk at it?"

Considering her theory, he decided it had merit. It was important that they found a way to appease these spirits, and finding the temple they identified with would be the first step in doing so. With a flourish of his hand, he gestured to the entranceway. "After you, then," he said with a smile. "Let's go take a closer look, shall we?"

Grinning back at him, she proceeded to walk down the pathway, moving beneath the arches while picking her way around piles of trash. He followed, and as they approached the large double doors, he reached around her to give the handle an experimental yank. But the doors were nailed shut and had signs tacked up that spelled out "No Trespassing" in big, bold letters. Whoever owned this place now, they wanted no uninvited guests, and that much was certain.

"Let's go around back," he offered, placing his arm around her shoulders to steer her away from the front entrance. As they began moving down the pathway together, he left his arm there in a companionable fashion, hoping she wouldn't mind. It didn't seem to bother her at all, and she even leaned into him further as they walked along, sending his heart to fluttering at her unexpected closeness.

"What did you find inside the warehouse?" she asked as they maneuvered past heaps of garbage.

He considered withholding the information but then decided it didn't matter. He trusted her, and it was all stuff she'd likely heard him talking with Mattie about when the officer had called him earlier. "There are a lot of dead bodies. It's one of the reasons I would have preferred that you'd waited for me at Demitre's. We don't know exactly what's happened yet, but it appears there was some kind of a struggle. There's no obvious motive, but it looks like our bug guy killed a bunch of street punks and smugglers with his pet insects. We assume they were all here to make a deal over handguns, and that's when he ambushed them."

Shivering a little, she snuggled closer within the encircling protection of his arm. "Do you have any leads?"

"No, not yet. We have a forensic team going over everything right now, but I did notice that there may have been a couple of people that made it out of there alive. I don't know if they escaped on their own or were taken captive—it's too soon to tell—but if we can find any witnesses, or any of those other gang members still living, it could be a huge break in the case. Any information we can gather right now is vitally important to tracking down these spirit creatures and discovering just what exactly it is that they want. If we find that out, then at least we'll have a starting point for negotiations. I'm not sure if we have any other means of dealing with them now, unless that old man can come up with a way to appease them somehow. They're just too powerful."

She nodded in understanding as they came around the side of the building and moved into the alleyway. Just a little ways away from the street there was an old broken couch resting up against a dumpster with a small, burned-out fire barrel in front of it. A forensics team was swarming around the location, busily gathering evidence and placing down numbered crime scene markers shaped like little tents. Jenkins removed his arm from around Lisell's shoulders, reluctantly stepping away from her.

"What have you got for me?" he asked the man in charge.

The investigator had a high forehead with thinning brown hair and was dressed in a see-through plastic overcoat. "There appears to have been an act of extreme violence committed here, sir," he said, standing up from where he crouched beside the broken couch and then walking over. Within his gloved hand, he carried a small evidence baggy. "We've recovered some hair and blood samples, but this event likely took place hours before the main dust-up inside the warehouse. We're currently trying to pinpoint the exact time based on what we've found so far."

"Okay, let me know as soon as you have anything more concrete," Jenkins told him.

The man nodded and then went back to his work while Jenkins studied the scene further. So much for his theory of escaped victims; whatever had happened out here was most likely unconnected to what had happened inside. But the couch had obviously been pulled from the interior of the herbal shop via a split in the boards covering a back service entrance. Walking over to it, he lifted the broken piece of lumber, bending down to peer into the darkened confines of the gap it created, but his view was blocked by pieces of fallen timber on the other side. It looked as if the roof had caved in at one point after the couch had been pulled through, and now debris blocked the rest of the opening. More "No Trespassing" signs were plastered across the walls here as well. Straightening back up, he reached for his cell phone.

"Mattie?" he said after the call was connected, "this is Jenkins out in the alley behind the warehouse. Can you get someone to check into the shop next door, please? Specifically, I'd like to know if we're gonna need a warrant to take a look around inside. I want to get in there and search the place, but it's boarded up tight right now and has official signage posted to keep people out."

"You got it, boss," she replied. "We're on it."

"Thanks, Mattie. Let me know when you've got anything, okay?" After disconnecting the call, he pocketed the phone before turning back to Lisell.

"I've got a few more things to do around here before we can leave," he said. "Will you wait in the car for me? I don't want you getting hurt out here."

"You mean you don't want me getting in the way," she replied with a sour smile. "I get it, Detective. I'll wait in the car until you're done then." With a wave, she turned and sauntered off.

As she walked away from him, he sighed. She really was quite a woman.

-31-

Getting to know this interesting young woman had been a rare pleasure. Charlie felt that they had much in common, and indeed, so did they all, Abraham included. Had they not all received powers on the verge of their deaths from a spiritual benefactor? Had they not all agreed to be bound by a pact with these spirits in exchange for the powers that they now wielded? It had been a real eye-opener—conversing with Florence—and he felt now, more than ever, that they'd been selected for a greater purpose, and one that had brought them together at the perfect time for it. All they had to do was complete their tasks, and the powers behind them would be appeased.

So it was that he sat in the foreman's office of the mining facility deep below the city discussing many topics of mutual interest with this amazing creature while awaiting Abraham's return.

"So you think our missions are intertwined, then?" she was saying.

"Of course!" he replied. "Why else would we have been given these powers, powers that are so very much alike, and all on the same night, if not to complete these goals as a team? Can you not feel the camaraderie that flows between us when we occupy the same room? As it was with Abraham, I feel a certain kinship toward you, and one that tells me that we were meant to work together on this. Even our objectives, although divergent, completely overlap. These spirits want the city to be whole again, to thrive with new life, and to be free of the corruption that now chokes it into stagnation. I'm telling you, it is a feeling that really resonates with me."

She nodded, considering all that he'd said, and he studied her as she did so. Her body was formed from pure electrical power, glowing from within like a fluorescent bulb. It appeared female in nature, yet lacked a certain definition, almost like an undressed mannequin without hair or other subtle embellishments. From time to time, crackles of miniature lightning would sizzle along the smooth contours of her physique, outlining it in greater detail, only to disappear back into the aether after a few scintillating moments. Her eyes, like twin points of fire, gazed out of a perfect heart-shaped face, yet the rest of her remained wispy and never truly solid. As a being made of energy, she shone and sparkled, the redness of her gaze blazing forth from a face that was like that of an angel come down from the heavens. The effect was quite breathtaking.

His insects alerted him of Abraham's imminent return, and as he walked through the door, they both turned to look at him in wonder. The changes he'd made to himself were astonishing.

The man's face was now dashingly handsome, with a straight, aquiline nose, a strong chin, and high cheekbones. In addition to that, his hair had grown back in, and now flowed in light brown waves from a wide forehead just above a sculpted set of expressive eyebrows. The eyes that gazed out at them were still pale in coloration, but the smile he favored them with was genuine. He noted their appreciation of his new looks, then gestured down at his clothing.

"What do you think?" he asked, striking a pose.

The elegant lab coat turned kimono was still there, but now it was covered by a tailored trench coat that flowed over the top of it, making it look like just another layer of his outfit. The suit beneath was of the finest quality, with a creamy-white shirt, red silk tie, and a matching vest, coat, and pants done in varying shades of gray. To round out this look of pure decadence, his feet were clad in shiny black wingtips. Overall, he now resembled a rich businessman venturing out for a winter stroll. Charlie turned to say something to Florence but noticed that she sat mesmerized, her mouth hanging open with a small, delighted smile tugging at the corners of her insubstantial lips. She seemed quite impressed.

"Why, Abraham," Charlie said into the stunned silence, "you look absolutely amazing! How did you manage to reform your face and hands so precisely? It is the most natural-looking work I have seen you do with your embryonic cells thus far. Well done, my friend, very well done indeed!"

Abraham beamed beneath the praise. "It was difficult in the beginning, but I think I'm starting to develop a knack for it. The first time I tried, I was in a hurry and simply needed a disguise. Now that I've had more time to exercise my powers, I seem to be able to do more refined work. In fact, I was hoping to speak privately with Flo, if you don't mind? I have something that—"

Charlie held up his hand, interrupting Abraham and causing him to fall silent. He was receiving images from the children he'd left with Demitre as a way to keep tabs and have an open line of communication. It appeared that the strange, reclusive man had written out a sign on a piece of cardboard and was holding it up to them. It said, 'Come quickly. New information. Need to act ASAP.'

"It would seem that Demitre has something for us," Charlie said. "I believe we should go there right away as this could be important to our mission. While we are there, we can also ask him about Luciano and see if he knows anything that will help us on that front as well. If I may, it would be a good idea for me to go in first so as not to startle the poor man. He knows nothing of our association as of yet."

Florence stood, her attention drawn away from Abraham and back to Charlie. "I'll dissipate now and await your summons from the ethereal realm. Once you get inside the man's home, just think of me and I'll come to you." She then looked Abraham up and down one final time, taking in his new appearance with a certain amount of cat-like approval. "You look marvelous, Abe," she finally murmured with a tenuous smile before vanishing in a crackle of cascading electricity.

Abraham looked very pleased with himself. Shaking his head a little as if to clear it of some inopportune thought, he glanced back over at Charlie. "What about you?" he asked. "I could get you some new clothes, help you blend in up there if you like?"

Charlie smiled, stroking Simon's wing casings from where he rested upon the back of his left forearm. Looking pointedly down at the chitinous flesh covering his body underneath the voluminous burgundy cloak, he laughed aloud. "No, my friend," he said. "It would hardly be fitting for me now. My own skin is clothing enough for me, and it suits me very well, I think. Would you not agree, Simon?"

-Father, you are magnificent, like all of your brethren.-

Chuckling at Simon's reply, he stood and moved toward the door. "Come, let us leave these warrens and venture forth to Demitre's penthouse. Whatever it is that he has for us seems to be quite urgent."

They left the trailer, walking along the pathway as thousands of insects parted and then re-formed behind them in waves as they moved along. While they were passing the storage container that housed the new queen and her hybrid warrior children, Charlie paused for a moment to look in on them. He found that there were now thousands of pupae scattered about, covering every square inch of the place and spilling out onto the path. The accelerated growth cycle of his new minions ensured that his troops would be mature and ready for battle far more quickly than he'd anticipated. It was something that he was looking forward to with great relish.

His mind reassured of their growth and well-being, he then led Abraham back through the tunnels toward the world above.

It took them almost no time at all to reach Demitre's building. When they arrived, it was still late afternoon, yet no other people were out and about in this part of town. His children had done a wonderful job of taking care of the undesirable tenants in this area. Now what was left of the local population stayed mostly indoors. It was a good feeling to have accomplished even this much, and Charlie took pride in his achievement. As they reached Demitre's elevator, he turned to give Abraham some final instructions about the eccentric apartment-dwelling survivalist.

"Demitre, as you will soon see, is not the most trusting of sorts," he said as they studied the many cameras placed at strategic points. "He has his ways about him, but can be very useful to us. So I will go in first and then have him send the elevator down for you. I am sure that he knows we are here by now, but since he does not know you personally as of yet, I will go and smooth the way for you to meet, so to speak. Please wait here a few moments."

With that, he turned and scuttled across the side of the wall, moving through the opening at the top of the parking garage, and then straight up the side of the building itself to disappear toward the roof.

Soon he was dropping down from the air vent located in Demitre's ceiling. As before, the man was sitting at his desk, only this time he was staring at his monitors, viewing the images of Abraham standing beside the elevator downstairs. As Charlie landed lightly on his feet with a small whoosh of air, the burgundy cloak swirling around him, Demitre turned to him.

"So," he said, "who's the suit?"

"That, my friend, is an associate of mine," Charlie replied, stepping forward into the light, his eyes glowing faintly. "I would ask that you allow him to come up so we may discuss this new information you have for us. And just so you know, it is not necessary to write things down and then show them to my children; I can hear you if you speak to them directly and I will know to get in touch with you simply from that alone."

He considered this for a moment, the anger at having a stranger waiting down by his elevator warring with embarrassment. "I didn't know that," he finally said, scratching at the stubble on his chin. "But it still doesn't explain why you brought someone here without my permission. I thought we had an agreement; I thought we had some sort of trust going on between us here."

"Ah, trust," Charlie murmured, "is a very fragile thing, or so it would seem. Perhaps you can tell me, then, why you have had a police officer up here and exactly why you were helping him without informing me of it first, hmm?"

Demitre looked uncomfortable. Clearing his throat, he turned and toggled the switch for the elevator. "If you're vouching for him, then I'll let him come up. But just who is he, may I ask?"

Charlie smiled. "He is a very close friend of mine and quite equally gifted, as you will soon see. Our missions coincide at this time."

Getting up from the chair, Demitre moved to go and open the doors that stood in the way of Abraham entering his abode. As the well-dressed man strolled past him, he locked the doors behind them before moving back into the main living area with a wary look in his eyes.

"Demitre," Charlie began, "this is Abraham. Abraham, this is Demitre."

Abraham extended his hand, a warm smile crossing his handsome features. "A pleasure to meet you. I'm Dr. Abraham Orson, and I've heard a lot about how you've been helping Charlie with our mutual cause to cleanse this city of corruption."

Demitre stared at the offered hand like it was a snake readying itself to strike. Then, mastering himself, he extended his own to clasp Abraham's in a brief handshake.

"Likewise, I guess," he replied. Then, glancing over at Charlie, he asked, "Are you going to explain to me who this guy is or not?"

"In a moment, in a moment," Charlie assured him. "But first, please say hello to my other companion, Florence."

With a blast of displaced air, Florence materialized within a globe of ball lightning, floating inside the crackling white orb at the center of the living room. Settling to the floor, her body solidified until it was almost fully corporeal, the electrical energy cascading around the room to sizzle into the darkened corners with an accompanying smell of burnt ozone. Her footfalls left little puffs of smoke rising from the carpet as her nude and hairless body strode forward into the computer area. Spying Abraham, a smile, seemingly brighter than the energy that formed her translucent body, lit up her face before she turned her fiery gaze upon Demitre.

He'd stumbled backward at her appearance, falling into his chair when it struck the back of his knees, and now gaped at her, his slackened jaw working but no sounds issuing forth. After a moment, he managed to collect himself enough to speak. "The Love Leach!" he exclaimed. "You brought the Love Leach into my home?"

Charlie and his companions stared at one another in confusion. Then, glancing back at Demitre, Charlie asked in perplexity, "Love Leach?"

"I'm sorry," Demitre added, managing to look a bit sheepish. "It's just what they call her in all the newspapers now. It's sorta stuck, you know, as a name people use to describe her. Since. . . well, you know, she kinda. . . sucks the love of life out of people, I guess. . ."

"That's ridiculous," Abraham scoffed.

"Preposterous," Charlie agreed after a moment of silent consideration.

Florence laughed aloud at their discomfort. "It's what the papers do, don't they? They make up silly names for things that they don't quite understand. Their readers eat that sort of thing up. And you have to admit, it isn't so far-fetched, after all." With a twinkle in her burning-hot eyes, she offered her hand to Demitre. "Yet my friends just call me Florence, or Flo for short, if you prefer."

He gazed at her in shock, then a silly smile spread across his features. Jumping out of the chair, he crossed to her in two strides and clasped her hand with his own. "It's a pleasure to meet you, a real pleasure. You've done more in the last three days to better this city than anyone else has done in the last three years!" Still shaking her hand, he turned to Charlie. "She's been taking out corrupt politicians and dirty cops all over town. It's positively inspiring!"

Charlie looked at Abraham and then back to the sight of Demitre still shaking Florence's hand. In a bemused voice, he asked, "Just out of simple curiosity, what have they been calling me in the papers these last few days?"

Releasing his grip on Flo's hand, Demitre's smile faltered. "Um. . . well, they're sort of calling you 'The Loathing.' It started because people were loathing to return to their homes down here after you began driving the bad guys out with your bugs. The papers made a big deal out of what someone had said in an offhand remark, and now it sort of. . . well, you know, stuck."

Charlie was not amused. As he stood thinking about it, Abraham stepped forward. "What do they call me, then?" he asked with a smirk. "Something equally absurd, I'm sure."

Demitre stared at him for a long moment before replying. "Ah. . . I don't even know who you are yet. What is it that you do again?"

"I take out the mafia and their henchmen," Abraham spat while some of his bulbous-headed minions materialized to float around him menacingly.

"Well, there haven't been any news reports on that yet," Demitre said, shuddering as he eyed the floating fetuses with a mixture of fear and loathing before moving to sit back down at his desk. "That's no surprise, though, since the mafia controls most of the newspapers anyway. I've seen some things about how a couple of clubs were destroyed, but it's all been passed off as accidents. You know—a fire at one and some sort of fumigation explosion at the other."

"Passed off as *accidents*," Abraham sputtered in outrage. "I crushed those men like the insects they were!" Then, glancing over at his friend, he added, "No offense, Charlie."

"None taken," Charlie said dryly. "But please, let us get back to business, as it were. Demitre here was just about to tell us why he is conspiring with the local police behind our backs."

"I'm not conspiring with the cops!" Demitre cried indignantly. "I work with a detective sometimes, just to help him out a little on his caseload. His name is Dan Jenkins and he's probably one of the only ones left in this entire shithole of a city who still gives a damn about upholding the law. Even though I've been helping him with what's been going on around here, I've told him absolutely nothing about you! In fact, he too is after the same sort of things that you want, I swear it."

Before Charlie could reply, Florence spoke up. "Wait, I know of this detective. His heart is pure, his intentions true and honorable. I've dealt with him before and have looked deep within his soul. He is most trustworthy, of that I can assure you."

"You see?" Demitre said, waving an open hand in her direction.

"We will let it slide for now, then," Charlie said. "So, tell us what you have found. You made it seem like this was an urgent matter, one that required our immediate attention."

"Yes, of course," Demitre said, swiveling his chair around so he could work his keyboard. "I've been monitoring all the cameras in the new hospital and also in the more privately funded laboratories within the connected compound, and something's come up that you just have to see. All of the doctors on your list have been summoned to some kind of secret meeting at the lab complex. And when I hacked into the security cameras inside the main building, I found this."

With a few more keystrokes, he brought to life an image on the central monitor. It was an opulent room featuring a large table. Seated at this table were a variety of well-dressed men. They did not sit easily, this gathering of individuals, but instead lounged in poses of tense, barely contained hostility. At the head of the table was an empty chair that seemed to be waiting for some final, mysteriously important occupant.

Gathering around, the three companions studied the scene unfolding before them on the screen.

"These men," observed Florence, "I can sense that they're the type of people that I feel the most compelled to harvest. Their souls are foul, and they cry out to me to be released from this mortal realm."

Charlie stared at the video feed in silence for a moment, then asked, "Who are they?"

"These are the leaders of every gang and two-bit criminal organization in the entire area," Demitre answered. "And at the head of the table will likely sit the most corrupt one of the whole bunch, the main reason we have organized crime in this city to begin with, the head honcho himself—Luciano Gargano. He's the only one who could have called all of these other underworld big shots into a meeting like this. He has to be somewhere in the building, probably on his way to this very table as we speak!"

Turning to them, he added in excited undertones, "If you act now, right this minute, you can bag them all in the same building, and all at the same time! Every one of the doctors and scientists on your list and every crime lord who has ever been a part of running this city into the gutter for years. You could kill them all."

-32-

This part of the building was perhaps one of his favorite places in the whole world. The entirety of its pristine, white interior, with its sealed, sterile environment and up-to-date equipment, was so cutting edge that it surpassed all others in the known scientific community. Currently, he was in the main observation chamber overlooking the central area, and he found the process that the doctors were using on his strike team members to be fascinating. Gazing through the double-reinforced safety glass into the room just below, he watched as machines pumped fluids into men who now lay on tables placed in orderly rows. The chamber itself was filled with silver cabinetry, wall-mounted computer screens, and modular stations full of racked, sterilized implements. As men in lab coats and face shields scurried about in well-organized chaos, Luciano was able to supervise every step of the highly experimental process, and all of it was being done to his precise specifications.

"I feel that I must protest this procedure, Mr. Gargano." A female voice interrupted his musing. "We don't even know what this process is going to do to those men."

She was a gifted scientist, but also a royal pain in his backside. With a twitch of his fingers, he motioned his bodyguards to stand down. They'd stepped away from the wall at her uncalled-for verbal outburst and now stood ready to silence her at a moment's notice should he so desire. But it really wasn't her fault; she simply didn't know him very well, not like the other doctors and technicians he employed. After all, her team was only here on loan from the labs uptown, the ones that he didn't yet own, so she didn't really owe him anything. But even though they were from the very same labs that had once housed Dr. Orson's special projects, that man's colleagues were still worlds away from him in brilliance. Abraham Orson had been working at a higher level than they would ever achieve, and that much was painfully clear. Turning his head to glance down at the woman, he gave her his most ingratiating smile.

"Please calm yourself, Barbara," he said. "These men are highly trained and all handpicked by me. They've undergone extensive mental and physical conditioning for years now, and they can most certainly handle it. And it's not as if I've had to coerce them—they volunteered for this process and knew the risks well in advance. I assure you that it will be just fine."

"I'm not interested in what they did or did not agree to," she snapped. "I'm worried that they'll all die! Or worse. We have no idea how this will turn out. Meaning no disrespect, but are you really willing to just throw their lives away for your own vain ambition?"

His features hardened as he resisted the urge to strike her. No one questioned him like that, especially in front of his men. Taking a deep breath, he regained control of his emotions. Her rudeness was unintentional, and he must remember that when dealing with her, or with any other member of her team, really. Staring at her pinched expression, he slowly relaxed, fixing a slightly more brittle smile in place as he continued to study her.

She was tiny as women go, yet fierce, with her golden hair pulled back into a neat French braid, leaving only short bangs up front. Upon her heart-shaped face rested glasses that were much too large for her, yet he knew they were currently in fashion, and it just so happened that they complemented her choice in makeup perfectly. This, combined with her lab coat and the sensible business attire she wore beneath, made her resemble nothing more than a young girl playing at dress-up, yet a very attractive one if you chose to ignore the anger so evident in every line of her severe expression.

He tried again. "These men are beholden to me, and their lives are mine to do with as I please. They all signed the necessary waivers when they joined the program, and I have a vested interest in keeping them alive. Besides, the process I've brought your team in to assist with today has been well tested, and the results have all been favorable."

"Testing it in a controlled, computerized environment is not the same as testing it on living organisms," she insisted. "What may have been favorable results within multiple virtual simulations could very well produce abnormalities, or even death, in your current subjects. This process should have gone through rigorous testing on lab animals before ever being sanctioned for use on human volunteers. I'm sorry, Mr. Gargano, but I just can't, in all good conscience, agree with your assessment of the risks involved here. This is. . . barbaric!"

"I don't need your agreement," he stated evenly, "only your obedience. Miss Crusher, I don't believe that you truly grasp the limits of your authority here. While you may be one of the senior staff in residence over at the labs you work for, your employers owe me a debt, and I have called that debt in. Simply put, you have absolutely no say in the matter. Now, you will proceed with the program as specified, or I will find someone who will and then cut funding to all of your projects uptown, thereby shutting you and your research team down indefinitely. Do I make myself clear?"

"You're not the only backer we have," she scoffed. "You can pull funding, but that will only set us back, not shut us down. Believe it or not, there are still people left in this city who aren't controlled by you, at least not yet anyway. But have it your way—I will proceed with the experiment as you specify. However, I will be lodging a formal protest with my superiors when we're through. Then we'll just see how keen they are to continue working with you when they find out exactly what's been going on over here."

As she turned and stalked away, he sighed. These scientists really had no appreciation for the power he held over them all. Well, they would learn. If she didn't toe the line, there were a dozen others just like her that would. Turning back to the window, he gazed down at the room below once more.

Laid out in a row, the men were strapped to the tables with sheets covering their midsections. Tubes and wires ran out from them and then into apparatuses which kept up a continuous flow of fluids containing doses of the all-important experimental serum. In recessed wall sections spaced evenly around the room, other machines kept track of vital signs while administering pulses of finely tuned electrical stimuli controlled by the computers themselves. Luciano glanced over to his right where another man dressed in a white lab coat sat at the main console typing in lines of code via a stationary keyboard.

His short, dark hair and aviator-style glasses made him seem younger than his thirty-three years as he worked to complete the necessary entries. Holding a pen between his clenched teeth, his hands flew across the keys, light from the monitor reflecting off the clear glass lenses of his dated eyewear. Taking the pen from his mouth after entering the last few equations, he reached over and made some quick notations on a clipboard sitting off to his right. Luciano appreciated his diligence, impressed once again by his professionalism and scientific demeanor.

"Well, Jeffrey," he asked. "What do you think?"

"I think they should have stolen more of Orson's ideas," he replied, turning toward Luciano with a look of pure derision written large across his blunt features. "Their attempts at expanding upon his findings are truly pathetic. Everything they've given us thus far is so derivative of his work that it should be considered plagiarism."

Luciano chuckled. Dr. Eastman's disdain for the other scientists was legendary. Unlike Abraham Orson, whose ingrained, although questionable, code of moral ethics had necessitated a not so-gentle coaxing to obtain his cooperation, Jeffrey Eastman had come to them eagerly and of his own accord. He'd grown tired of the limitations placed upon his experiments at the uptown facility and had sought out Luciano early on in order to pursue his own endeavors with a far greater freedom and more financial backing than he could ever have hoped for otherwise. His new facilities were located in another part of the compound, far away from everything else, and very private. Luciano had little idea of what he was currently working on there, but the few times he'd ventured into the man's research areas, his head had buzzed for weeks afterward from the effects of the strange machinery that purred and vibrated in those labs throughout all hours of the day and night.

Yet Dr. Eastman had quickly become invaluable to him in many other ways. In addition to his private studies, he also took care of the technological aspects of the entire facility, and his progress in perfecting the serum now being used was beyond compare. If they'd had another dozen just like him, Luciano would not have had to call in other scientists to assist. But because of recent time constraints, they'd needed help with the final equations to make sure this project happened without untoward delay. In fact, if they wouldn't have had access to others who were also familiar with Abe Orson's work, modifying these soldiers could have taken weeks instead of mere hours.

"I meant about our chances for success," he said tolerantly. "Do you think that we're putting the men at too great a risk? In your opinion, what are the odds that we'll be able to achieve our goals here today without any notable setbacks? Will these men be ready for combat, or will they merely be turned into mindless vegetables?"

"Crusher is a fool," Dr. Eastman replied dismissively. "With my processes entered into the computer, and the serum running at full capacity, there is no way this will fail. Barring the minute possibility of one of the subjects rejecting the enhancements, they should all come through it just fine."

"And what of our other modifications," he asked. "How are you coming along with the armor I specified?"

His deep brown eyes burning with the intensity of a man caught in the grip of a raging fever, Dr. Eastman reached up to adjust his glasses as a thin frown creased his clean-shaven countenance. "Those modifications are difficult but not completely out of the question. As you know, this type of technology has only ever been tried before on large transport carriers and tanks. The power needed to sustain the energy in order to produce a viable effect for any length of time is. . . limiting. Fortunately I've recently been experimenting with alternate energy sources and have come up with a solution. During the course of my own personal research, it just so happens that I needed a small, efficiently built battery to power my creations in a more portable fashion. The units I've devised will sustain the new suits indefinitely. There will be some side effects, though."

"What sort of side effects?" Luciano inquired.

"Well," Dr. Eastman replied, "any length of exposure to the batteries while unshielded is going to cause severe radiation damage. We can reduce this risk with additional lead plating, but that will encumber the men and ultimately slow them down. Also, the electrostatic aura you want to generate on top of all this is somewhat perplexing. Why exactly do you need a secondary field of this nature as part of the design?"

"We apparently have to be able to withstand attacks by large swarms of insects and reanimated fetuses," Luciano deadpanned. "Can you generate enough additional energy that it will fry anything that comes into contact with the armor?"

Jeffrey's inquisitive expression held many questions that he dared not ask; he knew his place in the hierarchy of things, unlike his fellow scientists from up the hill. With only a slight narrowing of his dark, hooded eyes, he nodded. "I should be able to give that to you, Mr. Gargano. Consider it done."

"Good, good," Luciano said. "Now, let us continue with the procedure. Is everything ready?"

"Yes."

"Then let us begin."

Turning back to the computer monitor, Jeffrey leaned over and placed his index finger beneath four large toggles situated on an electronic device resting next to the keyboard. Maintaining eye contact with Luciano, he then slowly moved his rigid digit upward until all four of the switches were at the maximum output. As the machinery cycled through its energy acceleration phase, his other hand danced across the keys once more before hitting "Enter." The lights dimmed as current was drawn from the power plant deep beneath the lab facility, energizing the machines in the room below.

Luciano stared down into the other chamber as the power surged, modified current flowing into his men, bolstering the serum that had been pumping through their veins for the past hour. All at once, their bodies heaved up from the tables, held in place only by the restraining bands that attached them to the platforms. He could see their muscles bulging, the blood vessels standing out in stark contrast to their pale skin. It was working. His men were becoming stronger than they'd ever been before. As he watched on with a growing sense of anticipation, their eyes flew open, dark red and shimmering as the energy coursing through them activated the serum levels that saturated their bloodstreams.

Within minutes, it was over, the men collapsing back to the tables in quivering heaps of enhanced flesh and bone. Luciano checked the monitor that held information on their vital signs and found that they were all stabilizing.

The experiment was a success.

"Please get these men up and into their gear as soon as possible," he said. "And don't concern yourself with the radiation levels; go for maximum team effectiveness for now. If they do what they're designed for, we won't have to worry about any damage they might sustain from the batteries. Now, I have a meeting to attend to in the conference room upstairs, but I'll be back down very shortly to collect them. And, Jeffrey, please make sure you have them outfitted with our latest weaponry while you're at it. We'll test those in the field as well, and I'll give you a full report on their effectiveness at a later time."

"Yes, sir, Mr. Gargano," Dr. Eastman said. "They'll be ready to go within the hour."

-33-

"Give me one good reason why I shouldn't just arrest you right now," Jenkins growled as he backed Demitre into a corner, his index finger planted firmly in the center of the man's chest. "You're aiding and abetting known felons in an ongoing criminal investigation. That makes you, by your own admission, an accessory!"

"Calm down, will you?" Demitre said, slapping his hand away. "In case you hadn't noticed, these 'felons,' as you call them, are no longer even human, so I hardly think the charges are going to stick. How do you plan on getting them to stand trial if you do manage to catch them? How will you hold them? Behind bars? The idea is laughable. Dan," he continued, grabbing the detective's shoulders. "They're doing you a favor! Doing us all a favor if you ask me. In the last few days, they've cleaned out the slums, taken down corrupt officials, and now they're dealing with all the underworld crime that's been infesting this city for years. We could have a whole new lease on life, and it's all because of them!"

Pacing back and forth, he waved his arms through the air as he continued his tirade. "Dammit, will you just open your eyes for a minute and see the bigger picture? I didn't have to tell you about my involvement with them; I could have just kept my mouth shut! Yet here I am, being upfront with you, trying to make you see they're not the sadistic criminals you make them out to be. But you know what your problem is? You're jealous! Why don't you just admit it—they're doing the job that you wish you'd been doing for these past three years, and more!"

Jenkins's left eye twitched as the smoldering anger within him burst into a raging inferno. He'd brought Lisell back to what he thought was a safe place, only to have Demitre tell them that he'd been assisting the very criminals that they'd been attempting to track down! Was he out of his ever-loving mind? People were dying, for Christ's sake! This was vigilante justice, and even if it benefited the rest of the population, it was most definitely against the law. In addition to that, it went contrary to everything Jenkins believed in, and he meant to put a stop to it no matter what the cost.

"Dan," Lisell's soothing voice murmured from over his shoulder. "She did save us, back there at the safe house. And afterward, the Love Leach said. . . well, didn't she say that you were one of the good ones? She has faith in you, Dan. These spirits, they can't be entirely evil. It's like the old man said—they have a duality, a drive to do what is needed, even if that means hurting the people who've always considered themselves to be above the law."

"That still doesn't make it right," he grumbled.

"Even so, the things they've done have only benefited us so far. You said so yourself, back at the hospital. That the people they're taking down are all bad people, right?"

"Yes, but even those bad people still have basic human rights," he insisted. "The right to due process, the right to a fair trial. . ."

Turning his head, he found that she was gazing at him, her eyes pleading, reflecting the raw emotions held deep within her soul. "You know as well as I do that most of those people would never have gone to trial if you'd caught them," she pointed out. "And many of them wouldn't even have been arrested in the first place. Can't you see? The people being killed are the very same ones that have been abusing the system for years now. They do what they want, when they want, and with absolutely no regard for the consequences. They've been hurting people, Dan, innocent, hardworking people like you and me. And they would have just kept on doing it if they were still alive now."

He thought about that for a moment and had to admit to himself it was true. But that didn't mean he had to like it. Shaking his head, he turned and stalked across the room to gaze through the windows, staring out across the city he called home, that he protected with every fiber of his being. Deep in his bones, he knew what the kami were doing was wrong.

So why did it feel so right?

"I'm sorry I didn't tell you about my involvement with them sooner," Demitre said from behind him. "But if it'll make things up to you, I'll tell you where you can find them. When they left here, they were heading for that new hospital complex. There's some kind of meeting going on over there with all of the city's most notorious gang leaders and mafioso in attendance. And even though these beings are trying to help clean up the city, I'd love to see some of those criminals go to jail instead. A good, long prison sentence would be more of a punishment for some of those scumbags than ending their pathetic lives could ever be. Death is a mercy they don't deserve, in my opinion. But before you go running off half-cocked, I have some other information you might want to hear."

The eccentric computer hacker had many valid points. Capturing the beings who were terrorizing the city was going to be difficult. But there was no real reason to argue the finer details of how they were going to go about it right this second. All that really mattered was finding out who and what these spirits were and then taking them off the streets for good. The whole city might be becoming a better place because of what they were doing, but he wasn't about to let them get away with outright murder. Not on his watch, and not if he had anything to say about it. But it seemed better to just let that go for now. Dampening down on his anger, he tried to shrug off his concerns while focusing on the tasks before him. It wasn't easy, especially when every fiber of his being was crying for him to lash out, to vent his rage by any means possible.

"What have you got for me," he asked instead.

"I've been doing some checking around on our new friends," Demitre began, sitting back down at the desk while tucking some of his long, stringy hair behind one ear, "trying to ferret out more info about them, and I was able to dig up some interesting tidbits from across the web. There's a lot happening out there that could be directly related to their appearance." As he typed away at the keyboard, blocks of data began to scroll across the main monitor.

"First of all, there was a body that was never recovered from that apartment fire. A Mrs. Florence Resario. I double-checked, and guess what? That was Nick Resario's wife right there. Isn't it strange she went missing during the fire and yet he never said a word to anyone about it? And didn't you guys tell me that he'd spoken to several of the survivors over at the hospital right after the incident, and they clammed up afterward? I think he may have been covering something up, something huge, maybe even his own guilt over committing arson and murder. And now he's dead, taken out by the Love Leach in a brutally vengeful manner, if what you've told me is accurate. Could his wife have somehow become what we now call the Love Leach? It's hard to say with any certainty, but it's one hell of a compelling theory, don't you think?

"In addition to that, there was a back alley abortion clinic located in the building behind that old herbal shop, and it looks like they closed down the day after the fire. There were reports that night of some type of underground explosions happening in the same area as well, which seemed a little fishy to me. So I checked around and found out Dr. Abraham Orson, who used to do research at one of those big, fancy labs uptown, was the main practitioner performing all the procedures down there.

"And get this, he's known to have had a bit of a falling out with the other scientists he used to work with. Something about his experiments being unethical enough that they fired him because of it. It's rumored that soon afterward he took out loans from the Gargano crime syndicate to start up that clinic. Big loans. Ones he was having trouble paying back. Maybe he could have had another laboratory secreted away underneath the clinic, perhaps one that was also somehow destroyed that night. Who knows what he might have had going on down there?

"But now, all of a sudden, he turns up here with his new pals, exhibiting supernatural powers of his own? Right after two of the Garganos' most lucrative businesses get taken out? That's real suspicious, don't you think? Then this team of extraordinary individuals all head for the new hospital complex that just happens to be owned by Luciano Gargano himself, and it's also the same place those doctors The Loathing is looking for now work? That's way too many coincidences for me to swallow all at once. There has to be some connection, maybe even a hint as to why they're here in the city to begin with. Perhaps it's even part of some vendetta for things that happened to them before they transformed. Of course, this is all supposition right now, but it would explain their actions and provide a hypothesis from which to build on while discovering their true identities."

He turned toward Jenkins, his earnest expression almost comical in the glow of the computer monitor. "I'm telling you all this so you can find some way to make peace with these beings, whatever the hell they are. The fact that these unusually violent events—the fire, the unexplained explosions—happened on the same night could be directly related to why these creatures are here now, or more accurately, how they were created. These people, missing or otherwise, could be the unlucky few these mysterious eldritch entities have chosen to inhabit for all we know. Although why they would want to do such a thing, I really have no idea. One thing there's no denying, though, is that they're powerful, and I don't know about you, but I want to be on their good side when all this is over.

"And that's one of the main reasons I've been working with them. But it doesn't mean I want to be subjugated by a bunch of supernatural dictators after they're done doing their thing here. My point is that we need to find some way to coexist with them so we don't get added to their list of targets. That's what drove me to make a deal with The Loathing in the first place. In exchange for my assistance in stealing those hospital records he promised, I'll have a say in the restructuring that comes after they're through. And even though he says they're here to clean out the corruption, he also claims they're not interested in taking control of the city afterward. I believe him, but I don't entirely trust him. We need to make plans to find people who can take up the reins of leadership once the dust has settled. That's something I think you and I can both agree on, am I right?"

Jenkins nodded thoughtfully. Getting qualified people in place to govern the city and put the pieces back together after all this upheaval was crucial. The police force would need new personnel, and they would also have to replace members at all levels of local government if the lists of those dead or missing were accurate. He couldn't bring back the deceased, that was beyond his powers as an officer of the law. But if he could have a say in choosing those who led the living into a better tomorrow, he would take it. It was the least he could do for the citizens he was sworn to protect.

"If we pursue this course," Jenkins said, "we're still going to have to do something to stop all the killing before we can rebuild. As part of the investigation, Lisell and I spoke with a priest of the Shinto order, and he says these creatures are spiritual entities known as kami, possibly ones that were brought over by an influential Japanese family several years ago to establish a new shrine. We think that the old herbal shop down by the docks could have been a front—it might just be the actual shrine cleverly disguised as a business to keep away American foot traffic. That would have allowed others of the Shinto faith to worship these ancestral spirits in peace and relative anonymity. You've made a good start in gathering information about whatever these things are, and perhaps even how they came to be here, but can you dig around in your database a bit more and find out who owned that dockside property? If we can discover where the actual temple is located, the old man we spoke to says we may have a chance to appease these beings at their point of origin before they can do any more harm."

"I'll get right on it, Detective," Demitre said. "But in the meantime, I think you should get over to Harlson Medical straightaway. There's that meeting going on up there, and if you hurry, you can catch up with these 'kami' before they begin their assault. I may have helped them out, but I still believe in most of the laws that you continue to uphold. When The Loathing and his friends left here, they were still trying to figure out the best way to break into the lab complex that's situated on the new hospital's grounds. That's where Luciano's having this gathering of like-minded criminals, and since it's locked up tighter than Fort Knox, you may still have a chance to intercept them."

"What about this other guy," Jenkins asked. "This Dr. Orson. What's his skill set? What abilities can we be expected to face from him if we have to confront them in open conflict?"

"I don't know," Demitre admitted. "He never used any of his powers around me. Although he did manifest some small, glowing fetuses floating in the air above him when he got upset. I think it's a safe bet that he has some type of power over aborted children or something linked to his previous research, whatever that may have been."

"Thanks, Demitre," Jenkins said, pulling out his phone to call for backup.

"And, Dan, there's just one last thing," Demitre added.

Pausing in the middle of his call, he glanced back at Demitre expectantly.

"It's that file on your old partner," Demitre said. "This will sound strange, but I haven't been able to find anything out about his disappearance. And that's unusual because I can usually find out anything I want about anybody. His entire existence has been wiped clean. It's like some super-serious black-ops shit here, Dan. He's been totally ghosted."

Jenkins was caught with his mouth hanging open. He'd completely forgotten about his missing partner over the last few days. With everything else going on, he hadn't had the time to even think about it or research what had happened to make him disappear the way he had. Considering what Demitre had just told him, though, he probably wouldn't have found anything out on his own anyway.

But even though this added another layer to the convoluted mystery he was trying to solve, considering where they were at in the investigation, it was one part of the puzzle that would just have to wait. Closing his mouth, he completed dialing up the station.

"Have all available units converge on Harlson Medical Hospital," he told the duty sergeant. "I'll also need a SWAT team to go on full alert and get a bird in the air to provide support. It looks like we may have an assault with intent to murder on our hands, and it involves the local crime syndicates, as well as those supernatural perps we've been tracking, so everybody gear up and look alive out there."

As he hung up, he was already heading for the door.

-34-

The guard lounged in the office chair at his security station inside the Harlson Research Facility, lulled by the tedium of an uneventful shift. Reaching up with both arms, he stretched to loosen his already stiffening joints but then caught sight of some unusual flickering on two of the monitors. Leaning forward, he lowered his arms, running agile fingers over the keyboard to try and stabilize the wavering images of the front lobby as they blurred across the main view screens. There seemed to be a battering movement around the cameras themselves, and as he fiddled with the controls, he was suddenly able to make out what appeared to be an eclipse of moths. As he watched on in disbelief, both screens became totally obscured by the flutter of their multitudinous wings. Leaning back in his chair, his face screwed up in confusion. *Now where the hell did all those moths come from this late in the season?* he wondered.

Part of his ingrained training already had him reaching for the call button. Punching through to the other control booth located beyond the second set of interior doors, he made contact with the man on duty there.

"Morty?" he said into the headset mic. "You better get out here; there's something going on in the lobby. It looks like the cameras are being blocked by a bunch of moths, if you can believe it. I need you to go check it out for me."

"Roger that," the voice came back over the speaker. "I'm on my way."

A few moments later, the large, hermetically sealed panels slid open, revealing another guard who moved with the bored nonchalance of a seasoned patrolman. Holding a flashlight loosely in one hand, he ambled toward the outer lobby with an air of unperturbed resignation, his starched black-and-white uniform looking crisp in the overhead illumination.

"Let me out, will you, Chief?" he called over his shoulder.

The man at the desk toggled in the door code, and after his partner left, glanced down to see a tiny spider sitting next to his hand. "Now how the hell did you get in here?" he wondered aloud, putting his palm down flat on the counter and watching as the arachnid crawled up the back of his fingers. "This place is supposed to be sealed up tight against the likes of you. But don't you worry, little buddy; when Morty gets back, I'll ask him to take you outside. You won't have anything to eat if you stick around in here."

Just then, a flash of light blinded him as tendrils of electricity coalesced and expanded into a sizable globe in front of his station. The outlines of a woman quickly formed inside of this fluctuating plasma-filled sphere, and in a matter of moments, Florence had finished materializing. As she stepped from within the orb's shimmering embrace, it broke apart, collapsing back in upon itself and sending miniature arcs of lightning crackling all across the pristine surfaces of the control room's sterile interior. Startled by her sudden appearance, the guard stared at her nude astral body, giving a spontaneous whistle of awed appreciation. But when her eyes, like twin points of fire, focused squarely upon him, he swallowed the dry lump forming in his throat and then blinked several times to see if he was somehow hallucinating.

Concluding that the spiritual entity standing before him was actually quite real, he regained his composure enough to reach for the gun holstered at his hip. But then a desire to please this beautiful apparition rose up within him, and he fell to his knees instead, basking in the warmth of her smoldering attention.

With a tiny smile teasing the corners of her insubstantial lips, Florence moved around to the back of the desk, then reached down to punch in the security code witnessed by the spider just a few moments before. Within seconds, the doors at the other end of the hallway hissed open again, and Abraham led the junior patrolman back inside with Charlie following closely behind them.

Ignoring the guard groveling at her feet, she admired Abraham as he moved confidently forward, realizing he was now by far one of the handsomest men she'd ever met. And what's more, she knew that his soul was pure, even with the slight amount of moral ambiguity that he suffered when it came to his research. Even though his powers tended to cancel out her own, there were some intimate details she could still read from him, and they'd shown her that he'd never intentionally hurt anyone during the long history of his scientific achievements. In fact, his highly trained mind had always rejected the theories of religious zealots who'd helped put a stop to planned parenthood by postulating that such a small collection of cells and tissues was already sentient. To him, the idea was preposterous. However, admiring how his thoughts worked didn't stop her from delighting in his improved looks. Even without the fancy overcoat he'd purchased, the new suit he had on was exquisite beneath the long, white robes that were a permanent part of his daily attire.

"We have the codes," she told them, refocusing on the task at hand. "There's no need to hurt these men any further. I can tell they're just hardworking citizens here doing their jobs and nothing more."

"Excellent," Charlie said. "I grow weary of always having to kill people in order to move forward with our plans. Now that we are nearing the end of our respective missions, I have hope that we can begin to rebuild and restructure this city to make it the place that it was always meant to be. For the time being, though, let us just simply contain them behind this desk where they can do no further harm."

Abraham, who had a hold of the second guard's arm, dragged him forward and sat him down at the duty station, moving the chair away from the controls. "If there's a way to perhaps put them to sleep for a bit, that might be for the best," he said. "We don't want them hitting an alarm or tipping off our enemies before we gain access to the conference room."

"Oh, I think I can handle that," Charlie purred. Raising his arms, he gestured with his outstretched hands, and thousands of arthropods boiled in through the open doorway. Soon, the entire foyer was filled with their buzzing, clickering masses. The guards cried out in pure terror as the insects surged over them, but within seconds both men were unconscious from a carefully regulated series of nonlethal bites and stings.

Abraham took the time to arrange them more comfortably before turning toward Charlie. "About how long do you reckon they'll be out?" he asked.

"Long enough for us to get in there and clean out this nest of vipers," Charlie replied with a grin.

"That was wonderful!" Florence exclaimed, resting a slim, semi-corporeal hand on Charlie's shoulder. "It's truly amazing what you can do with your children!"

Abraham scowled from where he loomed over the two comatose guards but managed to smooth out his features before moving to stand at Charlie's other side. "Well, now that we're in," he asked, "how shall we proceed?"

Florence was impressed by how well he was handling himself, yet was still confused by his overall demeanor. Before, he'd always been so quiet and reserved. But now, after changing his appearance and buying new clothing, he was like a completely different man. Ever since he'd gotten back from his shopping spree, he'd made it a point to join in on conversations and was always unfailingly courteous, but she still couldn't tell if he truly liked her or was simply being polite. She knew she wasn't anything special outside of her new abilities—just a closeted bookworm with very few other redeeming qualities. In fact, he must think her horribly dull. As a scientist and brilliant physician, surely he'd met hundreds of much more interesting people in the past. After they'd completed their tasks, especially now that he looked normal enough to blend in with the rest of modern-day society, he'd be able to spend time with anyone he desired.

Would he even want to be friends with her after this was over, let alone anything more than that?

It made her feel like a softhearted schoolgirl dealing with her first crush all over again. Mentally shaking off the tangle of confusing emotions, she decided to focus on the mission instead. The rest was just a distraction that she hoped would eventually work itself out on its own.

"Demitre showed us on the blueprints that the conference room is right through this next doorway and then down the connecting hallway to the left," she offered. "They don't know we're coming, so we should be able to surprise them just by walking in unannounced."

Abraham nodded, his pale eyes lingering on her as he smiled. "I want you to know that I appreciate this opportunity," he said. "I realize that you could have easily just swooped in there on your own and taken these miscreants out single-handedly, but I really do want to have the honor of killing the man in charge myself. Luciano has been a thorn in my side since before I even met him. Finding out that he derailed my entire career just to advance his own agenda was quite a shock, and it's not something I'm prepared to let slide. He's wronged me in so many ways now that I simply must have my revenge for what he's done. Being able to see him there in that room, in front of all his cronies, and then to be able to take him down and squeeze the life from him with my own two hands? Well, that's a priceless opportunity, and one that I have you to thank for."

His compliments warmed her, melting away any lingering resolve she had to ignore the longings of her heart. Yet still she had her doubts. What if he were only saying these things to be respectful of her contributions? *Now you're just being silly*, she told herself, denying that possibility. Dredging up a modicum of courage, she dared to emulate his directness, maintaining eye contact and then consciously willing him to see the passion blazing within her fiery gaze, the interest she could not bring herself to express in mere words. His pleased expression held firm for a few seconds more, then faltered beneath her impassioned regard. *Is he afraid?* she wondered. It was hard for her to tell; his thoughts and innermost emotions were obscured by the strength of his own spiritually given powers.

After a moment of uncomfortable silence, he glanced away, clearing his throat and rubbing at the back of his neck with one hand. "Yes, well. . . perhaps we should get on with it then and see this thing through to the end."

Charlie had already stepped up to the secondary doorway, collecting the multitudes of his insects behind him as he conferred with Simon, who was now perched on the back of his forearm. "Yes, let us do get beyond this portal, then I shall have the rest of my children clear the way forward. If we can do it with a minimum amount of noise, that would be ideal. We do not want anything to ruin our surprise now, do we?" He favored them with a mischievous wink as he prepared to probe deeper into the research facility's guarded interior.

Hiding her disappointment, Florence walked around to the back of the booth and toggled in the security code for the other entrance. As the doors began to decompress, she then joined Abraham, who had moved to stand just behind their burgundy-cloaked companion.

As the doors slid apart, Charlie was saying, "I wager they will be terribly upset once we barge in on their little. . ." But the rest of the comment died in his throat as the parting panels revealed a group of thugs standing just beyond them. These men seemed equally surprised to find intruders in the lobby area, but that didn't stop their leader from immediately aiming his Benelli M3 and opening fire. This unexpected point-blank discharge of the high-powered shotgun took Charlie square in the face. As he flew back into Abraham's arms, causing them both to collapse heavily to the floor, the insects in the entryway went berserk. The air was suddenly filled with clouds of swarming, buzzing arthropods led by a frantic Simon as the mafiosi backed away, covering their retreat with a crescendo of explosive gunfire.

Abraham's shields of ultra-hardened skin cells had manifested instantaneously, which was the only thing that saved them from the withering barrage of lethal projectiles. Holding Charlie in his arms, he gazed down in horror at the ruin of his companion's face. One of his friend's ocular orbits was completely shattered, a pulpy, gore-covered pit that now continually pumped green ichor out across the rest of his heavily damaged features. Bereft of life, he lay motionless in Abraham's arms, his directionless children filling the air above them with a terrible combination of rapid movement and deafening sound. Overcome with fear and a sense of soul-shattering remorse, Abraham turned his grief-stricken expression toward Florence, the muscles of his finely sculpted face contorting as his mouth opened and closed, soundlessly searching for words to express his intense feelings of loss.

"He's. . . dead," was all he could finally manage, tears coursing in wide rivulets down his ashen features.

Deep within herself, Florence felt something burst like a logjam being thrust aside by the waters of a seasonal flood. Without warning, an immense surge of unfettered emotions, stronger than anything she'd ever felt, rose up to overwhelm her. She wanted to kill, wanted to rend the flesh from the men who'd hurt her friends until their screams filled the air with vibrating shrieks of pain and terror. The two conflicting powers precariously balanced within her went berserk, battling one another in a sudden paroxysm of unstoppable violence. As the demons who constantly sought to dominate her soul found they were now unopposed by her own iron will, they quickly subsumed the brighter energy of the maiden spirit with red-hot malignant force. *"You killed Charlie!"* Florence shrieked as she prepared to make the men pay for their horrendous act of unprovoked violence.

The brutal slaying of her friend combined with the tears falling from Abraham's eyes were like the lash of a glass-coated whip across her already abraded emotions, goading her toward actions she would normally never consider. Feeling the jagged claws of his grief tear gaping wounds across her innermost soul, she experienced Abraham's intense misery, suffering it a thousand times over as the scalding heat of his despair branded her heart with unbearable pain. Promising herself that no one else would ever hurt him like this again, she rose from the floor in a bubble of scarlet-streaked electricity, her inner rage exploding outward to encapsulate her in a crackling orb of implacable destruction.

Saturated by the demon's unholy desires, the crimson-hued sphere eclipsed all other sources of light as she rose above the polished marble floor encased within its electrostatic embrace. The insects, sensitive to high levels of radiation, swirled away, instinctively fleeing her anger-infused emanations as they sought out the dubious safety of the much cooler lobby area. As the massively dense cloud of their airborne swarms parted around her, she focused all her burning attention on the men standing just beyond the open portal, transforming their endless stream of deadly projectiles into harmless liquid metal. As the hallway filled with a deluge of molten lead like a tropical storm of thwarted destruction, they dropped their overheated firearms and then turned to flee deeper into the building's shadowy interior. With a malicious snarl splitting her fearsomely glowing features, Florence followed, her powers scorching and peeling the paint from the walls as the orb of sizzling incandescence drifted after them with unstoppable rapacity.

Right then and there she decided that these men would suffer the most gruesome fate imaginable, their final moments on Earth filled with so much pain and anguish that their screams would echo through the corridors of time for all eternity. Floating down the corridor, she let the volatile fury of her unleashed demonic energy lash out unrestrained, watching as the fleeing men fell to their knees in a state of unimaginable agony. Within her, the minions of the underworld howled in triumph, blazing across the link they'd forged within her soul and eager to once more feast upon the living.

There would be no mercy for these murderous scum, no final release for the sadistic criminals who'd killed her mentor and made the man she now cared for weep such agonizing tears of deeply heartfelt sorrow. Dripping scarlet flames and charged with the hatred of a million unchained demons, she advanced down the deteriorating hallway, a veritable nightmare sprung to life from the unforgiving bowels of hell itself.

-35-

Luciano had arranged this meeting to discuss the very real threat of the supernatural forces now arrayed against them, but the people at the table were not exactly on the best of terms. Petore Mishnakov was a stern, volatile man with a shaven head and a scar running the length of his face from brow to chin. Even when he wasn't angry, the Russian oligarch looked like he'd bitten into a sour fruit, and his heavily accented complaints often rang louder than any of the other attendants gathered here today.

Itchi Suragami, on the other hand, was like a still pool resting within a shadowed glade, seeing much with his cold, dark eyes yet saying very little. Between the two of them, however, he was the far greater threat; his long silences were often punctuated by a swift and brutal death according to the ancient Bushido code he still followed.

Chavez Ramos Ramirez, the Latino veterano, simply looked bored. He sat slumped in his high-backed chair, stroking his expansive mustache, his smoldering gaze following the others as they continued to argue.

In contrast, the powerful black man seated next to him, Mustaffa Okaligacooni, was stiff and alert, the colors of his bold suit only accentuating his fist-pounding vocalizations.

That left Mickey O'Gillacuddy, the crusty old head of the Irish mob. His seamed and weathered face had seen more years of conflict than all the others combined, but he sat quietly with his hands on the top of his knobbed and intricately carved cane. As always, he watched from the sidelines, adding very little to the heated discussion, yet still a very palpable threat, nonetheless.

When Luciano had first entered, they'd been shouting each other down, their henchmen in various poses of imminent attack. Settling them enough to converse rationally had taken some time, but they were now about as calm as one could expect after ordering all of their goons from the room. His own bodyguards were the exception, of course, and still stood stationed behind his seat at the head of the table; he was the real power here, and none could dispute it. Coming from a well-established Italian Cosa Nostra, he had helped to usher in this recent period of stability by hammering out an uneasy alliance between these powerful men. They all knew that if it weren't for his efforts they'd still be killing each other off indiscriminately without reaping the benefits of having local government officials at their beck and call. The Garganos had built up this foundation of shared power, and Luciano meant to keep it firmly under his iron-hard control.

"Gentlemen," he said, bringing the meeting to a semblance of order. "We are here today to discuss the men and women who are systematically destroying our operations while killing off all of our most strategically placed assets. These interlopers have somehow obtained esoteric powers that, at this point in time, are still a mystery to us. I suggest that we put aside our petty squabbling and band together, strengthening our existing ties in order to rid ourselves of this ongoing. . ."

The sounds of gunfire erupting from beyond the outer doors cut him off mid-sentence. With a twitch of a forefinger, he sent his two remaining guards to investigate. As they left the room at a run, the meeting devolved back into a shouting match.

"What treachery is this!" Petore exploded. "You say this was to be safe meeting!"

"I'm out; which way to the closest exit?" Mustaffa interjected.

Within seconds the rest of them were on their feet, yelling and cursing each other as the gunfire in the hallway intensified. A rising crescendo of horrific screams reached them from beyond the doors, then one of his guards stumbled back into the room, half of his face melted away like it had been hit with a ray of molten energy. "They're. . . here. . ." he managed to wheeze out before expiring in a twitching heap. As his body stilled, the gathering devolved into unrestrained panic.

But Luciano hadn't made it to where he was today without being prepared for any eventuality. "All of you," he said, "follow me! Beyond these doors is an industrial blast shield covering a private escape route. Call your men waiting outside and have them draw your vehicles up to the west end of the building. Then have them prepare for battle; the people attacking us right now are the ones I was just speaking of. This could be our best chance to be rid of them! They came here to end us, but we will emerge victorious if we can but catch them while they're pinned down by our own henchmen. Now, all of you follow me, and be quick about it!"

However, as they clustered around him, pushing to be the first through the exit doors, the front wall of the conference room disintegrated into a cloud of fiery embers. Beyond it was a nightmarish scene straight out of Dante's Inferno.

The fused remains of men locked in various poses of flight were being slowly stripped of flesh, their blood and other bodily fluids streaming off them in a red haze of evaporating liquids. The effect was almost hypnotic, and it was already causing the white glimmer of bone to show through the exposed layers of their raw, interconnected muscle tissues. Warbling screams filled the air, and from that he knew they could still feel it all. With horrifying clarity, he realized they were somehow being held in a state of living death while they were each broken down into these sinewy skeletal statues. Only their hearts, lungs, and brains remained intact, along with their vocal cords, in order to facilitate the wailing cries of suffering, which now rose from them in lingering waves of unending agony and despair.

Floating behind this collection of macabre howling corpses was a woman suspended inside a globe of crackling electricity, the plasma-like discharges of the sphere's superheated circumference lashing out to caress the bodies of her targets with crimson-hued tendrils of electrostatic energy. Within this bubble of pure hatred and fire, the enraged spirit throbbed, wreathed in clouds of red vapor, as if she were bathing in the boiled blood of her hapless victims. Peering closely at the apparition, he saw that there were other shadows swarming around her, things seemingly called here to feast upon the souls of the men now being denied the mercy of a clean death.

Turning away from this uncouth sight, he was the first through the doors, turning to the blast shield controls as he ushered the others into the hallway beyond. In the conference room they'd just vacated, the walls continued to deteriorate, the metal and wood shrieking as the building materials sloughed away, the distorted sounds mingling with the cries of the doomed. It was this revelation of his enemies' true powers that gave him pause, making him doubt his own strategy. Could he really defeat something like that, something so destructive that it could command demons summoned from the very depths of Hell itself? Shaking a little in shocked uncertainty, he mashed his fist against the controls, sending the blast shield slamming down and cutting off the sounds and images from without. This part of the lab had been built to withstand a nuclear blast. He only hoped it would now stop whatever was raging its way toward them through the decimated hallways of the building's front offices.

Regaining control of himself with some difficulty, he gestured down the hallway to the left. "That way, and quickly now!" he told the others. "At the end of this corridor, you'll find another blast door. Once there, trigger the switch on a control panel like this one, and it will allow you to access the exterior parking lots. Gather your men there, then wait for my signal."

"Laddy," Mickey said in his thick Irish accent. "I'll be gatherin' up me men, an then I'll jus' be shovin' off. You canna fight against tha spirit an hope ta win; she's na from this world."

The others were quick to join in with heartfelt agreement. The general consensus seemed to be that there was no way to triumph over such a powerful adversary. This disavowal hurt Luciano's feelings, wounding his pride and then stoking his anger to new heights of boiling resentment.

"If you would leave, then so be it," he snarled. "But hear this now and understand it—the Gargano family protects its own. If you flee like a bunch of craven dogs, then there will be no part of this city left for you to rule over once the dust settles. These creatures will stop at nothing. If we don't band together now, all will be destroyed by their continuing attacks. Only I have the means to defeat them, only I have the technology and resources that none of the rest of you possess. So go now if you must, but think well on what I've said! Mark my words, for they may very well be the last ones that you will ever hear from me!"

"Maybe it's time for another family to lead us then, ay *ese?*" Chavez said, pulling a gun from beneath his loose-fitting jacket. "What's to stop us from just taking all that you own right here, right now?"

The others began to echo this sentiment, each pulling out a weapon and edging toward him. As Itchi drew a wakizashi from beneath his robes, eyes shining with murderous intent, Luciano took a step backward. Perhaps he had underestimated his rivals. This could very well be the last mistake he ever made.

Then from behind him there came the sounds of elevator doors opening at the opposite end of the corridor. Risking a glance over his shoulder, he saw a group of his own men approaching with guns held ready. In an instant, they'd formed up around him, bristling with hostility. Hiding the relief he felt behind a brittle smile, he straightened to his full height, brushing his hands down the front of his finely tailored suit.

"Gentlemen," he said. "I believe we are now at an impasse. Since you refuse to help, and indeed display a distinct disregard for my leadership, I feel that I have every right to kill you where you stand. But this one time, I shall allow you all to live. And I'll tell you why— these spirits, these things that wage war on us now, cannot be defeated by any one man alone. You will either get on board with me to fight against them or you will all die, one by one, alone and without the defenses that only I can provide. Now get out of my sight before I change my mind."

The men backed away, looks of disgust and thwarted ambition coloring their individual features. Then, with a final, calculated disregard for Luciano's threats, they turned and hurried away, the muted sounds of destruction from beyond the blast doors echoing after them.

Luciano motioned to his bodyguards and then headed back toward the elevator. He had to get down to the labs beneath the complex and collect his new soldiers. He didn't know if they were ready yet or if he could even make a stand with so few men now that he'd seen what he was up against, but he had to at least get clear of what was on the other side of those blast doors. Of that much he was certain. That raging female spirit had struck a chord in him, and it was one built out of primal fear.

How could he defeat such an avatar of living death? Dare he even try?

As his men gathered around him and the elevator began its slow descent, he mulled over the problem, seeking answers that he simply did not yet have.

-36-

The damage was extensive. Abraham didn't know if there was anything he could do or if it was even worth the effort to try. By all appearances, his friend was irrefutably deceased. Yet that simply could not be the case; they'd been granted their powers on the brink of death by spirits who now zealously controlled their prolonged existence. So there must be a spark of consciousness left somewhere within Charlie's remains. Glancing at Florence, who was currently engaged in fighting off the mafia henchmen, then back at the uncontrolled swarms of insects still filling the lobby area, he knew he had to at least try. Simon, Charlie's insectile lieutenant, circled overhead in a concerned frenzy as Abraham locked his shields together, encasing their portion of the embattled hallway in an impenetrable layer of ultra-hardened skin cells. Then he sank into a trance-like state.

Extending his powers, he cautiously probed Charlie's unresponsive mind as his hands lay to either side of his friend's lifeless head. There was no cerebral activity, nor even the faintest hint of a pulse, yet these were not true indications of death in this case. None of them had retained their full humanity after rebirth, so the normal signs of vitality no longer applied. However, there was another type of life residing within them now, and it was this unique energy source that he reached out for as he sought a way to repair the destruction caused by the shotgun's blast. Trusting in Florence's outraged attack to keep the mafiosi busy and in his own rigid shields to protect him while he worked, Abraham sank into an even deeper rapport with Charlie's inert flesh and began assessing the damage at a cellular level.

As he flowed through the ruptured cells, traveling the pathways of blood, bone, and tissue, he was amazed at how different Charlie's physiology was when compared to his own, or even to that of any other regular human being. The foreignness of it at first confused him but only for a moment. His scientific mind was already confirming that many of the bodily functions were modified, much like his own had been, yet in far different ways. Luckily, Abraham was able to determine just what those differences were and immediately set to work within this strange, new anatomical environment.

Much like the insects he controlled, Charlie's inner workings were now structured like those of an arthropod. It was really quite fascinating. Moving through this alien landscape of unusual systems and organs, Abraham held himself aloof from the changes around him to focus solely on the damaged areas alone. The bullet had penetrated Charlie's right eye and then torn through what had once served as his brain. The destruction that the projectile had caused was substantial; the eye was completely obliterated along with a large section of the brain's prefrontal cortex. For a moment, Abraham shied away from the alarming amount of devastation, concern warring with anger and shock. Then, stiffening his resolve, he made himself one with the surrounding physiological oddities and began his extensive repairs.

He didn't know how long he spent within the shattered remains of Charlie's skull, but the necessity to keep track of time fell away as he worked. Much of the area needing attention was beyond his level of skill, yet he was still able to encourage the natural rejuvenation process ingrained within Charlie's supernatural constitution to continue the restoration on its own. The effects of his manipulations were slow to reveal themselves but actually quite stunning to behold. As he eased himself back from the joining, he could already see that a lot of the damage was well on its way to being repaired. Would it be enough? Or would Charlie remain an insensate lump of organs and flesh, alive yet never quite conscious of his own surroundings? These were the questions that plagued him as he came up out of his self-induced trance.

Once he'd recentered himself, he studied his friend's current condition, accessing what he saw with the critical eye of a seasoned medical professional. It looked as if the bleeding had finally stopped and the horny plating around the socket itself was regrowing at an exponential rate. As he watched in stunned silence, the reconstructing tissues moved around the cheekbone and began to rejoin with the healthier carapace-like shell of Charlie's lower jawline. Sitting back on his heels, Abraham rolled his heavy shoulders and then stretched his neck, trying to shake off the stiffness and exhaustion he felt from all the energy he'd expended. Finally letting his shields drop away, he noticed the screams from the hallway were still ongoing. With deepening concern, he glanced in that direction and realized he now had an even greater problem on his hands.

Florence was suspended inside a glowing bubble of crimson energy, her body enveloped by a blood-red mist as her powers flensed the fluids and skin from the immobilized mafia henchmen. With their rigid bodies frozen in various poses of sustained agony, they continued to express their ongoing torment in a series of heart-wrenching screams. The flesh that the process was vaporizing floated in a particulate haze, the swirling trails of blood and evaporating viscera flowing back to spiral around Florence's waiting form. It saturated her aura, becoming part of a shiny red mantle that she now wore like a second layer of plasmatic skin.

Leaving the still frantic Simon to watch after his fallen comrade, Abraham climbed to his feet, his lab coat shimmering as it slithered back down and around his massive frame. Focusing on the sight of his beloved sealed within her electrified shell, he started forward, unsure of what he could do to help but willing to die trying if he must.

The walls around them were bowed outward as if a huge ball of fire had rolled through, the building materials twisted and scorched, covered in glowing embers and burning wisps of flame. It was a miracle the structure was even still standing at all. As he approached the lightning-streaked sphere, he studied her as she continued to bathe in the blood of their enemies. He realized then that there were shadows swarming around her, ones he hadn't noticed from a distance. Yet now that he stood in close proximity, he could feel the volcanic heat of her insatiable hunger, could see the beings that cavorted around her as she hovered with her head tilted back, spine arched, and arms flung out to either side.

They appeared to be demons.

This observation gave him pause, and he stopped right at the very edge of her circle of influence. Why were demons, if that's what they truly were, manifesting themselves here and now? He didn't have the slightest clue and yet it did not matter, didn't change the fact that he had to help her, had to save her at any cost. As he stood surveying the spectacle, trying desperately to figure out a way to rescue the woman that he'd come to care for so deeply, he noticed the heat radiating off her was beginning to intensify. It was apparent that if he couldn't find a way to quench her powers, and soon, they'd all be consumed in a searing conflagration, their mission failed, and the battle lost forever.

He had to find some way to communicate with her but didn't know how to begin. Taking another tentative step forward, he reached out, recoiling a little as her head snapped around, her crimson eyes tracking him while she snarled in uncharacteristic rage. The shadow demons spun crazily through the air, whipped into a frenzy by his mere presence, and this gave him some small hope that she could still be reasoned with. If they were so concerned about his potential interference, then maybe she still had a chance at redemption.

"Flo," he ventured, keeping his voice gentle yet pitched to carry over the shrieking of the dying men, "please, you needn't do this. Come back to me. Stop this madness and resist the creatures influencing you to commit such vile atrocities. Release these men and dampen down your powers before you destroy us all. Please. . ."

Eyes burning with nothing but blind hatred, she hissed like a feral cat, turning to face him as she continued gathering the blood and detritus being stripped layer by layer from the men around her. Then, with a series of truly frightening contortions, her astral form twitched and spasmed as it jerked its way toward him, the searing energy of her electrified undulations rippling over him in chaotic waves of unrestrained malice.

"Enough!"

The strident command came from behind him and had an immediate effect. As this vibrant vocalization echoed off the surrounding walls, Florence stopped, eyes going wide as they focused on a point just beyond where Abraham was standing. One by one, the bodies of the mafiosi began to collapse, their screaming cries of horrified anguish dwindling until the hissing of the overheated building materials and the crackling of her supercharged energy field were the only sounds remaining. The demons turned on her then, raking her with claws and fangs, swirling round and round as they ripped and tore at the layers of vaporized blood encasing her insubstantial flesh. But then, with a massive shake of her entire being, she threw them back, launching a counterattack of her own.

Twisting in midair, she began to spin like a demented ballerina, sucking the demons back into herself as she whirled with ever-increasing speed. In a cone-shaped vortex of roaring hatred, they flowed into her wide-open gullet like a blackened tornado, teeming with clawing, snapping figures. As the last of the shadowy assailants were consumed, she slowly stopped her mad gyrations, her glowing figure fading from deep red into ice blue and then back to her normal pure white radiance. Small bursts of electricity shot out from her then as the sphere collapsed, tracing the edges of the building's interior with a dazzling array of miniature lightning bolts. And as the excess energy dissipated around her, she stepped lightly to the ground, once more stabilized within the glorious incarnation of herself that he knew and loved so well. Eyes aglow with unrestrained emotion, she ran forward.

Just when he thought she was about to fall gratefully into his outstretched arms, she raced past, forcing him to turn in order to follow her progress. It was thus that he witnessed her enfolding a newly recovered Charlie into an overjoyed embrace.

"You're alive!" she cried, her voice heavy with unshed tears. "Oh, Charlie, we thought we'd lost you! Thank you! Thank you *so* much for saving me!"

Abraham's emotions were in turmoil. Part of him was ecstatic she was okay. He didn't have any idea what was going on with her, or even where those demons had come from, but the fact that she was herself again was like an immense weight being lifted from his soul. Yet at the same time, he was also racked by a searing envy. His relief that Charlie was back from the dead was almost completely subsumed by the jealousy he now felt as he watched them hugging each other with unmistakable affection. Like the odd man out, he stood waiting to be noticed, fuming in silent misery.

"But how?" she was saying. "We thought you were dead!"

"You will have to thank Abraham for that, I think," Charlie replied, gently disengaging himself from her embrace. "I believe that were it not for his timely medical ministrations I would be still bleeding out on the floor over there. Simon and I owe him a huge debt of gratitude that can never be repaid."

Abraham felt somewhat mollified by this heartfelt expression of appreciation, watching as Simon whizzed through the air to land on Charlie's outstretched forearm. But then Florence turned in his direction. Before he could even begin to offer an explanation, she'd flung herself into his arms, almost overbalancing them both as he staggered under the unexpected impact. As her electrified lips smothered him with butterfly kisses, he began to feel better about the current state of affairs, returning her hug with unabashed delight. "It was nothing, really," he demurred, grinning foolishly. After she was done thanking him profusely, he set her back on her feet, the expression of adoration on her glowing face melting the rest of his jealousy away. Feeling like he was floating on clouds, he yearned to spontaneously burst into song. But Charlie gently clearing his throat brought him back down to reality.

"We should get going before the police decide to storm the building," his friend said, indicating the faint sound of sirens that could now be heard above the crackling fires in the hallway. "We have to find a way past these security doors and then into the main laboratory itself. My children say that they have not seen anyone leaving the building as of yet, so that is the only other direction our adversaries could have fled."

Abraham searched Charlie's face, seeing pain still etched there, and studied the freshly closed layer of horny carapace covering what was left of his right eye socket. "Are you sure you're up for this?" he asked. "That bullet really did a number on you. Perhaps you should just sit this one out."

"Nonsense," Charlie replied. "It is merely a flesh wound. Come now, we must get past those doors, and quickly. Our final destiny awaits us!"

Abraham was not convinced; he'd been inside Charlie's mind and knew the extent of the damage done there. Frankly, he was shocked to see him up and about so soon; it was clear the healing Abraham had initiated was an ongoing process which still needed more time to continue its rejuvenating effects. Would the shattered eye ever be whole again? Perhaps, but perhaps not. At the very least, Charlie should be resting, not fighting or even walking if Abraham had anything to say about it. Unfortunately, judging by Charlie's look of determination, he could tell that this was one argument he would surely lose. Sighing, he released his hold on Florence, turning to study the immense doors located inside the conference room just beyond the partially incinerated corridor.

They were large and well-set, a heavy metallic safety measure designed as part of the interior structure which had come down from the ceiling to seal itself into slots on the floor. Abraham could tell that the portion of the lab the doors were protecting was built differently than these outlaying rooms and offices. Back behind that imposing blast shield was the real Harlson Labs, the ones owned and operated by Luciano Gargano himself. Flexing the muscles of his upper torso beneath the shimmering lab coat, he strode toward them with an attitude of unshakable determination.

"What are you doing, Abe?" Florence called after him.

The sounds of sirens were growing louder as he approached the thick steel plating, and he could hear the unmistakable chuff of a helicopter's blades whirling overhead. The police were right outside, and these doors were the only thing standing in the way of them completing their mission.

They had to go.

Steeling his hands into diamond-hard wedges, he ran the last few steps to the barrier, then rammed the tips of them into the thick metal surface. As his enhanced digits penetrated, he bunched the muscles of his chest and arms, using his legs to lift as he strained to drag the heavy portal open. For the briefest of moments, the massive doors resisted but then began to rise slowly from the slots in the floor with a shriek of metallic protest. With a final, tremendous heave, he powered his arms upward, letting go of the heavy panel as it shot back into the ceiling with a loud clang. As a small cloud of debris settled around him, he dusted his hands together, turning back to his astonished companions.

"Shall we go?" he asked with a crooked smile, waving an arm toward the opening in a sweeping, aristocratic gesture.

Florence's smile was like sunlight bursting through clouds on a rainy day. Charlie staggered a bit as he began to move forward, but she grasped his arm to steady him, then they both crossed to where Abraham was standing before continuing on into the hallway beyond.

With a somewhat smug feeling of accomplishment, Abraham followed, glancing around as they entered the corridor.

To the left, the hallway continued up and around a bend. Yet to the right there was a short section ending at a large freight elevator. Without hesitation, Charlie shook off Flo's help and walked over to push the call button. Within seconds, the double doors opened, and they all got into the car. Studying the control panel, Abraham selected the button labeled "Lower Level A."

As the doors slid closed and they began their descent, he couldn't help but wonder what they were getting themselves into. The thought of their last battle still weighed heavily upon his mind, and he decided it was time to change into something a bit more practical. Summoned from the depths of the aether, his armor rolled into place around him, covering him from head to toe in an impenetrable suit of articulated plating. Glancing at Florence, he watched her become fully immaterial, her feet lifting from the floor as she rose within a bubble of shimmering electricity. Charlie grinned at them both and then released Simon, who flew to the trapdoor on the ceiling and burst straight through it. Within seconds, the car was filled with the deafening roar of millions of his buzzing children following them down the elevator's shaft from above.

As they continued their descent, Abraham flexed his muscles within the heavy armor, rolling his shoulders and limbering up for the fight ahead. Whatever was waiting for them below, they were more than ready for it now.

-37-

On his way to the Harlson Labs, Jenkins got a report from the tactical flight crew saying they'd discovered a few suspicious cars and limos parked behind the west side of the building. Without hesitation, he'd ordered some mobile units to close in and detain the drivers. He was glad that he'd done so, for when he arrived at the scene, he was just in time to help arrest the city's most powerful crime lords as they emerged from a set of security doors located on that side of the complex.

They were all there. The leaders of the Russian mafia and Japanese yakuza, the head of the Mexican gangbangers, and the man who controlled all of the African American factions throughout the city. They'd even captured the crusty old patriarch of the Irish mob and now had them all handcuffed in the back of police cruisers. It was a banner day for the department, and it was a welcome change to have something go right after a week of unmitigated disaster. As he moved to establish a perimeter around the facility, he was hoping to continue this streak of good fortune by bringing in the murder suspects he knew were still currently inside. All the intel Demitre had given him had led up to this coup, and he was silently appreciative of the man's ongoing assistance.

However, the news outlets had also gotten wind of things, and they were there in force, their camera crews filming the arrests while broadcasting live on all channels. He'd been able to keep things quiet at the start of this investigation, but with everything going on in the last few days, the reporters were now frothing at the mouth to get an exclusive. At least this would be seen as a positive step toward finally putting an end to the chaos that had been plaguing the city. As he gave instructions to the line of officers holding back the reporters, they clamored for a statement.

"Alright, alright," he shouted. "Please move away from the blockades. It's for your own protection."

"Detective," one cried. "Can you at least give us an idea of what led up to this unprecedented arrest?"

"Why are you here to begin with?" another called out. "Can you tell us what's going on inside Harlson Labs that would require such a large police presence here tonight?"

Waving them into silence, he tried to come up with a professional-sounding reply. He wasn't used to interacting with the press. The bastards made him nervous.

"We're responding to an anonymous tip and working diligently to keep this city safe and protected. And you can quote me on that! But right now, you all need to back up and stay behind these barricades."

"Detective! Is there any truth to the rumor that Love Leach and The Loathing are inside the building right at this very moment?"

Shaking his head, he waved them off. "No further comment. Now please, for your own safety, back the hell up and stay out of our way." With that, he strode off, ignoring the rest of their shouted questions as he moved to where Mattie was overseeing operations.

"What have you got for me," he asked.

"Well, sir, there was definite movement inside a while ago," she said. "The helicopter crew reports that their thermal sensors are going crazy, but they can't get an exact reading. It's like the building was on fire in one certain area, but we've had no alarms or sprinkler systems going off. These scumbags were certainly here for some kind of meeting, but there's no sign of any of the Gargano family members and very few henchmen about, which I find to be odd for such a large group of high-rolling players."

Bringing up a schematic on her tablet, she pointed at the map as she continued. "The heat signature is coming from here, and this is where we are now, at the west emergency exits. We don't know much about the inside of the building as of yet; it's all private-sector construction and very hush-hush. There's suspicions that it's run by the Garganos, but that's mostly just speculation. I have a hunch that whatever's causing the heat signature is most likely one of our murder suspects. Only something with their kind of power could put out this much energy without tripping an alarm or burning the whole place down to the ground." She glanced up, waving her hand in an arc. "The perimeter is set, we have a SWAT team ready to go, and medical personnel are waiting on standby. I say we tighten the noose, sir. Let's get in there and finish their reign of terror once and for all."

"I want the streets cordoned off within a three-block radius," he told her. Then, pointing at the map, he continued. "Place snipers here, here... and here. Don't get too cocky; these perps are extremely dangerous. Let's not forget that the Leach has been taking down our men left and right all week without even breaking a sweat. We gotta watch out for that. Also, that bug guy is going to be a problem. While I'm thinking about it, find us some local beekeepers or exterminators and get them down here to deal with the insects in case we do get hit by them. There has to be something they can do, like with smoke or a repellent of some kind, that would break up any potential swarms. I want to make sure we have all our bases covered."

"I'm on it, sir," she said, then turned away to follow his orders.

Within the hour, he had the whole place buttoned up tight. But there was still no movement from inside the facility, and his officers were getting restless. Mattie walked back over to him with a handheld radio, and he took it from her, pushing the call button.

"Alpha unit, any movement?" he said into the mic.

"Nothing yet, sir. Area one is all clear," came the reply.

Systematically, he contacted the other carefully placed teams one at a time, checking to make sure everyone was in position. When there was nothing left for him to do to ensure the safety of his fellow officers and emergency personnel, he motioned the SWAT team leader over to join him.

She was an imposingly athletic woman in full tactical gear with a submachine gun hanging from a strap under her left arm. As she strode toward him, he could see the confidence she exuded in her every movement. The rest of her unit, also mostly women, waited behind a nearby barricade located a yard from the front entrance. They looked as if they'd been born for this type of assignment, and he was suitably impressed.

"This is Sergeant Roxanne Murphy," Mattie said by way of introduction. "She's in command of the SWAT team and one hell of a fine officer."

Sgt. Murphy eyeballed him closely and seemed to like what she saw. Standing straighter, she saluted him with a loose military-style hand to forehead, then offered him that same hand for a firm shake. "I've heard a lot about you, sir," she said. "In the last few days, me and my crew have taken up some of the slack created by our loss in manpower, and we've been following things as they've progressed within your own department. If it's not too out of line, I just wanted you to know that we all appreciate the job you've been doing. We're behind you, sir, one hundred percent."

He was momentarily taken aback by this unsolicited vote of confidence. In his mind, he hadn't really accomplished much of anything except a lot of fuck-ups and missed opportunities. Still, it warmed his heart to have the devotion of such willing and capable people. He promised himself that he'd do more from this point forward to try and live up to their expectations. Glancing at her team, he nodded in recognition, then turned back to her with what he hoped was an air of confidence. "I appreciate your support, Sergeant," he said. "What's your assessment of our current situation?"

"Well, there's been no further activity noted within the structure, and our eye in the sky hasn't been able to determine if there's anyone left inside. Except for that one massive heat signature, which has since dissipated, there's not much to go on. Once we get in there, we'll do a full sweep to try and locate the suspects. If we do get a bead on them, we'll pull back without engaging and request further instructions. I don't want to risk my team unnecessarily; it's a well-known fact that a confrontation with Love Leach typically leads to instant death. Not that we're afraid to face her. It's just that I don't want to go down like that, sir. Not without a fight, I mean."

He admired her dedication and outspoken declaration of personal intent. These people were ready to die for him, if need be, but they weren't going to just throw their lives away for the sake of glory. They knew the risks and were planning to act accordingly.

"Don't worry," he reassured her. "If you do get within line of sight of the suspects, I want you to mark their location and then retreat. I'll be going in myself to oversee their arrest, and I have it on good authority that these people, or whatever the hell they are now, won't attack me without provocation. It seems they only kill those who are corrupt in some way, and for whatever reason, that just isn't me right now."

The look on her face told him all he needed to know about her feelings on the matter. Apparently, abusing a position of power for capital gains was not high on the list of things she agreed with. Well, that suited him just fine. He was beginning to like this young hotshot officer.

"I'll tell you what, Detective," she said, "we'll pull back when we see them, but we'll be keeping them in our sights from then on out. Once you get in there, if there's any sign of trouble, you just give me the signal, and we'll do our best to take them down. They've still gotta bleed same as us, right? My team can handle it as long as that Leach lady doesn't hit us with any of her electrical mumbo-jumbo."

The statement was delivered with a lopsided grin, but he could tell she meant it. His opinion of her rose a few more notches as he waved over the exterminators who had just arrived on the scene.

"If you see anything flying or crawling around that entrance once we move in, pump the whole place full of everything you got. Smoke, gas, I don't care which—just get it done! You got that?"

The officers nodded, fidgeting with their equipment and clearly uncomfortable with the situation. Turning back to the SWAT team leader, he gave her his final instructions.

"I want this done strictly by the book. Canisters and full respirators to start off, with these civilians backing you up in case of swarms. If you catch sight of that female spirit, and she starts anything that even remotely looks like an attack, I want you to get the hell outta there. Don't be a hero, Sergeant; let me handle it if it looks like she's going to be a problem. There's just one other thing—this accomplice of theirs. We don't know much about him yet, but word on the street is that he can do something with fleshy self-animating blobs. They may look to you like fetuses, or even floating half-formed babies, but don't go anywhere near them. We have no idea how dangerous he is yet, and judging by the abilities of our other two suspects, I don't want you risking your neck unnecessarily. Your job right now is to scout out the scene, secure it if you can, and then back me up if it comes down to a fight once I get in there. You read me on that?"

"I read you loud and clear, sir," she replied. Reaching up, she pulled the gas mask down over her face, then signaled the rest of her team. Once they were all likewise equipped, she had them bunch up and move into position as a unit, rapidly advancing on the main entrance before fanning out and taking up covered positions. Canisters were launched through the open doors, then came a few seconds of waiting while the inside of the building filled with hissing tear gas. After that, they rushed into the partially obscured opening in rapid succession.

In a short amount of time, two of the squad members escorted a couple of security guards back out. They were coughing and tearing up from the gas but otherwise seemed unharmed. After handing them off, the two officers rushed back into the building. Jenkins waited somewhat impatiently, tense and silent as he scanned the surrounding area with a practiced eye. Finally, he got a call over the radio from Roxanne giving him the "all's clear". After waiting for the gas to die down a bit, Jenkins gathered the other officers he'd chosen to accompany him and then ran for the entrance with his weapon drawn.

Once inside, there was not much to see in the main lobby. A SWAT team member waved him through some heavy doors that looked like they could be sealed from the inside. In the short hallway beyond them, there was another security desk and a set of larger doors standing open. As he passed them by, he noted how thick they were and saw they were probably part of the lab's emergency safeguards. Hermetically sealed areas were supposedly a feature of the new facility from what he'd seen in the schematics. Whatever they were working on that needed such beefed-up precautions, he hoped it wouldn't interfere with the investigation. He had enough to deal with right now without having to face a biological or chemical containment hazard on top of everything else.

But once he was past the second set of doors, he pulled up short. The hallway beyond was practically a war zone. Bowed outward and blackened by some unknown force, the walls looked as if a gigantic ball of fire had rolled down their length, melting everything in its path. Toward the end, there was a wall that had been completely disintegrated, and beyond that, he could see a conference room with overturned chairs and a blast shield like the ones he'd seen in military installations.

Only this particular imposing portal had been badly damaged and was opened in such a way that it could only have been forced. His practiced eye had quickly taken in the details, but it was what he found littering the floor around him that stopped him dead in his tracks. There were several piles of smoldering human remains, mostly just bones and skulls, staring morosely back at him from their positions of horrifying destruction upon the scorched carpet. The officers behind him tensed with uncertainty, covering the area with drawn weapons while awaiting his commands.

Roxanne came back along the edge of the destroyed hallway, and he could tell that her team had things well in hand. The ones still visible were in positions that had a clear view of their surroundings, and they were covering every angle of the interior with laser-sighted precision. Roxanne pulled off her mask as she stopped in front of him, the remaining gas swirling around her booted feet.

"This area is secure, sir," she announced. "There's not much else to see, except for the obvious. Beyond those blast doors over there, there's another hallway that seems to be the route the mob bosses took on their way out. At the opposite end is an elevator, but it's out of commission. I have my team currently looking into getting it back online, but the rest of the facility is locked down tight behind doors that won't open. I'm not sure why they needed such heavy security measures, but we can't get past them. Down this way and through that T-junction off to the right, we found a civilian in a control room. He says he was attempting to reestablish auxiliary power, but his story seems kind of fishy to me. It may be that he's just trying to buy himself time before we arrest him. I think you should talk to him before we take him into custody."

"What about our suspects?" he asked. "Any sign of 'em?"

"Well, they were here alright," she said, indicating the surrounding destruction. "Judging by the damage, and the mob bosses wussing out like they did, the perps must have put on one helluva show. The remains on the floor are consistent with the missing bodyguards we were wondering about earlier. Seems like they may have gotten into a firefight with our suspects and lost badly. Of course, that's all just supposition at this point. We won't know anything for sure until we have the tech boys go over everything."

He nodded, already thinking things through. "We need that elevator operational, Sergeant. Get your best people on it and stay on top of it until it's up and running." Holstering his gun, he ran a hand over the lower part of his face, scratching at the stubble on his chin. "I think I should go and have a little chat with your fishy civilian now."

"Yes, sir, right this way."

"Wait," he said. Turning, he spoke to one of the officers standing behind him. "Get someone to question those guards we rescued, would you? Try and find out how we can gain access to the rest of the complex and see if they know anything about the elevators. Also, ask them where these elevators lead to while you're at it. The rest of you spread out, but don't touch anything until the tech team has a chance to go over it. For now, just see if you can find anything that will help our case along or allow us to discover an alternate route into the lower levels. If you do find something, get in touch with me ASAP. I'll be in the control room with Sergeant Murphy."

They all nodded, spreading out to continue the search as he followed Roxanne down the long, blackened corridor and then moved into another hallway untouched by the devastation. At the opposite end was an open door leading to a control room. Inside, there were several large banks of computers lined up along the left-hand wall, with a few chairs sitting in front of them. On the right was a small table, where two SWAT team members stood guarding a man dressed in a white lab coat. As the scientist noticed them walking in, he tried to rise, only to be pushed back down by the hovering officers. The look on his face was one of barely contained outrage.

"This is Dr. Jeffrey Eastman," Roxanne said by way of introduction.

The man glared at him from behind aviator-style glasses, the blinking emergency lights from the monitors reflecting from the clear lenses. "And I suppose that you are another policeman?" the man inquired coldly.

"Detective, actually," Jenkins replied. "My name is Dan Jenkins and I'm in command here. Can you tell us what happened?"

"I haven't the foggiest," the man said. "I was in my lab when I heard a commotion. I came to see what was going on and found everything like you see it now. I was trying to reestablish control of the computers and electrical systems when your fellow officers here detained me. Now, if you don't mind, I'd like to get back to work. This facility needs to be reinitialized and then locked down into safety mode. There's very sensitive research going on here—I'm sure you understand."

His attitude was pretty cavalier for a man in his position. Taking a moment to study him, Jenkins noted he was small and meticulously shaven, a thin, unobtrusive man with short black hair wearing a crisp, well-cared-for suit under the pristine lab coat. Outwardly he seemed normal enough, yet something about him, besides the open hostility, was sending up red flags. What was he even doing in the building at this hour of the night?

"Are you in charge here, Mr. Eastman?" Jenkins asked.

"Heavens, no," he said with a dismissive wave of one hand. "That would be Dr. Peterson. I merely run things while he's not here. I'm in charge of daily operations, you see."

"And where is Dr. Peterson now?" Jenkins asked.

"Oh, away on business," came the vague reply.

Pulling out a chair, Jenkins turned it around backward and sat down, staring hard at the presumptuous little prick. He didn't know what this guy was trying to pull, but his attitude was already wearing thin on the nerves. Time to take him down a few pegs. "Okay. Well, listen up, then. We need you to tell us everything you know about what goes on around here, and then we need those elevators back up and running as soon as possible. The people who did this to your facility are wanted criminals—even more dangerous than the ones who were recently gathered together in that conference room just down the hall. But I'm guessing you wouldn't know anything about that, now would you, Mr. Eastman?"

Folding his arms across his chest, the man smirked. "I've no idea what you're talking about," he said. "I've been in my laboratory all night. I only came up here after the power began to fluctuate. I'm in charge of critical systems, not conference rooms."

"Well, just who *is* in charge of those conference rooms then?"

"You'll have to ask Dr. Peterson about that, of course," the man replied, dark eyes glittering from behind the lenses of his eyewear.

"And Peterson is out of town. How convenient for you. What sort of research do you do in these labs of yours, Mr. Eastman?"

Rising from the chair, the man placed his hands flat on the table as he leaned forward. "I'm afraid that's confidential, Detective. In fact, I'm going to have to ask you all to vacate the premises. This building and its surrounding facilities are all privately owned. We have our own security in place, and if you'll excuse me, I have a lot of work to do. When we need you, we'll be sure to call and make an appointment. You can leave your card on the table if you wish."

It was Jenkins' turn to smile. Oh, the man had balls, he had to give him that. Reaching out, he stopped Roxanne from making a move; it looked as if she were about ready to blow. He wondered if the scientist knew just how close he'd come to getting a beatdown by the SWAT team leader. "We'd be happy to accommodate you," he said pleasantly, "but there's just a couple of things we have to look into here first."

Resting his elbows on the table, he steepled his fingers, staring into the man's unflinching eyes. "First of all, this is a crime scene. *My* crime scene. And before you get any ideas about that, let me tell you what is going to happen here at *my* crime scene. We're going to be going over this place with a fine-toothed comb. All your dirty little secrets will be coming to light, just so you know. And when you harbored the city's most notorious criminals here, you also became an accessory. Aiding and abetting is a punishable offense. Then there's the additional fact that three murder suspects have just torn through your lobby and killed a bunch of men in the hallway behind us. That makes your laboratory the scene of a multiple homicide. Are you beginning to get a better picture of what kind of trouble you're in here now, Mr. Eastman?"

"You have no authority here," the man stated, unperturbed. "Those hoodlums broke into our offices; we had nothing to do with it. Once we assess the damages, we'll be filing a complaint. As for your murderers, we have no control over where they appear or what they do in this city. They've been rampaging through town for days now, and you and your fellow officers have done absolutely nothing to stop them. From my point of view, we're the victims here. Those men, for whatever reason, were trespassing. And then they had a dust-up with your other suspects, who were also here illegally and without our knowledge or consent. It really has nothing to do with us at all."

"Oh, but I think that it does," Jenkins said. "They were here for a reason. Word on the street has it that the Gargano family runs this facility. Having all the other mob bosses here at the same time supports that theory. They were here for a meeting of some kind, and I think you know what that meeting was about. Not only that, but you still have dead bodies all over your hallway, men that were murdered here in cold blood. This is definitely a crime scene, and that gives us jurisdiction. We have probable cause and the right to investigate this area fully. Now, you can get those elevators back online, and you can cooperate with our investigation, or we can do this the hard way. The choice is yours."

"Even if I wanted to, that would be impossible," the man said. "The electrical surge has frozen all the systems connected to the elevators. The amount of energy that passed through those corridors fried our sprinkler system and took out all the wiring in this section of the building if I'm not mistaken. It will take days, maybe even weeks, to get everything back to normal. I was merely trying to get the auxiliary systems functioning properly until we can get a repair crew in here to—"

"Then how did you get upstairs in the first place?" Roxanne interjected.

"My labs are in another area of the facility altogether," he replied smoothly. "I wasn't in any parts of the building that are accessed via the elevator."

"There has to be a stairwell or something," Jenkins prompted. "You wouldn't be up to standard building safety codes otherwise." The man pressed his lips together in thin disapproval, clearly choosing to remain silent. Well, well; it looked like they'd hit a nerve. "We're going to get into those sections of the building with or without your help, Mr. Eastman," he continued. "You may as well come clean now and save us all a lot of time."

"Am I under arrest?" the man asked.

"Not if you cooperate."

The man continued to glare at him yet offered nothing in reply.

Jenkins gave him a minute to think things over, then sighed. "Take him down to the station and put him in a holding tank until we get some answers. In the meantime, get a tech crew in here to go over these systems. Let's see if we can figure out how to get that elevator working. Or at least find me some goddamn stairs! Down is the only direction the suspects could have fled; surveillance shows that no one has left the building since those other scumbags came out the west side exits."

"You better have a search warrant!" Dr. Eastman shouted as they led him away. "Our lawyers will hear of this! Mark my words, Detective. You don't know who you're messing with!"

The man's shouts echoed down the hallway as Jenkins stared thoughtfully at the computer screens. There were a lot of flashing red lights, that was true. He wondered if they could even get down to the lower floors no matter how hard they tried; none of the underground levels had been on any of Demitre's schematics when he'd looked at them earlier. The whole place could be designed to isolate those hidden areas if what the little prick had been saying was true.

He was still sitting there deep in thought when a team of technicians came in and got to work.

-38-

Charlie tried once more to shake off the dizziness, the thoughts in his newly healed brain coming thick and slow. He was functioning mostly by instinct and pure will alone at the moment and realized the dangers of doing so. Not only to himself but to his whole team. He glanced over at them, judging their disposition while waiting for the elevator to reach its final destination.

Abraham stood in front of him, his gleaming white robes flashing with iridescent stitchery as they flowed over the reddish-brown armor he now wore underneath. He'd erected several hardened flesh shields in preparation for leaving the enclosed space and now stood braced for action, the barriers floating in a tight, interwoven pattern in front of the sealed doors. Florence, her body arched with arms curving out to either side, hovered just to his right, a globe of crackling electricity surrounding her as she pulsed with barely contained energy. Eyes burning with internal radiance, she gathered the shimmering power into her fists, holding them like an ancient warrior brought forth out of legend. It seemed his friends were spoiling for a fight, and he could hardly blame them after what had happened upstairs.

But their main goal was to take down Luciano before anyone else got hurt. That man was a danger to everything they stood for and a threat to the bright future they were trying to create. Charlie knew that the spirits who'd given them these powers desired to usher in an era of peace and prosperity the likes of which the city had not seen in years. Now, if they could just find this one man and eliminate him, it would advance the spirit's agenda exponentially. The Gargano family had a stranglehold on this town, but once that was put to an end, Charlie and his companions could clean up the rest of the corruption, establishing the foundations for a new age of hope and enlightenment.

However, in order to do that, they would also need to dismantle the far-reaching empire he'd built and then destroy the military base located on the fringes of town as well. A few medical personnel to eliminate after that, and Charlie's part of the pact would be complete. He tried not to think too far beyond that goal for now; it was best to do these things one challenge at a time. Reaching out mentally to his nearby minions, he gave them last-minute instructions as they swarmed down the elevator shaft. They were likewise eager for confrontation, and he stirred in them the undeniable desire for retribution, making sure they'd be an unstoppable force once unleashed.

Watching the levels counting down on the electronic display, he attempted to clear the rest of the cobwebs from his mind while shoring up his failing reserves. He needed to be ready for anything when they reached the hidden lair of their enemy. Finally, the car came to a stop and the doors slid open.

"Wait," he cautioned the others. "Let my children prepare the way."

With a wave of his hand, millions of insects flew down through the broken trapdoor of the elevator's roof access and funneled into the spaces beyond the carriage, led by an enthusiastic Simon. The air of their tumultuous passing stirred Charlie's cloak and Abraham's robes as they flowed around them, invading the lower levels of the laboratory complex in all of their endless multitudes. Within minutes, the shaft was clear, and he mentally reached out to his children once more, seeing through their eyes, hearing through their tiny bodies as they covered in seconds the distance he and his companions would have taken vital minutes to traverse. Shaking his head in disappointment, he stepped from the compartment, turning back to face his friends.

"This place is completely cleared out," he told them. "We are too late."

"What do you mean?" Abraham demanded. "They were here just moments ago—how could they have gotten out so fast? This part of the facility is deep underground!"

Charlie focused on the images he was receiving from his legions of tiny infiltrators, seeking to discover what had happened to their intended targets. At the far side of the underground complex, he finally found what he was searching for.

"Come," he said. "It is this way. An escape route now guarded by one of those energy fields they used in front of the Gleaming Gypsy. Beyond it lies a door we must breach if we are to follow, but we have to move quickly; the children stationed above tell me the upper levels are now filled with police. Although I do believe they are mostly made up of officers who are uncorrupted. Many of the misbegotten souls on Luciano's payroll have already been taken out by Florence, their emotions collected for her own personal enhancement. Is that not right, my shimmering angel?"

Florence smiled at the flattery, but then grew introspective as she reached out with her own powers. "Yes," she said, "all of those above us are true of heart. And we'll need men and women like them in place once we're through with our tasks. It looks as if they're attempting to access the elevator, though, so we'd better hurry before they succeed."

Abraham, who'd stiffened slightly at their verbal exchange, allowed his faceplate to dissipate so he could communicate more easily. His revealed expression was grim. "Why would they leave a field generator in place by itself to guard their escape?" he said. "That doesn't make any sense. I think I smell a rat in the soufflé here." Turning his head, he studied the long hallway stretching out before them. "Are you sure your children didn't see any soldiers hanging around?"

Charlie agreed with Abraham's desire for extra caution. So, extending his thoughts outward, he reached for Simon and established contact.

-Yes, Father?-

"Simon, can you make another sweep of the entire floor? There is something not quite right about all this. We expected more resistance to our arrival. Are you sure there are no soldiers lurking about?"

-One moment, Father. We will investigate further.-

Charlie relayed that information and then they all waited, unwilling to move further into the complex until the report came back. After a few moments, Simon's thoughts reached Charlie's mind once more.

-Father, we can find no human presence within these corridors. Yet there are many rooms which we cannot enter, and the energy field itself prevents us from reaching the final set of doors.-

"Simon says there are no signs of other human life," Charlie told the others. "At least none that my children can detect. But there are many hermetically sealed doors here that they cannot breach, and of course the exit beyond the field is equally inaccessible. It looks like we are going to have to search this place ourselves if we want to be sure."

"But we don't have time for that!" Florence exclaimed. "Those officers could find their way down here at any minute. We don't want to be trapped between them and whatever's waiting for us on the other side of that final doorway. If we take the time to search, we'll wind up having to deal with whoever's coming in behind us, and you know as well as I do that they'll try to take us into custody no matter what we say to them."

"She's right," Abraham said. "We need to get out of here as soon as possible. Let me block all the locked doors with fetal material while we focus on our main objective. That way, if there's anyone inside those rooms waiting to attack us, the doors will be stuck and they'll have to force their way out."

"Can you cover the elevator as well?" Charlie asked.

"I don't see why not," Abraham replied. "But it won't hold them for long. We'll still need to hurry."

"At least it will buy us a little more time. Let us get to the other end of these corridors then and see what we are up against. Once we deactivate the energy field, we will have access to our enemy's escape route, and it will also serve as our exit point as well. We cannot be here when the police arrive; it would be a bad idea to deal with them now while they still wish to incarcerate us. There will be plenty of time later to work them around to our way of thinking."

The others nodded, agreeing with his assessment before turning to proceed down the hallway, Abraham placing fleshy membranes of hardened skin over each of the doorways they passed. With the elevator shaft closed off behind them and the rooms being covered as they went along, Charlie felt certain they were going to be fairly secure for the moment. Because of this surety, he spent the time focusing on regaining more of his flagging stamina as they moved along.

After traversing the maze of interconnected passageways for several minutes, they reached a central hallway large enough for the transport of heavy equipment. It had warning signage posted all along its length, as well as heavy rubber matting to prevent damage to the floor. Charlie briefly wondered just what they'd been hauling in and out of the facility before focusing on the end of the corridor itself. It was there that the generator was located, just as his children had shown him. Set in the center of the hallway, it transmitted an energy barrier across the last few feet, protecting a set of wide double doors. The scene was almost surreal, and Charlie stopped, motioning for his two companions to do the same. Something wasn't right—he could feel it. And as he tried to determine just what that irregularity might be, a stream of freezing-cold nitrogen shot out at them from behind the electrostatic field.

With barely a moment to spare, one of Abraham's floating shields rotated into place to take the brunt of the attack before disintegrating under its chilling onslaught. His last encounter with this type of weapon had prepared him well. Weaving a group of the newly designed multiphasic skin nodules before him, he turned his head slightly to call back over his heavily armored shoulder, "I thought you said there was nobody down here! If this entire floor is empty, then where the hell did that beam just come from?"

As he was making this observation, another focused stream shot out, this one consisting of the hot, sticky substance they were all familiar with from the last battle. Charlie waved his children away, and they scattered, using the dizzying maneuverability of their swarm to narrowly avoid the tar.

"Hey, Flo," Abraham said as he wove his barriers in intricate, self-replicating patterns, "can you sense anything going on back there?"

She'd paused behind him and was now floating in an increasingly agitated state, flashes of plasma flowing around her and intensifying into a succession of crackling eruptions. "I feel nothing," she said, "Wait. . . there is something—some kind of distortion. Can you not see it?"

Charlie focused on the area beyond the device yet could not discern what she was talking about. Glancing over at Abraham, he raised an eyebrow, wondering just how much his friend could really see out of the reformed helmet's bubbled lenses.

"There isn't anything there," Abraham said, still manipulating his fleshy defenses as streams of freezing nitrogen and boiling tar smashed against them. The constant attack was wearing them down, causing a congealing mass of slushy goop to collect along the floor as the shields were broken apart and regenerated in an endless cycle.

Charlie knew they had to disable that generator or they could be trapped here, potentially overwhelmed. Whoever was firing on them, their attacks were coming from one side and then the other, as if the weapons were wielded by foes who kept changing position. There had to be some way to get past them without sustaining further injury.

"Abraham, do you see that control panel?" he said, pointing at the device. "Could you not send some of your fetuses to materialize directly on those switches to shut the machine down?"

"I could, but I'm a little busy right now," Abraham said, manipulating yet another series of compacted cells to deflect the continuous barrage coming from the opposite end of the hallway. "Can Simon maybe get back there and take it out for us?"

"I am afraid that the field would fry him to a crisp before he could succeed," Charlie replied.

"I've had just about enough of this," Florence declared, her energy sphere now oscillating with a high-pitched, electrical whine as the resulting sparks sizzled out across the floor. Charlie stepped back, more than a little concerned. Whatever had happened to her upstairs, he did not want to experience it again. Those demons could have torn them all to shreds. He knew it was fortunate that she cared enough for him to have listened to his voice when he'd called out. If she had continued to let the rage dominate her personality, they'd probably all be dead right now. Or at least as dead as their guardian spirits would ever allow. As her crimson eyes glittered with malicious intent, he tried not to flinch, trusting that she was perhaps still in control and knew what she was doing.

Raising her arms, she aimed not at the generator but at a spot directly above it. With a thunderous eruption, huge arcs of lightning shot out from her fists and exploded against the reinforced panels hanging over that end of the hallway. As the bolts of pure electricity ripped through the ceiling, chunks of cement and plaster rained down, smashing into the generator and shattering it into a million pieces. As the energy field collapsed, dust billowed out from the avalanche of debris that had come crashing to the floor.

Charlie gazed at the destruction, marveling at the power which had caused it. It was then that he began to see the outlines of their hidden enemies. Coated by the settling detritus, whatever cloak of invisibility was protecting them now became far less effective. In the dimness of the demolished thoroughfare, he could suddenly see where they were standing, and he called to his children, sending them spiraling en masse toward these newly revealed foes.

But as his flying warriors swarmed the two men, their tiny bodies turned to smoke as they struck something that had to be a feature of the soldiers' protective gear. Like they were encountering an industrial-sized bug zapper, his children died in droves, and only the sheer volume of their concentrated attack was halting the deadly flow of their enemies' assault. As the men struggled to remain upright within the swirling cloud of insects, Abraham suddenly shouted for Charlie to call off his children's attack.

With his shields no longer needed, Abraham had instead created a huge floating ball of hardened skin that spun through the air with gathering momentum. Once the insects had scattered, he hurled this projectile straight at the now visible targets. With a thunderous crash that shook the building to its foundations, the dense ball of solidified embryonic cells struck the men simultaneously, hammering them both back against the exit doors. Crushed from the impact, they fell to the ground, debris raining down around their lifeless bodies.

Approaching warily, Charlie peered at them in curiosity. After the blow they'd suffered, their armor had malfunctioned and was clearly visible. It was more of the same design they'd seen in the previous battle, yet subtly different. The interlocking plates of these newer models phased in and out of focus, bending the light around them. Charlie had heard of this technology before but only on a much grander scale. To know that Luciano had access to this level of cutting-edge military equipment was a bit of a shock. For the first time since he had accepted his strange new powers, he began to feel afraid. Could they really win against someone who had unlimited resources and would stop at nothing to defeat them? And with the help of the military, his opponent now took on a higher level of threat than Charlie had previously anticipated. With a sinking heart, he realized they might actually fail at their tasks in the end.

"I couldn't sense them at all," Florence was musing aloud, staring down at the corpses. "It was like their minds were completely blank. As if they no longer had any emotions left at all for me to feel."

Her statement only reinforced his growing doubts. If even Florence, with her impressive range of powers, could not square off against these newly minted soldiers, what chance did he and his swarms, or even Abraham with his fetal minions for that matter, have against them? The thought made his head spin. What little stamina he had left exhausted itself, and Charlie saw the darkness closing in. Stumbling, he spun around, falling bonelessly to the floor as his friends turned toward him in shocked dismay.

-39-

"**A**re you out of your goddamn mind!" the general shouted. "I already gave you our most highly trained soldiers. And now you come here demanding more of me?"

Luciano flicked his fingers slightly, causing his two bodyguards to stop their menacing advance. They were fully aware that he didn't tolerate disrespect, but these were unusual circumstances. He'd come here directly from the escape route and needed these troops to be released expeditiously. The two enhanced soldiers he'd left to buy him some time wouldn't hold out for long against the powers arrayed against them, and Dr. Eastman was a smart man, but even he couldn't stall the police indefinitely. Luciano had instructed him to sabotage the elevators before the officers got there, then to misdirect them as much as possible. As long as they didn't gain access to the lower levels, and his adversaries followed him through the tunnels instead of remaining to investigate, then the labs would be safe.

It was a carefully calculated gambit that still had many weaknesses. If even one of his enemies decided to take control of those labs, or worse, destroy them, then he'd be unable to enhance more of the soldiers he needed in order to stand against them. That particular facility was crucial, and it was why he'd gambled on his foes coming after him instead of remaining behind to wreak havoc. In theory, their desire to eliminate him should far outweigh any urges they might have to stick around and destroy things. It was risky, but he felt confident they would choose to follow.

As for his underworld associates getting themselves arrested, well, that was just an unfortunate happenstance, and one that he hadn't planned on. He didn't know how the police or his mortal enemies had found out about the clandestine meeting, but that didn't matter right now. The damage was done, and all he could do going forward was attempt to mitigate the repercussions. He needed to focus on taking control of the situation, otherwise the city would run red with the blood of rival factions warring amongst themselves while their leaders remained incarcerated. Establishing the uneasy truce between the various criminal organizations had been a hard-won accomplishment, and it needed to remain in effect if his business interests were to continue unimpeded. Worrying about how the information had leaked would just have to wait until later; some things took precedence, and this was one of them. But first things first. Outwardly calm, he smoothed a hand down the front of his beige silk suit, eyes narrowing as he studied the general.

"You seem to think that this is a request," he observed quietly, "one of those favors I sometimes ask, which you believe you can safely refuse." Then, leaning forward, he allowed General Cooper T. Anderson to feel the biting edge of his closely held temper. "But I can assure you that it is not! All that you have, all that you are, everything that you've ever accomplished here is because of me. I have made it possible for you to get to where you are sitting right now, to have a nice home and security for your growing family. And I can take that all away instantly, with just the snap of my fingers."

Settling back into his chair, he let the smoldering anger fade, his expression once more calm and commanding. "You *will* provide me with troops, and you will do it *immediately*, or I will unleash such a storm of pain and anguish upon you that you will beg for death before this day is through. Do I make myself clear?"

The general stiffened in his seat, eyes snapping with impotent rage. "You might as well just shoot me right now, then," he said. "If I give you what you want, my superiors are going to go apeshit. I can't just authorize whole platoons of soldiers and massive amounts of military ordnance to be released to you from this base. The act itself would be career suicide! I'd face a court martial at the very least. What you're asking of me is impossible!"

"Ah, but there's where you are wrong," Luciano replied. "I have already made it possible with just one simple phone call. The men you will be assigning to me are all thugs and cutthroats, the dregs of society, who joined up mistakenly believing that the army would give them a chance to redirect their dangerous impulses. And their equipment has been more than paid for by my generous contributions to your superiors over the years. If you check your database, I'm sure you'll find that all the necessary arrangements have already been implemented. They simply await your final approval before the orders can be put into action."

With a look of disbelief, Anderson leaned forward and pounded some keys on the terminal in front of him. After a moment, his deepening frown disappeared as his eyebrows shot up almost to his hairline. "Well I'll be damned," he said, glancing over at Luciano with undisguised appreciation. "You're right. There are unit requisitions listed here made up of troublemakers selected from all across the compound, with enough armament and supplies to support them almost indefinitely. It seems that the necessary documents are in order, with falsified records in place to cover up the whole affair. 'Urban Peacekeeping Maneuvers'? That's clever. I have to admit, I am impressed." Easing back in his chair, he laced his fingers together over his ample stomach, a pleased grin spreading across his bewhiskered face. "It seems I'll be getting rid of all the scum under my command in one fell swoop. You're actually doing me quite a favor."

Luciano allowed himself a small, humorless smile in return. "As you'll be leading them, it would appear that this base shall soon be free of its most undesirable elements altogether, perhaps for the first time in years."

The general's swiftly souring expression was priceless. With lips puckered and jowls quivering, he tried to maintain his composure. "You're joking," he finally blurted out. "What the hell do you want me for? You got all the men you need and the squad leaders to handle them. I'm not sure what you're trying to pull off, but I want no part of it. This is still my command, and I intend to keep it, without sullying my reputation by openly associating with the likes of you."

"And there's where you'd be wrong again," Luciano said. "I require your expertise in this matter, and these men will need someone they respect, someone to keep them in line. There's only one person that they're all still afraid of, and that's you, my friend. I'll need you to oversee this operation and organize these wayward soldiers into an unstoppable force. As for this base and your command of it, well, it's never truly been yours to begin with. Your entire life has already been carefully orchestrated by my association, so you need not concern yourself with the notoriety that I have allowed you. If you do a good job for me on this mission, then I shall consider letting you keep it, with your precious reputation still mainly intact. At least for the time being. Are we clear on that?"

Pinching the bridge of his nose between two fingers, the general massaged it, sighing heavily. "What is it, exactly, that you're trying to do here anyway?" he asked. "You're not taking the city by force or anything stupid like that, are you?"

"No, nothing quite so dramatic, I assure you," Luciano replied. "We simply need to turn my estates into an impenetrable military compound and make sure that the entire area around it is completely secure."

"Whatever the hell for? You already got enough of your regular goons stationed over there to choke a damn horse! What do you need an army for?"

"There have been some further developments you're likely not aware of yet," Luciano said. "The people who have somehow obtained enough power to challenge me openly are now trying to take what is rightfully mine." Leaning forward, he stared into Anderson's eyes with unswerving resolve. "And I am through playing games with them."

-40-

The coffee was wearing off. It had been a long night, and Jenkins was starting to feel the effects of an increasingly frustrating day. Plus, he still didn't have much to show for it.

Stifling a yawn, he walked back toward the control room, passing the crime scene technicians who were still going over every inch of the hallway. The bodies they'd found were an unresolved mystery. Currently, the official word on the cause of death was extreme heat, but no one could really explain why the flesh had been stripped away leaving the bones and ligaments intact. Not to mention the eyes. They stared at Jenkins accusingly from out of blood-red skulls as he passed by, damning him for his inability to determine the exact cause of their gruesome demise. The only thing he could say with any amount of certainty was that it must have been one of the suspects, using an ability they hadn't as yet seen. Perhaps that doctor they were traveling with had some sort of heat ray. But, as for right now, they really couldn't say for sure what had killed these men. It bothered him the entire length of the hall while he was walking past the seared remains.

From reports he'd received so far, they'd made no headway down at the station in questioning the three civilians, either. The two guards had told a similar tale of having seen the suspects breaking in, confirming for Jenkins what he already knew, but Dr. Eastman had done nothing but complain and make demands, not the least of which was to see his lawyer. Attempts had been made to contact the facility's owners and management, but no one could be reached, which he found very suspicious. With a building this size, there should be people in the chain of command that could be contacted in case of an emergency. A board of directors, an owner, anyone in charge of keeping the security stations well-staffed.

But it was as if someone had gotten to them first. Every person they'd been able to identify as a possible contact was conveniently unavailable. It was too much of a coincidence that they were all otherwise occupied right now, and it was making him anxious. At any moment, he expected an army of lawyers to charge through the front doors with a cease-and-desist order, ending his investigation before it had barely begun. It was just one of the many worries nagging at him as he entered the control room and went to speak with the technician on duty.

"What have you got for me?" he asked, stepping over to the command center.

Jeanine Robello was the lead officer working on the electronic systems, and she was an excellent choice for the job. Recommended by Mattie, the woman knew everything there was to know about the type of mainframes they were attempting to access. She stood as he greeted her, wiping sweat from her brow with the back of one hand before setting down a diagnostic device she had connected to the central computer.

"This place is well-protected, I can tell you that much," she said. "We've tracked down the system that controls the elevator and found that it's isolated on its own power grid. I hate to be the bearer of bad news, Detective, but it looks like the guy who was in here when you first arrived sabotaged everything. With the elevator not connected to any other systems in the building, it was pretty easy for him to take it out completely. As far as accessing the rest of the programs here, he's initiated a ton of encrypted safety measures to ensure we don't gain entry. The man was incredibly thorough, and I can't seem to get past his fail-safes; every time I make any headway at all, something else pops up and blocks me."

"What about the blueprints we downloaded from city records? Surely there has to be another way into the lower sections of this building?"

"You would think so," she said. "But those blueprints are all forgeries as far as I can tell. Sure, they show the lower floors of the facility in parts of the layout, ones that are supposed to be there, but this elevator and whatever's underneath it doesn't appear on any of the schematics. I don't know how they did it, but the areas we can't get to aren't even on record. Since it's all privately owned and built by outside contractors, there's really no telling exactly what's down there."

It was infuriating to be stymied this way when he felt like they were getting so close. But he wasn't even sure if the suspects had made it down to those unknown areas in the first place. As far as he could tell, nobody else had left the scene, so that would indicate they were still inside the building. Or had they perhaps left by some other means? Rubbing a hand across his lower jaw, he absently scratched at his whiskers while considering the problem.

As he stood there musing, Mattie walked in and held out a file. "Here are some additional reports on everything we've gathered over the last few days. Some of the lab results from the other crime scenes have started to turn up—it's all in there. I thought you should see these right away, sir."

"Thanks, Mattie," he said distractedly, taking the folder and running his thumb along the crease of the spine. There had to be something else he could do to further the case along, but it seemed he was at an impasse here. With a heavy sigh, he waved the computer tech back to work and then cracked open the files to take a closer look. After flipping through several pages, he suddenly knew what he needed to do.

"You guys keep at it," he said, tucking the folder under one arm. "I have to go check on some things. If anything further develops while I'm out, you can reach me on the radio or my cell phone. And let me know as soon as you get the elevator up and running again. We're on borrowed time here. That egghead down at the station has lawyers, and as soon as he can get them rousted out of bed, we're going to have all kinds of legal difficulties. Do what you can until I get back."

As they acknowledged his orders, he turned and walked away, heading toward the parking lot and his waiting cruiser.

Demitre didn't sleep much, and Jenkins was eternally grateful for his late-night habits. By the time he entered the man's apartment, it was well after midnight, and Lisell came to greet him in the living room as Demitre allowed him access.

"Are you okay?" she asked. "You look awful!"

"Long night," he replied. "Why aren't you resting? It's very late."

She crossed her arms, rubbing her elbows a little as she hugged herself. "I couldn't sleep," she confessed. "I've been too worried about you and everything else that's going on. Demitre's been monitoring things on the police band and also using the cameras to try and keep an eye on you and your team, but we haven't gotten much information out of it. What's happening down there, Dan? We heard that you captured some of the crime bosses but nothing more after that."

Searching her face, he studied her features like a starving man seated at a banquet. He tried to shrug off the resulting rush of overpowering emotions, to explain them away as the by-product of too much work and too little sleep. But his heart told him otherwise. Now was not the time for such wistful yearnings; he had important work to do.

"We're currently trying to get past an encrypted computer system and a network of sabotaged power grids," he explained. "Once we got inside, we found that the suspects had either fled the scene or taken the one elevator that's not on any of the building's schematics down to a presently unreachable level of the building. I have a team analyzing the problem, but it's slow going. A scientist by the name of Jeffery Eastman put a lot of safeguards in place, and now we can't seem to get anything back up and running."

"I could maybe assist you with that, Dan," Demitre said, "but I've dug up some other information that I think you should look at first." Motioning him over to the desk, he gestured at the computer's main screen.

"I found out about the building owners you asked me to look into," he said. "It looks like they came here a few years back to establish a business presence in the city, and that's when the store you think may be a temple was built. According to my research, they were members of the Minamoto clan, a very prestigious Japanese family with strong ties to the nobility." Reaching down, he toggled a few keys on the keyboard, bringing up pictures on the screen with some accompanying charts and graphs. "What you see here is the main couple who led their branch of the family to America. They were shrewd business partners, smart, educated, owned a lot of high-profit ventures. These charts detail their steady rise in power and monetary gains here in our area. But it's not just that; they were also philanthropists, donating millions to programs designed to help those less fortunate."

Jenkins was intrigued, in spite of his exhaustion. "What happened to them?" he asked.

"I don't know," Demitre admitted. "Everything I've been able to dig up so far shows they simply disappeared. As there were no reports filed with the police, the whole thing seems to have been swept under the rug. In fact, the cover-up is so extensive that I can't even locate anyone who ever worked for them. Dan, I think we may have a mob connection here. If this family was amassing wealth and influence within the city, the Garganos would most certainly have wanted a piece of it. After their disappearance, all the properties and wealth they'd accumulated got funneled into dummy corporations, and these companies can all be traced back to the Gargano crime syndicate. I think they may have been taken out by Luciano when they refused to play ball with him."

"So what about this herbal shop then?" Jenkins asked. "Why board it up? Could it actually be a shrine, do you think?"

"The shop was not a money-making venture," Demitre said. "In fact, it never made any profits at all. Probably one of the reasons why the Garganos didn't try and keep it open. But the Minamoto's are well-known followers of Shintoism, and many of their ancestors are said to have gained kami status simply from leading exemplary lifestyles. So, if this couple brought some of these ancestral spirits with them to install in a new shrine, then I think that isolated herbal shop would have been the ideal place for it."

Jenkins thought for a moment, fingering the files he carried under one arm. The pieces were all starting to fall into place. Pulling out the folder, he rifled through it, then selected a report, scanning over its contents before handing it to Demitre. "Here's the information we got back from the labs on blood and hair samples found in the alleyway behind the warehouse. That alley is also right next door to the shop we now think is the hidden Shinto shrine. The name on the DNA report is real familiar; I think I remember the guy from a few years back. Can you run a quick search?"

"Sure," Demitre said, taking the page and then laying it out on his desk. Sitting down, he made a few entries on his keyboard, pulling up data on the main screen. "Here it is: one Charles Winston Murphy. He made a report at the police station about three years ago. His daughter was raped and murdered at his apartment while he was passed out drunk. It says here that the crime was gang-related, but the cops never caught any of the suspects—there wasn't enough info to go on, and they never got around to arresting anyone, even though they had plenty of DNA samples to prove who did it. Apparently, he was left as the child's sole guardian after his wife died sometime before that."

"What more can you find on the net?" Jenkins asked. "Does anything else come up as far as his history before all that happened?"

Demitre let his fingers dance across the keys, scanning through blocks of data and correlating information. "I'll be damned," he exclaimed after a few moments. "This guy was a highly decorated war veteran. Looks like he did multiple tours of duty and received several commendations, ultimately obtaining an honorable discharge for wounds taken in battle. The guy was a regular hero! What the hell was he doing in an alleyway behind that old shop?"

Jenkins rubbed his chin, thinking things through. Then, leaning forward, he placed his fists on the desk while scanning through the information on the monitor. "Now pull up what you got on that doctor. You know, the one who was running the abortion clinic just across the alleyway from the shrine."

Demitre's fingers flew across the keys again, and new blocks of data appeared. Jenkins grunted in surprise. "Look there," he said, pointing a finger at the screen, "this guy was working in a privately funded lab uptown before he got drummed out by his fellow colleagues. Something about unethical research into stem cell regeneration and tissue modification. And all his work seems to be related to using embryonic cells from human fetuses."

"What of it?" Demitre said dismissively. "A lot of scientists get shut down for delving into areas of research that are morally distasteful to their peers and other associates."

"Yeah, but this one wound up owning an abortion clinic across the alleyway from our shrine," Jenkins pointed out. "And according to your research, he got the funding for that clinic from the Gargano family, correct?"

"That's true, but I still don't see what you're getting at."

Straightening up from the desk, Jenkins collected his thoughts, putting things together. "We got a guy here who works for the Gargano family, whether he knows it or not; anyone taking their money is on the payroll. So, I think if we searched that abortion clinic, we might find a private lab, probably hidden underneath it or something. A place I'd wager he was using to continue his forbidden research, research the Garganos must have had an interest in seeing completed. You mentioned that the day after the apartment fire, this guy went missing and the clinic closed down. But then he shows back up, running around with our prime suspects. That's too much of a coincidence for me to overlook. My bet is that the mob probably killed him the night before."

"Killed him?" Demitre scoffed. "He was just here a few hours ago, and he didn't look dead to me. In fact, he looked great. Fancy suit, brand new shoes. He looked like a million bucks."

"Maybe so, but we got a war veteran whose blood and hair are all over a couch in that alley behind the shrine, and we got the wife of a corrupt cop who went missing in a mysterious fire on the very same night. Neither body was ever recovered," Jenkins said. "This shrine, these kami spirits, I think they did something to these people while they were dying—all three of them. Look at it this way: Resario had a long history of being abusive, so he probably beat his wife half to death and then set that fire to cover it up. We also got a whole bunch of dead gangbangers in a warehouse just down the block from the alley where we found Murphy's blood, all killed by insects that we know The Loathing can control.

"And in addition to that, we got dirty cops getting the life sucked out of them by this Love Leach character. It all adds up. What if The Loathing is Charles Murphy and the Love Leach is Florence Resario? Who would have a better reason to kill dirty cops than her? And the war hero's daughter was brutally raped to death by gangbangers. More than enough incentive to start taking them out, which is what he did the very same night. Joining forces with these kami spirits would have given them all enough power to enact revenge on their enemies, so maybe they made some kind of deal. Who knows? But what I just can't figure is why he stole those files from the hospital?"

Demitre had the good graces to look sheepish. "Well, I can help you out there," he muttered, staring down at his hands. "He needed to know about some doctors that used to work at Mercy General. I bet if we looked it up, they'd be the same ones who treated his wife before she died." He paused a moment, gathering his thoughts, then glanced back up at Jenkins before continuing. "That's probably one of the main reasons why The Loathing chose to hit the labs where your fellow officers are right now; I told him the doctors, not to mention those criminals, were all there at the same time.

"And since we know those labs are owed by the Gargano family, it's possible that these doctors transferred there because they're also indebted to the mob, right? And if this discredited scientist who owned the abortion clinic got taken out by Luciano's men, it would give him a reason to want revenge against organized crime then, wouldn't it? While they were here, he did claim that he was the one destroying the mob's businesses. In fact, he was practically bragging about it and got pretty upset when he found out the Garganos covered it up so well that he didn't get any press coverage."

Jenkins was nodding in agreement. Even though it didn't make much sense as to how they were all resurrected on the same evening, the fact that they were currently destroying the criminal elements in the city fit in well with what he'd learned from the old priest. He'd said that the kami were trying to reestablish a harmonious balance and eliminating the most disruptive elements in town seemed like the perfect way to achieve that. Also, the missing family who'd once owned the shrine was most likely dead, and now their ancestral spirits were righting that wrong as part of the package. And all of it led back to the Garganos. They had a hand in every part of it, not to mention the fact that their influence was the strongest negative factor in the whole area. It was the one thing tying everything else together. A light went off in Jenkins' head.

"I don't think that these kami spirits, or whatever the hell they are now, are even in the lower section of that lab anymore," he said. "And neither is Luciano. There must be an escape tunnel, one that we failed to locate. It's too late now to try and find the exit, but I can already guess where they're heading; they'll be hitting the Gargano estates next. It's where Luciano is sure to go to ground, so they'll have to follow him there if they still want to take him out. I'd stake my life on it."

Gazing down at Demitre, he decided what needed to be done. "Look, I know that I should try and stop them from going after Luciano," he said, "but the city is more important. I have to contact that priest and tell him what we've found. He's going to need my help getting into the boarded-up building that houses the shrine. If he can do this cleansing ritual, then maybe it will appease these spirits long enough to get them to leave the city alone."

"And I'm going with you." Lisell had come to stand beside him, hooking her arm through his as she stared up at him. Her facial expression left no room for argument; she was determined, and he didn't have the heart to tell her no.

Pulling out his phone, Jenkins got in touch with Mattie and gave her detailed instructions on what to do while he was gone. It was the middle of the night, but something told him that the old priest would still be up and waiting for them.

It was time to perform this ritual and put these kami back where they belonged, once and for all.

-41-

She took a soft cloth from the basin of cool water and once more sponged it across Charlie's heated brow as he lay on the cot in the foreman's office. His flesh was not like that of a regular man: it was hard and horny, pebbled like that of a crustacean, and colored a reddish hue not unlike his sprawling, burgundy cloak. It wasn't clear to her if this was normal for him, and her unfamiliarity with his altered anatomy only made her worry all the more. It didn't seem like he was coming out of the comatose state he'd fallen into before they'd breached the doors to the escape tunnel. His one good eye was closed while the other socket seemed to have healed over with something very much like a scab but subtly different.

Abraham had assured her, over and over again, that he could sense Charlie's own body was continuing to repair the horrible damage from the shotgun blast. Yet even so, she still had her doubts. This kindhearted man, who'd made her laugh while delighting her with his compelling stories, was much like a father figure to her now. Not like her real father, who'd been a drunken, uncaring brute, but like the father she'd always dreamed of having. He couldn't die, he just couldn't! Sighing, she thought back to their escape, wondering if she could have done anything differently.

After Charlie's collapse, Abraham had smashed through the doors barring the way out of the underground complex. It had not been easy; they'd been twice as thick as the first ones he'd opened and set more deeply into the walls. But once they'd moved past them, they'd found themselves in a huge loading area with trucks and offices like those found in an industrial warehouse. There were storage rooms as well, crammed from floor to ceiling with mysterious crates, all wrapped and ready for transport, but they'd wasted no more time on exploring.

Appropriating one of the trucks after finding keys in a nearby office, they'd followed the tunnel up and out of the shipping area to a hidden exit on the outskirts of town. Abraham had noticed they were close to the military base, so they'd spent a few hectic moments plotting a course around it, a heading which had led them toward the coast. Luckily, Simon had been able to guide them while Charlie was incapacitated. He'd taken control of the insectile swarms while his father was out of commission, and once they'd reached the ocean, had led them through a system of old drainage pipes, which eventually let out into the abandoned mining facility. Once there, Abraham had helped get Charlie situated before leaving to attend to some personal matters of his own.

She wet the rag again, sponging it carefully over Charlie's face while mourning the loss of his wise counsel. Her powers told her there was an ongoing buildup of the types of men she was meant to harvest; their collective emotions called out to her, tempting her with unsavory wants and desires. But without Charlie's minions to scout for them, and his friend Demitre to help them strategize, they couldn't go on the offensive, at least not yet. They would need all of their combined strength in order to overcome what was waiting for them now.

But ever since she'd failed to detect the two men guarding the escape tunnel, she'd been doubting her own prowess. If their enemies had somehow come up with a way to block emotions, she wouldn't be able to bring their fondest memories to the foreground of their thoughts. And without being able to do that, she had no way to siphon away their love and positivity, thereby causing them to beg for the sweet mercy of death. She would need to find other ways to eliminate her targets now, different from the methods she was currently using, and that thought terrified her. Since losing control at the lab, she'd been worried about her ability to constrain the demons raging within her. Plus, she secretly feared something else, something she didn't even want to admit to herself—she had loved every minute of their brutal attack. Giving into their twisted desires had made her feel more alive than she'd ever felt since dying, causing her to long for the experience again, like a drug addict jonesing for her next fix.

"How's he doing?" Abraham asked, interrupting her dark brooding as he walked through the open door. His attitude was as solicitous as ever, but she sensed there was something more going on with him. She just couldn't put her finger on what that could possibly be.

"About the same," she replied. "This scab over his eye seems strange, though. Are you sure it's normal for what he's going through?"

His knitted brow betrayed the concern he felt as he crossed the room, kneeling down next to the cot. Then, placing his finely boned hands on either side of Charlie's face, he went into what appeared to be a meditative trance. After a few moments, his pale eyes fluttered open again, and he gazed at her with a sigh of relief.

"He's going to be just fine," he said. "The energy I expended to increase his own metabolism has promoted new tissue growth and helped to repair the injury at an unusually rapid rate. That's why I think he fell unconscious; his body needed all of its resources to speed the recovery along. Frankly, I was surprised to see him up and about again so quickly. There was such a tremendous amount of internal damage; it's a miracle he survived at all, let alone made it as far as he did before keeling over. He must have been functioning on sheer willpower alone. . . if you think about it, it's really quite impressive."

"It was foolish of me to not realize the danger we were in," she lamented. "If I hadn't been so distracted, I might have sensed those men gathering on the other side of that door. It makes me feel in some way responsible."

Abraham raised his hand, cupping the side of her semi-corporeal face and then rubbing his thumb lightly across her shimmering cheek. His touch was warm and gentle, sending sensual thrills shivering through the rest of her electrified body. "It wasn't your fault," he murmured. "None of us were expecting goons to be waiting on the other side of that door. There was really no way any of us could have known Luciano and his cohorts had sent their bodyguards away from the conference room. You can't blame yourself for something we had no control over."

She closed her eyes for a moment, leaning into his caress and relishing the comfort of his touch. For some reason, it made her feel safe again, made her feel more alive. Almost as much alive as she'd felt when using the demon's power to destroy those guards. With a start, her eyes flew open, staring wonderingly into his own. Could the attraction she felt somehow be the key to regaining the pieces of her fading humanity? His gaze was forthright and lingering as he continued to stroke her cheek, and suddenly they were leaning toward each other slowly, like in a dream.

"Water. . ."

Charlie's muttered appeal broke the spell as they both turned to look down at him. Abraham immediately got up to pour him a glass, and a rush of heat moved through her as their intimate moment ended. Trying to regain her composure, she reached over, grasping Charlie's hand with a small, reassuring squeeze.

"You're awake!" she said brightly. "How are you feeling?"

"Like I have been hit by a truck," he grumbled. "How long have I been out?"

"Most of the night," she told him, trailing her fingers lightly across his forehead. It felt like he was finally cooling down a bit.

"We have to get moving," he said, attempting to sit up. "There is something big happening, something that requires our immediate attention."

She tried to press him back down, but he persisted, swinging his legs over the side of the cot as he leveraged himself upright. Abraham handed him the water as Simon came whizzing through the open door, buzzing happily around them. Charlie sat for a moment, studying them over the rim of the glass while he drained it. Then, clearing his throat, he set the empty cup down on the floor.

"My children have been watching while I was incapacitated, and the images I am now receiving are not good," he said. "Luciano has teamed up with General Anderson from the base outside the city, and military units have been digging in over at a large estate located uptown. It looks like we may be facing an all-out war, and one that will be difficult, if not impossible, for us to win, especially without causing more civilian casualties."

"What are you saying?" Abraham exclaimed. "Do you doubt our abilities?"

Charlie stood, favoring his friend with a look of mild reproach. "It is not our abilities I am concerned with. It is the advanced weaponry being used against us that I am worried about. Those men, the ones guarding that door, they had armor that bent the light around them, rendering them invisible, and self-contained electrical fields that repelled both my children and your embryos. Their minds were even shielded against Flo as well. Combine all that with the substances being fired at us, those streams of liquid freon and tar; how do we fight against whole squads of these men if they are enhanced and armored like the two we were barely able to overcome? How do we defeat ground troops armed with the same weapons that almost took us out twice in a row now? No, my friends, I do not doubt our abilities, much less our resolve. It is the power being brought against us that frightens me. Besides, just look at what a single bullet has done to my eye!"

Reaching up, he pulled at the puckered wad of tissues covering his right socket. As Abraham stepped in to try and stop him, he brutally ripped the scab from his face, exposing the newly formed section of carapace beneath it. The spongy epidermal layer appeared bright red and angry like a boiled crab. And as they stared on in shock, a fragile, semi-translucent eyelid drew back, exposing a freshly minted ocular orb of luminescent green. His new eye was smaller than the other and slightly malformed, sending a chill racing through Florence as she gazed at it in horrified fascination.

"That one unexpected attack sidelined me for hours," he groused, "and even now, I still feel sluggish and disorientated. I cannot simply regrow parts of my own anatomy every time I am wounded. My skin is tough, yet even I am not fully bulletproof!"

Abraham cleared his throat, unsuccessfully trying to hide a smug smile. "I, ah, sort of took care of that for you, Charlie," he offered, waving his hand off to one side like a showman introducing the next act. As they both glanced in the direction indicated, a reddish-brown panoply of armor appeared, hovering in the air, looking almost like the type of plated suit an ancient Japanese warlord might wear. "I can't make you invulnerable," he continued, "but this will protect against most firearms, as well as both blunt and bladed attacks. I modified it to fit your body and fashioned it from hardened skin cells collected from my own private reserve. It's much like the one I wear, but a lighter version that's more fully articulated so it won't slow you down. Would you care to try it on?"

When Charlie nodded enthusiastically, Abraham waved his hand once more, and the armored suit flowed through the air to cover his friend's body in waves of overlapping plates. The top half of the helmet's face mask had clear, hardened membranes protecting the eyes and twin horns jutting up from the forehead while the lower half was set in a fierce grin. The overall effect was stunning to behold, especially with the folds of his cloak billowing out around him. Simon whirred through the air to settle into his accustomed place on the left forearm, somehow completing the ensemble. Striking a dramatic pose, Charlie glanced over at her.

"How do I look?" he inquired playfully.

She'd never seen anything like it before, and his apparent return to high spirits, no matter how fleeting, was like a balm to her troubled soul. "You look amazing!" she exclaimed, then ran over to give him a fierce hug. He seemed a little taken aback at first, but then wrapped an arm around her briefly before she disengaged. Spinning into a delighted pirouette, she laughed aloud.

"I was so worried," she admitted when she saw their startled expressions. "When you wouldn't wake up, I thought we'd lost you. It's just such a relief to see you well again!"

"It will take more than a blast from a shotgun to kill me," he said, the helmet's faceplate emulating his typical grin. "I am a tough old man, or had you not figured that out yet?"

Chuckling in amusement, she turned to Abraham, her fiery eyes shining with gratitude. "And you!" she said with mock severity, shaking a finger. "You'd better watch this 'old man' more carefully from now on! See that he doesn't come to any more harm, you hear me?" Softening her tone, she continued, "Thank you, Abe. What you've done for him. . . well, it really means a lot to me."

Crossing the space between them, she drew him into a warm embrace, kissing him lightly on the cheek. As she released him, she wondered if he too had felt the searing desire their brief physical contact had inflamed within her. If she could have blushed, color would be staining her cheeks by now. Instead, she simply grinned ruefully, then winked. It was satisfying to watch the heat she'd so recently felt rise up to darken his own features as he favored her with a small, bemused smile of his own.

"Well, now that I am somewhat more impervious to gunfire, let us continue with our preparations for war," Charlie interrupted, regaining their attention. "Simon here tells me that the newest members of our family have assembled just outside and that they wish for us to inspect their battle readiness. Shall we go and attend this showing of our combined military strength?"

Florence exchanged a confused glance with Abraham and they parted to make room as Charlie strode between them, heading out the open front door. As they turned to follow, they both froze in the entranceway, her hand instinctively reaching for Abe's as they stared out over the stunning sight displayed before them.

Arrayed along the ground, and covering the exposed surface of every building, was a plethora of enormous insectoids. They were formed up in parade ranks, and their uncountable multitudes extended back further than the eye could see. Simon, his brown and black carapace shining resplendently in the overhead lights, launched himself from Charlie's arm, landing before this great horde of waiting warriors. Once grounded, he then began pacing back and forth in front of them like a four-star general inspecting his troops.

And at the very back of this swarm of newly minted soldiers stood an elegantly terrifying entity larger than all the rest. Its slender, high-crested head nearly topped the surrounding buildings while the long, spindly legs holding it upright made it almost as tall as a man. Yet even as frightening as this creature appeared, she was still obviously their queen, albeit as alien a queen as anyone had ever imagined.

Standing before his amassed children, Charlie turned to them, spreading his arms wide. "Behold!" he cried. "Our army stands ready, and they eagerly await my commands! Shall we take the war to our enemies and finally, for once and for all time, wipe them from the face of the Earth?"

Gazing out over this incredible amount of massed arthropods, Florence was stupefied. But Charlie seemed to have regained his confidence now that he'd witnessed the collected might of their new forces. At her nod of stunned acquiescence, and Abraham's more prosaic wave of a hand, Charlie turned back and gave the order to march.

Filling the air with clouds of deadly intent, the terrible host took to the wing, swirling into tightly controlled patterns that periodically blocked out the lights of the cavern, dappling them all in flickering, sporadic shadows that foretold of their enemies' imminent destruction.

-42-

Luciano was no stranger to confrontation, but like most of the rich and affluent, he'd had a danger room built into his main residence in case of emergencies. Yet the one he'd installed was more like a nuclear fallout shelter than just a simple hidden area where you could seek safety from unexpected threats. Located deep beneath his luxurious mansion, it had state-of-the-art technology, extensive living quarters, and a large stockpile of supplies. It was because of these features that he'd chosen this complex of ultramodern, hi-tech rooms for his current base of operations.

There was no doubt in his mind that they'd be coming for him. Their failed attempt on his life had shown him that, and he knew they would never give up until he was dead. So he had prepared accordingly. The troops stationed outside were ready for action, and they had the support of well-placed artillery units. Not only that, but he'd also been able to access his labs throughout the remainder of the previous evening, giving him enough time to upgrade many of the soldiers he'd conscripted from Anderson's military base.

Originally, he'd planned on drawing his adversaries away from Harlson Medical while he funneled his forces back in to be converted by Eastman and the rest of the scientific team. But as it turned out, the forward scouts had reported that his enemies had already fled the tunnels in a stolen delivery truck, escaping the lab complex shortly after he'd left there himself. They must have taken damage from the two soldiers he'd sent to discourage them, which was a fortuitous turn of events. All he had to do was spring his top scientist from a holding cell downtown, and then they'd been able to proceed with his plans unchallenged.

It had been problematic getting Eastman away from the authorities but not nearly as impossible as it had initially seemed. There was nothing they could really charge him with, so they weren't able to hold him once the lawyers arrived. Getting the other crime lords released would take additional effort, but he'd sent his lieutenants out to meet with their subordinates, ensuring that the peace would be held until he could manage it. And while his labs had technically been designated a crime scene, the attorneys he'd called in had simply converged on the police station in droves, cutting through the red tape with a practiced ease. It was their legal wranglings that had sprung Eastman and cleared the way for the overnight conversion of his remaining troops. With most of his best lawyers having been killed by the Leach, he'd had to do a bit of outsourcing to hire more, but his resources had always stretched worldwide, with access to operational funds that were nearly limitless. Being wealthy and connected did have its privileges.

These thoughts, amongst many others, swirled through his mind as he sat at the desk in his operational headquarters, watching the security footage of his troops digging in outside. It looked like a war zone out there, the pale light of the rising sun slowly revealing the blockades and trenches, illuminating the military units and ordnance which had been brought in throughout the early morning hours. And that was as it should be since the whole area was soon to become one.

Glancing up, he noted that the chamber beyond his office was now pleasingly filled with the technicians he'd hired for this operation, all busily manning dozens of other monitoring stations facing a huge wall covered with multiple display screens. The whole facility, with its bustling personnel and top-of-the-line computers, reminded him of the mission control center at NASA, and it was this very aesthetic that he'd originally intended when having the underground complex designed. No one would ever dare to threaten him while he was enthroned here, and the resources he'd stockpiled would make quite certain that he could resist any form of attack almost indefinitely. Redirecting his attention back to the smaller screen on his desk, he tapped a few buttons on the console, opening up a channel to Anderson's headset.

"General," he said, "is everything ready?"

"About as ready as it's going to get, you crazy lunatic!" came the acerbic response.

Luciano let the slight pass unanswered for now; Anderson was under a great deal of pressure and did not agree with many of the preparations being made. He had allowed himself to become lax with regard to the proper levels of respect that were owed, but they would sort that all out later. Now was not the time to castrate a man who would soon be leading his forces into battle.

"Good," he replied instead. "Make sure you have the front of the building covered with the fumigation tents like I instructed. We need to get the insecticides pumping into those rooms as soon as possible. Our adversaries should be arriving shortly, and I don't want them entering those areas until I'm ready. I still don't know how they were able to track my movements last night, but I'm certain that they're somehow watching us even now. You should be expecting an attack at any moment."

"Bugs and witchcraft!" Anderson scoffed. "This is all completely ludicrous, you know that, right? How the hell am I supposed to fight bugs and witchcraft? My men are trained for modern global warfare, not this trumped-up, supernatural horseshit!"

"Easy, my friend," Luciano soothed. "When they get here, the skies will be filled with so many insectile swarms that their unending multitudes will block out the sun. And once that happens, you shall finally see what my enemies are truly capable of. You'll have to take out The Loathing first, and then his arthropodal assault will surely dissipate. He likes to hang back and direct his forces from afar, so you may have to advance on his position in order to fully engage.

"The Love Leach, however, is a much deadlier foe; she drains the life from her victims with a centralized electrical discharge, so your men will have to be wary and avoid getting within close proximity. Let my special units handle her while you focus your efforts elsewhere.

"Which brings us to Doctor Abraham Orson. He manipulates resurrected fetuses and blobs of living protoplasm, so feel free to fire everything you've got at him until his minions are fully depleted. He'll need to get in close for his attacks to have any real effect, so I want you to take him alive. Make sure your soldiers are instructed to capture him unharmed after his powers are neutralized. Do we understand each other, General?"

"If it's really going to be that simple, then why the hell do you need an army?" Anderson asked. "This is insane! We've got hundreds of soldiers out here with a shit-ton of equipment, and for what? An old man, a little girl, and an effeminate doctor? You've completely lost touch with reality, do you know that?"

Striving to push his rising anger back down, Luciano took a long, deep breath, gritting his teeth while calming himself enough to reply. This was an inopportune moment to start an altercation with the leader of his ground troops, but after this was all over, he intended to make an example of Cooper T. Anderson. Oh, yes—he would pay dearly for his insolence! "Need I remind you," Luciano grated, "that this 'little girl,' as you so call her, has single-handedly taken out over half of the local police force? Her powers are so vast that we don't even yet know their full extent! And as far as the doctor goes, keep in mind that he easily destroyed an entire building filled with my top mafioso, all within a matter of minutes. Not to mention that this 'old man,' as you refer to him, controls millions upon millions of voracious, bloodthirsty insects. Enough insects, in fact, that he has successfully used them to clear out the entire west side of town! So you can rest assured that this will indeed be a hard-fought battle, and one that will need all of our combined resources if we are to succeed. And tell me, General, what do your military textbooks say about winning these types of engagements?"

"Though an obstinate fight may be made by a smaller force, in the end it must be captured by the larger one," Anderson quoted grudgingly.

"That is exactly right!" Luciano enthused. "Now, prepare yourself for a difficult confrontation and be ready to engage with the enemy the moment they arrive. I have more detailed instructions for you, but you'll get those in a confidential mission briefing here shortly. Once received, follow these directives unflinchingly while carrying out your duties and we shall surely grind our opponents back into the dust they sprang from."

"You better be right about this," Anderson grumbled. "We're going to be in enough trouble as it is when the Pentagon finds out about your little 'field exercise.' My superiors may have sanctioned this operation, but they have to answer to a higher authority, just like everyone else. We could have the Department of Homeland Security breathing down our necks out here at any moment."

"Let me worry about that," Luciano insisted. "You just focus on taking out our unwelcome guests as soon as they get here. Keep me posted as you continue with your preparations and I'll take care of everything else."

With that, he broke the connection, swiveling around in his chair and running a hand down the front of his newly designed tactical jumpsuit. He was ready for the next step in his plans, and although he did miss the style and comfort of his usual bespoke attire, these tight-fitting garments were an absolute necessity. There was a time for practicality, and that time was now.

There was one thing still bothering him, though, and it was the irrefutable fact that he had already failed. A great deal of time and additional expense had been put into obtaining Dr. Orson's discoveries for the family's exclusive use. His work with stem cells and tissue regrowth was beyond compare, light-years ahead of anything that other scientists were currently working on. Luciano's specific orders had been to make sure that Dr. Orson's research came to fruition, and then to procure all the relevant data as soon as possible. Now that Orson had somehow developed powers after his unfortunate accident, it would be nearly impossible to complete the matriarch's directives. After all, Orson's lab and all his scientific notes had been destroyed in the fire and were therefore irretrievably lost. But there had to be some way to convince the man that it was in his best interests to finish the work he'd started and then give the results over into Luciano's care.

Yet the more he considered the punishments that such an immense failure on his part were sure to bring, the more he realized that he no longer cared. This man, this self-important *figlio di troia* who now controlled forces beyond anyone's understanding, had made too many errors in judgment to be granted a reprieve. He'd killed Luciano's men, raided his properties, destroyed personal assets owned by Luciano himself. In short, he had made Luciano look like a fool, not only to the other local crime lords but also in front of the entire Gargano family as well.

It was time to teach the good doctor that his actions had dire consequences that could not be so easily evaded. Luciano's eyes took on a distant look as he considered all of the ways this trumped-up popinjay had wronged him. And there was one thing that became irrefutably clear to him in that exact moment—

Dr. Abe Orson must die.

-43-

They'd reached the old man's home in the early morning hours and found he had indeed been waiting for them. He said that he'd felt a change in the "harmonic energies" of the city and had known they'd be coming simply from that spiritual irregularity. Jenkins had no idea what he was talking about, but he took the explanation at face value. Soon afterward, they were speeding off to the boarded-up herbal shop with the priest and his grandson in the back of the unmarked squad car.

Now that they'd arrived at the location, Jenkins and Lisell were using crowbars to pry the boards off the doors as the priest and his young assistant assiduously cleaned the basin set just to the left of the entrance. Taking a break from wrenching on the tightly nailed obstructions, Jenkins studied the old man as the priest continued clearing the filth from around the bowl-shaped receptacle.

Currently, he was dressed in pure white robes with wide, flowing sleeves belted over loose trousers. In addition to that, he had on a black brimless hat with a bulbous, oval shaped protrusion sticking straight up from the back. This strange headdress also featured a wide, stiff tail that curved up, then trailed down behind him like the plumage of a bird of paradise. The peculiarity of the outfit fascinated Jenkins as he stood catching his breath.

He didn't know if the priest was truly legit or not, but right now he certainly looked the part. Whatever it was they were about to do inside this abandoned shrine, he sure hoped it would be a success; his city had been through enough, and right now Jenkins would take any help he could get, even if that help was in the form of a questionable religious ceremony. Shaking his head, he turned and got back to work, assisting Lisell as she pulled the remaining lumber away from the large double doors.

After a few more minutes of continuous effort, they had the entranceway fully cleared and began stacking the loose planks out of the way behind one of the stone lion-dogs guarding the front. The priest and his grandson had already removed the trash and rubble from the path and were now busily sweeping the length of it with brooms made from tightly bound strips of wood. Moving from left to right in a coordinated pattern, they progressed slowly down the walkway, the old man chanting some sort of mantra in his thick, Japanese dialect. The basin beside the door was spotless and filled with purified water now, with a bamboo dipper hanging from a hook at its side. Gazing up at the torii gates that soared above the path, Jenkins could almost imagine what the place must have looked like before the people who'd built it disappeared. It must have been one hell of a beautiful monument at one time. Then, wiping the sweat from his brow, he leaned against the nearest wall to await the completion of the ritualistic sweeping.

Once the priest reached the doors, he bowed, then spoke earnestly in his own tongue.

"My grandfather wishes you to know that we must purify ourselves before entering this place," the grandson translated. "Please follow our example at the *chozubachi*."

The boy, his own robes less intricate and looking more like a simple karate gi, first washed his left hand, then his right, deftly using the dipper from the side of the basin. Then he washed his face, briefly rinsing his mouth with water he'd dipped from the stone cistern. His grandfather waved them forward once his grandson was finished, and they both bent one at a time to copy the solemn procedure. After they'd completed this task, the old man followed their example, and then hung the bamboo dipper back on the hook when he was through. Turning to the doors, he reached into his belt and drew forth a wand and a pinch of something that looked like salt. Sprinkling the crystals before him, he began another singsong litany. It was soothing to the ear, and Jenkins found himself calmed by it.

Finally, after a lengthy amount of sonorous chanting, the priest reached over and opened the doors. If Jenkins was surprised that they weren't even locked, he hid it well as he followed the old man into the shadowy interior.

Once inside, his eyes slowly adjusted to the dim illumination coming from the early morning sunshine leaking in through the boarded-up windows. Now that he knew the retail sections were all a sham, he could see that they were arranged to look convincing enough to the untrained eye, yet were not actually integral to the overall aesthetics of the place. To the right was a sprawling indoor garden that took up a great deal of the main floor plan, and at its center stood a reflection pool with several simple pathways winding toward it through the overgrowth.

Light filtering down through a dirt-encrusted skylight speckled the water with intermittent rays of sunlight, creating a dazzling effect. And toward the back, next to the sealed-off exit where the couch in the rear alleyway had been pulled through, was a clutter of debris from where the roof had caved in. In the remaining sections off to the left, there were still bundles of herbs hanging from the rafters and rows of tidy shelves holding the remnants of assorted merchandise. The rest of the interior was spartan by comparison, the artistic simplicity of it still a fundamental part of the temple's age-old charm.

The priest spoke briefly to his grandson, bowing in their direction as he did so.

"My grandfather wishes me to ask you to please wait here," the boy said as he set down the large basket of supplies they'd brought from home. "We must continue to purify the temple, and he begs that you have patience as we do so."

Jenkins nodded in understanding, then respectfully gave a short bow to the elderly man. The priest's eyes lit with approval, and he returned the bow in kind before moving away into the area still hidden beyond the checkout counter. Jenkins spotted some sort of cording tied with multiple streamers back there, and the man followed this decoratively braided rope as he headed off into the shadows. The boy gave them a final bow before once more gathering up the heavy basket and then turning to follow.

As Jenkins felt Lisell's hand close around his own, he glanced down at her in pleased surprise. She smiled up at him and then snuggled in closer, sharing body warmth. It was cold this time of year, and now that the heat of their previous exertions was wearing off, she was probably chilled by the bite of late autumn air seeping through the cracks in the walls.

"Do you feel it, Dan?" she whispered after a moment.

Wrinkling his brow in thought, he tried to determine what she was talking about, but then suddenly realized that he did feel something besides just the cooler temperatures. All of his anxiety had faded away, leaving him with a sensation of inner peace. It reminded him of the contentment he'd found while resting in his mother's arms when he was only a small child. Taking a deep breath, he let it out slowly, enjoying the novelty of being stress-free for the first time in days. It felt truly amazing.

"Yes," he murmured in response to her query. "For some reason, I'm very relaxed here. It's like I can let go of all my worries and feel safe for a change. I know I still have much to do in order to save the city, but right at this very moment it's as if all of that is outside me, like I'm finally centered and whole again, free from all concerns. And. . . well, to be honest, it feels just like being loved by someone who truly cares about me."

Licking her lips nervously as a rosy color spread across her cheeks, Lisell glanced away, seeming a bit flustered. Then, shaking her head a little, she turned back, meeting his curious gaze squarely. "It's funny you should put it like that," she said. "I feel the same. And although I'd like to think it's just another effect of the shrine, now I'm not so sure I can believe that anymore. . ."

His heart was racing as he stared down into the liquid depths of her eyes. Could she truly mean what he thought she was saying? It seemed too good to be true. At a loss for words, he simply stood there, captivated by her beauty and hoping she could sense what he was feeling without him having to voice it aloud. They stayed that way for a while, the peacefulness of the shrine wrapping them in layers of blissful harmony.

After an immeasurable amount of time had passed, the boy came back, gaining their attention by respectfully clearing his throat. The spell broken, they both turned to see what he had to say.

"My grandfather wishes you to know that he has found the *haiden* and the *honden*. They are below, yet the *haiden*, which I am to tell you is the place of worship, has been destroyed. We have found that the false cellar in this building was at some point turned into what looks like a medical facility, and this room has caved in on the *haiden*, burying it in damaged equipment and shattered glass. There is no way now that we will be able to completely cleanse this area."

"Will that prevent you from performing the ritual to appease the kami spirits?" Jenkins asked.

"No," the boy answered, "it is a setback, but the *honden*, which is the sanctuary where the kami live, is still intact. You are not allowed in there; it is only for priests who commune directly with the spirits. But I am to escort you to a place just outside of this holy chamber, where you are to await the completion of the ritual. Even now, my grandfather prepares the *honden* for the final *norito*, or formal prayers, that he must intone to invoke the kami. He bids me to tell you that they may not answer—they will still be greatly angered by the desecration of their shrine and the loss of their family members. But I am to also inform you that my grandfather thinks they will want to hear us out. He believes they will desire to instruct us on how we may best serve them in restoring a harmonious balance to the rest of the city."

Jenkins remained somewhat skeptical, but he couldn't argue with the fact that there was definitely some sort of supernatural influence going on, something that had given certain people the ability to do extraordinary things. Lost in thought, he kept ahold of Lisell's hand as they followed the boy deeper into the shadowy interior.

Walking along the streamer-covered ropes, they were led toward a beautiful set of stairs hidden at the back of the building. Hand worked natural woods prevailed here, making it look as if every piece of the stairwell's construction had been fitted together with delicate precision. The whole area gave off a pervading feeling of peace and tranquility as they passed through the arched entranceway and then started down the wide, well-swept staircase. As they came to the first landing, Jenkins paused, his eyes going wide at the destruction he found just through the doorway to his right. Lisell gasped aloud when she peeked around him, horrified by the abundance of broken, twisted wreckage littering the room. After experiencing the serenity that the rest of the shrine exuded, the very wrongness of the *haiden's* destruction grated on the nerves.

As he studied the piles of broken equipment and glass, Jenkins realized something. "This must be the remains of Dr. Orson's hidden lab," he said quietly.

"What. . . I. . . I don't understand," Lisell whispered.

"Look there," he said, pointing. "There's a doorway you can barely see up there at the very back of the caved-in room. The abortion clinic is off in that direction, so I'm guessing this false cellar was once taken over by Orson for his clandestine research. Having his clinic next door, while also having access to the lower level of this building, must have been ideal. The experiments that got him kicked out of his cushy labs uptown were most likely still being performed down here. That is, at least until the night he was murdered. Something must have happened between him and the Garganos, something that got these labs destroyed and himself killed in the process."

"That seems pretty far-fetched," Lisell responded doubtfully.

"Well, I have to try and make sense of whatever bizarre evidence we stumble across. But I'm betting that if I sent a team over to search the clinic next door, they would probably find the entrance to the tunnel that's on the other side of that doorway up there. If Dr. Orson was doing his research in that cellar, and it disturbed the sanctity of this temple, wouldn't that be enough for these kami spirits to take notice? The missing persons who we now think of as our other two suspects—that old war vet and the abused wife—lived right here in this same neighborhood as well. I'm beginning to think that they were given their powers at the same time, on the same night, right before they were all about to die. In fact, it's seeming more and more likely that these kami must have made a deal with them, binding them all into some sort of death pact. Theoretically, it fits in well with everything else we've discovered so far."

"Let's not get too far ahead of ourselves, Detective," she cautioned. "I respect your powers of deduction, and it does sound somewhat more plausible now that you've laid it out for me. But there has to be more to it than that, doesn't there? I'm withholding my opinion until after we see just what these kami have to say for themselves."

He nodded in agreement, warmed by her words as they continued after the boy who'd waited for them on the next level down. The rest of the way, now lit by beeswax candles, was a study in flawless woodworking techniques. As they reached the final landing, there was another huge archway with a couple of those stone lion-dogs standing guard on either side. The old priest stood before a set of beautifully carved doors, holding a stick covered in white streamers. As they approached, he bowed deeply, then spoke to his grandson. Afterward, the boy turned to translate.

"My grandfather wishes you to know that he will now begin the final part of the ritual. You are not to enter the *honden* for any reason. He wishes you to also know that you should meditate only upon positive thoughts while you wait. He will perform the ceremony with great care and reverence so that we may hope for a favorable reply from those kami who are enshrined within."

With that, the boy settled to the floor in a cross legged position, resting his hands on his knees while closing his eyes. The priest bowed to them once more, then turned, beginning a long, sonorous chant that filled the air with a rhythmic cadence.

Jenkins sat, folding his legs beneath him, then shifted into a relaxed posture while trying to think only good thoughts. All his remaining worries drained away in the presence of the inner sanctum, and he allowed himself to close his eyes, floating within this peaceful aura of languid tranquility.

-44-

None of them were tacticians, and that had Abraham worried. Even though Charlie had been a decorated war veteran, he'd never been in a position of command. And Florence was once a housewife who'd worked at a bookstore. So even though she had many good and practical ideas from all the reading she'd done, she was of little use in planning a full-scale attack. As for himself, he harbored no illusions that his brilliant mind was capable of coming up with sound battle tactics; he was a scientist first and foremost, and then, to a lesser extent, a doctor. His work had always revolved around the saving and bettering of lives, not in the taking of them.

So they'd chosen to move quickly to try and get ahead of their enemies while they were still digging in at the Gargano estate. The palatial mansion was situated up in Green Derry Hills, a section of the city that was populated solely by the rich and influential. Their houses, and the grounds they were built upon, were sprawling compounds well separated by huge tracks of land that dominated the upper east side of town. It was here they lived out their self-indulgent lives, many of them never even knowing they had a notorious mafioso living right in the heart of their gated community.

Charlie's insects had been able to feed them intel until the air filled with pesticides, effectively concealing the grounds. From the images provided, they'd learned that most of the men Luciano employed were equipped with hazmat or beekeeping suits to protect against potential bites and stings. Of the soldiers themselves, they had no idea what percentage would be wearing the new armor they'd contended with in the lab's lower levels. With this modified gear having the ability to bend light and fry insects with an electrical discharge, it was going to be difficult to defeat them, especially if they were also armed with those experimental weapons. The cylindrical backpacks held either fire, tar, or freon mixtures, all formidable deterrents against the team's supernatural attacks. Not to mention the tanks and other artillery units these men had backing them up. Any way you looked at it, the coming battle would be challenging.

Now Abraham and his companions stood hidden in a stand of trees near the back corner of the property, just outside the decorative wall enclosing the grounds. From their position, they couldn't see much—just the rooftops of the manor peeking up above the clouds of pesticides like the ramparts of some ancient medieval castle. Its eerie appearance in the watery light of midmorning sunrise, coupled with the nearness of their enemies, sent fresh chills of apprehension shivering down Abraham's spine.

"How are we going to accomplish this?" he asked, glancing over at his friends. "They've got the air saturated with poisonous fog and probably have those shield generators set up all over the place."

Charlie smiled, his lambent eyes shimmering from beneath the lenses of his new helmet. "Worry not," he said. "I have had millions of my burrowing minions working on the problem for the last several hours. Look there." He pointed at the gates standing open to their left. "The soldiers have not yet made it this far with their fortifications. They still have military transports going in and out, and their preparations are mainly focused on the opposite side of the house. Luciano is not in evidence, but I have had some reports that he retreated to a secure area deep within the bowels of his mansion, a place which cannot currently be reached by any of my scouts. It seems that they are leaving this one gate open until the last minute, although it is heavily guarded on all sides.

"I propose we wait a little longer, giving my children the time to finish burrowing, then launch a simultaneous attack. While my warriors pour from the earth, unaffected by the airborne pesticides, we will hit Luciano's combined forces with everything we have, breaking through to the main residence. Once inside, we will then have a tactical advantage and plenty of cover to work from. What say you to that?"

"It sounds pretty risky," Florence said doubtfully. "There are a lot of men just beyond those gates, and they have a ton of firepower. Plus, I'm having trouble sensing them; they must have the same mental shielding as the ones back at the labs. I've been trying to come up with an alternate method to utilize my powers, but the odds against us are overwhelming. Couldn't we find some other way to do this? Perhaps if we snuck in and somehow took control of the house to begin with?"

"No, that wouldn't work either," Abraham was forced to admit. "There's no way we'd be able to sneak past all of these troops without being seen. What we need now is some kind of diversion. But even then, how will we overcome so many soldiers once we're inside the perimeter? I can protect us from a lot of the gunfire, but I'm not sure my embryonic shielding can withstand a direct hit from one of those tanks."

Charlie waved a hand in the gate's direction. "Well, if we wait until the next transport vehicle is being driven through, we may be able to—"

Something within Abraham's peripheral vision tipped him off, some type of movement, or maybe just a feeling of imminent danger. Instinctively, he called his multiphasic shields into being, covering them all in a swirling array of interlocking barriers. These hardened skin cells were like a perpetually moving gyroscopic model of Earth's tectonic plates. Gunfire immediately ricocheted off them, accompanied by the sounds of men dropping from the surrounding trees.

It had been a very close thing, and Abraham was relieved his instinctive reaction to the perceived threat had been successful. A nimbus of energy surrounded Florence as she rose from the ground, her electrostatic bubble protecting them inside his swirling shields as Charlie hunkered down, placing one hand flat on the bare ground beneath them.

"Stay close," Florence cautioned him. "My aura should melt any stray bullets that penetrate your defenses."

It was hard to see through their shielding, but Abraham could sense most of the gunfire was coming from behind them. When he started to feel the cold of freon and the heat of flames as well, he realized that their assailants, hidden by the light-bending technology, had been waiting in the trees. As the intensity of their combined attacks increased, it forced Abraham to move, keeping his shields rotating and re-forming where the unrelenting assault was shattering or burning them away.

"The gate!" Charlie cried. "My burrowing children are almost to the surface beyond. If we can somehow get through that opening, we can coordinate a counterstrike as soon as they are in position beneath the soldiers inside!"

"Do you think that's wise?" Abraham shouted over the sounds of machine gun fire. "I feel as if they're pushing us in that direction on purpose; I believe we're being herded into a trap!"

"There is nothing else we can do!" Charlie said. "If we do not coordinate with my children, we will have no opportunity to fight our way out of this at all. The suppressive gunfire currently battering away at your shields leaves us no room to counter their efforts. Flo, can you get a bead on any of them? Perhaps eliminate a few to even up the odds?"

With her brow furrowed in concentration, she floated inside the radiant sphere now filling the space within Abraham's rotating skin barriers. "I'm trying," she said, "but there are just too many. The ones behind us I can't sense at all, and the ones in front are all mingled together. Their intertwining emotional output is confusing my senses."

"Well, we have to do something!" Abraham exclaimed as they were forced through the gate by heavy bursts of gunfire mixed with heat and freon blasts. "I can't hold this together much longer!"

Little by little, they were maneuvered into the open space just inside the wall. Through gaps in the rotating shields, he caught glimpses of their surroundings, and the view was not encouraging.

The lawn of the estate had been turned into a military encampment. Through wisps of rising pesticides, he saw machine gun nests and blockades covered in barbed wire placed in front of trenches filled with troops wearing protective armor. These obstacles were arranged in a semicircle facing the gate, with tanks and mortar units deployed behind them for support.

As Abraham and his companions were driven into the center of this cleared area, the rest of the soldiers opened fire, and his shields were suddenly being battered from all sides. They shuddered under the impact of a motor shell, and the explosion destroyed a huge section of his rotational defenses, nearly knocking them all to the ground. When the tanks began to target them, the hardened cells of his embryonic plating crumbled under the bombardment, coming close to utterly failing. Hit from all sides, with explosions rocking them to the core, Abraham experienced true fear for the very first time. He quickly realized they would die here if they didn't go on the offensive.

"Abraham," Florence growled low in her throat, "can you expand your shields outward, buy us some time?"

Refocusing his energies, he summoned even more of the protoplasmic material from the aether, layering it into a further extension of overlapping plates. These larger barriers he then pushed outward, the newly formed constructs rocking from the explosions and heavy gunfire. "I can only keep this up for another few moments," he told her, "so you better do something before my energies are spent. Charlie, what about your subterranean assault? Are they in position yet?"

"Just. . . a little. . . more time," his friend muttered, the burgundy cloak flowing around him like a living thing as he kept one hand placed flat on the ground.

It's too bad the air is filled with these pesticides, Abraham thought, *since we could sure use the help of Charlie's other swarms right about now.*

Then, his white robes flaring out from his heavily armored body, he stood tall at the center of the ring of whirling barricades, Charlie crouching at his feet while Flo rose higher within her sphere of electricity. Her energy appeared to be building, a pulsating sensation that sent shivery waves flowing across his skin, and she soon had them encased within a globe of blinding white power. As he concentrated on keeping his hardened skin cells regenerating endlessly under their enemy's attack, he became aware of something happening just outside of her shimmering orb of protection.

Winking into being all around them, hundreds of ice-blue roses with fiery hearts suddenly appeared. They spun through the air in a pattern almost mathematical in its execution, perfectly spaced apart and twirling in unison as they emitted a flurry of snowy particles. As he watched on in growing amazement, they began spinning more rapidly, the frozen, crystalline flakes causing the sphere surrounding them to resemble a giant snow globe.

"Charlie," she warned, stress coloring her trembling voice, "you better tell those children of yours to hurry it up."

Her bravery and fortitude were inspiring. Something in Abraham's heart turned over with a wrench, and suddenly he went on the offensive. If she could remain calm and find a way to fight the men now arrayed against them, then how could he do otherwise? "Make some room at about shoulder height, would you?" he asked, already putting his half-formed plan into action.

As the roses drifted apart, splitting into two halves of a spiraling globe, he pulled more embryonic cells out of the aether. Some of his bolder minions popped into existence then, their floating fetal bodies hovering around his head and watching with wide, unblinking eyes. With these strange interdimensional beings bearing witness, he worked the modified cells into hardened, spike-covered cysts.

When he was finished, he had a multitude of spinning burr-shaped nodules gyrating through the air around him, filling the gaps in Florence's divided sphere at about shoulder height. With the roses throwing off their wonderland of snowflakes from above and below his ring of protoplasmic projectiles, the inside of their shuddering shield barrier was now filled almost to bursting. And through it all, his outer protective plating continued to hold off the unrelenting attack of their enemies, shedding bullets and explosive rounds in a multilayered, self-regenerating canopy of steel-hardened flesh.

Just when Abraham thought he could hold it no longer, feeling as if he were at the very limits of his strength and abilities, Charlie shouted, "Now!"

Through the gaps in the spinning shield wall, Abraham saw the ground rise up, engulfing the soldiers on all sides. But on closer inspection, he found that it wasn't actually the ground at all; it was millions upon millions of minor bees, yellow jackets, and other varieties of burrowing arthropods that Abraham didn't even have names for. The generators protecting the troops suddenly fell into the open pits made by Charlie's forces, exploding as their dampening fields were destroyed by thousands of industrious ants chewing through the electrical wiring. The soldiers wearing the new armor were so overwhelmed by the sheer volume of the attack that their power cells overloaded. Now clearly visible within the wisps of smoke and pesticides, they stumbled around, covered from head to toe in hordes of Charlie's insectile minions. All of this Abraham was able to view within seconds, and as the gunfire and large caliber explosions ceased, he let the outer barrier of protective skin shields fall.

As soon as his shielding dissipated, Florence's whole body arched, and the deadly rotational array of ice-blue roses shot outward, accompanied by Abraham's heavier spiked balls of hardened skin cells. Their effect was immediate and quite devastating.

The men, no longer protected by the failed generators, as well as every other soldier currently in range, were torn to shreds by hundreds of flowery darts and cannonball like cysts. The battlefield devolved into a wasteland of screaming, twisted bodies, fountains of blood erupting from torn and mangled flesh. What's more, the wind from this released energy rushed outward from Florence like a hurricane, blowing the lingering pesticides away and clearing the deadly fog entirely from the field.

Charlie rose from his crouch, smiling at the carnage. "Now, my children," he whispered, raising his arms on high, "strike to the hearts of our enemies and wipe them from the face of the Earth!"

The daylight dimmed, and Abraham glanced up, momentarily startled by this unexpected pall of darkness. Filling the skies, their vast numbers blocking out the sun, were thousands of Charlie's newly spawned warriors, led by the gyrating form of an enraged Simon. These carnivorous insects were huge, even more massive than the giant cockroach himself, with double sets of wings like a dragonfly and tails tipped by a highly mobile stinger. Their crab-like pincers opened wide as they swooped down upon their unsuspecting victims like a half-starved murder of crows, tearing into the soldiers who were still struggling to survive. It was a bloodbath. Abraham had seen a lot of death in his lifetime as a doctor, but this was different. Here the destruction unfolded around them, blood and viscera filling the air along with the screams of wounded, dying men. It was brutally repellent yet, in a morbid way, also strangely satisfying.

"We should take out those tanks before they can find our range again," Florence warned, pointing a glowing finger toward the large vehicles in the distance. A man was sitting in the commander's cupola on top of the lead unit, fiercely gesturing while shouting at his remaining troops. The generators on that side of the field were still operational, protecting the man from the lesser insects under Charlie's command.

"Ah, General Anderson," Charlie murmured in grim undertones. "We meet again. . ."

With a wave of one hand, he sent a swarm of his warrior brood arrowing toward this man's position. Unaffected by the remaining generators, his new children blasted through the electronic defenses, immediately covering the general in a writhing blanket of biting, stinging insectoids. Completely overwhelmed, he sank down inside the tank as the rest of the swarm invaded the armored vehicles through every crack and crevice. Within seconds, they had ceased operating, accompanied by the terrified screams of the soldiers still trapped within. Rising even further into the air, Flo then extended her powers outward, blanketing the field with overlapping waves of vibrant energy.

With deftly refined control, she drew forth the remaining soldiers' innermost feelings of love and contentment, siphoning up the emotions from the forefront of their thoughts, then swelling in size with the memories she stole from them. The men still left alive, now bereft of all hope, cried out for release, begging for a death that none of them truly deserved. It was amazing to watch her work, and Abraham was in awe of it. This woman, this beautiful creature of light and shadow, was all that he could ever ask for and more, and his heart suddenly filled with an insatiable longing so boundless that his spirit soared.

Rising above him, her sphere blazed brighter than any star in the heavens. Her glorious image suffused his senses, eliciting such an overwhelming response that it brought tears to his eyes. Some of his awestruck wonder must have reached her then, must have spilled over as she funneled up the emotions of the dying soldiers. When her eyes widened in recognition of his desires, seeking him out, he knew she'd felt his wild passions on a deeper level than he'd ever intended. Yet he suddenly no longer cared—in fact, he *wanted* her to know. Returning her gaze through tears of jubilation, he openly invited her to explore the depths of his feelings, holding nothing back.

It was then that a sizzling beam of electromagnetic radiation struck her full in the chest, tearing a gaping hole through her body of light that was terrifying to behold. Her fiery eyes, only just beginning to brim with delight at the feelings she'd sensed from him, blazed with excruciating pain instead as she cried out in total anguish. Then her sphere of crackling energy caved in upon itself, sending out streamers of fragmented lightning and showering him with a multitude of sparks as it collapsed. Watching helplessly, he witnessed her body disintegrate from the inside out, her final screams of tortuous suffering echoing through the morning air, rending his soul with a torment so great that he nearly died along with her. After one final ripple of displaced electricity, she was gone, leaving him standing there in shocked desolation.

"Look out!" Charlie cried, suddenly barreling into him from behind.

Crashing to the ground, he tumbled end over end, rolling to a stop just in time to see Charlie hit by another burst of the same infernal energy. It blasted him backward, hurtling him across the clearing to slam up against the trunk of a tree just outside the gate. His minions took to the air in an agitated swarm, partially blocking out the sun as Charlie disintegrated, leaving nothing behind but a pile of smoldering burgundy material.

Twisting around, Abraham sought out the source of these attacks, his anger building to a point well beyond his control. There, just atop the tallest spire of the mansion's rooftops, a glint of steel betrayed the assassin's position. As Abraham enhanced his eyesight to zoom in on this new threat, he saw it was a man dressed in an elaborate suit of armor, a large bazooka-like weapon resting across one shoulder. Yet this new antagonist did not continue his attack, almost as if he were waiting to see what Abraham would do next.

Rising to his feet, Abraham swept his arms out to the sides. As he called upon all of his reserves of power, his white robes swirled around his armored body, the Japanese symbols sewn into them flaring with a spectral radiance. His pale eyes, glowing beneath the lenses of his helmet, glared at this new foe as a deep, all-encompassing rage filled him with an unquenchable thirst for revenge.

Whoever this man was, he had completely obliterated Florence, destroying her with extreme prejudice, and then extinguishing Charlie's life with the same chilling finality. If it hadn't been for his friend pushing him out of the way, Abraham would be dead right now as well.

This man had to pay, and he would pay dearly.

Raising his arms higher, he utilized his latent abilities, drawing protoplasmic materials from all across the countryside, ripping them from every storage facility and hospital in a far greater geographical radius than he'd ever dreamed possible. Through it all, his eyes stayed locked on his assailant, the simmering anger within him churning like a massive caldera reaching the point of imminent eruption. And as he stood there trembling, striving to contain the vast amounts of cellular matter he'd gathered, more troops suddenly came boiling out from around both sides of the Gargano estate. There were hundreds of them, followed by a number of tanks and additional artillerymen, and they all rushed toward him, an uncountable mass of deadly force intent upon only one thing—

The ultimate destruction of Abraham himself.

-45-

Luciano had watched the confrontation with mounting excitement, but then as the day wore on, this sensation had slowly eroded into an uncomfortable feeling of impending defeat. In the beginning, victory had seemed so assured, with all his carefully laid plans swiftly coming into fruition. In preparation for the battle, he had commanded the back gate to remain open—a tempting vulnerability that none could resist—while also ordering the most promising of his modified soldiers to lie in wait nearby. And his enemies had walked right into the trap like a bunch of ignorant rubes.

In fact, from the very first moment they'd stationed themselves outside his back wall, he'd considered them as good as dead. From the safety of his control room, he'd ordered the soldiers to start their assault, and that first salvo had forced the trio into the ambuscade awaiting them beyond the gates as planned. Everything had been going splendidly. . . at first. But then his opponents had somehow wrapped themselves in a whirling barrier of overlapping plates, which had quickly proven to be impervious to all forms of attack.

He'd then wondered if the adhesive weapons in his arsenal might not have been the better choice for this engagement. Perhaps the glue guns could have stopped the rotating shields long enough for his troops to get in a kill shot. But there was no sense in fretting over it now; what was done was done, and dwelling on it was purely a waste of time. The reality of the situation was that his targets had somehow survived, and they'd managed to launch a counterattack of their own.

To quite devastating results.

That was when he'd decided to get involved. After all, he hadn't maintained his current position within the Gargano family's hierarchy by letting his underlings do all the dirty work. In situations like these, he'd found that sometimes just a modicum of personal effort was all it took to achieve the desired results. Besides, he'd been itching to join the fray ever since his enemies had first arrived. So, after giving strict orders to his immediate staff, he'd slipped into a small room situated just to the left of his desk where he'd donned the armor specifically fabricated for this event.

It was a variation of the combat exoskeleton worn by his soldiers, only far more advanced. Its highly sophisticated operating systems not only increased his overall strength, but also monitored his vitals while giving him a heightened range of mobility. Donning it was a process which necessitated the use of robotic assistance as he locked himself within its heavy confines. Yet once encased in this protective shell, he'd felt truly invincible. Collecting the sonic cannon designed to counter his adversaries' supernatural powers, he'd then boarded his private elevator, ascending to the highest point of the mansion's rooftops above.

Upon reaching those lofty heights, it had been surprisingly easy to obliterate the so-called Love Leach with just one blast of the hypersonic weapon. And then, as an added bonus, he had also managed to take out The Loathing when that strange little fool had pushed Orson out of the way. It gave him a sense of pride knowing that he'd single-handedly defeated these hitherto unbeatable foes. He may have failed to secure Dr. Orson's cooperation for the sole benefit of his family's scientific endeavors, but he had not failed to maintain the Garganos' stranglehold over the city below. With these superpowered pests out of the way, he would return to being the undisputed master of all he surveyed. As he peered through the scope once more, aiming for his last remaining target, he grinned, anticipating the satisfaction he'd derive from killing this final threat to his unquestionable authority.

And yet. . . was it not entirely possible that he could accomplish his great-grandmother's directives even now? Hesitating, he considered the doctor who now stood defiant in the middle of a field of death and destruction. If he ordered his remaining troops to take Orson alive, could he not still fulfill the commands of his family's matriarch, thereby securing the man's extensive knowledge for the Garganos' exclusive use? After all, Orson's co-conspirators were dead, and there was nothing left to hold him to this foolish course of self-destructive vengeance. With all the technology his research facility produced, surely there had to be something he could use to bend the man to his will. His own scientist, Dr. Eastman, was undeniably brilliant, and perhaps even now had the solution waiting in that private lab of his. Those unusual vibrations Luciano had felt burrowing into his own thoughts the last time he'd visited there were intriguing; could this unknown device somehow be used to subjugate Orson's mind as well? He would have to consult with Eastman first, of course, but he was fairly certain something could be done.

Tapping into his suit's communications system, he relayed his orders to the auxiliary units stationed on the far side of the estate; they were to subdue the good doctor with overwhelming force if need be, but otherwise capture him predominantly unharmed.

Thus assured of his impending victory on all points of the matter, Luciano peered once more through the weapon's scope as his rabid neophytes poured around the sides of the mansion like a horde of enraged fanatics. He knew his overzealous recruits would stop at nothing to capture Doctor Abe Orson alive. . .

Or they would simply die trying.

Through the magnified lens, he watched as his prey glared back at him. It was clear the man would not go down easy—but he would go down. That much Luciano was entirely sure of.

-46-

His powers had grown beyond anything he could have ever imagined. Fueled by anger over the loss of his loved ones, it had reached out almost of its own accord, drawing forth all the fetal materials available within several thousand square miles. And as his rage intensified, so did the power, surging inside him like a rabid beast with only one burning desire:

To kill the enemy standing atop the mansion before him.

But first, he had to get past the soldiers. Considering the forces arrayed against him, he decided he would no longer play by their rules; it was time to do things his own way. Simultaneously pulling all the embryonic tissues he'd gathered out of the aether, he formed a gigantic globule of protoplasm. Once summoned, the resulting blob filled the grounds below him in a writhing vein-covered mass. With focused intent, he then fed this pulsating monstrosity with seething emotions, pouring the intensity of his feelings into its cellular structure until the organism vibrated with the power of his innermost primal desires.

And then, with a final thought, he gave his creation life.

Shuddering into semi-sentience, it groped outward like an oversized amoeba, its pseudopods many times larger and more flexible than an elephant's trunk. And as it oozed toward the oncoming soldiers, Abraham traveled along with it on a platform made of hardened skin cells resting atop its uppermost ectoplasmic layer. With a flick of his fingers, he sent a cluster of floating fetuses to take care of the rooftop sniper's weapon; he had no desire to get hit by a blast of energy while he was busy defeating these bothersome ground troops. But as the tanks began firing and the mortar crews found their range, he was suddenly facing dozens of deadly airborne projectiles.

Snarling, he flung up both arms, his hatred allowing no room in his heart for petty fear. Following the fluid motion of his sweeping gesture, a large portion of primordial flesh shot upward in an undulating wave, absorbing the shells within its gelatinous folds. The explosions going off inside this membranous segment were severely muted, their volatile threat nullified within the confines of its muffling embrace. Slashing his arms down to either side, he then released this rippling expanse to collapse with thunderous impact upon the now fleeing soldiers, crushing them before turning his attention to the tanks themselves.

Following another twitch of his fingers, his creation shot forth multiple tendrils, snatching up the tanks and mortar crews like an unruly child manhandling its favorite toys. There were suddenly dozens of armored units suspended in the air around him, trapped within the mucilaginous membranes of the creature's repulsive filaments. Clenching his fists, he crushed them all, casting them aside and then watching as they broke through clouds of insects before disappearing over the far horizon. Seeing that Charlie's minions were still aimlessly swarming, his eyes were unwillingly drawn back to the spot where his friend had been struck down. But no matter how hard he stared at that empty patch of land, there were no signs of his closest companion; he had been vaporized and was now gone forever.

Just like Flo.

At the thought of his beloved's tragic death, his anger surged anew. Maneuvering the hardened skin pad to the apex of his monstrous mount, he flung his arms out once more, the shimmering fabric of his gleaming white over-robes flaring with radiance as the material swirled around him. Responding to his mental command, the organism surged forward, its rippling pseudopods creating utter chaos across the fields below.

More troops came pouring around the edges of the estate then, these both better organized and more lethally equipped. Forming into orderly ranks, they opened fire with freon, flame, and tar, filling the air with streams of chemically enhanced destruction from their cylindrical backpacks. This concentrated assault struck the mass of fetal tissues all across the front of its quivering form, tearing into it with unstoppable fury. For the briefest of moments, the creature's forward momentum ground to a halt, its upraised fibrils wavering in uncertainty. Then it shook off the chemical bombardment like a dog shedding droplets of water. Eyes the size of diving bells formed along its outer edges, peering down at its assailants while mouths filled with razor-sharp teeth began appearing at the tips of its undulating limbs. But these soldiers were resolute in their sense of duty and stood firm before the creature's advance, dying in droves as they were brutally cut down and consumed. Glancing back up at the rooftops, Abraham then zeroed in on his prime target.

The man still stood beneath the minaret, his now useless weapon held loosely in one hand. Stray sunbeams reflected from his armor as he watched his men being annihilated, not even deigning to notice the swarm of ill-formed fetuses still hovering about him. Then, shifting his attention, he sought out Abraham, staring down from behind the faceplate of his helmet as he spoke into a communication device on his opposite wrist.

Abraham realized he must focus all his remaining energies upon reaching this one man. To take vengeance for his fallen comrades, he must kill the enemy commander before more soldiers were committed to the ongoing slaughter. With that thought in mind, he gave a few commands of his own, and the gigantic lifeform he rode altered its physiology in response. Like a wave cresting before a tropical storm, the creature rose hundreds of feet in the air before crashing down with immeasurable force, shaking the ground like a massive earthquake as it struck. Surging forward in unstoppable waves, it then inundated the mansion through every crack and crevice, washing away all remaining opposition.

The battle before the Gargano stronghold was over.

Riding the hardened skin pad across the rippling expanse of pinkish vein-covered tissues, he stepped off onto the edge of the roof, then strode toward the man in the metallic suit. He had just one more thing to do here, and he meant to prolong the task, ensuring his enemy would experience the same level of torment he'd inflicted upon others. Flexing his enhanced muscles beneath the hardened plating of his own overlapping armor, he prepared himself for the brutal necessity of the upcoming beatdown.

The roof itself was angled, the structure his nemesis stood within like a decorative belfry perched at the very top. It was the type of architecture you'd find in many European-style homes, and, as he moved closer, the man stepped over the parapet, leaving the small staging area covered by the steeple.

Abraham was forced to admit that his adversary was quite impressive. His suit appeared to form a seamlessly fitting articulated exoskeleton, which covered him from head to toe in well-designed segments. And although it was definitely of military design, it also featured a number of fanciful embellishments purely there for ornamentation alone. The effect was rather stunning, strongly resembling fourteenth-century Gothic-style plate armor, yet with a contemporary flair. The piercing eyes staring back at him from behind the transparent face shield were shrewd, the man's expression a mask of studied indifference. With a nonchalance that betrayed none of his inner emotions, he absently tossed aside the now-defunct weapon, the goopy residue from Abraham's fetal minions leaking from the barrel as it clattered across the roof to disappear over the side.

"Doctor Orson," his voice echoed strangely from the helmet's speaker, "we meet again. But under less than ideal circumstances it would seem. And here, all this time, I'd considered us allies."

It was Luciano Gargano himself! Fortunately, Abraham's helmet hid his own surprise well. Stopping no more than an arm's length away, he took stock of the situation, trying to determine exactly what the man had hoped to gain by coming here in person.

"That all ended the day your hired goons destroyed my lab," he finally said, "and it never would have begun in the first place if I'd known you'd purposely maneuvered me out of my privately funded facility uptown just to get ahold of my discoveries—"

"Minor details," Luciano demurred smoothly, "not even worthy of consideration. The relevant factor here is your vitally important research. Come, let us set aside our petty differences—all this animosity is ill-suited to people like us. We are men of vision, men of science and industry! All of this brutality, this carrying on—it is beneath us. Think of the bigger picture! I can give you what you want, what you have always wanted—unlimited resources to perfect your scientific endeavors and all the acclaim that goes along with it. You shall once again have the unimpeachable regard of the world's scientific community, revel in the success you so richly deserve. You will be on the cover of magazines, your breakthroughs published and admired by millions. Think of it, Doctor! Just think of the possibilities!"

"I want no part of your underworld schemes," Abraham spat, "or your filthy blood money! It's people like you that give scientists a bad name. You take our hard-won achievements and twist them for your own selfish gains. But my research is no longer for sale, not anymore, and not at any price. This ends now. I will wipe you and the entire Gargano family from the face of the Earth! I will make you suffer like all those who have died here today in your cause. Yet the pain you'll soon feel will be magnified a thousand times over before I am through!"

The sound of Luciano's laughter rang hollowly from the helmet's speaker as he shook with sardonic mirth. "*Wipe out the Gargano family?*" he exclaimed incredulously. "Oh, my dear, sweet, ignorant fool! How naive you are! The Gargano legacy is bigger than you can ever imagine! Our lineage goes back hundreds of years, with a membership spanning the entire globe. We are *legion*! What can you possibly do to end us? Will you spend the rest of your days hunting us down one by one? That would take several lifetimes. You are nothing, a mere flea, a minuscule nuisance that barely concerns us at all!"

With a wave of one well-armored hand, he dismissed Abraham's threat like it was nothing more than the idle boasting of a willful child. Then, narrowing his eyes, he took a step forward. "We shall have your research," he said with overwhelming confidence, "one way or the other. Even if I have to rip it from your cold dead body to obtain it!"

Although Abraham had never been much of a fighter, his enhanced musculature and increased bone density gave him an edge that the other man was unaware of. Crouching, he slid one foot back, bracing himself as his armored toes dug into the shingles. If his preparations gave the gangster any cause for concern, there was no sign of it. Launching himself across the intervening space, the crime lord immediately captured his forearms in a vice-like grip.

Abraham was ready, but the man's speed had surprised him, and he suddenly found himself struggling against a foe far stronger than anticipated. Locked in a grapple, he was forced almost to his knees as Luciano bent his arms slowly backward. With anger surging anew, he repelled with all his might, twisting sideways to throw the man off. As Luciano spun past, he caught himself on the downslope of the roof, crouching there like a leopard ready to pounce.

"Excellent!" he exclaimed, "I was hoping this would prove to be more of a challenge."

With that, he charged forward once more, his speed a blur. As his armored body smashed into Abraham, the force of the impact sent him crashing through the railings of the steepled enclosure. Flailing wildly, he caught his balance on the other side, nearly plummeting off the roof's edge as fragments of broken wood rained down around him. Leaping over the shattered parapets, Luciano stalked toward him, his arrogance palpable.

Beneath them both, the house still overflowed with the protoplasmic entity Abraham had brought to life. And from its jellified mass, he drew forth enough tissues to form a spiked projectile, spinning it out of the aether and then hurling it at his opponent.

The ball of hardened skin cells struck Luciano full in the chest, burying itself in his breastplate and knocking him back a few steps.

But then, plucking the cyst-like burr from his armored plating, the man simply smiled, casting it aside.

"You wound me!" he mocked. "But as you can see, I am not so easily deterred. And now it is *my* turn!"

Covering the distance between them in an instant, he drove his fist squarely into Abraham's faceplate, the attack so accelerated there was no chance to block. Driven by the power of the man's energized exoskeleton, it felt like being hit by a sledgehammer. Knocked from his feet, he tumbled along the shingled roof like a broken rag doll. As he slid to a stop at the edge of the overhang, he shook stars from his eyes, his head reeling from the blow.

Before he could recover, Luciano had already leapt into the air, his arms upraised for a mighty two-fisted strike. Abraham was just barely able to roll away, avoiding being crushed as the man landed, his fists breaking through the roof with an earsplitting crunch. Using his elbows and knees, Abraham leveraged himself upright, staggering out of range. But Luciano was now stuck, his arms buried deep in the splintered shingles as he tried to yank himself free. In that moment, Abraham's anger and desperation allowed him to consider a move so underhanded that it went against everything he'd ever believed in.

Using every ounce of his power, he brutally kicked out at the man's unprotected head. It was a cowardly act, but one that this maniac almost certainly deserved. His heavily armored foot, energized by enhanced leg musculature, shot toward Luciano's helmet with unprecedented force. Yet Luciano was able to wrench himself free at the last second, pivoting so his raised forearms absorbed the blow. Even so, the kick landed with such velocity that the man was blasted into the decorative steeple. With a sound like a bomb detonating, the structure collapsed, burying him in falling debris.

And Abraham dared not wait for him to recover.

Rushing forward, he grabbed Luciano's armor-plated leg, dragging him out and then slamming him down on the shingles. The impact broke through the roof again, this time implanting Luciano in a jagged hole with his arms and legs akimbo. Kneeling on the man's chest, Abraham then began pummeling him with huge, sweeping blows. Luciano's head snapped back and forth, his eyes growing dazed as blood flew from slackened lips. After a few moments, his helmet's faceplate cracked, but by then Abraham was already running out of steam. Gasping for air, he stopped the deadly barrage, gazing down at his enemy while catching his breath. Peering groggily up at him, Luciano suddenly began making a gurgling sound in the back of his throat, a kind of wheezing cough that rapidly grew in strength.

He was laughing!

"Do you think. . . that you can beat me. . . so easily?" he burbled through bloodied lips, "I was taking. . . worse beatings. . . from far better men. . . *since before you were even born!*"

As he uttered this final, chilling statement, his right fist shot out, striking Abraham so hard on the jaw that it spun him around. Collapsing in a tangled heap, he barely retained consciousness as Luciano struggled to right himself. The man appeared completely embedded, but with the sound of jet engines firing, he suddenly rose up from the hole. Clearing the edges, he hovered briefly before settling once more, and Abraham saw it was thanks to his suit's onboard propulsion system. As Luciano's feet touched down, he was already readying himself for the next attack.

Hoping to give himself enough time to fully recover his wits, Abraham lurched to his feet, stumbling away from the mob boss. The man's armor was dented, his faceplate filled with a myriad of cracks, but other than that he seemed totally unfazed. Dropping into a crouch, he circled Abraham like a pro wrestler searching for an opening.

"I've been fighting my entire life," he boasted. "Street brawls, bar fights, turf wars—you name it. Working my way up from the gutter, I've become the man you see here before you today. This city, including everything in it, *belongs to me now.* And when I get done with the neighborhood I grew up in, you won't even recognize it. I will tear down the slums and back alleyways of my troubled youth and rebuild them anew, creating a utopia like the one I'd always dreamed of as a boy. And I won't allow you, nor anyone else, to stop me from making that dream a reality!"

His strategic circling continued, but Abraham matched him, keeping just out of arm's reach. It was clear now that Luciano was completely insane, but it only made him all the more dangerous. There had to be some way to beat him, but he knew he would need to do so quickly; his chances of winning were dwindling by the minute, and if he didn't finish this soon, he would surely be defeated.

But Luciano suddenly fired his jetpack again, shooting forward and then muscling him to his knees by recapturing his forearms in an unbreakable grip. Abraham struggled, but it was of no use; the man had him truly pinned. Gazing down through the cracked faceplate, Luciano flashed him a bloodied, bright red grin.

"You see, there is only one thing you need know about me," he said, "and that is the fact that I *always* win." As the man's eyes sparkled with barely contained madness, Abraham heard the electronic whirring of concealed motors within his gauntlets. "And now, whether you like it or not, I shall wrest all of your dark secrets from you one by one. It really makes no difference to me if you're alive or dead; I *will* discover the true source of your power, and then it will be *mine*, to do with as I please."

Pronged cables shot from concealed compartments within the man's armored gloves, punching through Abraham's hardened skin-cell plating to penetrate deep into his forearms. In mounting horror, he then watched as fluids began flowing up through these tubules, drawn into Luciano's suit to be stored away for later use. As to the purpose of this invasive procedure, he could only too readily guess.

His DNA was being stolen along with his modified blood. And with these spiritually altered samples, who knew what terrible experiments the Garganos could concoct? It was only a matter of time before they discovered everything about him, perhaps even unto divining the true origins of his mystical power. But the spirit who'd given him these gifts had intended them to be used to serve the city, to usher in a new era of rebirth and prosperity. Thinking of the bargain he'd made caused him to grow cold inside. This man, this unbearable megalomaniac, could not be allowed to obtain the secrets Abraham currently harbored.

Summoning his remaining energy, he reached out, mentally dismissing the gigantic lifeform oozing through the rooms beneath them. Then, glaring up into Luciano's smug face, he smiled tightly in return.

"This is not *your* city," he spat. "It belongs to the people who live here and will always remain so. The slums where you grew up will serve as a reminder—an undying monument to the pitiful life you've led and a warning to others who would dare to defy me!"

Releasing a portion of the embryonic protoplasm he held waiting in the aether, he allowed it to rematerialize inside of Luciano's armor, inundating the pores of the man's flesh as it filled the suit near to bursting. The man's eyes grew wide as the fluids filled the spaces within the exoskeleton, shooting from his mouth and nose as he choked on its sudden, overwhelming volume. Within seconds, he was hopelessly thrashing against his fate, rolling to one side and then clattering across the shingles. He was still struggling as his mechanized suit tumbled from the edge, plummeting into the bloody fields below.

It was over. Luciano Gargano was no more.

As Abraham gathered himself, wobbling upright to stand unsteadily at the top of the sprawling mansion, he wondered just what he'd gained from it all. The fight had lasted only a few minutes, yet now he found himself entirely alone. His friends were dead, blasted into tiny particles. And the victory, if it could even be called that, felt empty. Gazing out over the city, he couldn't even feel a sense of achievement from saving all the people who lived there. It still stood as it always had, and there was so much left to do in order to set things right. His pact remained unfulfilled. But how could he carry on now, alone as he was?

He was still deeply wrapped in these feelings of utter hopelessness as his body became insubstantial, slowly fading away like mists parting before the dawn.

-47-

The sonorous voice of the old priest was mesmerizing, falling in a singsong cadence as it floated out of the *honden* in clear, melodious tones. The meaning behind its ritualistic phrases was incomprehensible, but its effects were clearly apparent. A tremendous feeling of lethargic tranquility had fallen over them as they waited just outside the richly carved doors.

Jenkins had never known a greater impression of harmony, such a complete sensation of well-being, as he was experiencing right at that moment. Sitting there, holding Lisell's hand here in this mystical place, was incomparable to anything he'd ever done before. Almost as if she'd just come to the same conclusion, he felt her fingers tighten their grip slightly, then relax again, bolstering his perceptions of inner peace and contentment. It was a monumental feeling of pure bliss that wrapped him in layers of sensual wonderment.

There was a moment of complete silence before he realized the flowing recitation beyond the closed doors had ceased. With a languid curiosity, his eyes slid open, and he glanced at the finely tooled wood of the portal before him. The light of the candles within leaked fitfully from beneath the heavy panels, a warm, flickering glow that was suddenly broken by a flash of white light. From inside, he heard the voice of the priest raised once more in what sounded like praise, and then something he couldn't quite make out, which could have been a dignified response. It was definitely not the priest speaking to himself. The vocalizations were far too dissimilar. In mounting surprise, it dawned on him that the ritual must have actually worked. The old priest, even now, was inside the *honden* communing with the kami spirits! His astonishment in no way broke the spell surrounding them, and in this relaxed and receptive state, he glanced aside to see how Lisell was reacting.

Her beautiful, heart-shaped face was turned toward him, the lively eyes staring out from behind her horn-rimmed glasses like deep pools of mystery. Had any other women ever looked at him quite this way before? Falling under the spell of her gaze, he was wrapped in a whirlpool of tantalizing emotions. He felt a warm passion flowing between them, running outward from their clasped hands and suffusing their bodies in the pleasurable warmth of mutually shared attraction. The moment stretched into infinity, and yet he did not want it to end. When the doors opened and the old man stepped out, they were still so entranced with one another that they barely noticed his arrival. The priest spoke to his grandson in quiet undertones filled with the deepest respect, then the child rose from the floor, turning to Jenkins with a small bow.

"My grandfather wishes you to know that he has succeeded in calling forth the kami spirits and that they have agreed to speak with you. He also wishes you to know that none but those in the highest order of the priesthood are usually allowed inside. I myself am only allowed in to translate should it become necessary. I do not deserve this honor, but I will somehow endeavor to be worthy of it."

With that, he bowed again, then gave his grandfather an even deeper bow. After returning the boy's genuflection with a slight inclination of his head, the priest indicated that they should remove their shoes. Turning, he then reentered the *honden*, moving at a stately and dignified pace. Releasing Lisell's hand, Jenkins bent to slip off his footwear before following.

The interior of the shrine was warm and welcoming, and its wood partitions and eloquent flowing motifs showcased the simplicity of its form, highlighting the austerity of its spartan layout. Everywhere he looked, there were carvings that paid homage to the beauty of the natural world. Most of the materials were still in their rawest state, simply polished to a brilliant sheen by years of loving care. Candles lit the room, standing in sheltered nooks while three alcoves were built into the back wall, now shimmering with pure white energy. Within that ethereal glow, Jenkins could just make out three indistinct shapes standing serenely. And before these illuminated beings stood two other figures bathed in the essence of the kami spirits behind them. It was in front of these entities that the priest stopped, bowing deeply to each before beckoning Jenkins and Lisell to step forward.

Approaching cautiously, they peered at the motionless couple with overwhelming curiosity. The persona on the left was short and squat, shrouded in an overly large burgundy cloak which swirled around him in fluttering folds of rich, dark material. His features were horny and pebbled, like that of a hard-shelled crab, while his nose was long and pointed like the beak of a predatory bird. Standing with arms flung out and head tilted back, a sullen jade-green light leaked from between his parted eyelids. Jenkins recognized him instantly; he was the one everyone now referred to as "The Loathing."

The other figure was slender and completely nude, a hairless ghost-like apparition floating a foot above the floor. She was surrounded by a crackling nimbus of electrical energy, the perfect symmetry of her translucent form a wonder to behold as she hovered there within the energized field. Her eyes were mere slits, with ruby-red fire blazing from beneath the partially closed lids. She was definitely the being that was now called "Love Leach."

While he was gazing at them in awe, a light began to coalesce to the right, just in front of the last glowing niche in the back wall. Within this pulsating radiance, a new presence was forming. He was tall and stately, with a white high-collared robe flowing down around his well-muscled frame. Eyes like moonstones gazed out from a bald, slightly misshapen head that was lacking in both ears and nose while beneath the robes he wore an impeccably tailored suit. Could this be Dr. Abe Orson? Jenkins didn't know enough about the man to be sure, but it stood to reason that this would be the third person representing the kami spirits, their chosen avatars here on Earth.

The old priest bowed to the newly arrived figure, then turned back to Jenkins and Lisell. Inclining his head politely, he spoke in serious tones, the fluid Japanese flowing from his lips like a tumble of water rushing over smooth stones in a riverbed. After he was through, he glanced at his grandson with raised eyebrows.

The boy had the good graces to look embarrassed. It was clear he was overwhelmed at being allowed inside the *honden*. Stepping forward, he bowed low to the three kami and their representatives, then turned back to translate his grandfather's eloquent words.

"My grandfather wishes you to know that you may converse directly with the kami through their chosen spiritual conduits. He also wishes me to inform you that it is a singular honor to be approached by the kami like this and to speak with them personally. You have been greatly favored to be selected for their most worthy regard. Please be respectful. These kami are powerful, and we must show them we acknowledge their benevolence as the gift that it most assuredly is."

"We will be careful," he assured the boy, "and we're grateful to be honored this way."

The boy nodded, then translated their response for the old priest. The man gazed at them with gratitude in his eyes, bowing and then waving them forward with the streamer-covered staff he still carried. Shaking in mild trepidation, Jenkins and Lisell stepped up to the three entities arrayed before the glowing kami spirits whose presence filled the niches at the back of the shrine.

The floating woman opened her eyes wider, tilting her head down to gaze at them with fiery regard. After a moment of steady contemplation, she smiled radiantly.

"Detective Jenkins," she said, her cultured voice melodious and kind, "we welcome you here to our shrine and bid you to be at ease in our presence." Then, her gaze turned to Lisell. "And Dr. Pachenke, it is also very good of you to come. Your work is admirable, and we wish to see that it continues in the forthcoming era of peace and tranquility."

Glancing over at Lisell, he saw her blush under the praise of these powerful beings. He was feeling a bit overwhelmed himself, but he couldn't let that distract from the reason they were here in the first place. He must find common ground with these spirits and then convince them to stop their indiscriminate murders of the citizens he was paid to protect. There had to be some way to reason with them.

"About that," he began, "while we do appreciate everything you guys are doing, I'm going to have to ask you, respectfully, if you could please stop? The people you're killing. . . well, they have certain rights. You can't just go around wiping them out indiscriminately. There are laws in place, proper channels we have to go through, in order to uphold the peace. You have to follow the rules already set down by our own governing bodies. Do you understand?"

The woman glared down at him, her smoldering eyes narrowing as her lips clenched into a small, disapproving frown. "The governing bodies of which you speak were greedy and self-serving," she stated coldly. "And your law enforcement officials were eaten away from within by rot and corruption. Your city was *tsumi* and needed to be cleansed by *misogi harai*. It must be made *akashi* again."

Jenkins stared at her, the unfamiliar words sounding foreign to his ears. "I don't understand," he confessed.

The young boy stepped forward and bowed low. "Forgive me, but I must translate the meaning of these words for you. *Tsumi* is something that has been polluted and must be cleansed. *Misogi harai* is the act of restoring the natural process, and *akashi* is to be made bright and whole again. She is telling you that your city is dirty and corrupted, that it must be purified to be made beautiful and clean again. She is speaking of the process of renewal."

With a small sigh, Jenkins glanced back at the stunningly beautiful woman now controlled by the kami spirits. This was going to be more difficult than he'd imagined. How could he describe the ideals of "innocent until proven guilty" to these beings of almost unlimited power? Clearing his throat, he tried again.

"We do have some problems, that I'll admit," he offered. "But the laws that govern this great land of ours have to be obeyed. We have to follow due process, arrest people who are breaking these laws, and then prosecute them before we can sentence them for their crimes. They have certain inalienable rights; you can't just keep randomly killing them."

The small man with the green glowing eyes turned toward Jenkins, addressing him for the first time. "Your system is flawed," he said in a low, gravelly voice. "Just a few days ago, you yourself were powerless against what was going on in this city. Crimes went unpunished while your officials grew rich and fat off the suffering of those less fortunate. Your comrades were accepting bribes to look the other way while murders, rapes, and abductions happened right under the very noses of your highest officials. The criminal elements here were winning. Surely you can see that? Luciano Gargano and others of his ilk had a stranglehold on this entire area and everyone who lives within it. There can be no denying it, Detective."

He hated to admit it, but the spirit was right. Only a few short days ago, he had been all too ready to give up, at a point in his life where he was actually considering leaving the force. The loss of his partner, coupled with the corruption going on all around him, had been eating away at his resolve, steadily grinding him down until he no longer cared about anything. But he had taken an oath to uphold the law; he couldn't just sanction multiple homicides because they happened to be freeing the town from its criminal elements. That wasn't how the system was supposed to work. Vigilante justice was no basis for a functioning, law-abiding society. He had to somehow make them see that.

"By taking the law into your own hands, you have broken it," he said. "You can't just go around killing people because they deserve it. Where do you draw the line? What message does that send to the rest of the population? That it's okay to kill someone if they're already a criminal? That it's alright to gun someone down in cold blood if they've been doing bad things? That way lies chaos! In order to maintain the peaceful harmony you claim you're all striving for, there has to be law and order, there have to be people who run things and maintain the status quo. Without it, there would be total anarchy!"

"Calm yourself, Detective." This came from the figure on the right, whose pale, bulbous eyes had turned their sympathy-filled gaze toward Jenkins. "We understand the need for order and the basic requirements for a civilization to thrive. What you fail to realize is that there is no good or evil. Everything in the universe has the propensity for both. They are intertwined and cannot exist one without the other. It is a duality that many of your people do not yet fully understand. By removing the citizens who had become irredeemably tainted, who were strangling the growth and prosperity of this city, we have but set things onto a greater path, a path of healing and renewal. The governing of this new era of enlightenment will be carried out by those who have a clean inner spirit, who are *akashi*. And we will remain here in case the rest of you forget what can happen without a harmonious unity of purpose."

"That's all well and good—in theory," he told them, waving a hand through the air in exasperation. "But city officials are elected. There are a whole bunch of steps involved in getting the right people in place to govern us. How do you propose we do that? It's going to take money, and a lot of it, to pave the way for any candidates we put forth, and even then, it's still up to a vote. You can't simply choose handpicked people to lead us, then expect everyone to just roll over and let them do it! There's an entire process of elections and campaigning and a lot of other things involved that even I don't fully understand! Look, I agree with you on most of this stuff, but I'm just a cop, just one man. How do you expect me to figure out everything you want us to do, let alone implement it?"

"Do not worry," the glowing woman said, "we have made all the necessary arrangements. Your friend Demitre has been invaluable to us in the planning and restructuring that has been going on since we started this venture, and he knows the importance of his duties. The Garganos are no more, and all of their ill-gotten wealth has been very skillfully funneled into newly acquired accounts we've set up for the necessary politicking that will now take place. Do not consider that we are naive in any way about the nature of man; we know there will always be a criminal element to be dealt with. That is why we've chosen you to aid us, to be our liaison to the general public. While our anonymity must be ensured, there are many things you can do for us, things we can trust to no other. And the healing will continue long after this. Your partner, Dr. Pachenke, will be instrumental in taking care of those that have been adversely affected by our cleansing of this land. She will be invaluable to us as well while we usher in this new era."

He glanced aside at Lisell, feeling her shocked pleasure at having been acknowledged once again. A rosy glow spread across her cheeks, and he couldn't be sure if it was from being singled out or simple satisfaction at being referred to as his partner. Whichever it was, it certainly agreed with her. Yet there were still so many unanswered questions.

"What about this shrine?" he asked. "The old man told us there is something you need, something that will perhaps allow you to rest peacefully? Meaning no disrespect, but you guys have gotta go. For this whole thing to work, the city has got to get back to normal, without all these supernatural shenanigans going on. The population can't handle it, and there's going to be panic in the streets as it is. It'll take us a long time to calm everything down and get things functioning like you want, even without you still hanging around."

The spiritual conduits for the kami grew somber at this, all of them subsiding as the beings behind them conferred amongst themselves. This was not something Jenkins could see with the naked eye, but rather a feeling he got from the sudden silence and the fact that the energy levels within the *honden* had begun to fluctuate, causing the hair on his arms to stand straight up. For a brief moment, he was somewhat alarmed, tightening his hold on Lisell's hand and then glancing at the priest for reassurance. The older man gazed back at him, but his serene features betrayed nothing.

After a moment, the shining woman turned her fiery regard back upon them, pursing her ethereal lips as she chose her next words carefully. "We have decided," she finally said, "to trust you further with something that should not be revealed to anyone else. It is not something we wish to discuss, but we agree that it has now become necessary." Her eyes became twin pools of molten fire as she continued staring him down, causing the priest and his grandson to quickly fall to their knees, bowing their heads low to the floor. "Our family has been done a grievous wrong here in this land. The members who built this shrine were most foully murdered and their remains somehow hidden away. The three of us once led exemplary lives, so in death, we became our clan's spiritual protectors. Yet with the bodies of our kin defiled and missing, we can never fully be at rest. Their mortal shells must be found, and the ritual for proper burial must take place before we can be released from our sacred duty. We will not vacate this realm until this has been accomplished, and our avatars here will continue to uphold our will on this plane of existence until our clan's honor has been restored."

"Do you mean to say," Jenkins ventured, "that these three people who have been running around terrorizing the city with the powers you've granted them will still be a visible presence here?"

The woman rose higher, her eyes blazing and the globe surrounding her crackling with an intensity that had thus far been restrained and peaceful. The priest began to chant under his breath while his grandson trembled visibly.

"Do not presume to question our methodology!" came her booming response. "These spiritual conduits will remain, working from the shadows and doing our bidding as we see fit. You would do well to heed them, and us, if you wish to continue to go on living."

Lisell's free hand plucked at his sleeve, forcing him to glance aside. She was staring at him with a pleading look, warning him with her expression not to push things too far.

Turning back toward the kami spirits, she gave them a low bow. "We will, of course, play by your rules," she told them. "But if you would please explain things a little better, it will prevent future misunderstandings. We want to help, we really do, but we're concerned about the rest of the people who live here. We're simply trying to do whatever it takes to see that no one else gets hurt by your representatives."

The energy surrounding the floating woman slowly receded, the atmosphere in the room returning to its previous state of warmth and acceptance. The old priest and his grandson relaxed visibly as Lisell continued to stare past the three conduits, focusing solely on the spirits themselves. After a moment of heavy silence, the figure swathed in the large burgundy cloak grinned crookedly.

"We can see that you are trying and believe you will serve us to the best of your abilities," he said. "Do not worry—we will provide you with all the knowledge you need to successfully navigate this time of restoration. All of us here have the best of intentions for this city that you call home and for all those who live within its boundaries. There will be no more mass culling of the population as long as our instructions are heeded and a peaceful, harmonious balance is maintained."

Chewing on his lower lip, Jenkins tried to refrain from being overly pushy, but he just had to ask. "Does that mean you'll let the police and elected officials do their jobs without interference?"

"Most assuredly," came the immediate reply. "It is one of the main reasons we have chosen you to become the liaison between us and the mortal realm. Once the forces of law and order are reestablished, there will be little need for our direct supervision. Your affairs are of no concern to us as long as the city remains in a state of peaceful tranquility. We know that this will be an ongoing process; there can be no light without the dark, no flame without shadow. There will always be those who have their duality fluctuate to the point that crimes will be committed. We will trust in you, and in the people we put in place, to handle such things in your own limited way. It is only when the balance is tipped, and the city becomes irreparably tarnished by hatred, violence, and greed, that we shall again intervene, if only to set things back on the correct path once more."

"That sounds fair," he replied dubiously. "But can you be more specific about what you want from us right now? How can we. . . appease you?"

The figure on the right wearing the fashionable suit beneath glittering white robes turned to him. "First of all, contact will be made with our surviving clan members and funds will be diverted to restore this place to its former glory. This shrine will rise again, and you will ensure that it is a safe place for all those of the Shinto faith to visit. The old man and his grandson will be in charge of this until others can arrive from Japan, but you will hire workers to take on the rest of the cleanup and help with new construction. The money to do this will come from the accounts we've had Demitre set up with what we've taken from crime syndicates in this area.

"Secondly, all traces of our presence in the city will be suppressed and covered up. You know how to do such things, so we trust that you will get it done. Create cover stories, use misdirection in the media. We don't care how you achieve this, only that you succeed. Our spiritual conduits must remain anonymous and free from all repercussions for their part in the cleansing they've already done at our behest. And finally, and perhaps most importantly, you will find the remains of our slain family members and bring them here to us for proper burial. It is only then that we can truly be at peace."

Jenkins thought for a moment, considering all they had asked of him. "What about the deed to this property?" he mused. "How do we go about doing the work to restore it when the building's been condemned and there are no living members of your family left here to claim ownership?"

The man with the pale, nearly lidless eyes smiled. "Don't worry. We've had Demitre draw up the necessary documentation, and it will allow you to proceed until our clan representatives can arrive."

"And you want this shrine to remain as it once was?" he said. "Disguised as an herbal shop?"

"That is indeed our desire, Detective," came the reply. "And you will do everything within your power to ensure that it remains a safe location known only to those of the Shinto faith. There are no other shrines quite like this one; it is the first of its kind and must be protected at all costs."

"There will be questions, people that see the new construction and come by to poke around," he warned them. "I can't stop the looky-loos from flocking here or the press from making themselves a royal pain in the ass once they find out there's work being done so close to the crime scene next door."

"We understand," the floating woman said. "And we have our own ways of influencing things. Rest assured that all possible outcomes in this venture have been considered. You will have help in executing your administrative duties, and if you should ever need us, you may speak to the old priest. He will come to us with anything he deems of vital importance, never fear."

Jenkins considered what they'd said from all angles, deciding that it seemed reasonable enough. They were right about him; before all this had started, he'd been simply showing up to work day after day, yet not really accomplishing anything worthwhile. Now, in a manner of less than a week, these powerful beings had dismantled organized crime, gotten rid of corrupt city officials, and killed off most of the undesirable officers within the police force. Had it been an ideal solution? Not in the least. There had been too much upheaval, too many lives lost, to really count this as a win-win situation.

But even so, the city was in better shape than it had been in years. He had to admit that it seemed a small price to pay for the amount of freedom it now gave him to make the changes he'd always envisioned for this gloomy metropolis. This, for him, was a new lease on life, and he decided right then and there that he'd embrace it. Releasing Lisell's hand, he put his arm around her shoulders, drawing her in close.

"You have a deal," he told the entities. "We'll do our part while you guys do what you gotta do. But just remember, this city is protected by more than just you and your friends here; I'm on the job, and I have a whole bunch of other decent, law-abiding cops backing me up now. You start to step out of line and you'll have to answer to me, you got that?"

The old priest flashed a concerned look, unable to understand but reacting to the tone of the conversation. But his grandson's eyes grew as large as saucers before he hastily bent his head back to the floor, hiding his face from view while trembling uncontrollably. Yet the beautiful young woman floating within the cloud of crackling energy simply laughed, a light, melodious sound which rang out in the candlelit confines of the shrine's interior like the tinkling of bells.

"That is one of the reasons why we've chosen you, Detective Jenkins," came her amused response. "We have seen into your soul and know that you'll do a good job, as well as keeping us in check while you're at it. It is a precious balance that we look forward to maintaining for many years to come."

The shimmering lights in the niches at the back wall rose up simultaneously, and the three spiritual conduits began to fade from view. The old priest gave them a tremulous bow, then motioned for Jenkins and Lisell to proceed him to the exit. It seemed that the interview was at an end.

Turning, he steered Lisell across the polished wood floor toward the large doors standing open at the front of the shrine. It had been one hell of a week, but he was feeling pretty good about how things were panning out, aside from all the death and chaos it had caused. There was still so much more to do, but he could sense that he had a pretty good handle on it now. Reaching the entranceway, he turned and bowed to the old man as the priest ushered them out. The old man smiled as he bowed low to them in return. Followed by the grandson, they left the inner sanctum, pausing before the stairs leading up.

Turning, he gazed down into Lisell's eyes, savoring the closeness they now shared. With as much bravery as he had ever shown about anything in his entire life, he leaned in and kissed her full upon the lips. For the briefest of moments, she stiffened in his arms but then relaxed, returning his affections with a passion that was unexpectedly ardent.

All things considered, he began to think he was going to like this new era of prosperity. It suited him very well. Yes, very well indeed.

-48-

After the ritual, the spectral trio had somehow been transported back to their underground lair. Once the initial surprise and disorientation had worn off, Abraham had been overcome by a tremendous sense of relief. During the meeting, he'd been more or less just a spectator, the spirit who'd given him his new lease on life taking control in order to communicate with the priest and his guests. The experience had been unnerving, to say the least, but not entirely uncomfortable. A great deal of information had been exchanged, and he felt that he now had a much better understanding of what was to be expected of them in the years to come.

The fact that Florence was alive and unharmed was still sinking in. When he'd expressed concern for her well-being after reappearing in the abandoned mine, she'd informed him that the sonic blast had disrupted her energies at the very same moment the Shinto priest had been invoking the spirits. It was this summoning that had taken her from the battlefield, as it had done for each of them in turn, one at a time, as the ritual progressed. Being in the same room with her after believing she'd been killed was difficult. With Charlie present, he'd had to refrain from foolishly embracing her and babbling about his true feelings. And it had taken all of his self-control to maintain this semblance of decorum while they all compared notes.

To that effect, they'd held an informal meeting in the foreman's office, each telling their own part of the tale, with Abraham becoming the hero of the hour after his humble revelation of what had transpired once they'd both dematerialized. With the defeat of Luciano and his ground troops, Charlie announced himself well-satisfied that justice had been served. There were still others who deserved their attention, and this list included the doctors who'd allowed Charlie's wife to die, the politicians who'd somehow escaped Florence's wrath, and the remaining crime lords. But overall, they'd done well in eliminating most of the targets they'd been reincarnated to destroy. It was an accomplishment worthy of celebration. So they'd broken out a bottle of scotch left behind in one of the cupboards to toast a job that was fast nearing completion. The general mood was a festive one as they sat in familiar camaraderie, tossing back a few rounds.

"Did you see the look on the general's face," Charlie was saying, a grin splitting his features from ear to ear, "when Simon and my new children swarmed over him? It appeared as if he might actually soil himself!" Chuckling, he stroked Simon's wing casings where he rested on the back of his forearm. "He was not expecting the voracity of my soldiers, that much was certain! My children gave him quite a surprise as they converged on him from out of the clear, blue sky, did they not?" It was a rhetorical question, and they all erupted into fits of giggling, the feeling light and airy now that the alcohol was flowing freely.

"You should have seen Luciano's face when my embryonic fluids filled up his suit," Abraham added, wiping tears of mirth from his eyes. "He was so sure he had me dead to rights, so determined to use my research for his family's nefarious plans. I don't think he even realized what was happening until the protoplasm came shooting straight out of his nose! He was completely taken by surprise, the poor fool!"

Reaching across the space between them, Florence laid her hand on his arm, her fiery eyes sparkling with heartfelt gratitude. "Thank you, Abe, for giving that bastard what he deserved," she said. "After he blasted me with that sonic cannon, I thought I was a goner. It even still stings a little!"

The mock indignity in her voice had them all rolling again, the closeness of their association strengthening as they shared the gallows humor of well-tested veterans. Their unity had been forged in fire, hammered with the horrors of war, and then refined by the relief of unexpected survival. It was an attachment far stronger than iron, more deeply rooted than the ties of family, and shining with the beauty of the bond which had grown up between them. They were truly a team now and would back each other through thick and thin from here on out, no matter the cost. Settling further into his chair, Abraham heaved a great sigh of pure satisfaction.

"Well, my friends," Charlie was saying, "I should go look in on the queen now. She has been a bit broody since we refused to let her come on the excursion. I will need to find her a suitable mate, and soon. Breeding the next generation of our loyal soldiers should keep her occupied for quite some time after that."

Rising from his seat, he headed for the door, Simon whirring in exuberant gyrations through the air before him. The bulk of Charlie's insect minions had gone back to their ordinary lives after the battle, spreading out from the Gargano estates to return to doing the normal, everyday things that insects naturally took care of. The abandoned mines were now filled with only the remaining bulk of the arthropods from the new queen's clutch. They were large, aggressive, and required a lot of careful tending to, a role which Abraham was only too happy to allow Charlie to handle on his own.

Setting his glass down on the counter, his gaze returned to Florence where she sat next to the cot in the corner. Now that they were finally alone, he was suddenly at a loss for words. Her glowing, ethereal form nestled within its shimmering globe of ever-present crackling energy, her mist-shrouded beauty a breathtaking sight to behold. Yet now she was studying him with her lambent, fiery eyes, the hint of a smile playing across her lips as she rolled her glass back and forth between her finely sculpted, semi-corporeal hands.

"Well," she said, "it looks like we're going to be out of a job soon. What do you plan to do once our remaining tasks are complete?"

"Plan to do?" he repeated awkwardly, unsure of what she was getting at.

"You know—above, in the real world." She waved her glass around, indicating the interior of the small office. "Surely you don't plan to live here with Charlie, helping him to take care of all his unruly children?"

"Good God, no!" he said with finality. Then, gazing up at the ceiling, he put some real thought into it. "I guess I've never looked that far ahead," he admitted. "Now that we're about done with it all, I suppose I could go back to being a doctor, perhaps continue on with my research. Although I hardly see what good it would do anyone now. Everything I was trying to achieve seems rather pointless after what we've been through together. And we'll still be required to maintain the peace should things get out of hand again. I'd be willing to bet that the spirits will have a lot more for us to do in a very short time. Humans are so predictable in that regard. Always getting into trouble and whatnot. It's like they can't help themselves."

Slanting his thoughtful gaze back down, he found she was now staring morosely at the floor, her mood troubled and seemingly bleak. It was a shock when tears began falling from her smoldering eyes, tracing trails of burning, lava-like fire across her insubstantial cheeks. Crossing the distance between them, he knelt down next to her chair, taking the glass from her lax grip and then setting it aside before clasping her trembling hands between his own.

"Flo?" he asked softly. "What is it? Why are you crying?"

When she unwillingly glanced back up, he saw that her face was a mask of pure misery. Witnessing her distress was gut-wrenching, making his heart turn over in his chest. She was so lovely, and suddenly so fragile and filled with all-consuming pain. It made him yearn to resolve all of her problems, to rescue her from the unfathomable depths of this mysterious sorrow.

"I just don't know what I'm going to do!" she managed through the tears. "Charlie has his insects, you have your old life to get back to, but what do I have? I'm nothing! A ghost, a will-o'-the-wisp made from air and electricity. There's nothing waiting for me up there. I have no job, no husband—I can't even walk down the streets like a normal person anymore! What am I supposed to do, Abe? I can't stay down here in the dark forever. I just can't!"

Her distress created a pall of sadness that settled over the entire room, turning their recent victory into nothing but ashes. Rising from his crouch, he slowly drew her to her feet, his grip gentle yet firm. Then, reaching up, he brushed aside some of the fiery tears, not caring whether they burned his fingertips as they trailed across her glowing cheek.

When she stared at him in confusion, the wounded look on her face drove spikes of remorse into his very soul. He didn't know if she actually cared for him, but suddenly that didn't really matter. Even if she chose Charlie over him, it was more important that she was happy, truly happy, for at least one brief moment in her predominately tragic life. Having made that decision, he stepped back, releasing her hands as he gave her a reassuring yet tremulous smile. He was terrified. Of what she might think, of what she might assume about him once he revealed what he had done. But it no longer mattered what he felt; everything he had, everything within his power, he would willingly give to her. . . and more. He loved her that much and could do no less.

"I've taken the liberty of making you something," he said in a hoarse whisper. "I hope you won't mind, but I was concerned for your well-being, and so. . . well. . . I guess I should just show you and then see what you think."

Waving his hand through the air while twitching his long, capable fingers, he brought forth the female simulacrum he'd created at his apartment on the day he'd repaired his own features. It materialized in the air beside them, shimmering with a vitality that highlighted its inner health and natural beauty. He had refined it since its first creation, had spent many idle hours perfecting it, making sure that it would please her. With the bashfulness of a small boy offering a fresh daisy to a winsome young girl for the very first time, he displayed it for her approval. It was difficult to look at her now, but he tried his best to stand firm, ready for whatever response she might have to his well-intended presumption.

Marveling at the body suspended in the air before them, her blazing eyes grew wide. They were filled with either shock or horror, he could not tell which. As he stood there trembling and tongue-tied, she walked completely around the body, studying it from all angles. Then, with an arch of her insubstantial eyebrows, she finally turned back to consider him quizzically.

"Who is she?" she wondered aloud. "I. . . I don't understand."

"She's you, if you would like her to be," he replied with great difficulty, his voice quavering. "I created her. Grew her from the very best of my fetal materials, sculpted and refined in the hopes that you might someday desire a body to inhabit. There's no soul, no real personality inside of her; she's like an empty shell, a suit of new clothing, if you will. I know it may seem terribly forward of me, perhaps even inappropriate. But I had hoped that maybe someday you'd like to be seen walking down the streets again. Together. With me, I mean. That is, if you'd like that. As. . . as just friends if you prefer. . ."

His courage failed as the words trickled to a stop, ending in his flustered consternation. He had no idea how she would react, what she would think of him, and the fact of not knowing was slowly killing him. What if she thought he was a creeper? What if, by making this beautiful body for her, he had ensured that she would now consider him some kind of perverted psychopath? It was these thoughts and more that rattled through his mind, causing him no small amount of discomfort as he awaited her response.

"You made this. . . for me?" she asked, her voice husky with suppressed emotion.

"Yes," he replied hesitantly, nearly paralyzed by anxiety.

Her molten eyes stared at him, unreadable yet not seemingly angry. She was studying him, gazing at him with a perplexity that he couldn't quite fathom. With a tilt of her head, she continued to consider what he'd done for one more long, excruciating moment. Then, without another word, she ghosted into the body, her energy absorbing into the flesh until her bubble of crackling power was nothing more than a healthy sheen across its pure white epidermis. Stepping down onto the hardwood floor, she blinked her stunningly green eyes, then performed a pirouette, her naturally red hair flowing around her like a sun-dappled cloak.

"How do I look?" she asked.

He was speechless.

Standing on her tiptoes, she stretched, the lithe, powerful muscles rolling under the smoothness of her flawless skin. The freckles standing out on her cheeks were in just the right amount of profusion, and as she turned to face him, the waves of her hair trailed down like strands of silk to brush across the tops of her perfectly formed breasts. When she realized he was unable to articulate his admiration, that he was still frozen in silent fear, dreading whatever she might say, it brought a mischievous grin to her artfully sculpted lips. Arching an eyebrow, she sauntered toward him like a cat stalking its prey. Then, stopping less than an arm's length away, she laid a hand on his chest, gazing up into his pale eyes with penetrating candor.

"I see by your response that you approve," she murmured. Then, taking on a more serious tone, she inquired, "Why didn't you give this to me before now? Did you think I might be angry with you for creating it without asking first?"

Her closeness was electrifying. Fighting down his natural urges, he strove to maintain his composure. "There just hasn't been the time. With all that's been going on, there was never a free moment where we were alone together, a time when it was just the two of us. I didn't want to give it to you in front of Charlie. In case. . . well, in case it might embarrass you. Especially if you and he were. . . were getting along better than. . . well, I just didn't know where I stood, and I didn't want to get in the way if you two were already hitting it off."

"Charlie and I?" she exclaimed. "He's like a father to me! Yes, I do love him dearly, but not in that way!" Then, realizing the extent of his discomfort, she took pity. "Abe, this is the sweetest thing that anyone has ever done for me. But I'm an absolute nobody! You're a brilliant scientist with goals and a bright future. You could go out with anyone you want, anyone at all! But look at me—who exactly am I? Just some boring ex-housewife, a wannabe professional bookworm? I didn't think you'd even be interested. I mean, I'd always hoped, but I never dared dream you could have any real feelings for me. And yet, now that I see what you've done, what you've made for me, specially, just out of concern for my own well-being, well. . . you *do* have feelings for me, don't you Abe?"

As she'd been speaking, she'd leaned in closer, her other hand joining the first resting lightly upon his chest. He was having difficulty breathing now, her face, tilted up toward his own, so close, her deep green eyes so full of wonder. Could she truly be reciprocating his clandestine affections? He was dumbstruck, his thoughts whirling as he tried to come up with some heartfelt response, something that would reveal how much he truly cared. As he was searching for the appropriate words, her eyes suddenly went a little wider, her smile growing as it spread across her elegant features.

"I think your body is answering for you," she murmured, running a hand down the front of his suit to caress the bulge threatening to burst a hole in his finely tailored pants. As her fingers grazed his manhood, he groaned low in his throat, wrapping his arms around her to steady himself. Slipping her other hand up behind his neck, she brought her face even closer, her lips parted in desire. When she finally dared to touch her mouth to his own, the intensity of their first kiss nearly made him swoon. Then, rising to the occasion, he responded in kind, his hands now exploring her new body for the first time as their kisses grew more and more passionate. After a few moments, she drew back a little, staring up at him while trying unsuccessfully to catch her breath.

"I do. . . have to ask you. . . just one more thing," she panted, her eyes searching his own as she clung to him.

"Anything," he responded breathlessly.

"Do you think. . ." she began, "do you think that we might be able to find me some new clothes? I can't very well walk the streets with you wearing nothing but my birthday suit!"

Laughing in unison, they drifted toward the cot, shedding his clothing piece by piece along the way.

-49-

Once the ritual was complete, Jenkins and Lisell went back to his place, enjoying each other's company while further cementing their budding relationship. He couldn't quite put a finger on it, but there was just something about holding her in his arms that somehow made the world a much better place. After getting some rest, they made plans to see each other later that night, then he dropped her off at Mercy General before starting his own shift.

His first stop was the crime scene, and even though a mob of unruly reporters was still milling around outside, technicians and forensics personnel continued to gather evidence. In the middle of it all, some high-profile attorneys had also arrived. They were probably sent in by the Garganos, but no matter how many cease-and-desist orders they issued, they hadn't been able to cut through enough red tape yet to shut it all down. Either way, it didn't really matter anymore to Jenkins; the information obtained from the kami spirits had made the lab findings mostly irrelevant. His team would complete the investigation, but there was really nothing more to be gained by overstaying their welcome.

While wrappings things up, he was also informed there'd been a major dust-up over at the Gargano estates involving the local military. Consequently, they now had the USACIC to deal with on top of everything else. He was not looking forward to untangling that ungodly mess, but hopefully it would be the last major battle between the spirit's avatars and organized crime for the foreseeable future. Surprisingly enough, Luciano had been killed some time during the confrontation. And even though this wasn't the outcome that Jenkins would have preferred, at least the nefarious mob leader was no longer a threat. In that regard, he considered the man's untimely death to be an unexpected blessing.

Once his rounds were complete, he made his way back to the precinct, arriving at about two in the afternoon. All things considered, it felt like his life was finally starting to change for the better. Bursting with this newfound positivity, he strode into the building, hoping to just ease back into his normal routine.

But found utter chaos awaiting him instead.

It looked as if someone had kicked the proverbial hornet's nest. Unfamiliar officers filled the squad room, all bustling about while trying to appear busy. But aside from the regular roundup of dubious-looking perps being booked into custody, Jenkins couldn't see anything happening that would have necessitated this influx of additional personnel. Before he could ask someone what was up, the door to the captain's office banged open and Wolfe leaned out.

"Jenkins," he barked. "It's about time you decided to show up. Get your ass in here!"

So much for having a quiet day to settle in. With a heartfelt sigh, he headed for the man's office, trying not to appear too overly disgruntled.

As he walked through the door, Wolfe shut it behind them with ominous finality. However, the need for privacy was immediately apparent. Two city officials sat before his desk, and they didn't look happy. He recognized the Chief of Police, but the other man was only vaguely familiar. The captain saved him the trouble of having to puzzle it out.

"I'm sure you've met our Chief, Charles Lockwood," he began, "and this is the District Attorney, Montgomery Seldon. They've only just arrived back in town and wanted to have a word with you about some very important matters."

Moving around behind the desk, Wolfe wedged his bulk into the chair with a practiced ease. But something here was definitely off. The whole thing stank to the high heavens.

"We've heard a lot about you, Detective," the D.A. began, rising to greet him "You've done good work, absolutely fine work, in helping to keep this city running during a time of crisis. I wanted to personally thank you. We really appreciate everything you've done for us over these last few days."

Shaking the man's hand, he tried to assess the situation. Yet the D.A.'s thin, angular features were hard to read. "Thank you, sir," he replied tactfully. "It's a pleasure to meet you." Trying his best to appear humble, he then turned toward the Chief.

The older official looked impeccable in his crisply pressed uniform, but his slicked-back salt-and-pepper hair made him seem oilier than a used car salesman. When he reached out for a brief handshake, there was no warmth in his guarded expression. "Let's just get on with it," he huffed. "I have more important matters to attend to today."

"Are you sure he's even the right man for the job?" Seldon asked the captain while reclaiming his seat. "He looks a little too straitlaced for this."

"I'm telling you, he's our guy," Wolfe replied. "All the officers we got left follow him around like a bunch of love-starved puppies. Hell, if I wasn't in charge, they'd be taking orders from him without even flinching. The man's a goddamn hero, for Christ's sake. You get him to play ball, and the rest will fall in line soon enough."

"You better be right," the chief growled. "Too many of our operatives have been lost over the past week, and we need to regroup quickly. We've got a lot of irons in the fire, and the remainder of the force needs to be irrefutably under our control again before we proceed."

"I'm not sure that I follow," Jenkins ventured.

"There! You see?" Wolfe exclaimed. "He doesn't even know what the hell we're talking about. He's perfect. Spotless record, no disciplinary problems—he's a clean slate. Nobody in their right mind would ever suspect him. If we're going to stay ahead of the game, we need people who can stand up to intense scrutiny. And there's gonna be a lot of pressure once the Feds get wind of this. We already got Army Investigations on the loose over at the Gargano estates, and with so many politicians dropping dead over the last few days, you know the FBI will be crawling up our own asses next. We got to lock everything down while we still can."

They were all staring at him now, their expressions speculative. But after a statement like that, Jenkins was left wondering just whose side the captain was really on. Were his promises of support against departmental corruption nothing more than an elaborate smoke screen? The sensations of positivity from earlier began to evaporate as new doubts assailed him. Glancing from one to the other of these powerful men—men who held his very livelihood in the palms of their hands—he began to feel cornered. Trickles of sweat trailed down his spine while he struggled to keep his composure. He was so flummoxed that he wasn't even certain how best to respond.

"So, what do you say, Detective?" the D.A. asked. "Can we count on you?"

"I'm sorry, sir," he hedged. "But I don't know what you're referring to. Could you please be more specific?"

Seldon was clearly irritated by his apparent lack of insight while Lockwood merely clenched his jaw, considering Jenkins with a sour look. "Surely you've realized that there are certain procedures in place here," the D.A. began patiently, "a way things have always been handled? For example, you may have noticed that some of your coworkers have, shall we say, been operating more independently than others. These brave men and women were on special assignment, and ultimately only answerable to the chief and myself." Pausing, he let that sink in before continuing. "We would like to offer you a similar opportunity. Think of it as an unofficial promotion with a sizable amount of monetary remuneration."

Jenkins was starting to get the picture, and he wasn't liking it one bit. Now that he was being seen as an officer with some clout, they were hoping the other members of the force would fall in line once they had him hooked. At a loss for words, he stood fuming with impotent rage, practically bursting with suppressed emotion.

"There! You see his reaction?" Wolfe pointed out. "You're just confusing him. I'm telling you, this guy never knew what was what around here. I've had him doing scut work for years. It wasn't until we lost so many of our men that he started cutting his teeth on the higher profile cases. If you want him to understand what's at stake here, then you're just going to have to spell it out for him."

Jenkins glared at the captain, wondering what he'd done to deserve such an unexpected betrayal, but Wolfe's expression gave nothing away. Before he could open his mouth to set things straight, Chief Lockwood was up out of his seat, glaring at him like he was some sort of unrepentant jaywalker.

"We don't have time for this!" the man exploded. "The city's in an uproar, and we have to regain control before Internal Affairs lands on us like a plague of locusts. You say we can trust him, Wolfe, so that's good enough for me." Taking a step forward, he towered over Jenkins, invading his personal space. "Listen up, Detective, because I'm only going to say this to you once—the officers in this city look to me for leadership, and I am the absolute law around here.

"But since there's a lot going on that you obviously don't comprehend, I'm going to break it all down for you. From here on out, I'll be telling you which types of criminal activities to ignore and which ones to actively pursue. To start with, all of the Gargano business ventures are off-limits. We have a lucrative deal with their organization, and we're going to honor it, even without Luciano's direct involvement.

"In addition to that, I don't want you going near any of the gambling houses or escort services until further notice. Since we own most of them, I can't have you interfering with any of our ongoing operations. But once things settle down a bit, you'll be required to gather protection money from these establishments on a regular basis. There's a lot of cash involved, so don't go getting any funny ideas about skimming, or you and I are going to have some serious problems. Am I making myself clear? Is all of this registering with you so far, Detective?"

Yeah, it was registering all right. All the bullshit he'd been putting up with, not to mention the unexpected disappearance of his partner, it was all connected. And everything led right back to these two self-centered fucktards. Well, he wouldn't stand for it any longer. Reaching under his jacket, he unclipped the gun and badge he'd carried for his entire career. Without taking his eyes off the man looming over him, he then tossed them onto the desk in front of Wolfe.

"I'm reading you loud and clear," he growled, jabbing a rigid forefinger into the center of Lockwood's chest, "but if you think for one second that I'm gonna be your personal lapdog, then you are outta your goddamn mind! And in case you don't fully realize just how truly mistaken you are, I'd be happy to explain it to you in terms that will have more of an impact."

"Are you threatening me?" the chief snarled, slapping his hand away. "Insubordination against a superior officer is a punishable offense!"

"In case you hadn't noticed, you pompous jackass, I no longer work for you," Jenkins shot back, setting his feet in an open stance and raising his clenched fists. "So what's it gonna be? Are we taking this down to the streets, or am I gonna have to settle things right here?"

Lockwood bristled, but then turned toward the captain. "Arrest this man!" he demanded. "I've had just about enough of his insolent posturing!"

Wolfe looked them over, his heavy-lidded gaze roving back and forth between them as he weighed his options. Standing abruptly, he unholstered his own weapon. "You're right," he said. "I think we've heard just about enough."

Coming around the desk, he hesitated a moment, but then pointed the gun unerringly at the Chief and his accomplice. "You're both under arrest. I've been waiting a long time for this."

The door behind them suddenly burst open, and men wearing jackets emblazoned with the FBI logo rushed in. Quickly surrounding the two startled officials, they began reading them their Miranda rights while slapping on the cuffs.

Holstering his sidearm, Wolfe smiled apologetically. "Sorry I had to keep you in the dark about all this," he said, running a chubby hand back through his spiky hair. "But it was necessary to pull the whole thing off. Allowing you to continue working under the radar, so to speak, while we set this up was vital to the plan's success. Anyway, it's probably a good thing that they stepped in when they did—for a minute there it looked like you might actually clobber him!"

"And he totally would have, too," someone behind them commented. "Without me around to keep him in line, this guy gets all sorts of crazy ideas into his big fat head."

Jenkins, still flushed by his recent surge of emotions, turned to stare at the man now entering the room. "Tom!" he cried. "You're alive!"

"What? Of course I'm alive!" glancing at the captain, Tom frowned. "I thought we agreed that you'd tell him I got transferred?"

"We did!" Wolfe exclaimed. "He must have come up with this lamebrained theory all on his own. He's one smart cookie but can still be pretty dense at times. Whatever gave you the notion that he was dead?"

"His records were expunged," Jenkins replied faintly, relief coloring his tone. "And my sources told me he'd been ghosted. It looked to me like he'd been eliminated, that his records were wiped clean so the death couldn't be traced back to the killers."

"Well," Tom offered sheepishly, "the FBI did have to doctor my files so I could work undercover on this. I'm sorry, Dan. I never thought it would take so long. Back while we were still active partners, I'd come across compelling evidence linking the corruption in our precinct to the DA and other high-ranking officials. When the FBI approached me through Internal Affairs to lock it all down, I jumped at the chance. In fact, if Wolfe and I hadn't of fully cooperated, the higher-ups would have been on to us and we'd probably both be dead right now. We were supposed to bring you in on it, but it was decided that keeping you ignorant of the situation would be a safer option until we had everything all sorted out."

Jenkins took a moment to study his old partner, relief enfolding him like a thick, warm blanket. Tom appeared to be in good health. There was a scruffy new beard now covering his rugged features, but other than that, he looked like he'd done well for himself. Even the borrowed uniform seemed like a good fit.

Grabbing a corner of the FBI jacket, Jenkins rubbed the material between two fingers. "You switching sides on me?" he asked. "Looks like being a Fed really suits you."

"Are you kidding?" Tom replied indignantly, yanking it out of his grasp. "Who'd keep your sorry ass in line if I wasn't around?"

There was a bit of a commotion behind them as the agents finished placing the two suspects in custody. As they turned to watch, a tall man with a shaved head and bristly mustache split from the group, approaching them with a ready smile.

"This is Agent Brookdale," Tom said. "He's the lead investigator. We've also collected a ton of dirt on all the remaining city officials linked to the case, and it's enough to put the lot of them away for a good, long time."

"And we couldn't have done it without his help," the man stated as he shook hands with Jenkins. "Your partner here is very intuitive. Once we realized he was on to something, we brought him in straightaway. Not only for his own protection, but also to assist with the case we'd already been building. He's been an invaluable asset ever since."

The man seemed competent and secure in his job. As they were sizing each other up, the rest of the agents filed past with the two detained officials in tow.

"You won't get away with this, Wolfe!" Chief Lockwood cried out. "We have friends in high places! You better watch your back, do you hear me? You haven't seen the last of us!"

Brookdale motioned to his men. "Get these scumbags out of here," he ordered, waving them onward. Then, turning back, he shrugged indifferently. "I don't think you have anything to worry about; with all the evidence compiled against them, they won't be getting out any time soon."

Overwhelmed, Jenkins could only nod in return. His partner was back from the dead, the corrupt city officials were on their way to the slammer, and he had a date later that night with the woman of his dreams. Tugging distractedly at his loosened belt where the badge used to hang, he realized that he'd even managed to drop a few pounds along the way. Things were definitely looking up.

As they left the office, Wolfe caught hold of his arm, briefly stopping him. "Here," he said, handing back the gun and badge, "you're gonna need these, *Detective*."

With the utmost reverence, Jenkins took the proffered items, holstering the gun under his coat and then displaying the badge on the front of his belt. The gleaming metal of the cherished item faced outward as he clipped it into its accustomed place, indicating for all to see that he was a full-fledged member of the force once again. As Wolfe followed him into the squad room, there was a sudden lull in the general chaos. Glancing around, Jenkins realized that everyone had stopped what they were doing to stare in his direction. With a puzzled frown, he halted in his tracks, trying to figure out what was going on.

Then, from the back of the crowd, Mattie stepped forward, beginning a slow, rhythmic clap. The applause picked up gradually until the entire room was saluting him with this unanimous sound of heartfelt appreciation. He realized then that they were all gathered here today just for this, just to see him vindicated and wish him well. It was the single most gratifying moment of his entire life.

After a few minutes of continuous acclaim, Wolfe raised his arms over his head, waving his hands for silence. "Alright, alright, alright," he shouted. "We all appreciate what Jenkins has done for us, but we have work to do, people! Let's get back to it, shall we?"

Tom had moved to stand beside him during the ruckus, and with the respect of the entire force behind them, Jenkins felt that there was nothing they couldn't accomplish together. As he stared out over the sea of smiling faces, he finally felt complete, made whole again by their admiration and support.

But it was time to get back to doing the job they were paying him for.

"Well," he said to his partner, "should we go see what's left on the docket for today then?"

With a ready smile, Tom clapped him on the shoulder as they returned to their desks. And just like that, they were a rock-solid team once more, focused on their ongoing mission to keep the peace in a city so continuously afflicted with such perpetual crime.

EPILOGUE

The main Gargano stronghold was hidden away in the upper hills of northern Italy, situated on a private tract of land located far above the bustling cities residing below it. Built upon the ruins of a medieval castle, it had been there for hundreds of years, its inner courtyard protecting a sacred ring of mystical standing stones. Now this age-old place of power rested peacefully amidst the heady fragrance of flowers and lemons, surrounded by walled gardens of incomparable beauty. Birdsong filled the air, along with the deep, mechanical thrum of machinery coming from several outbuildings occupying the wards around the central villa. However, none of these scents or sounds reached the matriarch as she sat at her large, antique desk. Like a spider at the center of a complex web, she crouched within the confines of her private study, pouring over reports as they scrolled across her computer screen.

Much like the monoliths in her courtyard, Vanka Illustoria Gurguno was ancient. She had lived well past her hundredth year, sustained by the magic that was her birthright and by various scientific methods she'd used to bolster its effects. Born into a prestigious Romani family, she had gained her abilities not only through decades of hard work and sacrifice but also by inheriting the knowledge of those who'd come before her. Hers was a legacy handed down from mother to daughter throughout untold generations, an unbroken line of succession reaching far back into time immemorial. Now at the pinnacle of her power, she was undisputedly in charge of the Garganos' worldwide wealth and ever-expanding empire, a position she navigated with the calm rationality that had become her trademark.

But what she'd just been reading had completely shattered this legendary composure, causing a smoldering rage to build within her that was nearly beyond all of her iron-willed control.

Reviewing the reports a second time had only amounted to the same foregone conclusion: Luciano had failed. Leaning back in the well-cushioned cathedra, she let her gaze wander about her inner sanctum, seething with emotional turmoil.

The immense room, constructed like a domed observatory, was filled with the esoteric trappings of eons of intense study and metaphysical exploration. Banners inscribed with archaic insignia covered the walls while strategically placed display cases housed a plethora of books and other rare artifacts gained throughout a lifetime of ruthless acquisition. Not limiting herself solely to what she'd inherited through her Romani upbringing, she had instead sought to master all forms of forbidden occultism. And this had been no easy task. There had been many who'd opposed her over the years, people of considerable talent who protected their dark secrets with a savagery that was both a challenge and a thrill for her to overcome. Yet, one by one, they'd fallen before her, and she'd mastered their disparate ideologies to become the world's highest-level practitioner of the supernatural arts.

Mentally sorting through the multiple magics she had at her command, she began selecting those that would most likely benefit her cause. It would take some time, she decided, to come up with the right combination of spells and artifacts required to defeat her adversaries. For that was what they had irrefutably become—the sworn enemies of the entire Gargano clan. Glancing back down at the monitor, she ran a knob-jointed finger over the wheel of the mouse, once more pulling up images of her newfound foes.

A ghostly female spirit who sucked the life from people, a troglodyte who controlled insects, and the man formerly known as

Dr. Abraham Orson. In this case, the doctor was already considered a prized commodity. In fact, his research was such a vital necessity to her own personal agenda that she had specifically instructed Luciano to secure his cooperation by any means necessary. For unbeknownst to the other members of her far-reaching family, she had no intention of relinquishing her position to the next female relative in line of succession. No, she had decided that she would instead live forever. And this Dr. Abe Orson held the key to prolonging her unnatural longevity.

His research into the use of embryonic cell tissues was invaluable. It was the whole reason she'd originally had him separated from his independently funded labs. From there, he'd been relocated to a place where they could control his actions, feeding him only those resources needed to complete his experiments. With his discoveries and her financial backing, she would have eventually gained a freshly grown body to inhabit. And after obtaining this new lease on life, she could have then existed throughout time as the Garganos' immortal leader. Beyond all other things, it was his defection that had her truly outraged. It did not matter how or why he'd gained his strange new mastery over fetal materials; his unforeseen defiance was intolerable!

Therefore, recapturing him was now her highest priority.

Reining in her frustrations, she picked up a small, refrigerated container from the desk, unlocking it with a touch of the keypad before withdrawing a vial of opalescent liquid. Swirling endlessly inside of its glass prison, the translucent fluid shimmered in the dimly lit room, glowing like sullen moonbeams. Pursing her lips, she studied it for a long moment before pulling the bell cord hanging next to her throne.

The double doors on the far side of the room opened immediately, and her chamberlain stalked in, his tall, skeletal frame swathed in layers of black silken fabric. His skin, the color of ash, was inscribed with ritualistic markings, making his hairless head resemble a calcified skull. Pale, watery-blue eyes regarded her from out of his intricately tattooed face as he crossed to the desk and made her a low bow of total subservience.

"Malik," she commanded, "have the traitor brought in. I wish to question him."

The man bowed again, his expression unreadable as he turned and went back through the doors. Then, with a languid wave of one long-fingered hand, he summoned the two men standing in the hall to come forward.

Dragging a bruised and bloodied captive between them, the massive Māori warriors she employed as twin bodyguards strode into the room, their finely tailored suits straining to cover their hugely muscled physiques. Stopping in front of the desk, they let the man drop to the floor before assuming a respectful stance.

Vanka glared at the bedraggled figure laying on her priceless Persian rug. "You have one chance to save yourself, you filthy *bulangiu*, and if you answer truthfully, I may yet let you live. Why? Why did you leave my great-grandson to die alone? Why have you come here like a whipped dog, tail between your legs? You should have died protecting him, should have killed all that opposed him! Yet here you are, alive, while he is most assuredly dead. I should use every power at my command to make you suffer. I should have my guards slit open your belly and then summon the Djinn to feast upon your entrails! Tell me, *bengalo*, why should I not do these things to you? Why should I let you live when your master, Luciano, is forever gone from this world?"

Levering himself upright, the man wobbled unsteadily on his knees, teetering there a moment while regaining his equilibrium. Finally, he raised his battered features to meet her blazing scorn with defiant bravado.

"Because I'm the only one who can ensure that you have your revenge against those who've defied you."

Malik raised a hand as if to strike down the insolent fool, but she made a curt gesture of negation, and he let it fall back to his side unreleased.

"I would hear his words," she said. "I would know for myself why this cur believes he is the only one who can give me this thing."

"It's true," Marco Giovanni boasted, holding his head up high. "Because I have followed these vermin back to their lair. While everyone else was scrambling to defeat them, I alone located the place where they hide, deep beneath the city. And now only I know how to get there."

"Then why did you not say these things to my great-grandson? Why have you fled here instead of helping him to defeat these vile interlopers?"

"By the time I got out of the tunnels, the battle was over!" Desperately, he sought to convince her. "The man who controls the insects, he sees *everything*, like they're somehow all connected. You gotta believe me! I barely made it out of there without being spotted myself. You think I wouldn't have given this info to Luciano if I could have? You think I would have run from my responsibilities? Those were my own men dying on that battlefield! Now there's nothing left, and the rest of the city's gangs are getting ready to divide up our holdings like they got some kinda right to them. And those crazy, superpowered freaks had already killed off all of our strongest allies. I had to come here because there was no place left for me to go. Especially if I wanted to avenge Luciano. Those bastards have got to pay, Phuri Dai. We have to make them pay for what they done to us!"

She considered this minor crime lord, seeing him in a new light. He could indeed prove very useful in many ways. Glancing down at her fist, she uncurled her clenched fingers, staring at the vial of mysteriously modified blood which had been retrieved from her great-grandson's armored gauntlet. It was the stuff that dreams were made of, the very substance that now flowed through Dr. Abe Orson's veins. Her own research and development divisions had even greater resources at their disposal than Luciano. Could she not then discover the secrets held within their shimmering depths?

Snapping her eyes back up to focus on Malik, she waved a dismissal. "Take this man away," she commanded, "then ready my private jet and alert all of our scientific teams to stand by."

The man bowed again, his pale eyes betraying no emotion. Then, tilting his head quizzically, he gestured to himself, then around at the vast store of powerful magical artifacts surrounding them on all sides.

She answered his unspoken question with a decisive nod. "Yes, Malik, you and I will be handling this personally. And we will then see if these murdering *gadjikane* can withstand the full force of our combined might. I shall collect our recalcitrant doctor and have my revenge while I'm at it, even if we must destroy the very city he now protects in order to do so!"

Summoning all of her ungodly power, she rose from the desk, her ancient eyes burning with the flames of forbidden knowledge intensified by outlawed scientific experimentation. Sweeping her gaze about the room, she then began to select the accouterments that would accompany them on their mission, her indomitable will as hardened and implacable as the mountains surrounding her hidden Romani stronghold.

The defilers of her great-grandson would soon fall, one by one, beneath her wrath, and their precious city along with them. . .

AUTHOR BIO

William H. Nelson grew up in Anchorage, Alaska, where he attended college at UAA. During his time there, he was a regular contributor to several publications, including, **The Radical** (Radical Publications, 1992-94), **The Auroran** (Denali Publications 1993-96), and **Rainsongs** (Denali Publications 1995-96).

After moving to the Seattle area in 1998, he eventually met the love of his life, and they now reside in a small town just across the bay from the Emerald City. Although William continues to write every day, in his spare time he also enjoys reading voraciously, playing the drums like a berserk spider monkey, creating award-winning costumes and props for local conventions, watching movies with a passion bordering on obsession, and playing selections from his vast collection of truly epic fantasy board games.

Connect with William on Facebook!
www.facebook.com/williamhnelsonbooks

Official Website:
www.williamhnelsonbooks.com